Cook, Baker, Candlestick Maker

Frank Skinner

Strategic Book Publishing
New York, New York

Strategic Book Publishing
An imprint of Writers Literary & Publishing Services, Inc.
845 Third Avenue, 6th Floor—6016
New York, NY 10022
http://www.strategicbookpublishing.com

ISBN: 978-1-60860-098-4
        1-60860-098-X

Printed in the United States of America

Book Design: Suzanne Kelly

Acknowledgements

I dedicate this work, and everything I have ever done or will do, to my loving wife Susan and my two sons, Stephen and Michael. Their roads through life were made very difficult by my decisions. I love them more than anything.

I would also like to recognize two old warrior buddies who are no longer with us; Sid Telford (Department of State Special Agent) and Gus Holmes (U.S. Secret Service). We were known as the Three Musketeers and I raise my glass of Dewar's Scotch to you guys—our old tradition, no matter where we were in the world, or the hereafter. I have current buddies who I won't name as they are still "in the fight." You know who you are.

Table of Contents

Introduction

Captain Frank Skinner, Marine, began his career as do most young men in his profession—with all of the emotions engaged at once. Fear, anxiety, and homesickness battled with his intense drive to make a difference and do something that not all can do: become a United States Marine.

In the summer of 1967 Frank had no dreams of becoming an officer in the elite Explosive Ordnance Disposal field. He also had no dreams or aspirations of joining a unique group of professionals who developed and introduced "Explosive Entry (Breaching)" to the law enforcement (SWAT and bomb squads) and military special operations groups for the purpose of counter-terror (CT) operations.

Frank takes no personal or individual credit. His reward was the opportunity to work and train alongside that special group of warriors who intentionally took, and continue to take, the fight to the bad guys. These unsung heroes have done and are currently doing things that keep all of us safe and secure. We will never know or understand most of those selfless efforts. Frank takes us with him to the jungles of Vietnam as a young eighteen-year-old, then moves to Beirut in the early- to mid-1980s. This was the beginning of the current global war on terror and Islamic fundamentalism. This is an historical account, from the trenches, as to how and why this war began.

Frank retired from the Marines in 1990 and moved to the private sector. In this arena he performed as a security specialist and trainer. He has provided close personal protection to members of the Saudi royal family, political leaders (domestic and foreign), and Disney on Ice when the show traveled to Cairo, Israel, Belfast, and other hot spots. Frank provided a secure environment for expats working in war-torn Algeria in the late 1990s.

This book is written so as to take the reader on a personal journey with Frank as he moved through his career. A former 22 SAS (British elite Special Air Service) commented, "Reading this book made me feel like I was sitting in a pub having a pint with Frank while he told his story."

Frank's sense of humor weaves through his story as he not only jokes about others, but tells of comical situations that he created and how he endured their aftermath.

Frank reflects on the lives he's touched, sometimes in a positive way, sometimes in a very negative way. He says, "When I close my eyes at night, I think of each and every one of them."

Cook, Baker, Candlestick Maker

CHAPTER ONE

In the Beginning

I remember Explosive Ordnance Disposal (EOD) school like it was yesterday, even though the memory dates back to October of 1973. For some reason EOD, and explosives in general, captivated me. It was just one of those things that I was naturally good at.

Follow me from the heat and hell of Parris Island and Vietnam, through the alleys and streets of Beirut and Cairo. From jungle fighting to the gray world of diplomacy, anti-terror (AT), and the active pursuit of counter-terror (CT) operations. From closet meetings with international arms dealers, to transferring explosives behind a gas station at 0200 on a Sunday morning so that a Marine Amphibious Unit (Special Operations Capable), MAU(SOC), could deploy to Beirut.

Travel with me through the scientific development of Explosive Entry that is used today by some of the most elite law enforcement and clandestine units in the world. The birth and growth of Explosive Entry was the product of several curious minds. The need was established by the Federal Bureau of Investigations Hostage Rescue Team (HRT), Los Angeles Police Departments Special Weapons and Tactics (SWAT) and Orange County Sheriffs Department Hazardous Device Squad (HDS). When I started Schools Section at Quantico, the National Assets (Delta, Seal Team Six, HRT and LAPD) were constructing charges embedded in Ethafoam. Hard to jump and swim with that.

We had work to do.

As a kid I was clumsy as hell. I remember when I graduated from boot camp at Parris Island and they told my folks I was

Author left, Dong Ha, Vietnam 1968

gonna be Ammo or EOD. My mom asked, "What's EOD?" They told her and she about fainted. I was famous for my clumsiness. Another stressful thing was that the year was 1967 and TET (the North Vietnamese offensive) was only a year away...and so was I. I served three years as an Ammunition Technician before getting to EOD school, an all-volunteer field.

This book is a journey with me; personal, professional, and technical. It will give all readers a chance to experience the impact that my career had on my family while dealing with the intrigue within Diplomatic Security and the development of the United States Marine Corps, Marine Amphibious Unit (Special Operations Capable)...MAU(SOC). In the mid-1980s, Special Operations/Low Intensity Conflict (SO/LIC) was a new concept and in direct conflict with the Marine Corps mission and doctrine to date, "We come from the sea." Now we have to come from anywhere and everywhere at the same time without letting them know we're coming.

An old Delta buddy told me that we have to be the unseen cobra in the corner—unknown, terrifying, and capable of total destruction. In retrospect it is comforting to know that I was part of that evolution. It is also with a great deal of respect that I dedicate this work to the forward thinkers of those times, no matter how unpopular their positions may have been.

There were real men and women in place who put their country and the Marine Corps ahead of their careers. They are the true heroes. To the stumbling blocks and career-focused individuals: How much further along in this unconventional war would we be if you had backed us or, better yet, had retired and gotten out of the way!

For some unknown reason I took naturally to the explosive effects subject and material. It all made logical, clear sense to me, even the theories and concepts. I finished first in my class at Conventional EOD and second in Nukes. Nukes didn't hold the same interest level for me. Big-Assed Bang and a bunch of dirty air didn't excite me.

Funny side story and, again, those who know Susan and I will appreciate this. As you'll see throughout, my wife and I are very close. While I was out of the Marines my dad and I had two paint and body shops. I decided that I wanted to race. My dad and I looked at an old stock car that belonged to a friend of his and I was all set to become Richard Petty II. Susan would have no part of it—too dangerous—and it drove her almost insane. Susan isn't dumb but some things just don't interest her. When I was sent to EOD school it didn't mean that much to her except for career progression. She understood that because we were trying to have a family.

When I returned to Cherry Point as a fresh EOD sergeant, all was well. One night I had the duty EOD. We stood duty at home. I put a pencil and tablet next to the bed. At about 0130 I got a call from the Military Police (MPs). The enlisted club was directly across from the female Marine barracks. When the club closed, these ingenious young male Marines would take their beers outside and sit on the hill overlooking the female barracks. One of them would call in a bomb threat and they would observe all of the various arrays of non-dress of the evacuees. Once we searched and discovered nothing, I returned home to find my cute little wife sitting on the sofa. She had read the notes that I had taken from the MP.

When I walked in she said, "Where did you go?" I told her about the bomb threat.

She said, "So why did they call you?"

Bless her heart. She never again said a word about my work. Even the secretive trips to Beirut were never questioned. During this time frame she worked as a cashier for the base gas station. She did tell me later that she heard other wives, when asked, telling folks where their husbands worked—they would respond with "at supply" or "at the motor pool." She told me that it made her feel good to say that her husband was EOD. Of course the next question in those days was "What is EOD?" There were only about 120 officers and enlisted in Marine EOD at the time. It was an exclusive, all-volunteer outfit.

What did excite me is how some of the military and improvised explosive devices (IEDs) harnessed and focused their explosive effects: Misznay-Schardin, Monroe, shaped charges (linear and conical), platter charges, flex linear, etc. (See diagram on page 15.)

I remember when, as a young sergeant working on the bombing ranges at Chocolate Mountains, we would do "blow and go" operations. That meant we would walk in a line ten to twenty guys abreast. We had pre-cut time fuse with igniters (M60s) and blasting caps attached. As we spotted a bomb—up to MK84s or 2,000 pounders—we would place a block of C-4, cap it, yell "fire in the hole," pull the igniter, and continue in a line. (Hopefully, getting far enough away before we had to repeat the process.)

One morning in particular we were sweeping on line and I found four MK82s (500 pounders). The M904 fuses were mangled so I removed them, rolled up a small amount of C-4, and packed it in the fuze well. (Notice I spell *fuse* for a time fuse and *fuze* for a bomb fuze). For all four bombs I may have used one-quarter pound of C-4. Procedure was one pound and a quarter (M112 block) per bomb. I then proceeded to tie the bombs together with detonating cord.

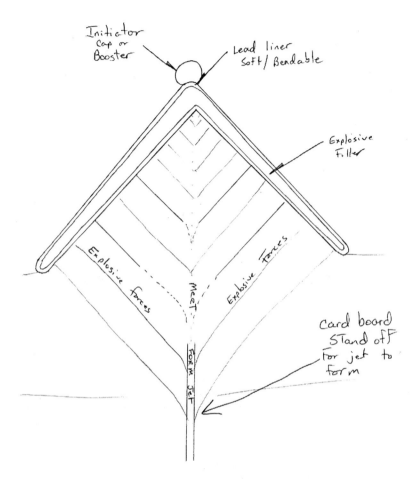

Initiator Cap or Booster

Lead liner Soft / Bendable

Explosive Filler

Explosive forces

Meet

Explosive forces

Card board STand off for jet to form

FORM JET

Taken from my basic demo lesson plan

The Master Guns ran over and politely asked, "What the fuck are you doin'?" To my knowledge that is the first time I ever said or heard "P=E Top"—short for "Plenty equals Enough, Top Sergeant"—one of the expressions I came up with when developing the courseware for the Quantico Explosive Entry course in August 1986. In my mind I had "used the minimum amount of explosives to penetrate 100% of the desired target."

Later we practiced with different explosive configurations. One of our improvised explosive device (IED) disrupters (.50 cal Dearmer or the MK2) used water as a projectile. It had sev-

15

eral projectiles but this one got my attention. I had always been fascinated how you could focus explosive effects to hydraulically force water through a hard target.

To me it was all based on FM—*Fuckin' Magic*. But I kept playing with it. I also kept playing with shaped charges. I gathered all the empty, expensive wine bottles from the Class VI store. (Had to get 'em out of the trash 'cause a young sergeant couldn't afford more than Old Milwaukee beer.) I would freeze them, soak string in lighter fluid, wrap it around the bottle just below the *ojive* (widest part of the bottle just below the neck), then light it. A slight tap would then break off the neck and with the dimple in the bottom it became a very effective "cold" shaped charge. These were excellent for blowing through the skin of a bomb without causing a detonation, but the explosive filler would ignite, allowing the bomb to burn out without detonation. Neat stuff!!

Arleigh McCree comes into my life abruptly one morning.

The captain yelled in the back of the EOD shop, "Who's in the back?" All the other guys were out screwin' off. I usually was, too, but I got caught this time.

I went up front and said, "I'm the only one here, Skipper."

"One's all I need," he responded, and proceeded to tell me that the Los Angeles Police Department (LAPD) bomb squad was gonna be on our demo range in about an hour and they needed one of our guys out there to make it legal. He gave me a list of powder (explosives) to pick up at the bunker.

So away I went. I got to the range a little early and started to set things up. I had no idea what the LAPD wanted to do—that was above my pay grade. All of a sudden two LAPD vehicles came bouncing over the dusty, rutted road that fed into our range. When they dismounted I was greeted by a tall (hell, everybody's tall to me), grinning sergeant of the LAPD bomb squad, Arleigh McCree. Little did I know that he and I would become good friends until that fateful day in 1986 when he and another buddy, Ron Ball, were killed by a booby-trapped pipe bomb.

After the introductions, Arleigh went on about what a *limp dick* the skipper was for not coming out to play. To Arleigh, everyone who was a bad guy or anyone who didn't think like him was an asshole. Didn't matter much to Arleigh what company he was in front of. (Later on, you'll read about me having him brief the MCAS El Toro commanding general about our plans for the security of the '84 Olympics.) What a treat that was, because Arleigh just didn't care.

After putzing around a little and doing gopher stuff I noticed that these guys were coming up with different charges and ideas—about how to penetrate walls, doors, ceilings, and floors—to initiate a hostage rescue.

During this time frame the *Rock Houses*—drug distribution/manufacturing houses in the days before crack houses and meth labs were well known—were starting to come into their own. The bad guys, or "assholes" by Arleigh's standards, would build a chain link cage inside the main entry or the front door. When the SWAT guys would knock down the door and assault they would be trapped in this chain link cage right in the middle of the *fatal funnel*—the area where SWAT officers are forced through a limited space, exposing themselves to concentrations of criminal weapons fire.

As I watched and listened I realized that while they had a good idea, they needed some help in the theory department. This very subject was at the center of my entire EOD and explosives interest. They tried kneading C-4, forming a thin line into an oval shape. This would be big enough to create a hole that an assaulter could run through. Yep, you guessed it, too much bang. C-4 is an RDX-based explosive.

Depending on who you listen to or what you read, C-4 detonates at 26,500 feet per second. Now some are gonna debate and show their vast knowledge but in everybody's book that is FAAMF (Fast as a Mother Fucker). To me that's close enough. You can imagine how long it took to knead a strip of C-4 into an oval that totaled about 12' long. Now make it Chicago in January and see how long it takes to knead frozen (or nearly frozen) C-4.

As I watched, I threw out a comment once in a while. Gotta remember I graduated from EOD school In 1974. It was then 1976 and I hadn't even earned my Senior EOD badge, much less my Master. Old-timers don't often listen to Basic Badge-wearers.

The captain had secured us an outdoor crapper—an eight-holer, as I recall. Someone out there is gonna say "No, it was ten" or "It was six," but as long as there was one when I needed it, that satisfied my P=E theory. The skipper was proud of this accomplishment. It needed some work but was in fine condition for its intended purpose.

I finally got Arleigh's attention and said, "Sarge…"

"Goddamn it!!! My name is Arleigh—don't call me Sarge. I ain't no fuckin' Marine. You got a name, asshole?"

That started a good, free-exchange relationship that lasted until '86. There were many arguments while having lunch with Arleigh or doing training together. He was into evidence pres-ervation and I believed in sifting and post-blast. Many was the time that we told each other that he was full of shit.

Anyhow, I radioed back to the shop and asked the skipper if we could use his mighty throne house for a test shot.

He said that as long as I blew a panel that was gonna be replaced anyway, go ahead. I told Arleigh that det cord, which detonates at about the same speed as C-4, was already in the configuration needed for the desired effect. Military det cord was fifty grains per foot. There are 7,000 grains in a pound, so that gives you the idea that Frank was thinking P=E. In addi-tion, I was thinking of the "V" that is formed when two pieces of det cord are taped together longitudinally. This "V" is a crude shape charge.

When I finished explaining my concept you could hear a pin drop.

All Arleigh said was, "No shit!"

I then took an "E" silhouette target which is hard cardboard with the general outline of a person's torso and head. I taped two strands of det cord around the perimeter and used a prop stick to hold it against the wall of the crapper.

Ooops!!!! Forgot about methane. Because this was a used facility, it had the lingering after-effects of waste in the form of trapped methane gas.

When the splinters stopped falling, and we picked ourselves up off the deck, I realized that my career was flashing before my eyes (as it will do often throughout this book).

The skipper's outhouse was no more. We did find the panel that we had attacked and there was a perfect oval cut out as if by a blow torch. I had now earned new respect from Arleigh and had one pissed-off captain of the United States Marines. I would, and still do, reflect on this day as the birth of Explosive Entry, or Breaching.

I later learned that a very dedicated friend, a former Marine captain, was doing the same thing for the FBI's Hostage Rescue Team (HRT). He became a good friend and mentor when I transitioned breaching into the MAU(SOC) program and conducted training for the Force Recon, SEALs, Army, and other federal agencies. Later, law enforcement got involved but liabilities were, and still are, a problem. So to any of you guys out there claiming to have started the Explosive Entry Program at Quantico—and yes, *I do know who you are*—you gotta beat that story.

I think this is a good place to begin the storytelling and get off the B.S. The above information is exactly how and when it happened, and it holds fond memories for me. Especially now when I quietly watch the "duty experts" who are grazing in the fields planted by guys like Arleigh and James. Funny thing…in all the expos I've been to, lectures I've heard, and expert opinions I've read, there sure are a bunch of "I's" and "me's." Never once did I hear a pioneer's name mentioned. Maybe a reason is that in those days our information became classified at the Secret level. We didn't want the bad guys to know that we could come at them from anywhere and FAAMF.

I remember teaching a class to some SEALs from Virginia Beach and they were so enthusiastic that you had to keep them under tight reins. They kept getting closer and closer to the placed charges until the lead liner of the flex began to tattoo their arms. It became a badge of courage (or stupidity). Gotta remember, we were all indestructible.

I made the statement, "If you can see it, it can see you." I later thought that cool and put it in my lesson plans.

Heard a guy the other day tell a class, "I used to have a saying for my students: If you can see it, it can see you."

All material was handled at the Secret level. As such, the National Assets such as Delta, Red Cell, and SEAL Team Six were not only willing to share but, thanks to James, I was invited to tag along on many training trips. The unwritten theory was that Delta and Six wanted me to train the tier two forces (Force Recon, Rangers, and conventional SEALs) because they saw the need but didn't have the time. The only restriction was that I couldn't teach aircraft or tubular targets. This relationship was excellent and the material was getting disseminated.

I was told by a recent retiree that this relationship no longer exists. Maybe the times changed, or the tactics, or the mentality. I heard from a reliable source that someone who came in after me decided that it was too much trouble to maintain all that classified material and did away with the classification of Explosive Entry. After that time, training trips ceased and there was no more information sharing.

I've always maintained that law enforcement needs this capability, but we need to maintain strict controls over how this info gets out. We are much more effective if the bad guys don't know what to expect.

I want this to be an enjoyable journey through the development of Explosive Entry (Breaching). The only way that my old head can get a handle on that is to take you on the journey with me. I will put each development phase in a separate chapter so that this may be used as a reference as well. Some of the illustrations are pre-1980 and are taken directly from the first curriculum that I developed for the Dynamic Entry School, Weapons Training Battalion (WTBN) Quantico.

NOTE TO READER

Breaching: Forcible entry via mechanical or explosive techniques

Explosive Entry: The proper application of the minimal amount of explosives to penetrate one hundred percent of the desired target.

Late Summer 1976

I had been assigned to the EOD platoon at Camp Pendleton after a one-year assignment to Range Company, Camp Fuji, Japan. The Marine Corps had started a policy for married Marines that if you were on an unaccompanied tour, and could afford it, you could bring your wife over and live off the local economy so long as it didn't interfere with your duties.

My wife and I had been married since September 1, 1970, and as our friends know, we are inseparable. Most folks don't understand how she puts up with me but she knows I love her and have since the day I was born—just didn't get to meet her 'til I was twenty. We dated twice, and the rest is thirty-seven years of history.

Japan proved uneventful save many drink-a-thons with the Japanese EOD guys. What a group of friends they turned out to be. I never could understand how they always out-drank us—we weren't slouches when it came to partying. EOD bravado is known throughout the universe. At one particular party, I went down to take a leak and found the Japanese lieutenant's wife holding a Japanese sergeant's head over a bowl, forcing him with her finger to puke. Hell fire, they were hitting us in shifts!!

My primary exposure to Explosive Entry began that sorrowful day that the skipper sacrificed his shitter to the Breaching god. Many folks have made sacrifices during the development of breaching but none that compares to that selfless sacrifice.

The platoon was a normal mix of Marine EOD types. Most of us were Vietnam Vets but not necessarily there in an EOD capacity. I, for example, was an ammo tech. That's a high-classed word for ammo humper. Like a sanitation engineer. It turned out to be a little less than boring. I worked at ASP-1 and ASP-2 (grade III dump) at Dong Ha, South Viet Nam.

I don't know (we didn't have Google Earth then) but I was told that we were about eight to ten miles south of the DMZ, well within range of NVA artillery and VC rockets. The dumps got hit again and again and you ain't lived 'til you spend two-plus days in a ditch about three feet deep in the middle of a major

ASP-2 Dong-Ha 1967 taken from one mile away.

ammo and bomb supply dump that is blowing up all around you
(see photos). Got decorated and received a Purple Heart for my
efforts. My truck was melted to the axles.

The doctor told me when they flew me to the hospital ship
USS *Repose*, and later the *Sanctuary*, that he was putting me in
for a Purple Heart. I wasn't much for medals and decorations. I

was, however, very proud of any rank that I achieved. Just to be a Marine was awesome, but to become an NCO was surreal to me.

I got out of the Marines in 1970 to attend college. When I rejoined in 1973, I had my new wife and a heart filled with ambition. I knew that I could not only be a Marine, but be a good one. But I needed rank. Rank meant money for my new family and money is something we didn't have much of in those days. After a few months at Cherry Point a smiling, cheerful Sergeant Steve checked in.

Steve was an Indian from Oklahoma. We became instant drinkin' buddies and ruled our world (providing our wives said we could). Steve and I spoke of rank, money, careers, and more beers. I wanted to be an officer and Steve wanted to be a First Sergeant. I told him Captains make more than First Sergeants. We had heated debates about that from time to time. He later retired as a college graduate with the rank of Lieutenant Colonel. Who says good doesn't come from the consumption of vast quantities of Old Milwaukee beer?

I then jumped to in my effort to become a warrant officer. That was to be a few years away. Still needed to get my record book sorted out and that was at Headquarters Marine Corps (HQMC) in Arlington, Virginia. Susan, Steve, and I planned a trip to HQMC to verify the correctness of our records. We went to the appropriate floor and requested our records. Young clerk complied and we took our time making sure that all was accurate. Upon departure we were walking past a series of buildings when I happened to glance up and see the "Awards and Decorations Branch."

I said, "Hey wait, back in '68 when I was wounded, my doc said he was putting me in for a Purple Heart."

Of course my dear, compassionate, trusting friend made the comment, "Bullshit, let's go, asshole."

It was noon and everyone was out to lunch except for a young black female Marine PFC.

I told her my story and she nonchalantly asked, "What was the date?" I told her that it was May 14, 1968, in Dong Ha, South Viet Nam.

She typed in some stuff and up it popped. She didn't say a word. Pulled out a Purple Heart certificate, threw it in the typewriter, clicked away, jerked it out, walked it into a back office (where some lieutenant was probably snoozin'), got it signed, brought it back, and handed it to me. She opened another drawer, pulled out a medal box, and handed that to me…still not a word.

Steve looked at me, grinnin' and shakin' his head, and all he said was, "I'll be. Kiss my ass."

That's the kinda story I'm glad Susan was there to see and Steve to bear witness. I feel sure that the Marine Corps takes Purple Hearts more serious these days.

My first exposure to a ground EOD Unit was the First EOD Platoon, Camp Pendleton, California. We had a good mix of guys and, as I reflect, it was almost like the movies. We had our goofball who defied all logic. We had our know-it-all. We had our pretty boy and all you had to do was ask him.

He and I stopped in a bar in the middle of the desert. Old gal tending bar was worn down from the desert life. My sidekick got up to go to the head when she had her head turned.

When she came back she asked me, "Where's Frank?"
I said, "Frank?"
She said, "Yeah—Frank Skinner, where'd he go?"
When my buddy came back he was all smiles (he was proud of his white teeth), thinking that would slay the beast.
He said, "Well, you didn't think I was gonna give her my real name, and besides that I never thought you'd be coming this way." Me and this guy cleared the path for trouble and how we stayed out of jail I'll never know.

Once he and I were commissioned we stayed at the El Centro, California, Bachelor Officers Quarters (BOQ). We had no transportation but there was a golf cart plugged in out front. I'm sure the area has grown but at that time it was a long haul to town. We shagged ass in the golf cart and ran through the gate, to the dismay of a very agitated MP. We found the best local bar, hid the cart, and proceeded to solve world problems.

Upon returning we nearly had to run down the MP but we got through, stashed the cart, ran to our rooms, and peeked out through the curtains like kids. We never got caught. You young military guys and gals reading this: Can you imagine getting away with that these days?

Short of peeing in the commandant's punch bowl, we EOD folks were left pretty much alone. Of course, if you were dumb enough to get caught, your ass was grass. But that was mainly for being stupid enough to get caught.

One guy who was there with us was a super good guy. His wife was a little promiscuous but he was great. Got tanked up one night and got a DUI. Captain bailed him out and took him home. Cops were pretty good in those days because we provided a lot of bomb support. This gent, being the good Marine he was, got up and drove in to work with a hangover. Only problem was that the MPs stopped him at the gate and gave him another DUI. This good guy, good sergeant, and good EOD tech hauled ass to Canada and stayed away for about five years. Finally turned himself in and got discharged.

We had a fantastic array of senior staff NCOs and officers. The skipper was straight-faced, seldom smiled, but had a dry sense of humor that could drive you nuts. Never knew when he was serious or pissed. Normally when he said, "We can settle this shirt on, or shirt off," he was pissed.

We had an old (old to us at the time, maybe in his late forties) master gunnery sergeant (E-9). He was as serious and meticulous as death. We grew to love the old man in our mischievous young Marine EOD way. We would get tickled when he lost stuff. Our favorite was when he lost his reading glasses. He would be looking everywhere and accusing us of stealing them. Of course we'd be laughing our asses off because his glasses would be on top of his head.

Only thing about the "Old Man" was that he would put our dicks in the dirt when it came time for the physical fitness test. He could run forever and fast. Never breathing hard and I don't think he had sweat glands. He sent me and pretty boy to the range one rainy cold morning. Unfortunately I was sitting on the mike for the radio and the base station was right behind the Top's (Master Gunnery Sergeant) desk.

All the way to the range we bitched and complained about that "old asshole" making us go to the range. "What a prick," etc, etc. It was Friday.

When we got back, not a word was said. We felt something was wrong but…total silence. We normally got off a little early on Fridays but the clock ticked right up to 1630. It was still cold and rainy, unusual for Southern California but I think the Top requested it for us and he always got what he requested. The EOD platoon had seven EOD trucks.

At 1631 the Top said to me and pretty boy, "Oh yeah, this *old asshole* forgot to tell you something. I want the trucks detailed for inspection by 2200 tonight."

To this day you can bet that I still look at my cell phone, or radio if so equipped, to make sure the Top ain't listening. When I was promoted to Warrant Officer the Top called me a traitor. It is customary for a newly commissioned officer, or warrant, to give a silver dollar to the enlisted person who rendered the first salute. Top was so pissed I had to chase him in my car to get the salute but I gave him the engraved silver dollar and I think it meant a great deal to him. By the way, this old fart was some high level surfing champion, either national or California. He was an old stud and commanded well-deserved respect.

I don't think anybody in EOD had the intense desire to study the effects of explosives like I did. Most EOD folks want to get the biggest bang. They want to hear the frag and feel the over-pressure. I always thought that was fun but the real power, the real use of explosive forces was to use Just the Right Amount. I used to love that cartoon of the bull with his horns being blown off. Caption sez: "Explosives Expert: Someone that can pack a bull's ass with enough TNT to blow off his horns and never bring water to his eyes." I always thought that kinda summed it up. Timing is everything, and the luck that I had that day on the range with Arleigh was uncanny at best.

Every subsequent trip that Arleigh made to Pendleton he would ask for me. He would always have some new idea or concept and some of them were really harebrained. But some of mine were, too. That was what was so healthy during that time. We were comfortable telling each other they were full of shit but we had to be prepared to defend our idea. Arleigh would invite me to L.A. for lunch and tours of their facility. I remember on one trip a bunch of the LAPD bomb guys were in trouble.

The bomb squad also did the ballistic testing. They had tons of weapons and ammo. They also had pellet rifles and air guns. Apparently several of the techs decided to use the winos and bums in the alley for target practice. They specialized in hitting the bottles when the winos took a drink. Some of them got fired over this slight indiscretion.

Arleigh's real fun came when he got to take new guys to the morgue. One afternoon after a plane crash he took me and a couple of new guys in.

Arleigh said, "Take a look at our crispy critters." Then laughed like hell.

As we started to come up with new ideas, Arleigh came to the range one morning and said, "I've got it figured out: Douche Bag Shot."

Of course, being the ever-critical individual I am, I said, "You've gone to the next level of full of shit."

He said, "No, hear me out." He proceeded to pull a Glad bag out of the back of his truck. He said, "We fill it with water, put det cord in, and use the water to knock down the wall."

"So how in the hell you gonna get a shit can liner full of water in the wall?" I countered.

He got a puzzled look on his face. But a light came on for both of us at the same time. Fill the bag after it's in the wall. Now you'll notice, especially you folks who have trained in explosive entry, that we continually refer to inside the wall. We had to think "outside the wall."

Be patient, we were still learning and developing. As we were bouncing ideas around about getting the bag in the wall, Arleigh said, "We'll rout a small hole, stuff the bag in, and fill it."

My response was immediate: "What do you think the bad guys are gonna be doin' while you're grinding away with a router?" Back to the drawing board. I've said many times—and I have friends and my wife who will verify—that when I used to go to sleep with a problem I could wake with an answer. The older I become, the less frequently it happens. Like everything else. Wish they had a blue pill for that. Arleigh and I had been hammering this Douche Bag concept like crazy. We called it the Water Impulse Shot.

We had even developed hydraulic equations for detonation velocity, water amounts, using antifreeze in the place of water...just idea after idea. Nothing was coming to us except that it was a good idea. Bingo...went to sleep thinking hard about it. Woke up and called Arleigh. He couldn't make it down until the next day.

That day the importance of the breachers' photo and logbook became important. I told Arleigh, Let's set our charge outside the wall, with twice as much water on the back to focus the explosive energy and hydraulically push the water through the whole wall. The tamping on the back would also serve to protect the assaulters.

Granted, this first charge looked like an abortion. Big, ugly, cumbersome trash bag, full of water, heavy as hell. Didn't look sexy enough to fit the SWAT image. We wrestled this big-assed bag up against the wall and used ten miles of ninety-mile-an-hour tape and several prop sticks. Our first charge we used four strands of det cord about three feet long with a trunk line that was eight feet long. Okay, what's the net explosive weight (NEW)? Yup: .14285714 pounds. We always believed in carrying out the decimals as far as the calculator did. We never rounded. A defense attorney or prosecutor would have a ball with that. Fifty grains per foot, twenty feet by fifty, divided by 7,000. (The amount of grains per foot, divided by 7,000 equals the pounds of explosives in TNT equivalence. There are 7,000 grains in a pound. This gives you an idea as to how small our charges were.)

Results? Worked like a champ. Problem was we soon learned that we were gonna have to deal with studs, electrical wiring, and plumbing. We achieved penetration. The studs were pushed in a little, but were still an obstacle. One important note here: If your first shot is successful do you consider this a sanctioned charge? No!! The best data you can develop is that your first charge doesn't penetrate and you second charge does. Keep lowering your net explosive weight (NEW) until you reach the point where you don't quite have total penetration. Then go back up to the next NEW until you get penetration. It may take twelve shots to refine and define your charge. This is the best test data. Log it, photo it.

The dialog in those days was amazing. A quick idea, then an immediate phone call. As was the case at the platoon in those days, we were always tasked to support somebody. Whether it was the San Clemente Island bomb sweep, Chocolate Mountains bomb sweep, or CAX operations at Twentynine Palms. To me this just interrupted my time that I wanted to devote to explosive entry. Given the tasks at these range sweeps I had to dedicate myself to paying attention to the job at hand. More of a nuisance than anything.

Then in 1977, on a Combined Arms Exercise (CAX) to Twentynine Palms, I was notified that I had been selected for Warrant Officer. I and a small staff sergeant were living in a Command Post (CP) tent. The staff sergeant was a real piece of work and quite the beer drinker. He had the funniest personality. One night I was in the tent getting my gear squared away. Harry had gone to the Staff Non Commissioned Officer (SNCO) Club. Somewhere around midnight I heard a jeep hauling ass over the desert and then a thump, thump as something was thrown from the jeep outside the tent. I went outside and it was Harry, full of sand and cactus, and quite drunk. I got him inside and put his sloppy ass to bed. The next morning he was sitting on the side of his bunk with the ever-present Camel dangling from his lips, rubbing his forehead.

He kept repeating, "What did I do??? What did I do??" He told me to make the morning runs to the CP. He was afraid to show his face.

I went to the company office and the WO looked at me and said, "Where is your little fuckin' staff sergeant?"

"In the tent, sir," I responded.

He said, "Well, let me tell you what that little fucker did. He started a major riot at the club then crawled out and was sitting on the curb with his Camel when the MPs arrived. He then proceeded to engage them so they locked him up."

Apparently Harry had the talent to really get the show rolling, then he would sneak out. Luckily the WO was the Duty Officer but when he got Harry out, Harry gave him shit all the way out to the camp. The WO just threw his ass out of the jeep at full speed.

A few days later Harry, the WO, and I went to the Army EOD camp to have a few beers. They always had cold beer. After a drinkathon, we headed back to our camp at around midnight. Anyone who's been in the desert at midnight knows you can't see anything. Darker than a Vietnam night. We were more lost than last year's Easter egg. We all had to pee so I stopped and we all got out. Couldn't see anything.

Harry was a bashful pisser so he snuck off behind the Jeep, very drunk. I got back behind the wheel, the WO got in, and I thought Harry was in the back. He had draped his arm over the spare tire for support while standing behind the Jeep. I hauled ass, dragging Harry along behind. Me and the WO were shooting the shit and didn't hear Harry screaming as we drug him along. Finally got stopped and there was Harry, again covered with Choya cactus and sand everywhere.

Once I got notified of my selection to WO, Harry asked, "Do you know why there are officer heads and enlisted heads?"

I said, "No."

He responded, "So that the enlisted don't have to watch the officers squat to pee."

I came home for the weekend and, just to let you know how broke we were, I loved Chivas Regal Scotch. Very, very seldom had the chance to get it but I thought it was the best. My little wife had purchased one of the tiny bottles of Chivas so that I could celebrate our selection with her.

As it turned out most people were happy with my selection to the officer ranks. Not the least was Arleigh. He was robust and jovial with his congratulations. Little did I know that a few years later this would pay off for us both.

When I pinned on Warrant I had to refocus my priorities. Had a six month Basic School to attend. Needed to get some college and all those other basic necessities for survival in the Officer Corps. My first assignment was as the station EOD officer at Cherry Point, N.C. This was a good tour even though I didn't get much time to play with entry techniques. I attended college at night and on the weekends and operationally we were covered up with civil war ordnance.

My commanding officer was an A-4 pilot with the call sign "Bones." Super guy and very supportive of EOD.

Our demo range had a fifty pound limit which we never got close to but we were near MACS 6, a huge radar facility. We were surrounded by trees that served to muffle our detonations. I was informed that the environmentalists wanted to cut down the trees around the range. This would have put us out of business. I made an appointment with Colonel Bones, and when I went in he wasn't at that time very familiar with me.

He said, "What can I do for you, Gunner?"

I immediately and without hesitation said, "Sir, whose dick I gotta suck to keep them tree huggers from cuttin' down our trees?"

He, also without hesitation, rose from his chair and began undoing his trousers and said, "Well Gunner, at least you know the right office to go to."

He and I hit it off big time after that...as long as I didn't get him into trouble. The Marine EOD at Cherry Point were getting several calls a week for cannon balls. Those dudes were as alive, and more sensitive than, the day that they were born.

There was an old guy in Newbern, N.C., who had a business inerting Civil War ordnance. He was doing quite well but it pissed him off that we were doing the same for free. If the item was safe enough we would inert it, research the history, and give the item back to the original owner with a write-up. If it was too dangerous we blew it.

The old man put an article in the paper that warned "the Marines are stealing your Civil War ordnance. If you give it to the Marines they will keep it and put it in their museum." This little battle went back and forth for several months. The old man eventually drilled the wrong item and it killed him.

His widow called our unit and asked us to get all the ordnance out of her garage. We responded and you would not believe the Civil War ordnance in that guy's garage. It would've taken out a city block. The old lady begged us to get it all. We took it and it was many months before that stuff was worked through. When I left in 1980 they were still working on it.

In early 1980 I had completed enough credits to be selected for the college degree program and I had been promoted to Limited Duty Officer (LDO) as a first lieutenant. I was lucky enough to be accepted at the University of Central Florida pursuing a degree in Business Administration.

There's a whole book about that 1½ year assignment. Let's see…active first lieutenant in the Marines…driving a new Corvette…with a twenty-seven-foot sailboat in the Marina twenty miles away on the intra-coastal waterway. Let your imagination run wild. Although I was happily married and have been for many years, that was a fun tour. Only problem was that I wasn't blowing stuff up. I did, however, have some lengthy conversations with the engineering department. The results of those discussions were some very good ideas that I was anxious to apply. BUT…where was the Marine Corps gonna send me? I got a call from the lieutenant colonel who handled officer assignments.

He started the conversation off with "Frank, I need your help." My heart sank. I felt an EOD school, tech center, or worse—his job—coming down the pike. The EOD god was smiling on old Frank…again. He proceeded to tell me that he had a combined team, one station and two wing teams, that had failed an Inspector General (IG) and was on the edge of mutiny.

The Officer in Charge (OIC) was a good guy but his command had assigned him the additional duty of Armory Officer which is a more than full time job for two guys. He had tried to hold it together but had a very ineffective Non Commissioned Officer in Charge (NCOIC). At least it was a team.

I would have preferred a ground team but what the hell. At least it wasn't an admin weenie tour. Now I'm thinkin' Cherry Point again or Iwakuni as I hadn't been overseas in a while. Nope!! Good news…El Toro!!

I got right on the phone with Arleigh and, man, was he elated. He said, "I got new shit for you. You are behind the power curve now." I told him, "You ain't shit!" I had a degree and had been working with the engineering department. Still had to wait a while. I needed some leave and my wife and I were gonna drive across country.

After leave we began our trip in a little Jeep (CJ-5) pulling a trailer that my dad and I had built. Looked like the Beverly Hillbillies but we were happy and on our way home. We both liked California and it was just Susan and me. Life was an adventure.

CHAPTER TWO

Explosive Entry

When I reported in to the Station Team at El Toro, things were a mess. I had learned from previous leaders that it is best to observe for a week or two then make the needed changes. The situation didn't permit that luxury.

My first morning there, at around 0900, a young sergeant approached me with a beer in hand and said, "Want a cool one, sir? We do this all the time."

I don't have to expound on which direction that conversation went. Suffice to say that the young sergeant no longer thinks that beer in a Marine EOD shop at 0900 is appropriate.

The former EOD officer offered to come by and do a turnover. I told him that I preferred that he didn't. This one was best handled my way.

As I analyzed each individual I realized that there was some real talent there. Just boys being boys and being given too much leash. I told you about my antics so I knew where their heads were. You got the broad brush of this in my intro but I can say as a professional this was truly the best tour of my career.

As I listened I heard conversations referring to E-5s and below, and "Tell that E-4 to come here." Another one that really sent me spinnin': "Get the troops together."

I also noticed that there was a shit hot gunny who organized the men for morning Physical Training (PT) every day.

The senior gunny would sit on his ass and never join in. One morning, after a few days I walked out and asked the gunny if I could join him and the Marines.

He grinned ear to ear and said, "Hell yes, sir."

I replied, "Good, now we just have to wait on the other gunny to get his PT gear on."

The guffaw started.

"Er…Sir, I don't do that, I've got a medical chit…"

"Let's see it," I said.

The day before I heard him telling the Marines, "You guys hurry and get this PT done."

He said, "Sir, I live in Riverside and that's where my PT gear is."

I said, "Go get it, we'll wait." Couple hours later he returned but couldn't run, do pull-ups, or sit-ups. Don't want to spend time on him but that was the atmosphere. Got rid of him. I held a formation.

Announcements:

1. *From this point on you will be Sergeants and Corporals, not E-5s or E-4s. I worked hard to make Sergeant and Corporal* (I was so good they let me be a corporal twice) *and no prick ever called me an E-5 or E-4. E-5 is a pay grade and we ain't here for the money. If you let ANYBODY refer to you as that, I don't want you.* (Later I had a young, hard-charging sergeant tell a lieutenant colonel that he was a Sergeant, not an E-5. The colonel looked at the EOD badge and just nodded. Sure swelled that sergeant up and made me feel good, too.)

2. *We are not Troops, we are Marines. If you want to be a Troop I'll arrange an interservice transfer for you to the Army.* (Had no idea if I could do that…but neither did they.)

3. *We will PT every day just as the gunny has established it. Gunny, I request that you let me lead PT on Fridays.* (Got a sharp "Aye-aye, sir.")

4. *We will field day* (very detailed cleaning) *the office and shop space once a week with a detailed cleanup every night.*

5. *Also, I want an ordnance museum in this shop that the Queen Mary would want to visit. Gunny, assign someone to make it happen.*

You would not believe the transformation of those men. They had it in them. The junior gunny saw it, too, and had tried his best but got cut at every turn by the senior gunny.

I told the good gunny, now senior because the other guy got shit-canned, "Gunny, you have twelve sets of footprints in front of your desk. I have one set in front of mine and they belong to you." From that point on *he* ran one hell of a shop. Pride swelled; the decks were spit-shined. Commanders brought VIPs down to see the museum. I think the real reason they came down was that the EOD Marines shouted "attention on deck" and that is something the Air wing ain't used to.

We partied, as EOD folks were expected to do. We raised hell. I received many a call at 0100 or 0200 from the Marines.

Susan would answer the phone and I could hear a drunken voice ask, "Susie, can the skipper come out and play?"

"No, Mac," would be her answer, but they loved her nonetheless. Mac would always be the one to call because the other Marines figured he was Susan's favorite. They knew that at any time, day or night, they could come by and get a bowl of spaghetti or chili or a sandwich.

Once, during a disagreement, Susan told me, "You love those Marines more than you love me!"

I responded, "That is as it should be. If we get thrown into the shit, those guys are gonna bring me home to you." Never heard that comment again. She didn't mean it anyhow—she loved 'em, too.

The young hard-charging sergeant who informed the lieutenant colonel that he was a sergeant was a particular challenge. Might have weighed 120 pounds, but was hard as nails. I had a lot of EOD parties at my house, and on every occasion after having a few he had to invite me out. We'd go in the front yard, I'd whip his ass and we'd go back to partying. It was a rite of pas-

The pride of my career, combined EOD teams, El Toro, California

sage. It was like a son thinking he can take Papa Bear. He never did, but he did something else I instilled—he never stopped trying. Bet you guys can't get away with that now.

On Fridays I would take them on a long run around the perimeter of the air station. Man, this really bumped up the pride. We became the envy of El Toro.

When the Headquarters Marine Corps, Explosive Ordnance Disposal (HQMC, EOD) Officer in Charge came out to do our IG inspection, he about had a kitten. We all received Excellents but I strongly felt that the Marines deserved an Outstanding. I was told that nobody gets an Outstanding.

That's the backdrop on the climate and personnel. Needless to say, I was honored to have guys like this on the team. One of those fine officers is out there teaching breaching to you folks out west. Go get 'em! Just don't tell 'em that you started the program—Howdy Doody!

I had made a new friend in the civilian bomb community. He was the commander of the Hazardous Device Squad for Orange

County, California. Another super man with a super team. Now let's see: you have two cocks of the walk in the same grid square. Yep, no love lost between Arleigh and Charlie. I used to laugh my ass off at those two guys. Reminded me of the movie *Grumpy Old Men*. Of course, bein' me, if it got too quiet I'd make a call to one or the other and get it stirred up again.

One thing I never made fun of was the professionalism and pride that they took in their jobs and their people. They were the best, and Charlie still is. We were developing charges left and right. We had discovered flex linear shape charge that was lead-lined and could be conformed to any shape. As mentioned earlier, you weren't a seasoned breacher unless you had lead tattoos on your shoulder. This almost got out of hand.

We conducted many training exercises in and around L.A. and Orange County. Charlie was very good at getting training sites through the fire department. People would donate the structures (that they were going to tear down anyhow), we would blow holes everywhere, then the fire department would set it on fire and practice putting it out. Most of you folks who are breachers will be familiar with the first evolution of charges:

Oval Charges

The first, and least likely, to be used at that time was the Oval and Folding Oval charges developed for getting through doors. We later developed an Oval charge that really focused explosive effects and was used against frame-constructed buildings and residences.

Two "E" silhouette targets taped butt to butt with the heads cut off. Flex linear of various grams were taped around the perimeter using the thickness of the cardboard as a standoff. Now let's talk a little about flex linear and the shaped charge effect, or the Monroe effect. Explosive forces leave the surface of explosives at right angles always. If it is a wrinkled-up gob of powder, then you have numerous forces leaving in every direction. Monroe harnessed this as illustrated (Figure 1):

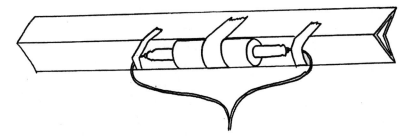

FIGURE 1 Opposing blasting cap priming system

I spoke before about using a wine bottle. In a conical shape the forces leave at right angles in the cone to meet and become one central point jet. Linear, on the other hand, creates a jet that is a straight line. Flex linear came in assorted grains-per-foot configurations. The largest I've seen is 600 grains per foot. I never advocated using anything that large.

I will now discuss the different Oval charges and their application and fill in how they evolved. The Oval is really the first breaching charge to evolve into an operational charge. I want to talk about the smallest to the largest charges, how they were constructed, the thought process behind them, and how we improved upon them. Just cutting a hole is not magic. How can we do it effectively, with no injuries inside, and, very important, do it quietly? Remember Arleigh's router. We'd gone beyond that.

Now keep in mind that, except for a few items, all of the explosives used in breaching were commercial. There was no flex in the Marine allowances. Commercial detonating cord came in other than fifty grain-per-foot and was much more applicable. We discovered that to effectively penetrate an interior hollow core door, twenty-grain flex was perfect. The edges were a little ragged but we got 100% penetration with minor effects inside the door. We were keeping meticulously detailed log books. Guys today are lucky with computers and digital cameras. Beats hell out of a Polaroid and a stubby pencil. Bunch of Marines and cops trying to work out 354 grain divided by 7000, times how many feet. That was comical.

39

A common problem that we faced was attachment. In my early notes and lesson plans I cited the two biggest problems were finding targets to train on and methods of attachment. I taught that you always had to have two methods of attachment for each shot. In those days, axle grease and a prop stick were the quickest and quietest. Only problem that we encountered was axle grease would ignite if placed under the explosives.

Then we got the bright idea...HEY!! Let's make a fireball and let the assaulters appear to be coming from hell!! Well, it worked but it created the need for assaulters to be wearing Nomex fire retardant flight suits.

So there ya have it...Frank had to get flight suits and Nomex gloves for Arleigh and Charlie's teams. I must sound chauvinistic now because one thing Charlie had over Arleigh—Debbie filled out a flight suit better than any of us knuckleheads. In addition to that, she was a professional and held her own against all comers.

We experimented with hollow doors (20-grain flex), solid wood (normally 40- to 60-grain flex), depending on the gut feeling when examining the door. Up to and including metal fire doors (normally from 75- to 125-grain), again dependent upon the door recon. We blew door after door. I had gained access to a source at the base. They were remodeling housing and office spaces. I got all the doors.

Charlie was doing one hell of a job getting targets. Now that we had doors down pat we started thinking about tactics. Knowing what we knew about explosives, could we control the plug that went into the room, with or without fireball? We found if we had intelligence that the bad guys were at the right of the door and the hostage at the left (or vice versa), we would construct our oval as follows:

- Solid door (wood) studded walls
- Oval construction as described earlier. We would put 40-grain flex on the side of the bad guys. We would put 60 or 75 on the side of the good guys. Now let's slow it down and start thinkin' like me: 40 will cut, 60-75 will

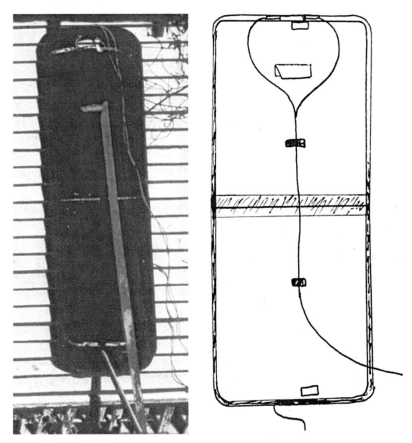

FIGURE 2   Folding Oval Charge

cut faster and cleaner. This pushes the 60- to 75-grain side first and faster while the 40-grain side holds a little longer and slower. This spins the plug into the room in the direction of the bad guys.

Conversely, maybe it's a small room and you want to take extra care not to harm hostages. We would construct the same oval but we left a gap in the charge at the bottom so that the bottom remained attached. This just laid the plug inside the room still attached at the bottom. It worked very well with steel doors. Only problem is the grease. The assaulter will have to run down

41

that ramp created by the plug and it could have, and has, looked like Keystone Kops as they stumbled all over each other. Not a pretty picture with loaded MP5s at the ready.

We experimented with every variation. As we played and developed we had one nagging word that kept dragging us down—Liability. Would the bosses ever okay the use of Explosive Entry? Please remember, at this point I was dealing strictly with law enforcement. I hadn't even thought about introducing it to the Marine Corps. Shit, Marines didn't care about surgical entry. Not yet, anyhow. General Gray hadn't become commandant yet.

At some point during this evolution we started thinking about how difficult it would be to transport our charge. Not too tough on a cop moving in an urban environment, but what if we throw in a fast rope situation? What if the target were in a secluded area and the SWAT had to move quietly? "Careful Hurry," "Smooth is Fast"—we've all heard the terms. What if we could fold our charge in half? Charlie said, No way, because it would break the explosive continuity. Well, we had these little 20-gram DuPont boosters that were red and looked like a one-inch-long small piece of garden hose. Actually looked like a piece of bubble gum. Which my three-year-old son was to discover. Later, in my exposure to the Spec Ops world, I'll relate that.

My concept was we could take a booster, cut it longitudinally. We would run two pieces of flex, top half and bottom half. Attach the "E" silhouette targets as before but give the tape slack so that the charge could fold in half. We would attach the two cut booster halves to each side with an overhang. When unfolded, the booster would lie over the other half of the flex. Worked like a champ and was half the size (Figure 3).

This was all really cool stuff and tons of fun. But, what if we couldn't come through the door? What if it were booby trapped, or the hostages were placed against it, or the door was blocked off? No sweat—let's come through the wall. As you recall, we did that with the Douche Bag Shot but the studs were a problem.

You'll also remember that we had learned to control the plug from the door most of the time. Now we know that we could cut through an outside wall of a wood frame structure, but what about

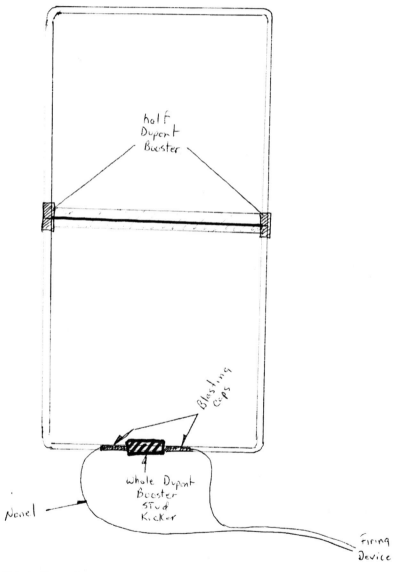

FIGURE 3   Oval charge

that big-assed stud? Especially in older buildings that used real 2 x 4s and long nails. If you believe it when someone says homes today are built better, don't believe them. I know: I've blown my way into old and new. Give me a new, hurricane-proof building any day. I'll huff and I'll puff then I'm comin' to get ya!

Charlie came through with a super training site. It was an old house with lap strap siding, real wood and 2 x 4s. It had a real roof with tongue and groove, a real brick fireplace. Hell, as a young Marine I'd have loved to live there. Beat hell out of Slum Village at Cherry Point. This was our opportunity to play with real walls. We'd heard that the SAS was playing with explosive entry and was using balloons inside to test for overpressure and frag. We did it, too.

We even blew up condoms because we were told they were closer to human skin. I don't think I ever convinced Susan that I needed to carry 100 condoms with me when I traveled. Never used 'em, so I wouldn't know.

I must admit, it was funny watching Debbie blow up those condoms. Believe me when I tell you, we didn't give her any ribbing about that operation. Needless to say, we abandoned that practice because we decided it didn't matter. If it got to the point you needed explosive entry, the use of force continuum had already been satisfied. I knew the Marine Corps wouldn't give a shit about blown-up rubbers.

We constructed our standard Folding Oval but we had to figure out how to take out a stud. Remember: studs are normally placed on sixteen-inch centers. No assaulter with gear can get through a hole created between two studs with sixteen-inch centers. Some structures are built on twenty-four-inch centers but it's still too small.

I'm a dumb ass when it comes to handyman stuff so I ask the logical question, "How do we find the stud?"

Debbie replies, "With a stud finder."

I said, "Smart ass."

She says, "No, you can buy a density locator at the hardware store." Oh well, there ya go. Had again. We wasted no time obtaining one of these and practiced all morning on locating the studs. In the old days it took a lot of practice because they weren't as accurate as today. But we got very good.

In the early days if we were off a half-inch or so, it didn't matter. As we grew and enhanced the explosive effects, even an eighth of an inch mattered. This really got our heads spinning. Anyone can blow through a wall, but we're breachers and we have to control it. It ain't gonna control us.

We developed two wall charges. We determined, first, do we want the plug to go up or lay down? To have it go up we placed a 20-gram booster at the bottom of the oval exactly where the stud was determined to be. We initiated at that point so that the cut started at the bottom, the booster snapped the stud or pushed it off the nails (preferred), and as the cut went up each side of the oval it spun upwards. If we placed the booster at the top it would cause the plug to lie down.

We experimented and played with this until it became second nature. I was to that point by then and used to convey this to my students: Whenever you go out to eat, go to church, any office space—when you find yourself examining the structure and determining in your mind what it would take to breach, and what the best charge would be, you are morphing into a breacher.

I've had many students come back and tell me "at first I thought you were full of shit, but now every time I go into a building I catch myself doing a recon as to what it would take."

I always say, "That ain't a bad thing, keep it up."

The Oval charge used to penetrate shingles, tar and tar paper, and wooden sheathing, then crack the rafters (Figure 4 and 5). The result was that the drywalled ceiling just fell harmlessly to the floor. It would have startled the tangos (terrorists) and made them dodge but the debris would have harmed no hostages. We had two personnel inside the living room, sitting on a couch, when this shot was fired. Just in case, we wore helmets, eye protection, and body armor. Never once felt overpressure or frag. There was a great deal of dust and small debris but that was it. "We can come from anywhere and everywhere at the same time."

FIGURE 4

I used to tell my students to imagine Murphy everywhere. I don't think I've ever seen a discipline more susceptible than breaching to the effects of Murphy. I also insisted that they "what if" everything until they're sick to death of it. As a breacher, I would ask my teammates during the chalk talk: Number one, give me two what ifs, number two same, and so on.

You would be amazed at how many clusterfucks were cut off during those exchanges. During training, "what if" was a byword. I know that's a no-no in most training circles, but you'd better do it in breaching. Normally by the time folks reached the level that they were training in or experimenting with breaching, their "what ifs" made sense.

We even discovered that a liberal amount of axle grease applied between the charge and the target was an excellent form of adhesion, plus it threw a huge, non-lethal fireball into the room. You can imagine what it looked like to the bad guys inside at 0300—large explosion, huge fireball with black-clad warriors emerging from the fireball with sub guns ablaze. Quite the distraction.

FIGURE 5

"C" Charges (later called ATT charges)

Nothing glamorous here, but an important part of the evolution and one that should be on every breacher's mind. How can I achieve the same goal with less explosives? If I want to get through a door, is there a way that produces less frag, less overpressure, and less chance of injuring who I am trying to save? The next logical question: How is the door attached? Normally by two or three hinges on one side and a door knob, latch, or throw bolt on the other. Biggest drawback here is a drop bar on the back side of the door. We'll talk later about how to defeat that.

47

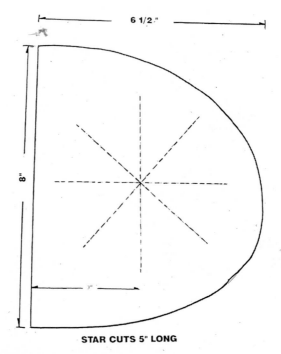

STAR CUTS 5" LONG

"C" Charge

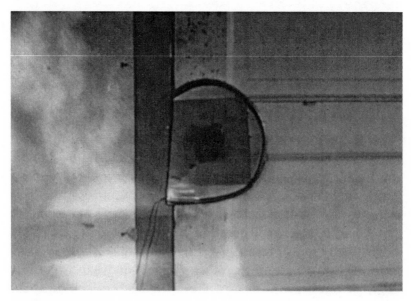

C Charge in place

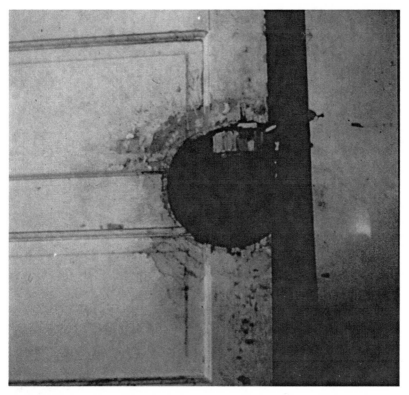

Notice the clean, knife-like cut. This is 100% penetration with minimum amounts of explosives.

Up until now we had been using about twelve feet of flex or detonating cord to get through a door. Now we take the same flex or detonating cord (I never was a detonating cord fan but it's easy for the military to get), say, forty grain per foot. We cut a piece of cardboard that looks like the outline of a "D." We cut a star hole in the middle as illustrated. Tape the flex around the curved edge, not the straight side. Now we have approximately 1½ feet, which is forty grain=.00857143 pounds, Net Explosive Weight (NEW) to get through the same door. You got it. Now we have a charge that each assaulter can carry and if s/he runs into locked interior doors, s/he can attach, yell fire in the hole, and blow and go. I understand that most units have phased out this charge. What a shame.

Gun ports

LAPD, the Orange County Sheriff's Office, and the L.A. County Sheriff's Office SWAT teams were becoming very interested in what we were doing. This was when the learning curve accelerated beyond belief. We began the real tactical application, from an operator's standpoint. "What ifs" totally shifted, egos bumped in to each other. We had been doing this for a number of years and now the new guys were trying to horn in. But that grew and evolved and new respect was given and taken by all. We really had the team now.

One question kept popping up: What if (love those two words) we breach a door and make entry to discover that there is an L-shaped or a T-shaped room and the bad guy is around the corner? It's okay to be able to cut the pie but our assault has been delayed and the bad guy has time to do harm to the hostages. Good point. Someone brought up the idea of diversions but I'll explain how that evolved later. What about a gun port that is blown in the wall to provide coverage of the blind areas? We worked this out to a science with our assault planners. We just made a circle charge, just like the oval, only smaller—about two feet in diameter. This was mounted at a predetermined area that, when blown, would create a hole for a shooter to provide coverage. As you can imagine, this required coordination. Didn't want our guys shooting each other. So I gave a little class on fields of fire and chalk talk coverage. Now to coordinate while not trying to get ahead of myself. This is how it would go.

The gun port charges would be placed at a predetermined and agreed upon location. Each SWAT member would verify verbally the location of the gun ports and the fields of fire. The gun port shooters would be on standby. The assault team would move to the objective. The breacher places the charge. Green light comes from the command post (CP). Control is normally assumed by the CP in the form of "Assault team you have a green light" followed by "I have control," then a count-

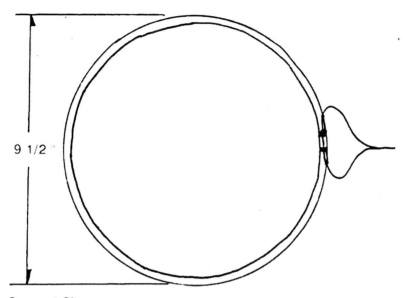

Gunport Charge

down: five, four, three, two..... After "two" is verbalized, the gun ports are fired. On "one," the main charge is fired and the team assaults. That is very basic (with a bunch of stuff left out that I will cover later).

We decided to reinvent the wheel: water hydraulically pushed through the target. All we could remember was that nasty, ugly, heavy, hard-to-handle Douche Bag charge that Arleigh came up with. The only thing that nagged us was that it worked.

I don't want to sound melodramatic but we were at a training site and had taken a break. I forget who, but someone was drinking from a one-liter soda bottle. Either that person or someone else said, "Hey, why don't we use a soda bottle?" Well, great idea, but how do we get the explosives inside? None of us was talented in that and we didn't know who knew how to erect them little ships inside of a glass bottle.

So we kept playing, talking, discussing, cussing, and what evolved was very simplistic and required another trip to the

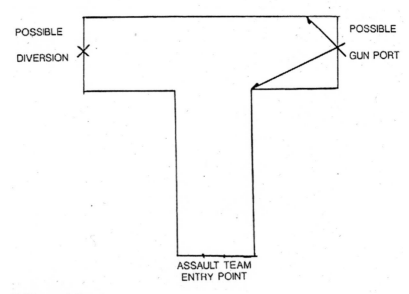

POSSIBLE
DIVERSION

POSSIBLE
GUN PORT

ASSAULT TEAM
ENTRY POINT

T Shaped Room

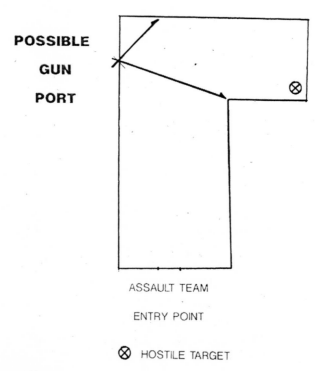

POSSIBLE

GUN

PORT

ASSAULT TEAM

ENTRY POINT

⊗ HOSTILE TARGET

L Shaped Room

hardware store. In those days, plastic soda bottles had a plastic boot on the bottom. This was easily removed. We poked a hole in the bottom and a hole through the cap. We fed detonating (det) cord through the hole in the bottom, up through the opening, and through the cap. We left enough detonating cord out the bottom and top to rejoin and tape for an initiation point. Once in place we hot-glued the bottom. This created (hopefully) a water-tight seal. We then filled the bottle with water, screwed the top on, hot-glued where the detonating cord came out of the top, joined the ends, and there was our charge.

If you felt that you needed more detonating cord you could feed the detonating cord out the neck of the bottle, tape additional detonating cord to the main line (making sure your pieces were short enough to go back in the bottle), then pull it back into the bottle. You were only restricted by the neck opening. Later, plastic milk containers with flat sides and larger openings were preferred. Now this thing looks really cool and is bound to kick ass with little or no explosive effects.

But remember the two biggest problems with breaching??? Yep, attachment. How do we attach this cool guy charge? Nylon-reinforced tape became the answer. We ran a piece of tape from the neck to the bottom with lots of slack. This formed a loop that held neatly over a doorknob. This little piece of ingenuity became the mainstay for blowing a door open. Worked great. Commercial folks are making a fortune on it today.

With three additional strands of 50-grain detonating cord, it would also override the latching mechanisms of inward-opening steel doors.

What about outward-opening steel doors? With a little thought we overcame that with the Bellville spring theory. We attached the bottle to the center of the door (dead in the middle) at the same height as the latch. This would push the door in, bending it to the point it extracted the lock then the metal would tend to want to go back to its original configuration which would cause the door to just swing open without even blowing a hole.

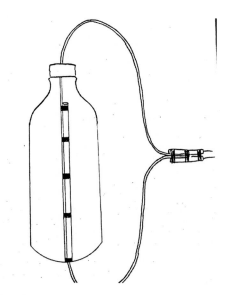

Water impulse charge

Water Impulse charge in place

Block dropper (mail tubes)

It was determined that plastic mail tubes were the perfect tool for transmitting water hydraulics to concrete block walls. Dependent upon the reinforcing factor of the blocks, you could increase the size of the detonating cord to increase the brisance that would effectively drop the block in place with no frag inside the room. It is this principal that most of the commercial items use today. Dick Marcinko's boys proved invaluable by bringing operational applications to the development phase of this charge.

After all, my layman definition of breaching was:

"Use explosives to rapidly penetrate a barrier—wall, door, roof, or floor—in order to engage the bad guys with ultimate and complete surprise, causing no injury to innocents inside the objective. No injury to assault team members." For law enforce-

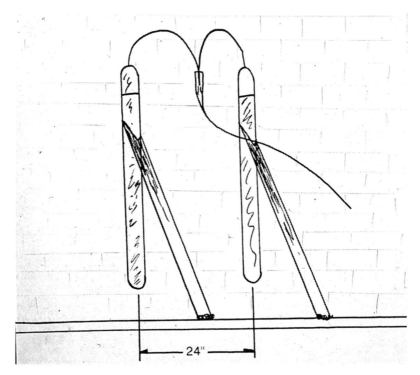

Mail Tube Water Impulse Charge

ment I add, "While limiting the liabilities within the scope of the use of force continuum."

I will cover more on water charges when we discuss the training evolutions. Water seems to be the trend today with the advent of the Sidney Alford tools and Chris Cherry's water tools. Sure do wish I had been smart enough to market my ideas.

We developed the remote wire cutters being sold today. Anybody wants to challenge that, I have the original drawings. I had MSgt Gregory make the first one for me at the armor repair facility, Weapons Training Battalion, Quantico. It was a tube just like the one you see today, with a piston driven by a squib. You guys can make this stuff. We did and it worked.

Slant Charge

The Slant Charge is one of my favorites for its simplicity and failsafe use. As you may have noticed, I am a simple man with a simple mind. I like to take the straight route from point A to point B. If you'll recall, a door has two or more hinges on one side and at least one latching mechanism on the other. The best way to positively open that door is to separate the hinges from the lock(s). I came up with a six foot or less piece of flex taped to cardboard (flex grain size remains the same as for an Oval, just half the amount). I cut a right angle point on each end so that it could be leaned either way. I would place the charge with the bottom being below the lowest hinge and the top above the highest latch. If the door was recessed in a doorjamb, all the better. The jamb gave support to my charge.

Even if you have a dead man or drop bar, you can jerk (normally it's already clear) the bottom half of the door and go in under the top half. If there's no dead man, the top half will swing freely. Works great...every time. When we did dog and ponies later in my career this was my charge of choice. Murphy couldn't find many ways to screw it up short of mechanical or component failure which only he had control over. The slant charge could also be folded in half for easy transport but remember—the more moving parts, the more Murphy likes it.

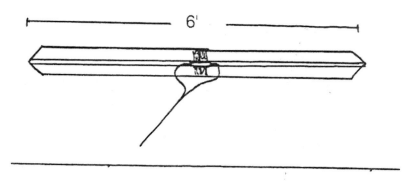

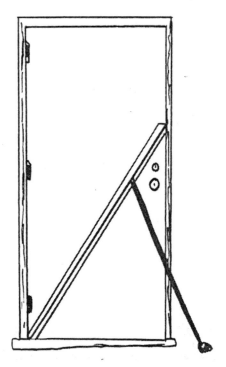

Slant Charge

Window Charges

We all have to have a little fun and adrenaline push. We began by learning a great deal from our SWAT partners. They had a deal going with windows and glass that really sucked. They went in by break and rake. They would break the glass inward with a baton or flashlight then rake the loose glass that was left so that they had a clean hole to go through without getting a piece of glass in their ass.

I was no SWAT guy, but let me put it in perspective: you're up there at the window; you have to expose yourself to break the glass, and then stand there like a big dummy raking the glass out of the edges. Wonder what Bobby Bad Guy is gonna be doing all that time? One of the targets that Charlie had graced us with had ample windows for us to play with. What evolved is the "Window Charge." We built an L-shaped device out of 1 x 2 stripping. It was approximately six feet long with the L part being about two feet long. We attached this with copious tape.

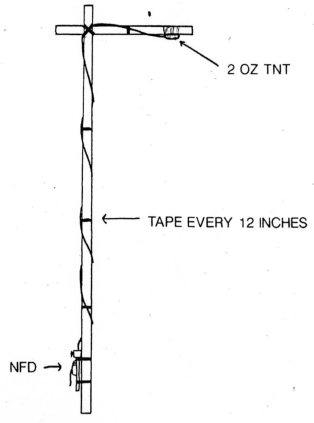

2 OZ TNT

TAPE EVERY 12 INCHES

NFD →

Window charge assembly

No nails—remember, "If you can't eat and digest it, don't put it on your charge." We crushed one wafer of TNT to powder (one-pound blocks of TNT are packaged as a number of wafers). We put this in a plastic sandwich bag and taped it to the short end of the L. We then ran Nonel (or shock tube, as it's called today) to the firing device on the handle. I will cover the evolution of initiation later.

That is a story in and of itself. Then, like before: five, four, three, two, and on one the breacher swung the device like a bat plunging the short L through the window and fired the device once it was in. This blew all the glass out and if you were real lucky it removed the entire window frame. The fun part was that the breacher had to hold onto the stick during detonation. What a rush.

I was a guest speaker for the International Association of Bomb Technicians and Investigators (IABTI) on Explosive Entry. I had put the Los Alamos guys through training several years later and they invited me to tell 'em my tale. Well, we had a demo day and the guys wanted to see a window charge. They overdid it and were using a small concrete building to boot. It removed the window, the doors, and the roof, and the breacher was a little shaken up. P=E.

First Force Recon Breacher Course

Fracture Charges

Satellite Charge One of the charges under
"Fracture Charges"

Don't ask how we came up with these names. It is good to see today that most of the original charges have the same name. Of course Sidney Alford had to give the British twist but that's understandable—he's British. On a trip with him we were discussing water charges and I don't think he knew or cared about my background. I mentioned that we had worked with water back in the '70s with the LAPD.

He didn't say anything for a few minutes then with an utterance he said, "That was over thirty years ago."

I said, "I know." As you've read, water impulse is not new.

Subject was never addressed again. Good on him. He, as we all were, is an innovator. He has taken the original concept to the next level and has gone commercial. Gotta remember, in my day this stuff was classified.

Anyhow, back to the Satellite charge. All was well and dandy as long as the doors and walls were stick wood. What about blocks and concrete? Oh shit, that one seemed tough. It was, and still is. There was no magic to getting through concrete. It took ample amounts of powder, pure and simple. We taught and advised to go through concrete as a last resort. I still don't think law enforcement is ready for that. Way too much Net Explosive Weight (NEW). NEW is based on the TNT explosive equivalent.

We used "E" silhouette targets. We cut two-inch squares of deta sheet, an explosive that is pliable but not so much as C-4. It comes in a sheet that is in a roll. It comes in various "C" designations. The number after the "C" is the grams per square inch. Therefore C-3 is three grams of explosives per square inch. Easy math for your NEW calculations, right? The satellite was all guesswork and still is. We just kept adding deta sheet until we got through. How do you know that will work every time? You don't. One wall may be ten inches thick and an adjacent wall in

Satellite fireplace results

the same building may be fourteen inches thick. Just too iffy. However, this is how we built it.

We would cut two-inch squares of deta sheet, normally C-4 or larger. In most cases we would double stack the deta sheet so that it was in fact C-8 or larger. We spaced these around the

We come from anywhere and everywhere

cardboard as illustrated, then tied it all together with detonating cord. Kinda ugly, and not a charge I'd want to use if I were rescuing my family. That was another point I always used: Before you push that button, would you want your family behind that wall? One SWAT guy from L.A. said, "Hell, yes—all I got is an ex-wife."

Ghost Buster

This charge created too much bang for the return. We ran a strip of deta sheet two inches wide around the perimeter of the target. We then ran a strip diagonally from one corner to the opposite corner, making the "No Smoking" or "Ghost Buster" indicator. Again this was a SWAG (Scientific Wild Ass Guess).

Ghost Buster

Ghost Buster results (bricks drop in place)

I never got excited about these because it violated my theory of P=E. These charges did, however, penetrate. They were just unpredictable and heavy duty. Maybe okay in a rural area or a combat zone but not for downtown L.A.

Door Knockers

Another less-favored charge was the door knocker. It was just too much powder for the target and would send doorknobs and locks flying through the room as frag. It does warrant explanation as it, too, was part of the evolution. The tactical guys wanted something small that they could all carry in case they encountered an obstacle inside the objective. We would take a 20-gram booster; if you'll recall, it looks like a two-inch-long

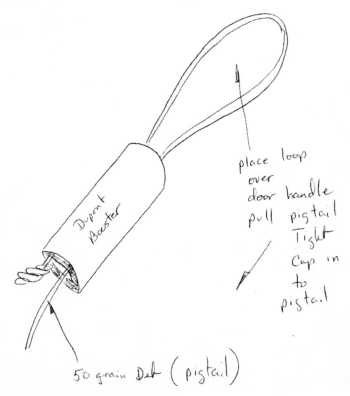

Door knocker or Gumby Charge

piece of garden hose, but it's red. We ran a strand of detonating cord through it, then back through, forming like a hangman's noose. This was slipped over the doorknob, and then the booster was cinched down. Made a hell of a bang and was a threat to the hostages as well as to the tactical team.

Initiator Development

All you old salts bear with me for a second. Want to give a little basic demo to the green peas out there. There are and have been basically two forms of initiation. Electric and Non-Electric (interesting concept, you say). In the '70s when we wanted absolute control we used an electric system. This was made up of an electric cap with leg wires, a firing wire (in breaching, except for fracture charges, the leg wires were enough), and an electrical generating machine, normally called a hell box. Electric is what we started with but the hell box was too cumbersome. We devised a system using a nine-volt battery and a button. Very small and could be managed one handed.

If you wanted complete safety most people agreed that non-electric was the way to go. We didn't have to worry about static or Hazards of Electromagnetic Radiation to Ordnance (HERO). Now in a SWAT environment, radio traffic is crazy all around. The chance of having an accidental detonation is remote but could happen. That's when we learned about Nonel (a commercial non-electric system). It was a small plastic tube similar to an IV tube that came in various lengths. It was dusted with HMX (a British Explosive) and aluminum powder. Crimped to one end was a non-electric cap. This cap could be instant or have a built-in delay. We wanted no delays for breaching.

This gave the best of both worlds. Total control with the safety of non-electric. We developed a firing device that had a firing pin, a trigger, and a twelve-gauge shotgun primer that initiated the Nonel. It was cool stuff because you could see the flash go through the tube...ZAP. We used to run a strand through the class with the cap removed. The students would hold the Nonel in a grip and we'd initiate it with the lights off.

Hard day training

It gave a flash and an impulse as it passed through their grip. Sexy firing devices both manufactured and homemade were the thing of the day. I developed a bang stick device that could be manipulated with one hand.

These systems did not work for the small "C" charges and Door Knockers. For these we used non-electric caps with a very short piece of time fuse and an M60 fuse lighter.

A typical training day was intense. We started early and were excited about results. Time seemed to slip away and it was dark before we knew it.

Avon Rounds

Breaching with a twelve-gauge shotgun was no new concept. What was new was the development of the original Avon round (named for the commercial, "Avon calling"). Until that point, a twelve-gauge shotgun slug round was used to break locks, tear hinges loose, or generally disrupt any door attachment. The problem with this was obvious—there was a flying slug going somewhere and, because of ricochets, you could not tell where that slug was going.

The .50 cal Dearmer (MK2) was a tool commonly used by EOD Teams. I was intrigued by its use of water and/or nickel powder, forced at high velocity by a blank .50 cal impulse cart, to disrupt an Improvised Explosive Device (IED). What I noticed was that all the kinetic energy was depleted on the IED and no "slug" was unleashed. I started by playing with water and nickel powder but the twelve-gauge lacked the push to be effective. Carrying a .50 cal machine gun was out of the question so I went back to the twelve-gauge.

Eventually, after much gnashing of the teeth and nerves, we determined that a mixture of sixty percent dental plaster and forty percent S70 steel shot (the steel shot in old copy machine carts used to keep ink mixed) was ideal. It was light enough to be pushed by the twelve-gauge at high velocity but dissipated after breaking the lock or hinges. There was much debate as to the exact mixture but I think so long as it's fifty-fifty or more dental plaster it is functional. I still say this is a cheap way for law enforcement to breach without buying all the high speed stuff on the market today. Of course, I also say that our original breaching charges were cheaper, safer (less NEW), and more dependable. Don't believe me?? Just take a look at some of the NEWs required for this new-fangled stuff. You just have to maintain logs and photos.

Force Recon nailed me at Lejeune. Being a Cook, Baker, and Candlestick maker (that is what all the operators called strap-hangers like me), I always had to be on my toes. They tested me continuously. We were conducting breacher training at Stone Bay, Camp Lejeune. We had made a batch of Avon the day before because twenty-four hours of dry time is required. If the mixture is not 100% dry you have a wet, heavy slug instead of frangible material.

Some of the Recon guys made a fresh batch and mixed it in with my dry rounds. Funny stuff. I was wearing a Marine green t-shirt and UDT shorts. I had given the class to the boneheads and was going to demonstrate on a solid wood door with a lock and three hinges. I grabbed four rounds and loaded them in to the 870 and positioned the shotgun for a lock attack. My philosophy was to make contact with the door with the muzzle of the weapon, back off about an inch and fire.

Well, sir and ma'am, said first round was a wet one. The wet slug bounced off and penetrated my left thigh and abdomen. The S70 steel shot penetrated the skin and tore up some capillaries but nothing serious. Blood flew everywhere. From the armpit down to my boots (left side) was covered with blood. I knew I'd been had because there was no reaction from the class. Just blank stares. I could read their minds: What's the old bastard gonna do now? Therefore, I continued to teach as I downloaded the shotgun, got three new rounds (which I verified were dry), and proceeded to attack the door successfully.

Afterwards the Corpsman came up and handed me a wet rag to clean up with. A young black corporal came up to me later and said, "Suh, you one hard mutha fucka." I still wear that comment and the steel shot tattoo as a badge of honor. You can bet I checked all rounds from then on. It must have impressed them, because most young corporals don't address captains in such a manner, at least not to their faces. Later, as we grew together and these guys became my instructors, we had some laughs at my expense.

I don't want to dwell too much on the charges, as I will get into more depth in later chapters. I just wanted to cover the birth and development as they were just ideas, concepts, and experimentation at the time. We all thought, "What a great idea," but we didn't know how well this new technology would be accepted. Liabilities were, and still are, obvious. It is imperative that each breacher keep a detailed log and photos of all shots in the event the charges have to be justified in court. This is the main reason that water emerged as the tool of choice when it came to law enforcement.

From the middle of 1983 until my assignment to State Department I got heavily involved with assisting Arleigh and Charlie Stumph in preparing for the 1984 Olympics in L.A. This was to become a turning point in my career and life. I had no idea what I was in store for.

In the summer of 1983 the planning for the Olympics had built to a fever pitch. All jurisdictions were competing for their piece of the pie. Territories were being marked off and egos were rampant. I realized early on that my little game of pitting Arleigh against Charlie would not be wise. We all had too much to worry about.

The traffic in L.A. was already horrendous. Those of you who live in Southern California know what I'm talkin' about. We were set up in an area called Piper Tech. This was our planning center and would become our operations center during the Olympics.

As it turned out, the traffic was nothing because most residents left town—most of the time the freeways were a ghost town. All that was missing was the Santa Ana winds blowing tumbleweeds down the 405 freeway.

Unknown to me, wheels were in motion that would dramatically change my role during the Olympics and my entire career path was to not only take a fork in the path, but a right angle…a sharp turn. Things had started to get a little weird. I sat in meetings where it was discussed not if, but how much, explosives we would use on a wheel of the Olympic athletes' bus in the event they were hijacked. We could blow a wheel off and the SWAT guys could assault. Man, would the news media love to sink their teeth into that. That comes later. Let's get back to breaching.

Shipboard Breaching

Just when I thought we were well on the road and we could breach anything, a SEAL asks me, "Frank, do you know anything about breaching on board a ship?" I looked at him and thought to myself, here I am Mr. Breacher and I never even thought of a mission that would more than likely fall to the SEALs or Force Recon. Of course they needed shipboard breaching. More importantly, they needed the data from a breaching training trip. I called around and got put on hold, transferred to this guy and that gal until I finally was about to give up. Then I remembered

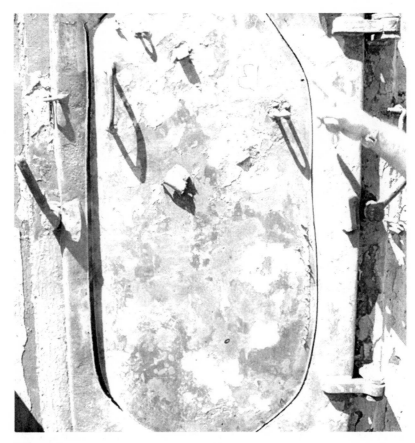

The cut

my buddies down in North Carolina who had gotten all those ships from the graveyard that we sank off Kitty Hawk.

I called Dave at N.C. Fisheries and told him what I was up against. He said to hang on a second. He came back to the phone with the number of a sand crab in Norfolk who was in charge of the salvage program for old Navy ships. Luckily he was also a retired Master Chief and you never had to worry about stuff falling through the cracks when those guys started playing. They just made it happen. Master Chief answered on the second ring. I re-introduced myself as we'd met when I first went down to survey the ships for N.C.

Doug, another unsung hero who now has only one hand. The best at P=E.

Long story short, the Master Chief locked on an old Liberty Ship and training commenced.

We were soon to learn that explosive effects were considerably different aboard ship. Reflective overpressure took on a whole new meaning. An assault team could no longer stack against the breach. More importantly they could not stack in a

71

reflective area. Reflective overpressure, in most cases, was more devastating than direct overpressure.

Couple that with the fact that you are in a solid steel hull. It's like taking a solid steel rod and striking an anvil. The vibration is indescribable.

Doug wrestled with overpressure and we determined that the standard breaching charges may not be applicable below decks on a ship.

We focused on smaller charges, attacking the "dogs" on compartment hatches. Oval charges were still acceptable above decks. Water was not a consideration as steel is considered a hard target.

Shipboard training was completed with many lessons learned. Just another tool in the tool box.

CHAPTER THREE

Diplomatic Security

While at El Toro, the Marines and I went through a big change over the two years that I had spent there. We had grown together and formed an exemplary unit. I would've stacked these guys against any in the Corps. The officers who had come in during those two years were also top shelf and Master Sergeant Fox, the NCOIC was a rock as long as he didn't have to do administrative work. I think the guy broke out into hives if you asked him to do an after-action report or do some filing. Put him in the field or in charge of a run and he was good to go. He and I became a team and life long friends.

We were all neck-deep in getting ready for the Olympics because we knew, regardless of the territorial battles, if something big happened the military was gonna be called in. The Marines at El Toro were the closest. I gotta hand it to my generals and Commanding Officer's at the time. Other than that colorful brief from Arleigh, I was left alone to put it all together. We had developed emergency disposal procedures and locations, and evacuation routes for the bomb trailers. We had stocked L.A. and Orange County with enough explosives to deal with any situation, and if they fell short we were there to pick up the slack.

I had a ritual at El Toro. We would periodically have a family day at the range. In the morning the EOD guys would put their wives and kids in the bleachers then put on a demolition demonstration that awed them all. We then grilled hamburgers and hotdogs and had Cokes. (Yeah—EOD had Cokes in them days.) At about 1400 I received a land line call on the phone from Bev, our Woman Marine (WM) EOD officer assigned to the State

Department. She was an outstanding EOD officer and a Marine personified. The billet that she had was unpopular with the old-timers in Marine EOD at the time. Little was it known that EOD was going to play such an important role in our War on Terror.

Like our EOD folks in theatre now. Where do we get these kids? To me it's hard to comprehend. I heard one story of a Marine EOD master sergeant who responded to eighty IED calls in a twenty-four-hour period. Not to mention our famous gunnery sergeant who, in an attempt to win hearts and minds, gave the bad guys a thumbs up…just got his middle finger confused with his thumb. God bless him, his parents for having him, and everything he stands for. I don't restrict my praise to Marine EOD. The entire community has suffered together. As a result of the conflicts today the EOD community has grown closer and mutually supportive in every arena. It is amazing to see the learning curve leap when information sharing is the common effort.

When Bev called I was surprised, as it was unusual to get a land line call on the range unless it was the general or colonel wanting to have a talk and listen session…they talked, I listened. It was good to hear from Bev because I always respected her transition into the all-male field of EOD. Her question rocked me back a little. "Frank, would you be interested in relieving me at State?" Before I could respond, she continued that since I was so deeply involved in the Olympic planning, DSS wanted me on board because they were going to have fifty-one operational protective details during the Olympics. I had no idea what her job even was. I knew that she traveled a lot but that was it.

Here's what was in my head:

Law school—I was living my lifelong dream.

We had adopted my oldest son.

I was in the battle for the Olympic preparation.

I was developing the breaching program with friends.

This wouldn't make any friends for me in Marine EOD.

I asked how long before I had to give my decision.

She said, "Before we hang up." She further told me that I would travel a great deal but I'd see stuff others only dreamed of or didn't know about to dream of.

"I'll do it!!"

Bev was happy and I finished out the day with a bunch of stuff runnin' around in my brain housing group. Not the least of which was I'd made a decision without talking to Susan. Not only not smart, but not in line with the relationship I had with my favorite girl. Later we would both learn that this decision had cast me into a theatre that would require me to make many decisions without consulting her. Much of it I couldn't even tell her about.

Now don't get the impression that I was a spook working on this "black" project or that "compartmentalized information" because I was the "Cook, Baker, Candlestick Maker." I was just fortunate enough to be involved with guys and gals who were on the cutting edge at the time. I won't mention names as these are the true, silent heroes who will never be known. It is unfortunate because these days, some are successful in consulting, contracting, and training positions, and doing well. Others are not doing as well through fate or luck but if the truth were known about these true Americans and what they did for this country in the '80s and '90s it would astonish you.

As for me, I am thankful for my decision because I got to work with these folks. I traveled with them, trained with them, and partied with them. And as with the Recon Marines, they always tested me. I think I passed with flying colors because most of these folks are still friends. For more details refer to *Rogue Warrior* and *Red Cell*. Don't know if all stories are true but I do know that most were. I learned early that the author, Richard Marcinko, was one of a kind and what was needed at the time.

As it turned out, the United States was hosting the NATO Ministerial at the Wye Plantation in Maryland. It was coming up soon so I had to get back to D.C. ASAP so that Bev could train me and tell me about my new job. I was excited and apprehensive at the same time. Had no idea what to expect. I knew that two former Marine EOD captains had retired and taken positions at State. One was the senior firearms instructor and the other handled the Marine security guard training. I had visions in my mind...U.S. Department of State...marble...big offices. I'm sure that existed but not at my level. Got to peek in a few of those places once and a while when on protective detail, but it wasn't for me.

When I arrived at State Annex 15 (SA-15) in Roslyn, Virginia, I looked up at the cold, contemporary office building. I think it may have been about ten stories and brown and square. I took the elevator to the fourth floor and met the boss. He introduced me around, then showed me to a gray metal desk haphazardly positioned amongst other gray desks.

"I think this is you." Bev had to travel at the last minute and was not there to meet and greet me. That was okay; I kinda liked to look around on my own and get the lay. I've never been a real bashful person so introductions were easy. You wouldn't believe how easy it was to make the personality types of people in that environment. You had the career types who were all about the political aspects and did a good job. You had the ones who pretended to be career types and had all the vernacular and polish but down deep they didn't give a shit—just didn't want the boss to know that.

Then you had the good guys—didn't give a shit and didn't care who knew it. They did their jobs; if they objected to an issue they let it be known. I read that place in just a couple of days. Welcome to the Diplomatic Security Service (DSS). That sounds negative but I don't mean it that way. I think I just described a cross section of corporate America. At least that's been my experience since, whether with Kellogg/Brown and Root, the Disney on Ice show, or Ringling Brothers, just to name a few.

After I checked in, which took a few days, I was given a sheet that listed all the equipment I was to draw. It was somewhat free time while I accomplished this. My son Stephen was two, and my best buddy. It was hard to go anywhere without him, nor did I want to. I had to go to the firearms range to draw some equipment and I knew the range master so I took Stephen along. We had a white 1984 Corvette at the time and I was feeling good—headed to Lorton, Virginia, as a new State Department guy, with my son strapped in next to me.

76

Stephen was big into cowboys and Indians and he was forever configuring his finger like a pistol. He would point his finger and go, Pow! Pow! Pow! Everyone thought this cute. I'm sure the gun control freaks would find some kind of Freudian screw-up on my part that made him do that.

Our heroes in those days were John Wayne, Clint Eastwood, and Don Shula—not dope dealers, gang-bangers, millionaire athletes, and movie stars that degrade everything this country has stood for, from a jail cell. Forgive me; I'm just a little to the right of Attila the Hun.

When I arrived at the range I was happy to see my old friend the range master. We had compared notes before and we both had been at Dong Ha, South Viet Nam at the same time. Didn't know each other but when you've eaten the same real estate it establishes a bond. I was taken aback when he started pulling out weapons, magazines, holsters, bullets…it just kept coming. I was issued an Uzi 9mm sub gun, twelve-gauge Shorty shotgun, Model 19 Smith & Wesson (.357), and a Browning Hi Power 9mm pistol. Of course I got all the goodies: holsters, magazines, pouches, Velcro forever, more bullets.

Hell, I looked like Mel Gibson in *Thunderdome* when I lugged everything out to the 'Vette. Now I'm thinkin,' like most Marines would at the time, I ain't ever been trained on any of this stuff except for this short-assed little shotgun. But it all looked cool, 'specially the little Israeli sub gun. Been seein' 'em in the movies and reading about them but never had one. One thing kept buggin' me, or exciting me…what do I need all this hardware for? I would find out soon enough.

In this state of deep thought Stephen was asking a million questions followed up by a million more as only a two-and-a-half-year-old can do.

His eyes were as big as two trash can lids when he saw all that stuff. Now to set the stage, I am not a gun nut. I do believe in the right to bear arms. That's an inalienable right. I just never got into the gunslinger mode. I did become quite a good shot which pissed off most of my guys later on, but for now I was just the bomb guy.

I popped open the back of the 'Vette and stashed my arsenal. At least I was smart enough to put the ammo up front. As dumb as it sounds today, kids weren't required to be in a kid's seat so Stephen had the run of the car. It was about 1630 and Beltway traffic was, as usual at this time, all shiny. So many cars you couldn't even see the road.

Stephen was in the back, very quiet, then he started his Pow! Pow! stuff. I chuckled as usual and asked several times, "Did you get 'em, son?"

"Yeah, Nanny" (couldn't say "Daddy" yet). I noticed the cars in my rearview mirror were backing off or pulling into other lanes. I thought perhaps an emergency vehicle was coming. The void got larger and larger. Stephen was really into the Pow! Pow! by then.

I was gettin' concerned so I said, "Quiet, son, there's traffic." I turned to look at him and about defecated.

He had the Uzi up in the rear glass, Pow! Pow!-ing all the cars behind us. I saw my short-lived State Department career flash before my eyes. I finally got the Uzi away from him, got him seated in the front seat, then hurriedly took the next exit. Many days went by with me expecting the Law to come and arrest me or having the boss come in and say, You're headed back to the Corps and they've got something waiting for you.

Nothing happened but I learned a big lesson. Weapons security was a household word. I had never had guns in the house before, but my entire perspective changed that day.

Bev returned and she began giving me the dump. Up until that point several mobile training teams had been sent out worldwide with emphasis on Beirut and Bogota. I was just holding down my gray desk and following Bev around, trying to learn what I could. Bev was a bunch smarter than me but she was patient and made sure I got what info I needed.

CHAPTER FOUR

First Mission

NATO Ministerial meeting, Wye Plantation, Maryland, late 1984. That was a whirlwind and my memory catches bits and pieces. There are points that stand out that will never be forgotten. We stayed in a real nice hotel, something I wasn't used to in the Marine Corps. We had several Army EOD types assigned to the detail to perform searches and provide IED security. I wasn't sure how that worked because I was EOD, so what was I gonna do with them? Soon learned that one, too.

Man, when it kicked off we were getting calls left and right… search this limo…search that restaurant…go search a boat… search that hotel. It was enough to drive you nuts. Bev took it coolly and in stride while teaching me along the way. In the midst of that she also took the time to take me around to all the posts at every shift change to meet the agents assigned to the detail. It was obvious that everyone had a great deal of respect for Bev.

As anyone who has ever worked a detail will know, time runs together. Days are lost, meals are skipped, night becomes day, and vice versa.

With what downtime you have, you party. I tried to be careful in this regard since I was the new guy, but I knew I had the proven potential to be a Marine Corps Animal if the need arose. A local bar had an all-you-can-eat-and-drink night, so we went. Bev was not present.

An old State Department guy was there, a former Marine chopper pilot in Vietnam. As the night progressed, one of the Army EOD guys was a little loaded and started mouthing off to the female Army EOD tech. It escalated and the State guy got into the discussion. For some reason, we all decided to walk back to the hotel. When we got back we sat on benches outside the front of the hotel. The State guy went up to his room and I stayed down to make sure the Army folks were calmed down.

All seemed well until, all of a sudden, the State guy came running across the porch, jumped over us and went after the Army EOD guy. I caught the State guy mid-flight but I was too small to have much effect on his big ass. He and the Army guy whaled away for a couple of slugs then we broke it up.

To this day I don't know, nor does the State guy know, why he came back downstairs to jump the Army guy. The State guy was really a good guy as a rule, so I'm sure he had a reason.

The next day there were some bruises but all tried to act like nothing had happened. I continued going to the posts and talking with the agents. It was cold and miserable so the conversations centered on that. The plantation was donated by the Corning family, I was told. There were deer stands on the property that hadn't been used for years. In some cases rusty shotguns were still leaned against the rails of the deer stands where they had been left after a hunt. I was amazed. I was to be further amazed by the activities of rich and famous people as I worked my way through State and as a private security specialist upon retirement.

We were almost finished and the Ministerial was winding down. We had two military bomb dogs assigned to the detail. Bomb dogs are normally passive and subdued.

One of these dogs was the "Hound from the Baskervilles." He would attack his own mirror reflection. His handler was the only human that could come near him. They had to keep a muzzle on this one. We were in the command post, which was made up of two adjoining rooms. We were shootin' the bull and drinking coffee, just happy to know it was almost over.

We were already thinking about L.A. and the Olympics. We had heard that the Secretary of State, George Shultz, was coming to address the Ministers. Again it was drizzly raining and miserable. About mid-afternoon an agent came bustin' in to the CP. We had the two dogs locked in the heads, one in each room. The bad ass was in our room.

The agent was dressed to the tee, earpiece and all. In a big hurry, no doubt, he yelled, "Where's the head?" He then looked at the door which was obviously the head and yelled over his shoulder, "In here, Mr. Secretary!"

Mr. Shultz came steamin' in, grabbing at his fly, obviously in need of the facilities. As his hand reached for the doorknob my hair stood on end.

I yelled, "No, Mr. Secretary!!" He hesitated as the handler approached the door and grabbed the handle. I pointed to the next room, where that handler was already removing his dog.

I said, "There's a bad-assed dog in there." Mr. Shultz probably doesn't even remember that.

Now I was thinkin', "This diplomatic stuff may not be for me." Three times in as many weeks I'd seen my career flash before my eyes at a high level. I could see the headline: "Secretary of State Accosted by Bomb Dog While Tryin' to Take a Piss—Frank's Fault."

As you can imagine at this point, I was one happy camper to get the hell out of the Wye Plantation. I asked Bev, "Is it always like that?"

She said, "No, not normally."

I was never happier to see a gray desk in my life. Little did I know that the firestorm had just begun. The vultures were circling. All of the people that thrived on the misfortune of others were spreading the word. Somehow made them feel more important to throw you under the bus. You've seen them in all arenas. They use the backs of others as their ladder to success. It all came back to me in one form or another. New guy...Frank... causes riot at NATO Ministerial...big fight...Marine officer in the middle. Gets here and within two weeks has already started trouble. We don't need him.

I went to my boss and said, "That ain't the way it went down. I know I'm the new guy but I broke it up."

The boss told me he would look into it. I later heard that the State guy who was in the fight had a huge set of balls. He went to the boss and told him he started it and that if it hadn't been for Frank, things would have been far worse.

Didn't hear any more for a week or so but then we all had to go to a Basic Agent graduation ceremony. I felt like a fly in a jug of buttermilk. As I went through the reception line I was introduced to the Deputy Assistant Secretary of State for Security (DASS).

He said, "Captain Skinner, the new Marine, I appreciate all that you did to calm the situation at Wye." My butt drew up like a shower curtain. I looked hard to see if he was being sarcastic but he was sincere.

Whew…off the hook again. That has seemed to be the story of my life—right to the brink and somehow the black cloud blows away.

Before Bev departed she told me that she and I were to give an IED-awareness class to the U.S. Mission to the United Nations. Ms. Jean Kirkpatrick was the ambassador. We prepared and got all of our slides ready; our homemade bomb-training aids were packed and set. The morning that we were to depart I was to pick up Bev and we would ride to the airport together. We never even thought about the training aids. Just to give you an idea: we carried the bomb-training aids on the aircraft and no one said a word.

When I arrived to pick her up, she wasn't quite ready. She came downstairs in a t-shirt and skivvies. Now I can assure you that Bev wasn't promiscuous or even thinking like that, but I have to admit she got my attention. Enough dirty old man stuff. Class went off without a hitch and we both got letters of appreciation. Just a point to make about how much terrorism has changed our world. We carried our IED training aids as aircraft carryon luggage with no questions asked.

I still lived in a self-imposed shadow of doubt. I was definitely out of my element. I was a Marine and used to being amongst Marines. This was an unreal adjustment. Those Marines reading this and especially those who spent time on the hill know what I'm talkin' about.

Now, all of a sudden the boss says, "Frank, you need to go to Wang computer training."

That's it...I'm screwed. A fate worse than death. My first laptop was an etch-a-sketch and some prick knocked it off my desk and erased everything I had stored. I'm a stubby pencil, legal pad kinda guy. I know that sounds dumb today but I was a product of my environment. I remember the first time I navigated our sailboat offshore with a GPS—I felt like I was cheating in school. Just didn't seem right.

'Nuff whinin.'

Frank the Bomb Guy was off to Wang training. What an appropriate name. Luckily the training was across the street. When I think back on this assignment, I laugh as I sit at this computer at the kitchen table tryin' to bang out my story. The first day I walk in, all these young girls were lookin' at me and it was obvious I looked like a set of tits on a boar hog. There were a bunch of desks all over the place—at least they were gray so I felt at home—but I must've looked like a turkey on Thanksgiving eve.

They took pity and put me behind a keyboard but never let me solo. Maybe that's because I was always complaining, crying, kickin,' and gouging. That was the toughest two weeks I've ever experienced. Got my certificate, walked back to the square, brown building, and gave the certificate to the boss.

He said, "Good, now you're our duty expert and can train the rest of us."

Oh, shit!! The deck is always stacked at State.

I realized that I would have to get smart fast to survive there. I later learned a famous State Department saying: "I'm on board, pull the ladder up." I say that in jest; met many hard core State guys and gals. Just on a different frequency but then again, most of the world is on a different frequency from Marines. We like it like that!

Los Angeles 1984 Olympics

Now it was time to get serious about the Olympics. I had been in communication with Arleigh and Charlie. Both were a little pissed that I had taken the State assignment and abandoned

Arleigh, seated far left, and author, standing far left, 1984 Olympic security planning dinner

them. They were good friends and pouted like good friends when they felt betrayed. Love 'em dearly.

Bev could not spend the entire time in L.A. She was about to get out of the Corps and go to work for USAID or whoever. She took the first portion and I flew out to relieve her for the last three weeks. As I recall she was in a rush but gave me a whirlwind spin-up. With her professionalism that was like a two-week brief from an analyst. Once I got the reins, she was off. Now it was my turn, sink or swim. As it turned out, it was a lot of worry and stress for nothing. Except for the L.A. cop who planted the bomb so that he could be the hero, it was uneventful except for some fun stuff I'll share with you.

Once I settled in my room I went to the CP to see what was up. The first guy who I met was an Army EOD captain who informed me he was in charge and he'd let me know if he needed me.

Those of you who know me can imagine what transpired at that point. Once the issue was settled as to who was in charge, I informed the young captain as to what his responsibilities would be. He agreed totally and we had a wonderful relationship thereafter. As it turned out, he was invaluable and was instrumental in making things move smoothly. Hell, he probably should've been in charge. He wasn't, though.

Not a big story line about the Olympics but it did open my eyes as to the grandeur and pomp associated with high-level protection. By now the State guys had accepted me so, initially, they would ask me to stand post whiled they peed, or relieve 'em so they could eat. That was a rite of passage. Eventually I was riding motorcades, carrying a weapon, and pulling the full load. As EOD I was familiar with Posse Comitatus, the old law that precludes the use of the military for law enforcement. As a matter of fact, to get around that at El Toro I had a recorder hooked to the phone. If Charlie or Arleigh called they had to say into the recorder "In the interest of public safety can you respond?" I would answer, "In the interest of public safety I can respond."

The State Department required a great deal of support from external agencies. The U.S. Marshals provided support not only for the Olympics but for the United Nations General Assembly (UNGA) as well. There was a marshal who stands out in my mind.

We were all overworked, tired, punch drunk, and in some cases just didn't care. We were tired, the detail agents more so than me. I got a tasking to go to the marina to search a boat for a Kuwait prince.

I rolled out and got there with the Navy divers and this prince has contracted an offshore fishing boat and a 150-foot luxury yacht. Seems as though he wanted to deep-sea fish but wanted the option of transferring to the luxury yacht if he and his son got tired. Don't blame him—that's how I go fishin.'

When I get there the 55-foot fishing boat was there and the Navy EOD guys were there but no yacht. The Navy guys conducted their underwater search, I conducted the search below decks, and life was good.

The yacht pulled in at about the same time as the detail with the Prince and his son. They had to wait for the search. The prince went off for coffee, leaving his eight-year-old son with his U.S. Marshal protector and me.

I asked the marshal, "How goes it?"

"Wow," he responded. "How goes it? How the fuck goes it?? This little fat motherfucker called me at 0230 this morning and says, 'Me want Ham Bugga.' Every night this little prick calls me and wants a Ham Bugga. I'm gonna get him out on this boat and drown his ass."

I was tickled but concerned. I'd had enough goofs at State. I said, "Easy, man, he might understand English."

The marshal turned to the kid and with a big smile said, "You're a fat little asshole, aren't you?" while nodding his head. The little guy smiled and nodded back. Mr. Marshal, if you're still alive and read this, you've brought me many laughs.

We had a real easy go of it. Nothing developed and I think Arleigh was pissed. He wanted something to happen just to make it worthwhile and to make him a hero. That's why he was really pissed when the LAPD cop planted the bomb. 'Course Charlie busted his ass over that one.

One evening in my hotel room I got a call from my Army captain. I think he set me up, but good on him, bad on me. You've gotta respect a good trick. There was a package at a specific address in L.A. that needed to be checked because it was going on the flight with Prince Phillip and Princess Ann.

I noted the address and told the captain that it was on my way in and I would handle it. Next morning I got ready, suited up, earpiece, lapel pin—ready to rock. Got to the address without the hindrance of traffic and pulled into the parking lot of a funeral home.

As I pulled up, this very distinguished black gentleman approached my car. He waited patiently until I got out.

He addressed me, "You must be Mr. Skinner with the State Department?" Very baritone, articulate voice. He was balding on top with a gray side splash and long sideburns. He was in a jacketless tux with a bow tie.

I responded, "Yes, sir, that's me."

He almost bowed, then said, "Please follow me."

I knew that I was at a funeral home. (That kinda limits what kinda package I'm gonna be checkin.') As I followed him in, it was a circular hallway around the perimeter of the building with alcoves on the inner side of the circle. Within these alcoves were caskets. After passing a few alcoves he glided to the left and entered an occupied space. In this space was a coffin containing a young black male. He was wearing an ornate, short-sleeved white shirt with Michael Jackson gloves.

As I looked down I was thinkin,' What now, smartass? I looked at the director and he had a knowing smile on his face. I'd seen a bunch of dead people and even seen folks killed. Not a high point in my life but facts are facts. I tried to take charge but that old gent was wizened beyond belief. I was hesitant and nervous and he picked up on it and relieved the tension.

He said, "Would you like to inspect under the body?"

I'm sure I hesitated, but said, "Yes, is that possible?"

He took a small wrench-type device and cranked the body up. I looked under and gave him a thumbs-up. Still smiling, the old gent respectfully lowered the body.

I saw the pillow and said I should check that. With his hands folded across his front he nodded acknowledgement. He raised the head and I rapidly massaged the pillow. At that point fluid came from the body's nose.

The old gent then retrieved a plastic bag and covered the white shirt. He was extremely graceful and meticulous. I felt nervous and totally out of place. The old guy continued to sense my discomfort.

In order to break the tension I said, "What a shame—young guy, looks like less than thirty years old."

The old director responded in his deep baritone, "He was twenty-six."

"What a shame," I said. I added, "How did he die, was it cancer or an accident?"

Being the wise old guy he broke the tension. He said, "Mr. Skinner, I do believe that the mutha fucka was involved with narcotics."

I started laughing and so did the old guy. As they say…wise old men/women. This situation exemplified the expression, "experience and age will always overcome."

Of course, when I got to the CP the Army captain wanted to know if the "package had been inspected."

In passing, on the way to the coffeepot I said, "Yeah, mission accomplished." I didn't elaborate and it drove that captain nuts. If you're readin' this, you got me, but I wasn't gonna tell ya!

I got to visit every Olympic venue in the L.A. area. There were some equestrian venues outside L.A., that I didn't attend. There was one equestrian in L.A. that I did attend. I was assigned to Prince Phillip and Princess Anne. They were up in the bleachers and I stayed down on the ground.

There was an L.A. cop there on post and he and I were shooting the shit. I was suited up with all the stereotypical gear: suit, earpiece, radio, lapel pin, etc, etc. People on detail today probably just have a cell phone.

All of a sudden, out of the bleachers came Muhammad Ali. He was all grins, and walking straight toward the L.A. cop. He put his hand out and the cop talked to him like they were old buddies.

Ali looked at me and said, "Secret Service?" I responded, "No, sir, State Department." He smiled big and then shook my hand and said, "Good to meet you…good to meet you." Very quiet, subdued, nothing like I saw on TV. Then he departed as abruptly as he had arrived.

About five minutes later an attractive lady came down and went straight to the cop. "Did you see Muhammad?"

He responded, "Yes Ma'am, went that way." It was Muhammad's wife.

Apparently he forgot he was with her and just got up and left. The cop told me that Ali loved cops. When he could drive he would stop and hold up traffic to walk over and shake hands with a cop. Very sad to experience.

Shortly thereafter William Shatner walked down and spoke with us for a short time. What took me by surprise was his height. I'm short but he was shorter. Still a tall man to me, being the old country boy, high school dropout, Marine done good. I was star-struck but I knew I couldn't show it—kiss of death for a bodyguard.

The end of the Olympics was approaching. Now they were talking about the closing ceremonies. We had a number of Army EOD troops assigned to us, in addition to my captain. These kids had been working their asses off. Before the closing ceremonies I secured seats for them all with the State Department dignitaries. Shitty seats, but at least they could attend.

Just before the ceremonies the Agent in Charge (AIC) approached me and said, "Frank, we can't let the EOD guys in. Deputy Assistant Secretary for Security (DASS) is coming with his family."

I was pissed beyond belief. How do I tell these troops that crap? Well, I'd networked a little and made some friends. The athletes had reserved seats at the end of the stadium. Best in the house.

I went to the security guy and presented my dilemma to him, "My folks have worked this event since day one. I had seats for them but some pompous State Department asshole took their seats. Any chance of seating them here somewhere?" He must've been former military because he said, "Follow me." We had the best seats in the house. I had my binoculars so I looked over at the State Department folks. AIC was lookin' at me through his binoculars with a less than happy look. This time I didn't give a shit. I did my job as a leader and Marine officer.

Prior to that, I was approaching the closing ceremonies. Again, you have to know that if you are in a protective scenario you can't approach a celebrity. My son Stephen was an O.J. Simpson fan. All he knew was the Juice. I saw O.J. running full-out toward the closing ceremonies. I decided, Son's more important.

I approached him. "Mr. Simpson, I know, as do you, that I could be in trouble for this. However, my son is a "Juice" fan and I couldn't live it down without your autograph."

He stopped and said, "You got something to write on?" We sat on a small block wall and he asked, "What's his name?" I said, "Stephen." He wrote an entire page to Stephen then signed it. Handed it back then took off. That always impressed me.

1984 United Nations General Assembly (UNGA)

The Wye Plantation was still fresh in my mind as I was informed that I had to coordinate the 1984 UNGA bomb security effort for the Diplomatic Security Service (DSS). I was again going to get U.S. Army EOD support and Air Force bomb dog support. Fortunately, Bev was still on board and would be my tutor for this entire evolution. That made me breathe easier. We arrived in New York and proceeded to the Summit Hotel. This was my first visit to New York, so I was awed. I still didn't know what to expect but I was sure about one thing: no altercations with Army EOD. As it turned out we had some tremendous technicians assigned and encountered no problems.

One young PFC from Kentucky, country as a butter bean, came into the CP one morning and I noticed that his eyes were bloodshot.

I said, "One too many beers, son?"

"Naw, suh…I don't drink."

I don't think he'd ever been out of the hills of Kentucky. I also noticed that his right front pocket was bulgin' out.

"Whatcha got there?" I asked.

"Quarters, suh."

I guess I seemed surprised, and he just couldn't contain himself anymore.

"Suh, I seen tha damndest thing last night! A donkey screwin' a gal."

Seems that my little country boy had discovered the peep shows on 42nd Street.

As we geared up, I found that this operation had been performed so many times that it was like clockwork. As the foreign ministers arrived, we had to search their limos, then their hotels. Any event or dinner they attended we had to advance it and do a bomb sweep. Became mechanical. I have to admit, the UNGA was fast-paced, fun, and exciting. All of the old hats hated it, but they had done it many times before. This entire evolution was about four weeks long, arrival to departure. This was the thirty-eighth annual UNGA. My last one was the fortieth anniversary UNGA and it has stories galore (to be covered later).

On several occasions I was asked to do an airport pickup or delivery. If we had a "High Threat" protectee, DSS liked to have one of their own bomb folks with them. I rolled on the minister from Iraq, the now-famous Tariq Aziz. We called him Aziz the Sleaze. Actually, Aziz was the only Christian in Saddam's Cabinet. (He was still an asshole.)

We would pick him up at JFK and he would pile his nasty ass in the back of the limo and immediately fire up a big Cuban cigar. Of course, the windows didn't roll down in the limos, so whoever was trapped in the limo with him got to smoke that nasty cigar as well.

The Cuban foreign minister was just as bad. We were all convinced that they did it on purpose. They were rude and crude as they come.

When Aziz was nailed in Iraq I took special pleasure in that event. Bet there's no limo or big cigar now. Should bring him over to our penal system and introduce him to our inmates. Would give him a new appreciation of long, cylindrical items.

On one such motorcade from the airport we had a U.S. Marshal in the right front of the follow car. We had NYPD motorcycle cops in front and back. It was an impressive sight. People would jockey to get alongside and yell at us, "Who's in the limo?"

Al, the marshal, would yell back something like "Michael Jackson" or "Pierre Cardin."

Sometimes people would follow us back to the UN Plaza Hotel all excited, just to see some fat little balding or gray-headed dude, all rumpled from travel. Man did they get pissed. Al always got a big chuckle.

Bev was cute, in that when Al was around she digressed from being the cool, professional Marine EOD officer. She got all mushy about Al. He was a dapper little guy and a definite Type A personality. To my knowledge, he had no idea how Bev felt.

CHAPTER FIVE

Mobile Training Team (MTT)

When I got back to the gray desk sometime in October, 1984, I had no idea what was coming next. Bev had either just departed for her new job or was about to. One job I had was to teach a one hour bombing awareness class every Monday afternoon to people from all agencies who were about to travel overseas. Bombs were kinda hot since all of the bombs in Beirut and Europe.

There was still that Liberal element within the diplomatic corps that said, "It can't happen to us."

It did, time and again, over the next few years. But for now it looked like the gray desk for a while. Beirut was still a hot topic since the Marine Headquarters (HQ) had been bombed and the embassy had been bombed twice. It seemed like things were heating up in a big way.

I went to the firearms range one morning to see if I could help out there. The range master (I'll call him Joe) told me that he had a firearms instructor course starting up.

I said, "I'm in."

Joe was a grumpy dude and seemed to even hate himself. It was all a front. Joe was a retired Marine EOD Captain and had made a way for himself within Diplomatic Security. He realized early that to grow within the diplomatic community the best defense is a good offense. It worked for him. Nobody wanted to suffer the wrath of Joe.

All the agents would call to see if he was at the range or not.

If he was out they'd say, "I'm on the way...Need to qualify." If he was there they'd say, "I'll call back."

M60 machine gun training

It became a standing joke. I mainly ignored him; he never got to me that much. Guy had a lot of experience and I wanted to learn all I could as fast as possible. Besides that, I liked him. (He will call me a fag for that comment.)

I breezed through the firearms course and Joe took us out to Bill Scott Raceway (BSR) to go through the anti-terror driving course. Man, was that fun!

Joe and I went out for a beer and he told me, "We may be going into Beirut because the embassy just hired a load of guards and we had to train them."

That got my interest. Here I was a Marine officer with a chance to go to a combat zone.

It was early November, 1984, and I couldn't believe my fortune. Protective details, gunslinging (as best I could), driving fast and banging into cars on purpose, blowing stuff up at will.

I met some Navy SEALs at BSR who were working in the kill house. I heard loud bangs, then weapons fire. Curiosity got the best of me. Went over and discovered they were BREACH-ING!! Basic stuff with det cord, but breaching nonetheless.

Turns out these were Red Cell guys. I suppose there were some Team Six guys mixed in. Those guys were hush-hush at the time so they didn't have much time for me. Didn't run me off either, but just kind of ignored me. I picked up fast and didn't say much either. It was just fun watching.

Beirut, Lebanon, 1984

The first stage and most delicate phase of this operation was telling my little longhaired mess cook that I was off to Beirut. All we really knew about that pretty little city was that it had claimed the lives of a bunch of Marines and a Navy Corpsman. Not a good way to set the stage for telling Susan that I was headed over. To be realistic, I wasn't going over as a Marine; I was going over as a diplomat, with a diplomatic passport and all the privileges. Nobody bothered to tell the militias in West Beirut that there was such a thing as diplomatic immunity. To them you were just a bigger target. To compound that, if they found out that I was really a Marine officer, I would have been a bigger trophy and certainly a desired target. You can bet I started growing my hair out—I was trying to push that stuff through my scalp.

Over the next two-plus years we made eight trips into Beirut. The initial mission changed over the course of those trips. This first trip was dedicated to training the recently hired guards. We also had to equip them. The State Department had purchased Mini-14s, which are small rifles that fire 5.56mm rounds. They have a folding stock and a three-round burst selector. I later discovered that they were cheaper than the M-16 or the M-4. They did, however, use common NATO ammunition.

We also loaded up on LAAW anti-tank rockets. We were gonna train and equip the old-timer guards on this system and put them at posts to engage Large Vehicle-Borne Improvised Explosive Devices (LVBIEDs). The initial leg of our trip was on an Air Force C-141 out of Andrews.

This wasn't a spook trip but we also didn't want to advertise it. I suspect now that was due to keeping the media in the dark, as opposed to informing the bad guys. Due to this, Susan couldn't even come to see me off. She was not a happy camper, but she knew that I wanted to get into some of the world events. That is what I trained for, and it's where I needed to be. We had come a long ways from the days when she wouldn't let me have a stock car because it was too dangerous. Then again, I never really gave her all the details. Not that I had secrets from her, I just didn't want to worry her.

I had become an adrenaline junkie but on a small scale compared to what was in store for me in the future. I thought I was a Bad Ass, but later I was to become indestructible...or so I thought. Me and the guys I hung with would push and push... right to the very edge. Those of you then, and today, know what I'm talking about.

Back to Beirut...

The C-141 had been loaded with the pallets and I had been advised by Joe to bring along a sleeping bag. Wise advice. The belly of the C-141 was full but there was plenty of room forward and around the edges to lay out our sleeping bags. The first leg took us to Rhoda, Spain, for refueling. I had never been to Spain, or Europe for that matter. I've been to or through Europe over one hundred times since. But that early morning landing was exciting to me.

I was thinking, "Wow...get to see some Spaniards in the flesh." We landed and they had us deplane while they refueled. We went into the Air Force terminal and I looked around wide-eyed. Looked like any other U.S. military airfield operations tower in the U.S. Remember, I had worked at Cherry Point, N.C., and this joint looked just like it. What a bummer. I never saw one Spaniard.

After retirement, I was on contract to Kellogg/Brown and Root (KBR) in Algeria. I met the family in Majorca, Spain. Saw plenty of them then.

We went to the Air Field Operations (AirOps) office and got some of the typical jet black, thick coffee that is prevalent in AirOps world wide. Tasted like shit. The crap they gave us on the C-141 was better. After a few hours we loaded up and were off to Larnaca, Cyprus. Now ya gotta keep in mind, we had no Google Earth, no laptops, no GPSs.

All I saw was a world map that told me where Cyprus is. Cyprus is a small island about ninety miles west of Lebanon in the Mediterranean. November or December is not a good time to go to Cyprus. We landed just about daylight and taxied to the end of the airfield. Because of our cargo, the customs folks wouldn't let us into the terminal.

In addition to the armament on the pallets, we each had our "Go Bags" with all of our weapons and ammo. This was my first exposure to assassination grenades. With my whole five years in EOD, I had never seen or heard of them. Looked like a baby M-67, round hand grenade with a spoon and fuze like the M-67. However, the ball was smaller than a golf ball. They fit nicely in your pockets and were excellent for disrupting an attack or covering your E&E (Escape and Evade)…'nuther words, un-ass the area. I was given a handful and told to keep 'em handy over the next few weeks. That sent me a message that these folks in Beirut might be serious.

We had a lot of trouble getting the Cypriots to provide ground equipment to offload the hardware. Eventually they provided assistance and we got all the stuff off. The delay caused the crew of the C-141 to be really pissed at us.

I think that at one point Joe threatened the pilot to get him to stay as long as he did. Now Cyprus was not a high threat environment but it was windy, rainy, and cold as the hubs of hell. I've never been so cold. At the end of the runway there were a few conex boxes, but they were locked and there was no other shelter. The 141 had departed and we were hungry, thirsty, wet and cold…cold!

At this point I hated Cyprus, an attitude that was to change 180 degrees over the next months and years. I now consider that place paradise and when I finally die, I'm sure I'll be walking the beaches of Ionopa, with a bottle of Aphrodite wine and a huge ear of roasted corn made so delicious by the old Cypriot ladies who roasted the corn on the beach and sold them to

CH-53 Being loaded on tarmac at Larnaca

tourists from their small concessions. That is, if God feels I'm worthy of heaven. As you can tell from some of the photos, Cyprus was a very enjoyable, relaxing place. Especially if you had just been pulled out of a war zone and your nerves had been stretched to the max. I'm not sure Cyprus is all that perfect, but the contrast from the streets and alleys of Beirut in the mid-'80s made it seem like the most perfect place in the world.

We waited and waited. A CH-53 was to pick us up. The 53 was from the Marine Amphibious Unit (MAU) that was floating off the coast of Beirut. These guys were also to be our primary emergency evacuation out of Beirut if the shit hit the fan. Now I'm thinking, "We been sittin' here—freezin,' wet, and hungry— for hours." No choppers. How was it gonna be if we needed emergency evac out of town? Eventually we saw two 53s headed in. They hovered then set down. They kept churnin' and burnin' while the pallets were loaded. This seemed odd to me because of all the safety that is forced at you stateside. Nobody believes in the old warrior adage, "Train like you fight!" General Al Gray came along and changed that for the Corps. General Gray had the foresight to see Special Operations/Low Intensity Conflict

97

(SO/LIC) on the horizon. He also insisted that Marines, once again, carry loaded weapons. But he made sure that adequate training was implemented that put Marines back in the fight.

We got all the equipment loaded with the help of a disgruntled Cypriot forklift operator. We had to hurriedly break down a couple of pallets because the forklift couldn't get them in the chopper. That pissed the pilot off because he had to shut it down. What was funny about this entire operation that I've described is that it sounds like at least a squad-sized team was headed in. Nope—there were three of us: me, Joe, and Rob.

We had enough weaponry to have decided the Civil War at Gettysburg with three guys. The Air Force folks were just shaking their heads. You can only imagine what was going through their heads. When the 53s lifted off I heard something that I hadn't heard since Vietnam and it made me feel warm and fuzzy.

Joe yelled, "Gentlemen…Lock and Load."

We grabbed our weapons and inserted the magazines and charged the chambers. We were hot!!

This was to be a tactical landing. I think the pilots weren't threatened, just had a chance to hotdog and took it. When we landed, it was on a hilltop that was all sand and dust. The rain had stopped since leaving Cyprus; it was dusk and the choppers wanted to get the hell out before dark. Can't say as I blame 'em. The Regional Security Officer (RSO) had brought a group of embassy guards (Lebanese local hires) to help offload the choppers. They were one hell of a lot more efficient that our Cypriot forklift operator. Those guys had the two choppers unloaded and the trucks loaded while I was still being introduced to the embassy security staff. The choppers lifted off and I watched their lights as they slowly disappeared over the Med.

It got real quiet. It was a clear evening. As the sun went down I realized it was like California. Sun going down below the ocean horizon. I felt a twinge of nostalgia. I missed Susan and was a little homesick. I was inside my own head, as I have a tendency to do when I need to sort stuff out. I was sortin' but getting nowhere. Ninety miles away was safety. No Marines or U.S. military here at all. No support or lifeline except through the delicate safety of "diplomatic immunity." That would later prove to be almost comical—"almost" being the operative word.

The embassy on the west side of Beirut had been blown up a few months back. All embassy operations had been moved to the ambassador's residence.

The ambassador was Reginald Bartholomew. We made the trip to the embassy compound and again watched the efficiency of the guards who unloaded the trucks and stowed the "war gear" inside a bunker. The RSO took us into the office spaces and showed us around. He, Joe, and the Assistant RSO were old buddies.

I was tired and jetlagged and just wanted to sleep in a warm bed. Didn't even care about the bed as long as it was warm. A hot shower sounded good but I suspected that the living arrangements in a war zone were less than top line. Was I ever wrong. When we finished, the RSO put the team in an armored Suburban. This was to be our vehicle while there. We followed the RSO to the embassy living quarters. Our team was to occupy one apartment.

Oh boy, I thought. Sharing rooms with these guys, traveling with them, eating with them, and working with them. Gonna be a long, grumpy trip.

When we finally got the elevator to work, we went to the second floor which is actually the third floor in Americanese. (Everywhere else in the world the first floor is called the ground floor, with the numbered floors up from there.) Joe took the keys and opened the front door. Rob was an old Diplomatic Security guy and very moody. Joe was the grump and Rob was the Mood Maker.

We walked into a huge kitchen area that opened farther to a large dining room with a conference-sized dining table, then into a large living room with a TV and overstuffed chairs and a sofa. Wow…better than home. We then broke off in to our separate bedrooms. Very nice, with all the comforts. We each had a bathroom with tub and shower.

After we stowed our gear, Joe gave us our marching orders. At 0700 the next day we would head to the embassy and get sorted out. It was now about 2200 and we were all tired. Rob had slipped into his non-speaking mode. Never knew what the guy was pissed about but he did, and I guess that's all that matters.

We were up and at it about 0600. We all loaded our gear into the Suburban and off we went. We hadn't been assigned a driver yet. Oh yeah…we were also to get a set of bodyguards to tag along.

Joe had been to Beirut several times in the past but wasn't much on sharing his experiences. If you asked you usually just got your head bit off.

He got in the passenger seat and Rob piled in the back. That left the driver's seat open. I wasn't offended. Just the opposite: if the shit hit the fan, I wanted control of the vehicle. Those guys could do the shooting and I would haul ass, running over what bad guys I could on the way out.

Off we went. It was becoming daylight and I got my first real look at Beirut. You could look across the bay and see all of Beirut from the hillside where our apartment was located. It was breathtaking. The Mediterranean was blue-green and the ripples on the surface sparkled like diamonds and green emeralds, each complementing the other. It wasn't as cold as it had been the night before. A light haze hung over the city.

I could see why everyone referred to the old city of Beirut as the "Pearl of the Middle East." I was in love. To the east you could see Bikfaya and the Shoof Mountains. They had small, snowcapped peaks. Turn your head right, you could see gorgeous white beaches; turn left and see snowcapped mountains. Breathtaking.

As I witnessed all this beauty, I felt for my Uzi to ensure it was locked and loaded, felt for my Browning Hi-Power, completed a press check to see that a round was in the chamber. I was ready for war in a postcard-beautiful country that I had immediately wanted to call home.

We wound down the mountainous road to the beach highway. This was called the Porifin. It wound westward towards town.

Joe pointed to a small shop and said, "Pull over there."

I complied.

He said, "Let's grab us a breakfast *minuche*."

"What the hell is a *minuche*?" I asked.

He looked at me and said, "Don't matter, you hungry, you eat."

I followed his lead and bought two. He had Lebanese money from a previous trip. Both sandwiches, or roll-ups, cost about twenty cents.

Man...I fell in love again. These were great; I wish I'd have bought a half-dozen. They went down fast with the Turkish coffee that we'd purchased. At first the Turkish coffee tasted worse than the stuff in Rhoda, Spain. But after a while you couldn't drink regular coffee—it was too weak. Nescafe was the only other coffee available. When most folks use one pack per cup, I'd use two.

As we drove along, with Joe giving directions and us eating our *minuche*, I was amazed at the traffic. I don't know what I expected but it certainly wasn't the hustle and bustle that I was witnessing. No war torn buildings or armed troops. Just normal people going about their daily routines.

We turned left at an intersection and headed towards a large, chain linked compound on a distant hill. It was either a prison or the embassy offices. Yep, embassy offices. Once we got cleared in, most of the Lebanese guards recognized Joe, and I must say he was never grumpy with them. He would raise hell when they goofed up or couldn't shoot well, but he was normally very gracious with them and treated them better than us.

I later learned that he did that because he felt guilty leaving them behind when he headed back to the states. I later experienced that same emotion. To this day I wonder what happened to my friends in Christian East Beirut and even some Muslims in West Beirut. I learned in my travels that we are all people first. Then we are exposed to our individual cultures, religions, and governments. We are born a product of God and become products of our environments. That feeling always kept me from hatred and allowed me to function in a more professional manner. I've never enjoyed the anger emotion and I don't know what it is to hate. This ain't a sermon. There are certainly some people that I'll never take a warm soapy shower with and there are some things that I don't like, but I never let those emotions control me.

We carried our go bags and made our way up the endless steps that covered the compound. Everything in Beirut was uphill! I honestly can't remember going down steps or hills to accomplish anything. We finally made it to the entrance and we went inside. As I later learned, this was sparse compared to most ambassador residences. Still, we went into a huge marble foyer. Most of the downstairs had been converted to temporary office space.

The embassy was in the process of relocating to a temporary office space (TOS) not far away. It, too, had been blown up so now they were repairing it for occupancy. The RSO was a jovial, very professional type. He definitely did not allow the environment to get to him.

I was surprised a few weeks later, while en route to our apartment at a rapid rate of speed up the winding road, to see the RSO out jogging. He was perfectly safe from the bad guys, but had to jump in the ditch to avoid being run over by me and the Suburban. Thank God, nothing was ever said to me about that. Just accepted, I guess. We were all in Dodge City and lived life accordingly.

The first day the RSO informed us that when we finished training the new local hires, he would have the second-largest militia in Beirut. Now a little about the militias. Operating in West Beirut was Hezbollah, Hamas, the Progressive Socialist Party (PSP), and other various factions.

The big, bad guys in the west were Nabi Bari and Whalid Jumblat. In the east you had the Christian groups Lebanese Armed Forces (LAF) which were Government, and you had the Force Lebanese (LF) which was headed by the warlord Elie Hobeika. There was also a smaller, non-violent movement headed by Michel Aoun.

Amine Gemayel's brother, Bashir, had been the last great hope for all of Lebanon. He was elected to be President but was assassinated prior to taking office, as was Hobeika.

The President was Amine Gemayel. Aoun was to replace Amine Gemayel later. If all that sounds confusing, try being us attempting to figure who our friends were. I think every time we went into Beirut it changed anyhow. This trip we were buddies with the Lebanese Forces or Force Lebanon as they called themselves(LF). The LF was normally a friend to the Gemayel regime. *Normally* is a word that doesn't always fit in Lebanon. All of the militia's, Christian and Muslim, were primarily thugs out to advance their own agendas. Under the leaders were the "sub-thugs". These guys were also out to get what they could for themselves.

For the RSO to say that he would have the second-largest militia was a big statement. I think at that time the embassy guards numbered over 300. We had about 100 to train this trip. Not all would make it through training. Firing a guard was extremely difficult because the embassy was a top payer and jobs were hard to come by. Never enjoyed that part of the job.

We then went out to the bunker and conducted an inventory. That was fun, given the fact that Joe was grumpy and Rob wasn't speaking. Some things in life seem real dumb to me and this was one of them. We spent all day going through that stuff. It was in sealed containers, making the job that much more tedious. We had to break it all open, count it, and then reseal it. It wasn't like we were gonna get resupplied or that anyone else would have access to the junk. As a matter of fact, when we left Joe wanted to do another inventory to sign it all over to the RSO.

RSO was cool. He said, "I ain't wastin' my time with that. This is Beirut—if I run out, I'll just buy more."

Right on, I thought. I think it did deflate Joe because he liked that packin' and unpackin' stuff.

Once that was settled, we took a look at what translators we would need. We were assigned a very sharp young man named Edgar. Super, super good guy. We had another one also assigned but I can't remember his name. He was quiet and moody like Rob. They became instant buddies complimenting each other on who was in the shittiest mood.

Ernest

Then we learned from the RSO that Elie (pronounced eye lee) Hobeika wanted to assign two bodyguards to our team. "No" was not an acceptable answer so later that afternoon we were introduced to two of Elie's boys.

We called them the Spider People. Their logo was a big red spider on a black and silver spider web background (pictured in the photos). Their headquarters (HQ) was an underground complex that we never got to visit. We did take some photos outside that I've shared with you. Our two young bodyguards were even pissed that we had those. We could only imagine what happened down in the bowels of that facility. I'm sure many actual and suspected bad guys were questioned to various degrees of stimulation. When I used to joke with the bodyguards, they would only laugh and shake their heads. I think waterboarding would look like "patty-cake" to those guys.

The two assigned guys were Imad Kassas, a very handsome, well-built young man who was hot-headed and always full steam

Montemar bar Imad, standing

Spider hole

ahead. When he drove, he scared the hell out of Rob to the point that once, when Imad slowed for a traffic circle, Rob bailed out and refused to get back in the car. Imad was always trying to outdo us either at shooting (which he could never do, much to his chagrin) or driving (and after I showed him my skills he gave up on that one, too). He then reverted to being a bully to the locals. If traffic pissed him off he would merely force the muzzle of his Shorty AK-47 at an opposing driver and threaten to shoot them.

On another occasion we stopped in a market to get some beer. I waited in line with some Hindu workers who were getting snacks and supplies. Imad grabbed me by the shoulder and forced me to the front of the line, pushing the Hindus away with his weapon. Now I got testy and went back to the rear of the line. Imad and I had a discussion and I told him that in America we respected folks and took our turn. He smiled and said, "You not in America now—you in my country."

Ernest Hatem was the second guy. Ernest was the opposite of Imad. Older, homely, but very efficient. He was not aggressive and only shook his head at Imad. I could tell just by the way that Ernest manipulated his weapon that he was the guy to contend with. His AK seemed like a natural extension of his body. Everything was fluid and effortless. When walking or sitting you hardly even noticed that he had a gun. But he always did.

Over the next couple of years I became very close friends with these guys. I had to remind myself from time to time that these were bad guys, too; they just happened to be on our side. They were both to die in a .50 caliber machine gun ambush just after my final trip to Beirut. Prior to that ambush Ernest had lost a couple of fingers in an earlier ambush.

Just to drift ahead a little in an effort to emphasize the Good, the Bad, and the Ugly. Ernest had an uncle (Fred Frem) who lived in Miami. Now it was well known that the militias in and around Beirut relied on the drug trade to support them. Ernest's uncle was a Lebanese mobster in the drug trade.

Ernest had made a trip to visit his uncle and was caught with several pounds of heroin in the trunk of his car. I received a call one evening from the uncle. He explained that Ernest was in jail and going to court. Apparently Ernest was copping the CIA defense.

The uncle initially wanted me to "pull some strings" to get his nephew out of jail. He told me that he would fly my wife and I to Miami, all expenses paid in luxury surroundings, if I would testify on behalf of Ernest. He insinuated that money would be of no object.

I told Joe of this and we agreed to write a letter to the court. We expounded on the fact that Ernest was to have intervened (I'll tell about that later) and saved the team's life when attacked by a rolling roadblock. The courts accepted this but Ernest still got a couple of years. Later I was told that he got out early for good behavior. I don't care who you are or what you've done—if you traffic heroin in America, you need to die.

Our day had been full, so we secured and made a trip to the local market. Joe was the cook and took to it with vigor. You couldn't even help the guy. After a very nice dinner of beef, lentils, and rice, I offered to clean up the kitchen.

He jumped me hard and said, "I made the friggin' mess so I'll clean it up."

By now I was tired of it.

I said, "Have at it, Ace."

He looked at me funny but then later was extremely nice to me.

I learned something about Joe. I will tell you later how I made it work in my favor. I also discovered something else that I loved about Beirut: Almaza beer and Cuban cigars. Heineken beer was only six bucks a case and Cuban Montecristos or Upmans were about four bucks for a box of twenty-five. I loaded up.

The next day was range day. We had some classroom stuff but the range was the most interesting. I was to be a firearms instructor but I also had to teach an IED recognition and search class. Joe was anal about the range, like he was about most other stuff. He was right. One thing I have to say is that when he set up a makeshift range, with all his little idiosyncrasies, it very seldom failed.

Training continued, uninterrupted by falling targets and other mishaps. Joe was very adamant about giving the students every chance. He knew what the job meant to them and was sensitive to it. We had old guys, young guys, fat guys, and skinny, unhealthy guys. One common thread ran throughout: they all wanted and needed this job. Joe still would not compromise his standards. The standards were fair and he gave them every chance. If they still couldn't do it, they were gone. After all, Joe also considered that these guys would have to protect Americans assigned to the embassy.

Just a side story as to the value of these guards. Prior to the TOS bombing Joe had trained all of the guards to date. The road approaching the TOS was a right-angle turn off the main road onto a drive access that ran in front of the TOS building, then turned left down the side of the building and then left again to an underground parking area directly under the offices. At ten-something the morning of that fateful day, a large, explosive-laden truck turned onto that access road.

One of Joe's guards started engaging the truck driver with his weapon as the truck drove directly at him. He never flinched or ran. It is guessed that he killed the driver as the truck careened to the right and ran into a large palm tree where it stopped. There was a remote control device on the bomb so the trigger man saw that the bomb was gonna go no further so he fired the bomb, killing the guard and others. We can only guess as to the rest. Let's imagine that the driver was headed to the underground parking garage. It makes sense. We can only speculate as to the death and injury that would have resulted had the driver made it to the garage. This little Lebanese guard, who only wanted a good job, stood his ground and saved God only knows how many American and Lebanese lives. I venture to guess that not too many Americans even know about this little guy with a set of balls as big as the truck that he stopped.

Upon reflection, I suspect that this is why Joe took this so serious. Rightfully so.

Marines who were on embassy duty were a good source. I met with them and introduced myself but didn't mention that

Author standing at the spot where the guard was killed (TOS)

I was a Marine. All those guys automatically assume that you are CIA because they'd never seen a diplomat carrying so many guns and running around in town.

If you're gonna run around in town, make sure that you establish some safe havens. This proved invaluable in later trips into Beirut. Every Friday night the Marines had a TGIF night. It was a party that every embassy employee attended. Locals could come if invited. Being good Marines, there was always an array of cute little Lebanese girls, some of the prettiest girls in the world. I attended my first Thank God it's Friday (TGIF) and had a great time. In other Arab countries it is TGIW as Wednesday is their Friday. Friday is their Sabath.

It was good to be back amongst Marines even though they didn't know I was one of them. It was fun to see how they never really accepted me as one of theirs but they were courteous with the "yes, sirs" and "no, sirs." They were a little star-struck because they thought we were out doing all this cool spook stuff. Yeah, buying Almaza beer and Cuban cigars.

Back to the safe houses. I always enjoyed going out, away from town central, when I traveled. I liked to see how the real people lived and thought. It helped you keep a thumb on what was really happening. One of the Marines had a girlfriend and I spoke with her. Her father and mother had a mom-and-pop grocery store in a little town on the Green Line, Ashrafiya.

I was shopping in Ashrafiya for some gold and I saw the store. I went inside and started talking with the old woman behind the counter. Of course, I couldn't tell her I'd met her daughter and that she had a Marine for a boyfriend. So I just started chatting about this and that. She asked if I worked at the embassy and I said yes. She smiled and then we started talking politics.

As was the case all over Beirut, the Christians couldn't understand why America had abandoned them. I never could come up with a story that set well with me. The bad guys had blown up the Marines, our media had crucified the effort, public opinion turned and out we came. Sure would've been nice if the media told the story about the little Lebanese guard who gave his life saving Americans. I doubt that it would've mattered at that point.

After a few minutes of chatter this little old fat guy came out of the back room with a box of vegetables. He said something in Arabic to the old woman, who was his wife. She responded and I could tell from her gestures that she was telling him about me. Some words we can all understand and put two and two together.

I could tell from his mannerisms that he was not impressed with the fact that I was a.) American, and b.) worked at the

American embassy. It was clear that all of his problems centered around the Americans pulling out of Beirut. It was, therefore, all my fault—in his eyes. It would be many more trips before he trusted me. A trust that I'll always feel I violated because when I left for the last time in 1986 I never again communicated with him. It was to happen many times in countries that I had to violate a trust just to ensure the team's and my own safety. Sure am glad I didn't make a career of that.

Since this was my first trip to an Arab country, even though East Beirut seemed as Western as any big city that I'd ever visited in the States, I'd like to share something that became quite pleasurable to me over the years: Lebanese food or, better yet, the ritual of the Arab evening meal. One thing that was a common denominator was the manner in which all Arabs enjoyed their evening meal. It held true on subsequent trips to Egypt, Saudi, Kuwait, Algeria, Tunisia, Morocco, and any other Arab place that I forgot.

Lebanese food was particularly good. Other Arabs also enjoy Lebanese food. When protecting the Saudi prince and his family (to be covered later), we visited Lebanese restaurants all over the world: London, Paris, New York, Beverly Hills, just to name a few.

On the day before we left, Imad wanted to take us out to eat the next day. It was out of character as they seldom ate large meals during the day. Apparently there was a tourist attraction on top of the mountain just outside the city. You take a cable car up the mountain and there was a huge statue of the Virgin Mary on top. Tradition was that you scratched your name in it for a blessing. I scratched away, as I felt in need of a blessing at the time.

Rob was being his old non-speaking self so he refused to go along. After the first week we had moved out to the Montemar Hotel because they had to put some permanent embassy folks in our apartments. I was a happy camper. Nice hotel, with a room to myself, bar downstairs, right on the Mediterranean with a pool. 'Course it was the wrong time of the year for that stuff. Still was nice and we didn't feel like we were stuck up each other's butts. Still, Rob would get pissy and not speak for no reason.

Montemar Hotel

Joe, Imad, and I finished our duty at the Virgin Mary and off we went walking to a "special restaurant" that Imad was taking us to. It was mid-afternoon and the place was packed. You would have to be there to understand how unusual this was. This was a tourist attraction but due to the war there were no tourists. Joe and I were the only Caucasians but Joe had black hair and a big black mustache so he fit right in.

He used to laugh and look at my blond hair and blue eyes and say, "What you mean we, white man?"

As it turned out, this place was very famous for a delicacy known throughout the Middle East. It was a delicately sautéed selection of baby birds that were retrieved just prior to hatching.

They came complete with eyeballs, beaks and feet. They were called *duri* (pronounced "doo-rhee"). I picked up on that fast as I had been trying to learn Arabic. *Khara* (pronounced "kha-draa") means, literally, shit. So *khara* means shit and *duri* means bird...guess what? I'd applied English and Arabic to form the term of endearment for a young Marine, *Khara-Duri*, or Shit

Bird. I was very proud of myself. Apparently it didn't translate directly but it became a byword amongst us and the guards.

Also at that time Red Fox was popular and he had done the skit about how Yuma, Arizona, was named. He was a Calvary trooper outside a fort with a bunch of arrows stickin' out of him. As he lay there in the throes of death, he kept yelling, "You... Muh, You...Muh." This was how Yuma got its name. Well, we were all joking about it and on the range Joe or I would yell down the firing line, "You...Muh." This took off like wildfire even though the Lebanese guards didn't have a clue as to its meaning. Everybody, American and Lebanese alike, knew the phrase "Yu-Muh."

You laugh or ask yourself, Where is Frank going with that? Later I'll tell how that saved the lives of me and my other team members on another trip into Beirut. It is funny what little things settled in your mind when you're in a combat or hazardous environment. I'm sure that thousands of similar stories will come out of Iraq and make no sense to anyone but those who were there.

Needless to say, I didn't even try those little sautéed birds. They were nasty-lookin' and lookin' back at me on top of that. The grease surrounding them was just as nasty. Joe and I got a real chuckle out of those little birds. They were just standin' there lookin' at us. Imad was very upset that Joe and I wouldn't partake. To him he had paid us the highest compliment and we had paid him the largest insult.

No matter, I wasn't gonna eat that crap no matter whose feelings got hurt. Joe and I did feel that it would be a good idea to take a little doggy bag back to Rob. He was still at the hotel and not speaking to us. There we went, with Joe holding the little bag of birds out from his body like toxic waste. We knocked on Rob's door and we were both giggling like kids.

Rob opened the door and said, "What do you want!" He started to mellow and smile a little when he saw that Joe brought him a peace offering. He timidly took the bag of little birds, smiled, and said thanks. He turned into his room and slowly closed his door.

Joe and I looked at each other and grinned. Man, Rob must've opened the bag and there was all them nasty little birds lookin' at him.

His door busted open and he yelled, "You assholes!!" and he threw the bag at Joe.

The bag hit the wall next to Joe's head and busted open. There were little birds everywhere…still lookin' up at us.

We laughed like hell. Many months after that if we brought it up to Rob he wouldn't speak for a week. Man was he pissed. At least this time I knew why he wasn't speaking.

We departed Beirut via helo and when we landed in Larnaca the pilot motioned for me to come over to his window. The chopper was churnin' and burnin' and I couldn't hear anything. Crew chief came around and gave me a headset. I'm thinking, "What can this guy want from me?"

Once I figured out how to work the headset (with the help of the crew chief), the pilot asked, "Hey man, you comin' back this way?"

I answered, "More than likely. Whatcha need?"

He replied, "Anything to read, like *U.S. News*, *Time*, sports… anything; we get no news out here."

On my next trip and every trip thereafter I loaded up on news and sports magazines. Never had the same pilot but the ones I did have were very appreciative. It's the little things that you miss in those environments.

On the way out, there was a young guy who approached us along with the RSO. He was carrying an orange diplomatic pouch. He was a Delta guy who had been there for a number of months on mission. He was to lash up with us to leave Beirut as a team member. This was to be his cover.

Upon arrival in Larnaca Joe told him to lock his pouch in his hotel room. This guy would have no part of it. Larnaca was about twenty-five or so miles from Nicosia, where the embassy was located. He wanted to follow the book and lock up his pouch. We Mobile Training Team (MTT) guys weren't quite that letter of the law.

Relaxing with a cold beer, Larnaca

We preferred staying in Larnaca because it was right on the beach, we were having a spurt of good weather, and the topless girls were out in force. No Nicosia for us. We ended up laying over in Cyprus for a few days. When it came time to depart we headed for the airport. When we arrived and checked in, there was no Delta guy. A young lady from the airlines attached herself to us because we had the diplomatic pouches and they just wanted to get us the hell out of there. She collected our passports and tickets, and off she went. We told her there was another guy coming from the embassy. We had about an hour until departure. We waited and waited.

She came out every few minutes to ask, "Where is the other guy?"

We didn't have a clue. He had been told to be there one hour prior but now it was a half-hour 'til departure. No Delta guy. Finally all the other passengers were boarded and only the three of us were at the gate. We could see the entry to the terminal from where we were at.

All of a sudden, with about three minutes to go, this cab came flying up to the terminal. Out piled this Delta guy and he looked like Pig Pen from the Charlie Brown comics. Stuff was flying everywhere. He came running toward the entrance and I ran to get his documents. The girl had already decided that we were too late. Joe was talking to her smoothly and I was getting the Delta guy collected.

I said, "Give me your ticket and passport!"

He handed his ticket over then started searching for his passport. He didn't have it!!

"What the hell!" I yelled.

I ran outside to where the cab had dumped him. There were these concrete poles spaced about four feet apart, four feet high, and a foot in diameter. There, bigger than life, was his black diplomatic passport, lying on top of one of the poles. I grabbed it and ran inside and told him to follow me and don't get lost. Joe had schmoozed the girl and the flight was waiting. I handed her the docs and away we went.

Of course we forgot to tell her that we all had diplomatic pouches, and by international law and treaty they had to go on the aircraft last. Not only that, we had to put them on and watch them go on last. Once we got on the ground, at the belly of the plane we were watching the last of the passenger luggage go on. The Delta guy hefted his orange bag onto the ramp before I could grab it and it was headed up the conveyor. Joe saw it go into the belly and went nuts. He threw a fit on me.

He said, "You dumb fucker, you know that the pouches go on last!" We still had some stuff to load but this stiffened me a little. Here I had single-handedly got this Delta guy sorted out and all was well and I get called names like that.

I turned on my heel, put my face about two inches from Joe's, and said, "Fuck you!" then proceeded to get on the aircraft and take my seat.

Now if you'll recall, a little earlier I mentioned that I learned how to make Joe's outbursts work for me. I had learned something about him. He was grumpy and extremely hard to get along with but down deep he didn't like to hurt feelings. I guess after I boarded he started thinking about what an asshole he was.

When he got on the plane he walked by my seat and laughingly said, "Fuck you, eh?"

I looked at him and said, "If you didn't understand it the first time: Fuck you, asshole."

It shocked him and he moved to his seat. We didn't say much to each other for the remainder of the trip.

When we arrived at Dulles we were picked up by a State Department van and transported to the firearms range at Lorton. We had our wives meet us there. We broke open the diplomatic pouches and took out the weapons and ammo and stowed them.

Susan's eyes got really wide when she saw that arsenal but to this day she never said a word. We also took out our goodies, gold, cigars, new Browning Hi-Powers, Czech CZ 75s new in the box. We bought CZ 75s and Brownings for $180, new in the box. Susan was tickled with all her gold. I was still cold to Joe.

We took a few days off and then returned to the range. I just didn't feel like going to the gray desk. Just a mental letdown after the last six weeks or so.

Joe was a big gun collector. Probably had more guns than ATF. He had a Remington .357 lever action rifle that I'd been looking at, drooling over, and playing with.

When I walked into the range classroom Joe says, "Here ya go" and tossed the rifle at me. He said, "It's yours now so that I don't have to keep wiping it down after you handle it." Just Joe's way of apologizing.

From then on if he had a knife or a gun or a range bag or whatever that I liked, I would just get pissed at him and it would usually become mine.

Over the months and years since, Joe and I grew to be close friends. Since retirement we lost touch, as is the case in many military or combat friendships. I hear he's doin' well, mellowed out, and enjoying retirement.

Things settled back down but I began to spend more time at the range teaching classes with him. Most of the agents couldn't understand how I voluntarily subjected myself to the wrath of Joe on a daily basis. Like I said, I made it work for me. Plus, once you got by the gruff, he was a wealth of knowledge about weapons and other things related to the Diplomatic Security Service (DSS).

Bev had put together an IED recognition book for DSS. It was a great work and when she left, it was up to me to see that it got published and distributed. It was a collection of tons of intel and info on IEDs. Typical Bev, it was perfect. As I went back and forth to main State and the printing office, a neat softbound book emerged with "Written By Bev…" at the bottom.

The chief of our division at the time wasn't a big fan of anyone but himself.

He saw that and said, "We're not going to put that on the street. I know that it violates copyright laws."

I told him it didn't matter who, what, when, or where, what mattered was getting the information out to the folks who needed it. He still held it down. I waited. I'd talked to Bev about it but I got the feeling she thought that I was dragging my feet.

The number two guy was a super individual. He was one of those number twos who never bad-mouthed the boss but could find ways around when needed. The director went out of town for a while so I went to the number two. He was aware of Bev's book and also the trouble I was having getting it cleared. He couldn't outright overrule the boss but he found a way around.

He said, "Change that to 'Compiled by Bev…' and I'll sign off." This I did and away it went.

The boss returned and never said a word. I don't know if there were any private conversations, but I suspect so. Bev did more than just compile. She collected the data and weaved it through her own editing. It was a very informative and helpful reference document. This book was distributed worldwide and we can never know how many lives it saved just by creating awareness.

I took advantage of this downtime to get as much training as possible. I wanted to get instructor certified wherever possible. Long and short, I stayed glued to the news about Beirut; I wanted to go back.

We were sending our Basic Agent and Regional Security Officer (RSO) classes to Bill Scott Raceway (BSR) located at Summit Point, West Virginia, for driving, surveillance detection, counter surveillance, follow-on firearms (shooting from vehicles), motorcades. We would run protective details in Winchester, Virginia. I wanted to play. I nudged myself into a driver instructor class that in those days lasted two weeks. It was really intense. Walked away with my instructor card punched, ready to teach.

The BSR Director of Training made the comment that another guy was the best natural driver but I was the best driver and natural instructor.

I made fast friends at BSR and ended up going through their entire instructor package. I even went through the CIA's surreptitious entry class (lock picking). This proved scary.

After I had a few basic and RSO classes under my belt as an instructor I was feeling pretty cocky. Met some new friends and we were having a ball.

These new friends were from SEAL Team Six, Red Cell, and Delta. Matter of fact, the Delta guy has been a lifelong best friend. This was during the era that Dick Marcinko was in charge.

This and a little before was also the time frame that Dick came up with the works *Rogue Warrior* and *Red Cell*. Like I said about his books before, I don't know if it was all true, but I know that some of it was, at least the stuff I knew about. Didn't have the need to know for the other stuff.

We were on the verge of out of control. Not quite there yet, but getting close. Of course if you had to do the things that we did, you had to be on the verge. Just make sure you never crossed the line. We did at one point, and it woke us all up.

We conducted periodic "Instructor Development" classes supposedly to keep our skills honed. In reality it was just another opportunity for us to stretch it to the limit. Me, the Navy guys, and the Delta guy were hanging out at "Pit Out." (The place where vehicles returned to the race track from the Pits.)

We looked over and saw the large refrigeration units that were used to store beer and sodas for race days. Of course they were all locked. That was no hill for a hill climber. We had just graduated from lock-picking school. Piece of cake. In about two minutes we were into the beer. We drank, toasted, partied, drank, and toasted some more. There were a few State guys there who were to become plank owners in the new Mobile Training Teams (MTT) that I will cover later.

Still, tough guys, mostly former Special Forces of some type. Somebody had the bright idea to run the track in the cars for time to see who was the fastest. Of course we all thought that we were the fastest. Faster and faster. Spin outs, off-road recoveries, bent fenders. Still wasn't enough adrenaline. Needed more.

The best idea came out. Put a guy on the hood, standing like a hood ornament, then see who could go fastest. Faster and faster. Up to over 100 mph down the straightaway with a nut on the hood yelling, Don't hit the brakes. Delta guy was the smartest. Called everyone in to the Pit Out area again and said, "That's it, shut 'er down! We've been lucky." And we were.

But!! We weren't done yet. Remember my '84 'Vette? Yep…had to have a go with that. We stopped, locked up the beer, and said, Let's go to a bar. Me and the State guys had federal credentials and badges. The Navy and Delta guys didn't. We load up in four vehicles and hauled ass to town. We got on 81 North and the Navy guys were in front. We're in motorcade formation—chrome to chrome—doing 110.

As we got off the exit, a local cop fell in behind us. Navy guys pulled in to a roughneck beer joint (which is all we looked for in those days), we followed, and so did the cop. He went straight for the two Navy guys. He was young and new and nervous. All of us with badges descended on him with badges out. He was surrounded by four guys with badges held in his face.

After talk and apologies, all was well and the cop departed. We went inside to renew our party. Such was the way it was in those days.

On a more docile note: I talked with the number two and told him I wanted to get into Beirut again. He told me to chill as that was already in the works. He was a sharp guy and told me it would be wise to learn a language.

I checked around and learned that the Foreign Service Institute was right next door and that they offered classes before work. I went over and looked at their program. You needed to score a 60 to study Arabic. A 50 was needed for French. Well, after all, they speak French in Lebanon. So I took the test, passed, and got into French 101.

After a few classes I felt like a homo trying to *parlez vous* everything. I was out on French. I went to the head instructor and told him I wanted Arabic.

He said, "Fine, score a 60."

It was a tough test. There was an old guy in there taking the same test. His wife was to be the ambassador to Madagascar. Don't know what language he was gonna study but I knew that I was gonna sit next to him—real close—for the test. I did and he and I both passed with flying colors.

CHAPTER SIX

Beirut MTT Number Two

I attacked Arabic with vigor. To me it came easy because it sounded more manly, plus I'd spent time there and had started keeping my legendary black language notebook. All of my current and future Arab friends knew of my notebook. They loved it. They would even bring strangers over and introduce them, then say, "Frauunk, show notebook." Then the stranger would try to come up with a new word for me to add to my book. I tried to learn ten words a day then, in addition to the classroom. I studied classic Arabic, which is spoken in Saudi and Kuwait. On the ground I learned Levantine Arabic, which was spoken in Lebanon. To this day, all Arabs say that I have a Lebanese accent. I'm out of practice but hope to redevelop my skills and learn to read and write it. Too many gray brain cells these days but I'm gonna try.

During this downtime I was still giving the Monday afternoon awareness classes. It seemed like the same old stuff week after week. Periodically I'd go to Quantico to teach the Marine security guards headed out to embassies the world over.

When I returned from Beirut I reported to the commanding officer of the Marine Security Guard Battalion. He was a full colonel destined to be a general and hero of Desert Storm. One hell of a man. I gave him a courtesy brief on my trip, which wasn't required. Early on in my career I learned it best to keep the colonel informed. At least then he knows you're not hiding anything and he'll tend to leave you alone to do your job.

He asked about the Marines and I gave him a full report. He asked how often I'd be taking the trips and I responded as often needed and required. He asked to get a report on all the

Marines that I visited. He knew that I was in the long hair mode and made no issue of it.

The Executive Officer (X.O., second in command) was another story. I came down to give a class and I wore a suit. My hair wasn't regulation but it looked like a businessman's haircut. This major jumped all over my ass.

"Captain, when you come down the next time you will be groomed, wearing dress blues, and looking like a Marine officer."

I saw that there was no reasoning with this bonehead so I simply said, "Aye-aye, sir."

I went to see the colonel. I said, "Sir, it appears I won't be able to give you an objective report on the Marines when I travel."

"How's that?" he said without looking up.

"Major Numb Nuts (not exactly what I said but the feeling came across) said that I had to tighten up my haircut and wear uniforms to give the classes."

You could tell the colonel was steamed but he simply said, "Just go ahead as we discussed and keep your hair at the necessary length to do your job."

Didn't hear any more about the hair but me and this guy were to tangle again in a much more serious venue.

In addition to my Arab language studies, my instructor courses, and classes that I was giving, I decided to revamp the IED training packages and come up with an IED Awareness video. Just another example of "Don't volunteer for anything." When I sold the idea up the chain of command it went crazy. "What a great idea...we'll get real actors...we'll have a movie set...we'll send this to all the embassies."

Hold on—send to embassies? That means Frank wouldn't have to go. Time to downsell this operation. I went back to the drawing board and resold the idea that *Frank is the bomb guy*, not an actor. This video could be used as a fill-in only when Frank was traveling to the embassies. Okay, they agreed.

Whew!! Almost let my alligator mouth talk me out of a job. Had to watch that with the State folks. I learned that day to present them with your final goal then show 'em how to get there. Don't let them determine your goals for you. So suddenly Frank was a movie producer, director, and actor.

The first one was just me as a talking head, lookin' like a goof, showing pictures of IEDs and bomb scenes that were well-known throughout the world. Goofy. Goofy. I understand that this movie is still alive and well at State somewhere.

The second version was a little better. I used some local talent (agents and secretaries) and we pulled it off good. Showed some protective details, a bomber placing a device on a limo... ooops!!! We forgot to take it off and it turned up again on a protective detail in D.C. Had some explaining to do on that one. At least by then I didn't see my career flash before my eyes anymore. I'd learned how to bob and weave like a true diplomat.

While all this was going on I also decided to build some new bombs for my IED class. After all the bombs going off in the world, everyone wanted and was getting Frank's IED class. Not really Frank's—Bev's. I wanted to put my signature on it. I was tired of teaching other peoples stuff.

I was sitting at the gray desk one morning trying to figure what else I could do to look busy because I'd learned that my job was hours and hours of boredom interrupted by moments of sheer panic. I was in the hours and hours phase right now. I was getting ready to make a bus trip over to main State when I noticed a couple of strangers in the boss's office doorway.

One guy was older and about my height with a mousy-looking face. Seemed to always be smiling with his mouth but the rest of his face told a different story. This guy had the mechanical ability to read right through you with a glance that left you cold and disarmed.

The other guy was just the opposite. He had a free laugh and a warm, genuine smile.

As I walked by, the boss grabbed me and said, "Abe, Joe, let me introduce you to Frank. He's our duty Marine and bomb guy." Both shook my hand in turn and I could tell that Abe was in charge of whatever was going on. Abe's face looked like the pivot point for an Amtrak. He had scars everywhere.

Turns out Abe was the RSO when the embassy was bombed in Beirut. He was undergoing plastic surgery at the time. Turned out to be one great guy and the easiest-going personality I've ever dealt with.

Abe said, "Where's Bev?"

"I am her replacement; she moved on to bigger and better things," I replied.

"Good meetin' you and maybe we can get together later," Abe said.

"Why would he want to get together later?" I wondered. Maybe just more of that diplomatic nice guy stuff that makes you feel warm and fuzzy for about five minutes until a little later that same person says, "Have we met before?" "Yeah, asshole, about fifteen minutes ago."

Didn't matter to me, I was headed over to Dignitary Protection (DP) to see my old buddy Dick. Maybe he knew of something that was coming up that I could hook up with. Sometimes there would be an off-the-wall detail in D.C., New York. or Los Angeles. I was bored as hell and nothing was going on. Man, was that about to change. I walked into DP and ran into Tony. Tony was the logistics and a make-it-happen guy in DP. Retired Army and busy as hell at all hours.

I grabbed a cup of coffee and peeked into Dick's office. On the phone, as always. He finally hung up and told me to come in. He started talking as I was walking.

"Well, you in on this new Ninja MTT that they're starting up?" I must've looked surprised because he immediately told me, "Look, you didn't hear it from me. Just wait 'til somebody in your chain tells you...if they do."

"What the hell are you talking about, Dick?" I already saw new guys coming in and taking over the MTT mission and booting me, Joe, and Rob out on our asses. Not quite, but close.

I went outside and sat on the bus bench just to think about what Dick had just said. New Ninja MTT?? What was that all about? Dick was a no-nonsense kinda guy and wasn't big into rumor mill. He obviously thought I knew about whatever it was. Oh well, had to wait and see.

MTT Beirut Number Two

On the bus ride back to Roslyn I was running all kinds of stuff through my brain housing group. Man, was I gonna be pissed if I got edged out of any more MTTs. I jumped off the bus and grabbed a cup of coffee at the downstairs coffee shop. Stuff upstairs tasted like battery acid and they still made us pay a quarter for it. The elevator seemed to take forever.

We had a new Agent class in and these folks seemed to be everywhere. I got off the elevator, sipping my hot coffee as I approached my gray desk. To my left there had been an old storage room about fifteen feet by fifteen feet. In the couple of hours since I'd been to main State, somebody had gutted this storage room to bare walls and now there were two more gray desks with chairs.

Joe, the mousy guy who I had met, was at the desk on the left and the second desk was empty. I sat down and tried to look busy but curiosity was killin' me. Finally couldn't stand it anymore. Picked up my coffee and walked over to the doorway and leaned in. Joe looked up with that neat little smile but no warmth in his eyes.

I said, "Hey, Joe, you gonna be with us now."

He was actually a fairly open guy once you got to know him. Apparently he had retired from State, or wherever, and had been brought back on contract.

Abe came walking in and sat down at the other desk. He was obviously occupied in thought because he ignored the fact that I was standing there.

Those of you who know me realize that I didn't let this last long.

I asked, as if to both, "So what are you guys up to?"

Joe ignored me but Abe looked up and said, "We're standing up the formal MTT program. We're starting the interview process next week. We figure to bring on about twelve guys. It will be a permanent posting and we hope to have at least one four-man team out at all times." He immediately turned back to Joe and started discussing a list of names that he had on his desk.

I drooped back over to my gray beast and plopped dejectedly in my chair. Al, the number two, came in with a big grin on his face.

"Frank, you up for a trip to Beirut as early as next week?"

I jumped up and said, "Hell, yes! I can go this week and do the advance if you want."

He laughed and said, "No, it'll be Monday or Tuesday of next week. This one is classified so don't spread the word."

Classifications were not of a spooky nature. We weren't doing anything weird. It's just for travel security and OpSec they didn't want anyone knowing our plans.

As it was Wednesday, I had a lot to do. I had to do some shopping for my little buddy with the Almaza beer. Had to pick up some trinkets up for Ernest and Imad. Like kids, they'd be pissed if I didn't bring 'em something from the land of the big P.X. I also had to buy some news magazines for my helo buddies. The rest of the week was a whirlwind. Apparently this was to be the last of the ad hoc MTTs. It was going to be three of us again—Joe, me, and a new guy, Mike. Mike was an old hand at DS but was new to the MTT game. Wasn't real thrilled about going to Beirut but was also the kinda guy who took it in stride.

Next big hurdle was telling Mama that I'd be gone for a few weeks. Friday night was the right time. We went out to dinner and, as always, we took Stephen. Susan and I were and are the types who didn't look for excuses to be away from our kids. I was away enough as it was and Susan was the consummate Mom. (Nothing or nobody comes between Mama Bear and her cubs; even if they're wrong, she says they're right.) I learned early on to not come home flexing my muscles as the new parent in town. It confused the boys and kept me out of the dog house.

We went to our normal pizza joint and ordered our pizza and a pitcher of courage. Once I had downed one of those (Susan normally drank one glass and that was it) I told her I had some news.

She said, "When do you leave?"

I told her it wasn't set yet but probably Monday or Tuesday. The previous trip we had gone in on an Air Force C-141. This time we were going commercial. Things had heated up in Beirut and it was going to be a fast one. I think the RSO also wanted the additional firepower, and as it turned out that was true. We went through the motions that weekend but neither of us was looking forward to my departure.

As usual, I assumed the task of telling Stephen I had to go on a short trip. Even though Mama knew where I was going she never questioned and I never told her. It was just accepted.

I went to work early on Monday, early even for me. I've always been the type to be two hours early but never one minute late. A quirk of mine. I went straight to the range because I knew Joe would be there. He was there all right, and going about his little packing routine. He loved to pack and catalogue and stow, then unpack and do it over again. He just loved it. I grabbed a cup of coffee and sat on a student desk. Joe hadn't said a word and neither had I. Finally he grabbed an old, oily rag and began to wipe his hands.

He pulled out a couple of cigars and said that his wife found them locally. "They're not Cuban, but I like 'em better. Got a nutty taste to them." They weren't in a wrapper so I say, "Where'd she get them?"

"Hell, I don't know," he responded.

Turned out to be Muniemakers from Connecticut Valley. (Any cigar guys out there, give 'em a shot—not bad.) As we puffed away out in the parking lot, Joe asked how Susan took it. I said like the sergeant major she is. Nose down, butt up, and continue to march.

He rolled his eyes at me and said, "Bullshit!"

I asked, "So when're we goin'?"

He responded, "We're on a Pan Am flight to London tomorrow. Leaves a little after 1600."

Cool thing was that we would be flying first class. We had courier letters for the dip pouches that contained all of our weapons. I knew what I had to do that day; haul ass to main State, get our courier letters, pick up three orange bags (dip pouches), head back to the range, and pack up. Mike was at the office so I told him I'd get his stuff and he could meet us at the range.

I was all done by 1500 and back at the range ready to pack. As expected, Joe was standing by all packed, sunglasses on, guns laid out, clean and with a light film of oil. Boxes of ammo were stacked on a nearby table.

I said, "Shit, looks like we're goin' to war."

Joe responded, "No shit, white man!"

We were all done by 1730 and ready to go.

There was a favorite watering hole in the complex so we strolled over. After a few beers we headed our separate ways.

The next day went fast. I kissed Susan and Stephen goodbye. Susan said, "Call me if you can. I worry."

"Don't have to worry about me," I said. "Worry about the other guy." I tried to make light of the situation but it was and still is hard to leave her. I made my way through the traffic around the Beltway to get to Lorton.

Finally made it, and Joe was there but Mike hadn't made it. We goofed around cleaning the place. Joe then decided we needed to shoot a little. He broke out a couple of Browning Hi Powers and away we went. We never said a word, just shot, pasted our targets, then shot some more.

I felt that Joe had some advance info on where we were headed but couldn't share it with me. Oh well, I learned long ago that if you don't have the "Need to Know" you probably don't want to know. Just as well.

I was pumped up and ready. Didn't want or need any rain clouds messing up my excitement.

By the time we got the weapons cleaned and put away, Mike had shown up. I could tell that he was a little nervous but ready. Anybody in his right mind should be nervous. The U.S. military had pulled out of Beirut as a result of the MAU HQ bombing.

There were a few Security guys at the embassy and about twelve Marines. That was it, in a country torn by civil war. As Richard Pryor once said, "You go in lookin' for justice and that's what you find—just us." It was also a time when nobody could be trusted. The locals and the government folks were very upset with America and Americans. As I said before, they felt abandoned. I felt that they were, too. But I wasn't a politician, I was a Marine. I did what Marines do: follow orders.

We got to Dulles in time to have a beer, which is not really by the book as a dip courier. We didn't pay too much attention to that stuff in those days. As dip couriers we were permitted down on the tarmac to load the pouches. As always, they went on last.

Didn't have the Delta guy, so it went off without a hitch. We then went up the stairway and were directed to our seats in first class. Joe was a strange traveler. Once he got in his seat he didn't want to be disturbed FOR ANYTHING! No food, no water, no booze.

He would put on his black blinders (like those you see on TV sitcoms), kick back, and sleep. In retrospect, I think he pilled up so that he could sleep. Not me—too wired. I told the stewardess to keep the drinks coming 'til I fell asleep. That normally didn't happen until an hour before arrival. Sometimes it was tough getting off that plane, climbing down the ladder, grabbing the pouch, then finding our way to the terminal to hook up with our next flight and do it again. Not good practice going into a hot area.

Getting through the terminal was easy enough. Next came security. Heathrow was not diplomatic-friendly in those days. There were international laws that govern dip couriers. It was accepted worldwide that the pouches were never to be out of our sight. They instructed us to lay the pouches on a belt that went through a wall to the space on the other side. Joe went ballistic. He was not the personality to mess with when he was pissed. Not really the type to mess with when he was happy, either. He yelled and screamed and threw his bags around.

The little lady security guard was unflappable. I am sorry, sir, but that is proceedya (in that snooty accent). Needless to say, we finally complied. Even if they X-rayed they wouldn't see anything—we had thin sheets of lead that we wrapped our weapons in. We reconfigured the shape so as to look like anything but a gun. That had to drive 'em nuts.

We got the bags and checked the lead seals. All was well. Then we continued through security and, even though we had

Larnaca, seafood salad, Aphrodite wine

dip passports, we were made to empty our carry-on bags. My bag had a lined cardboard bottom. Bitch even took a razor knife and cut it to expose the cardboard. Joe just stared. Never said a word. I told her that a good friend of mine was in charge of Customs at Dulles.

I was gonna call him and tell him to jerk every Brit around who came through. Guess she wasn't headed to Dulles because she didn't give a damn. Of course I had a friend but that call would never take place and even if it did I'm sure my friend wouldn't give a damn either.

After that, the trip was uneventful. Changed planes, flew to Larnaca, and lady luck smiled. Weather was beautiful and the MAU choppers were too busy to come get us. Looked like we were gonna be stuck in the hotel for a few days on the beach, damn the good luck. We lounged around, ate fresh seafood salad like I've never tasted, sipped Aphrodite wine, chewed on the roasted corn still provided by the same little old ladies, and enjoyed the scenery provided by the topless and, in some cases, bottomless European ladies who seemed to litter the beach in front of our hotel.

CHAPTER SEVEN

Beirut Continues

We finally got the word from the embassy at Nicosia. The choppers would be in at around 1000 the next morning, adjacent to the same conex boxes that caused our previous discomfort. This time the embassy sent the "ice cream truck" and a little Cypriot facilitator. He was jovial and seemed really happy to see us. Joe knew him from a prior trip. Sure wish we'd had this guy on the first trip. We loaded up the ice cream truck and bounced out to the end of the runway to meet up with the choppers. Man, what timing. No sooner had we unloaded our gear than we heard the whop...whop...whop of incoming helicopters (choppers). We strained our eyes and were happy to see Ch-53Es again.

We just didn't feel like a UH-1 Huey or a CH-46 Sea Knight venture. Just more secure and comfy in a 53. Size does matter. I passed the news magazines up to the pilot and he gave me the thumbs up. With his visor down I had no idea if it was the same guy but he was appreciative nonetheless. Again, it's the little stuff that we take for granted. A newspaper, a cup of real coffee, dry/clean/starched clothing with shined shoes, a haircut, a shave.

Once we were loaded up and ready to go we piled on board. Mike was funny-lookin' with his headset on, trying to look serious. Joe had his headset on with his ever-present dark glasses, looking very much the part of air crewman and operator headed for action. I just felt the adrenaline.

Granted, we weren't going into a typical "hot landing zone," but in Beirut one never knew. The militias seemed to have better intel about our actions than the embassy did. We flew in nap-of-

West Beirut

the-earth style, which is almost at ground level in the haul-ass mode, dodging hills, buildings, and vehicles.

Man, what a ride. The pilot was shit-hot and obviously trying to prove it to us. He would stand the bird on its side to turn between two large buildings then stand it on its nose to pick up air speed.

When the chopper was on its side you could look out the open door and see the upturned, startled faces of the pedestrians on the streets. It felt like you could reach out and touch them. We had removed our weapons from the dip pouches and had "locked and loaded" prior to coming into Lebanese airspace. We were on "rock and roll."

It appeared that we were leaving the populated areas but the pilot had just headed north over the foothills then swooped back into East Beirut. What a contrast. I was to see it up close and personal on a future trip, but the difference between East and West Beirut as seen from the air was amazing.

In the west it looked like an old WW II movie set of bombed-out Germany at the close of the war. East Beirut looked like any large U.S. city with hotels, restaurants, and casinos. Clearly a system of the haves and have-nots.

In the west the warlords were the haves at the expense of the population. In the east it was capitalism at its finest. Of course there was corruption there as well, but at least the common person had a shot at a piece of the pie.

We again felt the familiar pull of the g-forces as the pilot feathered the chopper. It felt like your whole body was trying to fit itself through your butt hole. We thumped down and the crew chief obviously didn't want to spend any more time on the ground than was necessary so he was hustling, yelling, throwing our stuff off the back ramp, grabbing his headsets. You can only imagine how Joe reacted to this. I was pleasantly surprised. He just rolled with the flow and got his butt offloaded with the rest of us and our gear.

As it turns out we were just on the outskirts of town. The RSO had turned up with two blacked-out Suburbans and a handful of embassy bodyguards. About 100 meters away I saw two guys standing next to a small, white Toyota.

I had to squint but was happy to see that it was Ernest and Imad. Imagine that. Elie Hobeika and his boys knew our schedule as well as the embassy. They had not been tasked to "protect" us this trip but we told the RSO we'd like their company again. The RSO said, "I'll fix it with Joseph Sphere" (Boss of the Spider People directly under the warlord Elie Hobeika). We knew that Elie and Joseph already wanted this so that they could keep tabs on us. It was a standing joke between us and Imad and Ernest. We were CIA (they pronounced see-ya) and they were the Spider Spooks (SS).

We didn't get them assigned to us for a few days and we had to get hot on the range. We had another seventy-five new-hire guards to train and get posted. We headed to the range the first day, with Edgar driving and me in right front. We had been issued the new Hechler and Koch MP5 submachine guns.

This was new to us because our old Uzis fired from the open bolt position, meaning that the bolt would be to the rear. When you pulled the trigger the bolt would slam forward, picking up a round out of the magazine, chambering, and firing the round in one movement. Pressure created by the round going off would slam the bolt back to repeat the process. This created what we called a chunka-chunka feel when firing.

The MP5 on the other hand fired from the closed bolt position. The bolt would be home with a round in the chamber. It was much more reliable and more stable than the Uzi, with no chunka-chunka. Eventually the MP5 came out with new models: MP5N, Navy model; MP5SD, silenced.

The SD created a problem for us when we were training. The FBI and BSR had shooting houses, or kill houses. They were made of stacked tires that prevented the rounds from going out of the facility. These houses were very large and had several rooms. We were concerned about round penetrations so we started playing with 147-grain, subsonic ammo. Only problem is that they wouldn't penetrate the tires and become captured. They would bounce off and ricochet. Banged us up a bit before we realized what was going on.

The next MP5 was the K model. This was a very small, short, machine pistol affair. It was designed primarily for protective details. It fit into a metal briefcase and was carried as such. Just looked like a normal businessman with his/her briefcase. The trigger was in the briefcase handle and a designer stripe down the length of the case was for sighting. Sexy little rig. I never carried this because it seemed too limited for me. I like the ability to make quick magazine changes—hard to do inside a briefcase. This system was designed to provide covering fire while you E&E'd the protectee.

Back to the range. Joe and Mike were in the back seat. In the back cargo area we had fifty pistols and loads of 9mm ammo. We also had fifteen Remington 870 shotguns with twelve-gauge slug and number seven buckshot. Number seven put out twenty-seven bee-bee-sized shots of lead that would stop even the most demented terrorist.

We stopped and got our standard *minuche* sandwich and steamy hot Turkish coffee. This was all new to Mike but he was buckin' up like a trooper. Another thing about Mike, he was a

Minuche Sandwich Break

devout Christian and a deacon in his church. Joe and I were at the other end of that spectrum but we both respected his belief and dedication. I later learned that this is a good way of life.

We were bouncing along and turned off the main highway. We went past the small house on the left that was on a little hillside, just a hut with a big front porch. Set up on the front porch was a homemade weight bench and bar. Hanging from each side of the bar were two concrete blocks as weights. I can't remember a morning that we didn't go by and see the young Lebanese guy working out. Edgar said that he was trying to make the Lebanese Olympic team. He was well known in Lebanon. I always wondered why Lebanon didn't buy the guy a set of real weights. Oh well, not mine to reason why.

As we wound upward on the small, two-lane road, we were eating and joking with Edgar. He had a pretty little wife and a brand new baby. Heavy traffic and crazy drivers were not uncommon in Beirut. I have to admit, we were not alert. What was to happen next gave us a lesson in situational awareness.

A military jeep (M151) with an M60 belt-fed machine gun and gunner passed us on the left side. Initially I didn't think about it until immediately behind the jeep and pulling along-side us was a white Mercedes sedan. Up until this time most attacking vehicles and car bombs were white Mercedes sedans. I looked ahead and alarms started going off in my head. The gunner in the jeep was pointing the M60 right at our windshield with his finger on the trigger. One thing we were always trained to do was notice the condition of the antagonist's weapon, including the position of his trigger finger. Here we are in the classic "box" with no way out. Jeep with the M-60 machine gun in front, white Mercedes along side and a vehicle behind closing the door. No escape to the right because of the dirt bank.

Now I jerked my head to the left and saw all the windows down on the Mercedes and several AK-47s pointing in our direc-tion. A quick glance to the rear verified my biggest fear—there was a third attack vehicle closing the back door. Now if I had been driving, the story would have turned out very different. We would have made a dramatic escape or we would be dead. Edgar just slowed the vehicle to a stop.

Mike and Joe were shouting conflicting orders to Edgar, "Go...Go!" or "Stop, see what they want!"

I glanced at Edgar and, for a moment, thought he might have been an inside man and involved with the attack. He was calm and had a slight smile. It turned out to be a mask that all of these folks wore to convince their attacker that they are innocents and have nothing to hide.

There was no shoulder on my side of the road, only a three- or four-foot rise where the road had been cut from the hillside. Edgar pulled over to a point where I wouldn't be able to fully open my door because of the embankment.

Another reason I was a little concerned: Joe, Mike and I all had MP5, 9mm submachine guns. We had backup Brownings that are also 9mm. Our antagonists had an M60 and AK-47s, all of which are 7.62mm. Now, 9mm is bigger around but the cartridge and muzzle velocities are totally different.

Little armor lesson: We were in an armored Suburban rated at B-4 armor level. This will stop twelve-gauge slug and .357 Magnum as well as our 9mms. So we couldn't shoot out. Their 7.62s would penetrate us like a hot knife through butter. They immediately jumped from their vehicles and surrounded us, yelling and screaming. Our windows wouldn't go down so we just looked at them.

Edgar started to open his door and I grabbed his arm and told him I'd shoot him first. The smile went away because he knew I was not bullshitting.

By now I understood enough Arabic to know that they wanted our guns and ammo. As a Marine, that was not going to happen.

I yelled through the glass "*Safara 'Merikee*" (American embassy). Didn't do a bit of good. Guns were pointing and banging against the glass.

They kept yelling to put down our windows and we responded with what type of sexual intercourse they could conduct with themselves. I was *scared shit*. Things started to cool down a little and I placed my dip passport against the glass. That didn't help.

The yelling started again and the weapons' muzzles kept banging against the glass.

Then I heard the click...click. I looked back, and Joe was holding up his MP5 just enough for them to see him clicking the safety off and on.

"Holy shit," I said. "Knock that off."

As it turns out, he was right. As I studied the culture more I realized that the only thing the Arab mind understands is strength and balls. Joe was showing them how he felt about the situation with action not words.

I had by then heard enough to know that these assholes worked for Joseph Sphere and were Spider People. It became easier to see who was in charge as one guy started talking on the radio. I overheard Sphere. I called him back over and he walked up to our vehicle with his rifle on his shoulder and pointed directly at my face. We were all yelling through the bullet resistant glass, which seemed to intensify the situation.

"*Shoo...shoo?*" (What...what?)," he asked.

I said, *"Enta ardiff* Joseph Sphere?" (Do you know Joseph Sphere?).

"Shoo ismock...shoo ismock?" (What is your name?).

"Anna ismooa Frank (My name is Frank). Call on your radio and tell Imad Kassas and Ernest Hatem to come here!! They are friends. Tell them Joe is here and Yu-Muh!!" As my Arabic was limited, it was a mix of Arabic and English. Through gestures and verbage the thought was expressed.

I was taking a little chance because I wasn't 100% sure who these guys were. Given the circumstances I felt it worth the risk. A gunfight was just moments away given the status.

He went to the radio and yelled and screamed for a while as only Arabs can do when they're holding a normal conversation. Eventually he said into the radio, *"Naam...naam"* (Yes...yes). He strolled back over and shouted an order, *"Halla...hallas!!"* (It was over, finished).

All weapons were lowered, fingers off triggers. Nobody in Beirut took it to the next step of putting the safety on. *"Ah Hallan...Ah Hallan"* (Welcome...Welcome).

Everyone started laughing. At least *they* did—nobody in the Suburban even broke a smile. We were left alone and continued to the range. Once we calmed down, the banter started between us. Mike got me to the side, very upset by what Joe did with his safety. I just shrugged it off to nerves. Mike said he thought Joe had a suicide wish.

We unpacked all of the ammo and weapons and locked them in the storage facility. A few hours later the students showed and we began training. About 1430 we see this red Mercedes convertible winding up the road toward us. It was as red as I've ever seen. Turned out to have white leather interior. Pimp ride from hell.

It was Imad at the wheel with Ernest riding shotgun. They pulled up on the range, laughing and joking. "You have big problem this morning?"

"Yeah, couple of your boneheads almost got killed."

"Ha! Ha! You scared, Frank?"

"Damn right, couldn't open my window or door, three AKs in my face. I was just not a happy camper."

Edgar and author relax after the day's events with the LF

They began to relate the story from their end. They were in their CP. Apparently Elie Hobeika was in the immediate area and we were stopped as a result of the fact that we'd penetrated their security perimeter. Imad and Ernest had heard the initial radio traffic that men in a Suburban had gotten through with guns and ammo. The attackers received orders to turn us about after they confiscated our weapons and ammo. Imad and Ernest got interested when the lieutenant radioed back that we refused to open up or give them anything.

They were then ordered to assault us and take the weapons and ammo. The lieutenant informed them that we had the advantage because we were in an armored vehicle. We could shoot them but they couldn't shoot us. It was just the opposite, but thank God they didn't know it. After a while Imad heard his name, my name, and Joe's name. Then he heard "Yu-Muh!" Imad screamed, *"Ya Allah...*That's Mr. Joe and Mr. Frank. Let them go, let them go. Besides they can shoot better than you and you will all be killed." But for the grace of God.

This time we stayed at the Montemar Hotel for the total trip. Much better living conditions. We had the seventy-five guards to train and the tempo was fast. We had brought the LAAW rockets over on our first trip but had been unable to train anyone on them. We had decided that we would accomplish that on this trip. In addition, I was to take a look at the security procedures to see if I could harden things up a little. I made several attempts to penetrate security. I did it personally but this wasn't fair because they knew who I was and what I did. I then solicited the help of a female secretary to take in a fake bomb. Got right through. Of course I was on hand when she came through because I didn't want anyone to get shot.

As it turns out, the guards weren't comfortable with searching a female because of their culture. Better to have a bomb than violate a female. I then immediately advised the RSO to hire four girls, which he did. They did not receive firearms training but they did extensive search and recognition training, including psychological profiling: looking for nervous activity, sweating, jabbering, etc.

The next step I took was that I made six small plastic boxes. I attached some PVC pipe and a handle on top. I mounted a small green light and a small red light on the top with a button. When they waived the PVC over a package and pressed the button the green light would come on. If it ever turned red that meant that there were explosives. Very first explosive detector. I had a training box that I made up that would always turn red and buzz. I held it over C-4 or TNT, pushed the button, and off it went. These "detectors" were nothing more than empty boxes. The bad guys or surveillance teams didn't know that. It was a show for surveillance. The guards caught on to this after about four to six months but we can only guess how much explosives were kept out. We'll never know our successes, only our failures.

My next little trick lasted longer. I took two old huge movie cameras, like the ones you see from old movie sets. I mounted them on poles looking in opposite directions down the road. I surrounded these poles with chain link fence and barbed wire on top. I then put a shotgun-armed guard inside the fence. They were hooked to nothing but they sure looked high tech and important. I was putting on a show for terrorist surveillance teams. Something worked, because after our efforts ended in 1986 there were no more attacks on the U.S. Embassy in Beirut. We did other things as well that are still classified but the simplicity and cost effectiveness are uncanny.

We went through a selection process to determine who would be the best LAAW rocket guards. We were going to put one hell of a lot of firepower into the hands of a little Lebanese guard. Most of the posts were within the range of town for this weapon. If we selected one bad apple and there was an incident or accident there would be hell to pay. After we selected twelve guys we headed off to the Bikfaya mountains just on the town side of the Baka Valley. It was beautiful. Just a little snow on the ground, but clear and crisp.

We had taken probably sixty rockets with us. This little weapon is a device used for anti-tank warfare. Not a little toy. It has a high-explosive head and a shape charge that can penetrate nine inches of steel. We got everybody lined up, unpacked the rockets, and were all set to go. We took a bed sheet and attached it to the cliff face. We painted a circle on the sheet with fluorescent orange paint. Joe and I were to demonstrate the first few rounds. Joe got all set, cocked the weapon and clicked the fire button. Click...nothing. Recocked, click...nothing. He tried again and again; it wouldn't fire. We repacked that one and got another; same thing. On the third attempt the rocket launched from the tube but failed to detonate when it hit the sheet. Joe went through about six rockets, with all being failures in one manner or another.

The two loudest noises: Click when it should go bang and bang when it should go click!

He gave up and said, "Frank, you try...maybe it's me."

I did the same thing. After we had fired or attempted to fire twelve to fifteen rockets, I finally had one explode. Now imagine this. Here we are, the gurus putting on this show with American weapon super technology, and nothing worked. Embarrassing ain't the word.

Joe was extremely pissed and didn't care who knew it. He was really in a rage this time, throwing stuff around, kicking rocks. All I could think about was these LAAW rockets that we'd placed back in the containers that didn't fire. Didn't think it wise to be throwing that kinda stuff around. What the hell, Joe was an old EOD guy, too. He knew the odds of something blowing up. Anyhow I wasn't about to get between him and his tantrum.

Next morning we met in the hotel lobby. Joe had a smile on his face like the cat that ate the canary. I knew he had something up his sleeve but he wasn't ready to share it yet. We ate at the hotel that morning. We feasted on hot fresh croissants, fresh cheese, jellies of every type, and fresh fruit that was sweet and juicy. All this was washed down with copious amounts of Turkish coffee, also made sweet by the amounts of sugar we added. It's no wonder that I put on about fifteen pounds during this tour. That, too, was to come to a screeching halt.

We mounted up and headed to the embassy. After yesterday's events it was determined that I would do the driving until Imad and Ernest joined us. We were a bunch more alert and Mike was particularly animated. His head bobbed and swiveled like a plastic toy in the back of a Mexican's car. This is one time I was thankful for his nervousness. We made it without incident and got through the gate with numerous Yu-Muh's back and forth from all the guards.

Once inside the RSO's office we were introduced to the new embassy nurse, a kindly little lady of about fifty who looked very much the part. She had only been in country for a day, so she was brand new. Joe, Mike, and I grabbed a cup of coffee and settled in to wait until the RSO had time for us. He was always busy, as you can imagine with a post like that. As we laughed and bantered, the nurse, Kay, realized that we were there training guards.

She said, "I assume that I know who you guys work for and it ain't State." We had heard that before and were to hear it many times after. We assured her that we were State but she never really believed us.

143

She made the comment that she would like to meet the guards at some point.

Joe said, "Frank, why don't you and Mike take Kay and introduce her to the guards who are on duty?"

I could tell he was trying to get rid of us, Mike more so than me because he gave me a sly wink.

I said, "Sure, let's go."

Kay asked, "Is it safe to go out now?"

I said, "It's as safe as Beirut ever gets."

She wasn't convinced, but away we went. Mike begged out and headed to wherever it was that he always found to disappear. He would be gone for hours on end, then reappear as if nothing had happened. We stopped worrying about his little sabbaticals.

Kay and I went outside and headed to the main gate entrance area. There were four guards posted there. Three were old-timers and one was a guy who we'd just trained.

Me and the guards started shouting "Yu-Muh" as soon as we saw each other. The new guy was like a recruit and snapped to as soon as he saw me. As I approached each guard I shook his hand then placed my hand over my heart, as is Arab tradition.

In Lebanese I said, *"Kaey fuck"* which is Levantine Arabic for "hello." In Egypt it is *izaick* (eye-zay-ick); in Saudi it's *keef hallick*. But the *kaey fuck* is truly the greeting, and not making fun or saying a four letter action verb meaning sexual intercourse (didn't know I could talk like that did you?).

After we made a few rounds and I introduced Kay to about half the guards, she said, "Frank, I am very uncomfortable." Kay didn't speak Arabic.

She said, "It may be macho and cool, but I don't like it. When you say '*Kay fuck*' to these guys then say 'This is Kay,' it just doesn't seem appropriate."

I looked at her like a deer in the headlights. Wow, how embarrassed she must have felt. My dumb ass never even thought about it. I gave her a quick lesson in Arabic and tried to teach her a few words but she never could bring herself to say "*kay fuck.*" She'd just shyly say "hello." That worked, too.

When we were done I headed back to the RSO's office. The secretary was there and welcomed me with a fresh cup of Turkish coffee. She knew I preferred it. Joe was in with the RSO with the door closed.

After a few minutes Joe came out and headed toward the exit.

He said, "Where's Mike?"

"Prayer circle, I guess. He split off when I took the nurse around and I haven't seen him."

"Good," he responded. He took off like a shot. He had some documents folded up in his hand and we headed for the stairwell. Normally we went up but this time he headed down. Oh well, been around Joe long enough to know: Don't ask, don't guess, and worst of all, don't worry, because he was gonna do it anyhow. He went down to the basement area and entered a small office there.

One desk, a secretary, and an old guy standing in the corner, looking at a newspaper. Joe greeted the secretary but went straight to the old American guy. The gent seemed to be perturbed at being distracted from his paper. Joe handed him the documents and the old guy scanned them. He walked over and took a pen from the secretary's desk and initialed or signed the top document. I couldn't see the contents of the paperwork.

He then handed the paperwork to the secretary and went over to a small safe against the wall. He manipulated the dial and it opened. He took out several bundles of U.S. currency. I couldn't see but they appeared to be $10,000 bundles of 100-dollar bills. There were two or three bundles. Joe stuffed them into the range bag that he carried everywhere. Out we went.

What amazed me is that not a word was exchanged. Joe looked at me as we approached the stairway and asked, "Ever heard of the 'Black Bag Man'?"

"Yeah," I said, more joking than not.

Joe responded, "You just had a transaction with him."

After a split second I responded, "I didn't sign shit."

Joe said, "Doesn't matter—you were there, Mr. Commissioned Officer."

The only thing that kept me in my skin was the fact that he was laughing as he said it. But only his mouth was laughing. His eyes were dancing with excitement. Hold on white boy, going for another Joey ride.

One thing was for sure, it wasn't 100% sanctioned because Joe said, "We need Mike to teach protective operations for the next few days." There was a Lebanese detail on the ambassador supported by some Tour of Additional Duty (TAD) guys and a State Dept RSO. It was a chance for Mike to do some good and give Joe and I room to do whatever we were going to do.

It was now early afternoon and Joe had successfully convinced Mike that the team relied on his expertise and experience and that the training for the detail was best handled by him, as neither Joe nor I had his vast knowledge and background.

Mike went for it like a trooper and no doubt did a superb job. I think, in retrospect, that Joe trusted Mike, he just wanted for him to have deniability if the shit hit the fan. Joe and I departed the embassy to get some lunch and, I assumed, for Joe to let me know what was going on.

I was right about lunch but Joe didn't tell me anything. It later turned out to be a test. Joe liked to put people in tough spots just to see how they performed. This entire evolution was to be my test. After a lunch of *shawarma* sandwiches and hot tea, we headed back to the range. Every time we went to the range, one of Joseph Sphere's boys would show up. We had reliable Edgar with us but we had dumped Imad and Ernest.

We pulled up on the range and got out. Joe still hadn't said a word. He opened the weapons storage bunker and took out a couple of boxes of ammo. He threw me one and for the first time spoke. "Let's shoot."

I grabbed a target as did he and we went down range to set them up. On the way back up range we saw a military style jeep pull up behind our Suburban. Little Lebanese guy gets out, as did his driver and they sauntered over to our firing point. We started to talk and he spoke good English. Joe was overly nice to the guy.

The guy pulls out an M1911, .45 pistol that was very new and obviously this guy's pride and joy.

"Look," he says time and again, "Look, new 45." It was all pimped up, with pearl handles and engraving. At one time it was a nice gun. It was his and he was proud. That's all that mattered.

Joe took the gun and looked at it closely as if he were completely in awe. I knew Joe better. He loved guns and I knew it killed him to see this fine weapon all pimped out. Joe did a press check to see if a round was in the chamber.

The 45 is a single-action weapon. The hammer has to be cocked for it to fire. Thus the saying "locked and cocked"—safety on, hammer back on a live round in the chamber. As always this was the normal Lebanese carry. Joe liked that because we carried our Brownings the same way. All you had to do was draw, rotate muzzle to the target, as you bring the weapon up you take the safety off, then engage. I was never comfortable having a gun on my person that was ready to go. I know, from training, that it is best in a threatened area to carry ready to go but I couldn't help checking from time to time to see if the safety was still on.

Joe told the LF officer, "I have never seen one like this."

The officer said, "Yes, it is very good gun."

"No," Joe said, "this is an automatic. I've only ever seen a semi-auto."

Officer said, "No…no, not auto."

Joe suddenly turned his back to the LF officer and flutter-fired his 45. Joe was so good that the 45 sounded like a machinegun. The last round went off before the first brass hit the deck. I'd never seen nothing like it.

Joe locked the slide to the rear and said, "I've gotta get me one of these." Shaking his head again, said, "Never seen an auto 45." Little LF guy couldn't see what Joe did. All he heard was the seemingly-auto fire coming from his gun.

Joe handed it back to him and asked, "Will you sell it?"

"No…no," replied the LF officer. All of a sudden this little guy is examining his gun in great detail. He was looking for the selector switch. He rotated it over and over in his hands. (I'm still thinkin' about that bundle of money in Joe's bag.)

I was asking, "Is he gonna try to buy this Julio 45?" .45 ammo was very difficult to obtain in Lebanon. Plenty of .556, 9mm, 7.62 (both X 39mm and 51mm). Just no 45. Joe was talking and joking with the officer.

All of a sudden Joe said, "You need some ammo for that?"

"Yes...yes, that would be very good. You have...you have?" asked the officer.

Joe said, "I have boo-koo," which meant something in Vietnam but luckily most Lebanese speak English and French. So "boo-koo" meant "a whole bunch" to the officer.

Joe said, "I need something, too."

Now the officer was wary, "What you need?"

Joe said, "I don't know, nothing real difficult here, but I'd like to have two Rocket Propelled Grenade (RPG- an anti tank weapon) launchers as souvenirs." The officer tried to not look excited but Joe and I both realized that the chance of Joe getting two rocket launchers was very good. The officer tried his best Arab negotiation skills but he had tipped his hand and I think he knew it. All that was left was for him to get as much 45 ammo as he could.

He said, "Maybe I can get one but not two."

Joe said, "Okay, one today and one tomorrow."

"No...no...no. Only one."

Joe said, "That does me no good. I need two. One for office and one for home."

"What in the hell is Joe up to?" I wondered.

Finally the officer said he could get one tomorrow and one next week. That part was settled.

Now for the ammo. Joe said, "1,000 rounds per RPG launcher."

"No...no...2,000."

Joe said, "Okay, 2,000—1,000 when you give us the first launcher and another 1,000 when you give us the second."

The little guy didn't realize that Joe had just screwed him out of 2,000 rounds. They shook hands and said we'd meet there at the range the next day.

That night I couldn't hold back. We went down to the hotel bar where we enjoyed an Almaza or two and BS'd with the bartender. It turns out that the bartender was with the PSP, a West Beirut militia. He was planted there to get intel from Western visitors.

We didn't know this until a later trip when we went to the bar and had a new bartender. New guy said he didn't know where the old guy was.

Imad looked at me and drew a knife gesture across his throat. Imad said, "He PSP...dead."

Back to the story. Joe and I were enjoying our beers when I said, "Okay, Joe, what are you gonna do with RPGs?"

Once again he said, "What you mean me, white man? You mean 'we'." Oh shit, here we go again.

Joe started his story. He'd been a busy little beaver, unbeknownst to me or Mike. He was so pissed about the LAAW rockets failing to function that he met with the RSO and said, "Look, this LAAW thing was a bad idea from the get go. RPGs are common in Beirut, everybody knows how to use them, they're easy to maintain, and re-supply of ammo is not an issue." He talked the RSO into it.

RSO said the only problem was the launchers. The embassy could not buy them because they were a Russian/Chinese weapon, but the embassy could buy the rockets. Now figure that one out. The RSO told Joe if he could get the launchers, the embassy would buy the rockets. Joe had been talking to the folks on the seventh floor. No matter how many floors an embassy has, whether it's two or fifty, there is always a seventh floor. That's lingo for the CIA offices.

Apparently the seventh floor had contacts to purchase the rockets, an arms dealer in West Beirut. Only problem there was that West Beirut was where the bad guys lived. The arms dealer wouldn't bring one hundred rockets across the Green Line that separated East from West Beirut. We had to go get them. Another fine mess Joe got me into.

Time was short because we needed to get all the launchers and rockets transported back across the Green Line, even if we

149

survived all the checkpoints getting in to West Beirut. Then we had to get all that equipment back up to the mountains and conduct the training. Seemed easy enough…if you were Houdini.

The next morning we went to the range and started shooting again. The LF had a secret camp nearby because every time we started shooting someone would show up. This time it was the same little officer. He bounced out of his vehicle, no driver that day. He came over to Joe and went through the greeting ritual; nothing could transpire until that was done.

He told Joe, "Come, look." Joe followed him to the rear of the vehicle and they pulled something out of the back that was wrapped in a rug. Once unrolled, we saw that it was a very nice RPG launcher with an optical sight mechanism. Joe operated it a time or two then motioned for me to come over. I took the launcher, then rolled it back up.

The officer said, "No, no." What the hell, I thought. Now what? Apparently the rug belonged to his wife and wasn't part of the deal. I unrolled the package and gave back the rug. I carried the launcher over to the back of the Suburban and placed it in the back. I then covered it with my jacket. In truth, there wasn't a problem with us having a launcher. They were as common as any other form of armament in Beirut in those days. I think even most kids had at least one.

Joe made a big deal of escorting the officer over to the ammo bunker where he ceremoniously laid out 1,000 rounds of 45 in fifty-round boxes. It made it look like one hell of a lot of ammo. The LF guy was happy as a clam. You'd have thought he'd won the lotto.

One down, one to go, plus the ammo.

That afternoon we went to the RSO and told him we'd scored one launcher. He picked up the phone and spoke softly into the receiver. Couldn't catch all of the conversation but I did hear enough to know that someone was headed to the RSO's office from the seventh floor. The secretary brought us fresh coffee and we shot the bull about folks we knew, who was where, and general gossip. Ladies are right—men gossip a bunch more than they do.

Eventually this extremely Arab-looking guy comes into the RSO's office, complete with worry beads. Even though he was dressed in Western clothing he wore the same type stuff that the Lebanese felt was popular. An off-white Cuban doctor shirt with little waist pockets and frill on the front. It was worn outside the black slacks with black nondescript shoes. He was thick in the middle and had a hawkish nose that protruded over a bushy mustache. He was slightly balding and what hair remained was salt-and-pepper gray. Introductions were made; he spoke perfect English with no accent at all. He also spoke Lebanese with no accent.

At first I thought this must have been the office manager for the seventh floor. He would have fit right in at a local *souk* or at a local mosque. He turned out to *be* the seventh floor. He was the station chief, second only to the ambassador. This guy was good.

I ran into him a couple of years later. I was teaching the Monday afternoon class for the folks headed overseas. As people were lined up registering, I saw him in the line. He looked more American with his suit. It was obvious that this guy was a chameleon. He would fit anywhere.

I walked up, greeted him, and said, "Good to see you again."

He said, "I don't think we've ever met." That was my cue.

I looked at him closely and responded, "You're right, you just look like a guy I met at a conference in D.C."

Back to Beirut. The guy told us he had a contact who could provide as many rockets as we needed. We had to supply cash, we could never include the embassy in any dealings (we were on our own), and, above all, we couldn't mention the seventh floor guy's name or any knowledge of him. I guess this guy was doing us a real favor by hooking us up with the arms dealer. It was a human intelligence (HumInt) source that he used in West Beirut and if we screwed it up it could cost us dearly in the form of human life and info. He kept reminding us that using the RPGs instead of the LAAWs had to be our idea. We were just using our own initiative to help protect the embassy, etc. In other words, if we got nailed in West Beirut, the embassy would disavow our mission. Not a real spook trip, but when it comes to my rump, then somebody telling me, "Get caught and we ain't comin' to get you"….It feels a little lonely.

Once that was over Joe said, "We understand all that. Time is our only enemy. We have one launcher so we can start training if we can get some rockets (we had gotten the second launcher the following day). We need to move fast."

We were getting good solid intelligence that the Hezbollah were gonna come after American interests in East Beirut. Many firefights erupted along the Green Line as bad guys were intercepted by the good guys. You could hear bombs going off all around the city at odd hours. It was really heating up. The bad guys knew that if they got the press behind them the American public would force our withdrawal totally. Things were moving fast so we had to also.

Seventh floor guy said, "If I can set it up, can you go tomorrow afternoon?" Joe said, "Yes, but not before." Again, Mike was completely out of all this. He didn't have a clue.

I was the new guy and had to trust all those around me. That trust had waned a little when the RSO and the number two at the embassy said that we were on our own and not sanctioned. Later learned that the seventh floor guy short-fused us so that the tangos didn't have sufficient time to plan an ambush.

I was a Marine officer. Was I supposed to be doing stuff like this? Well, I justified, commandant sent me to State, State sent me here, so I'm doin' my job. One thing is for sure, this stuff wasn't goin' on any After Action Report (AAR). The seventh floor guy said he would get back to us. He departed with no fanfare.

After he left the RSO asked, "So, what do you guys think?"

Joe stood up, drained his coffee, and said, "When did we start getting paid to think?"

After a nervous chuckle we departed and headed to the Montemar. Mike met us downstairs and was all excited about the training he was conducting with the bodyguards. He even made a comment from time to time that once I got some experience I could be his assistant instructor. Wow…I was thrilled.

We ate an early dinner as the next day promised to be busy. Mike was going to have his practical exercise and was neck-deep in planning. Joe and I just wanted to break away, have a few beers at the bar, then turn in. As a Christian, Mike didn't drink, but being a good team guy he would come in, have a Coke, and socialize. Lucky for us he had one Coke, and then said he had a big day and wanted to turn in. It was still early, so Joe and I had time for a few. We didn't discuss the next day because the bartender was listening and hanging on every word. It came as no surprise to us when Imad said he got wasted.

The next morning came quickly. Sleep never seemed to solidify itself during the night. I wasn't afraid or anxious, even though I should have been. I was really thinkin' about Mama and Stephen. Sleeplessness was due to good, old-fashioned homesickness. I had to get my mind off that for now. As I went downstairs I saw Mike all loaded up with maps, charts, memos, and lesson plans. He was goin' to war and in a focused state of mind. He never asked nor did he care how Joe and I were passing our time. Just as well because it was hard to come up with a good lie.

Joe was downstairs eating his croissants and cheese. Every move was meticulous. I sat and the waiter began serving me immediately. I suspect he was waiting for me because Joe and I always ate together. After I got my Turkish coffee and began to spread my cheese on the hot bread Joe looked up and said, "It's a go. We'll head out just after prayer. We will be taking Edgar and he drives."

I didn't object because we had a few checkpoints to go through. My blond hair and blue eyes and Southern accent might tip our hands.

Joe said we'd carry our MP5s and Brownings, and I could carry my Berretta 70S mini magnum 22 cal. I would ride shotgun so I could take over the wheel if Edgar got hit. We had trained and drilled on Man Down scenarios at BSR: We, as instructors, would drive at high speed. A training explosive would go off next to the car and we would slump over the wheel and generally

153

be in the way. The trainee would have to force us out of the way and continue to drive at high speed from the passenger side.

Joe said he would have a twelve-gauge in the back seat to provide cover if we had a troublesome checkpoint. We were ready. Now all we had to do was tell and convince Edgar. Edgar came to the hotel just as we were finishing up. He nibbled at our leftovers and Joe told the waiter to set Edgar up. Edgar protested but Joe was hearing none of it. Joe was on the hunt again. Edgar ate and noisily sipped his coffee as is Arab tradition and custom.

Joe said, "So Edgar, what ya wanna do today?"

Edgar, ever smiling and pleasant, responded with what he thought Joe would like, "We go range and shoot."

Joe said, "We may get to shoot but we won't be going to the range."

"We need to go to the embassy first thing, and then we thought we may go take a look at West Beirut." I watched Edgar closely for any sign. He didn't even flinch. He continued to munch, then that same survival smile crept across his lips.

"I think you no joke," he said.

"No joke," Joe responded.

"Edgar, you don't have to go but it would be much appreciated if you did and there's a bonus for you if you do."

We trusted Edgar implicitly.

Joe asked Edgar if he knew his way around the west side, knowing that he did. He had lived in the west before the civil war and still had family there even though he was Christian.

"Where in west we go?" Edgar asked.

Joe said, "We have to get directions at the embassy."

Edgar pushed back from eating and said, "We go, must cross just after prayer."

We loaded up the vehicle—no Suburban for this trip. It was a Toyota SUV. The type you see all over the Middle East. Joe positioned himself in the center of the back seat. He had guns everywhere. He dug into his little range bag and pulled out a couple of the little assassination grenades. He then handed them over the seat to me. I just shook my head and dropped them into the waist pocket on my travel vest. Just like an alcoholic says, "One is too many, a thousand is never enough." I wanted about a dozen of these little brain scramblers. If we got hit I was gonna look like one of them wacky pitching machines that go bug-fuck. We gave Edgar a Model 19 Smith & Wesson revolver with .357 Hydra-Shock ammo. Makes a hell of a hole and takes the fight outta folks.

We passed through embassy security and once again went to the RSO's office. He wasn't there but the secretary handed us a thick envelope. No RSO, no seventh floor guy—we were definitely on our own. Joe grabbed the envelope, obviously pissed that the RSO wasn't there but now driven to do the mission with or without the pencil necks, as he put it. We fast-paced it back to the car and loaded up. Joe got in the back and recharged all his weapons. I did the same, making sure that a round was in every chamber and that I was "locked and cocked" (or *deek muff too ah* in Arabic).

We left the embassy compound and Joe directed us to pull over at the little sandwich shop. He opened the envelope and glanced through. He passed each sheet to me once he had looked at it. The first sheet was directions in detail. The second sheet was a map. The third sheet a letter of introduction to the arms dealer. Nowhere was there a name of office of origination. No ties. I showed the directions and map to Edgar. No problem, he said. We'll see about that, I said. Joe gets out of the car all of a sudden and goes in the shop. He ordered four sandwiches and a cup of coffee. Don't know when we'll be able to eat again, he said. I bought Edgar four sandwiches and four for myself. Edgar wanted a Coke and I got coffee.

One thing foremost in our minds at that point was that several Western hostages had been taken and were being held for concessions. We knew there would be no concessions for us. Several hostages had been killed. We would be dubbed CIA and that would be that.

We loaded back up and rechecked our gear. Edgar had his Smith in the issued leather holster.

I told him, "Edgar, put you gun between your legs so that checkpoints can't see it."

He said, "What about *zebi* (penis)?"

I said, "Don't pull the trigger while it's there."

We had a chuckle—"nervous banter" we called it in Vietnam. Everybody trying to be tough and macho before the shit hits the fan. Knowing down deep that you are scared as hell but you have to do it anyhow. That was us as we approached Ashrafiya. I remembered my old buddy at the mom and pop shop where I drank Almaza beer. It was comforting to know that if we had to run and could get across the Green Line the old man would look after us. Mama would, too, even though she bitched about the old man drinkin' beer. Safe house.

As we maneuvered through town, Edgar was very reserved. Normally our driving was aggressive. I thought it might be best to act as we usually did but Edgar was the native and I was gonna let him have his way. We approached a concrete wall that had tons of barbed wire hanging all off the top. It was haphazard and unlike any I'd seen in the Marine Corps (neat and tidy). As we drove along, there was a turn to the left and an opening in the wall. About twelve vehicles were lined up to go through. We were at the Green Line.

I'd heard so much about this spot it was somewhat mystical to me. I had expected a two-hour drive and a bunch of crap. Twenty minutes after leaving the sandwich shop we were there. Like being put into the big game, expecting to go in the fourth quarter, only to have the coach tell you five minutes after kickoff, "You're in!" As we cleared the wall and could see across the expanse between East and West Beirut, there was a span of about 300 meters of no man's land.

On our side there was a Lebanese Army (LAF) checkpoint then a bouncy, rutted, pot-holed track across to West Beirut. On that side there was another checkpoint but it wasn't manned by uniformed soldiers. They were in olive drab uniforms and Arab headdress, and armed with AK-47s. As I watched them check vehicles, about six of them would surround the vehicle being checked. One guard would approach the driver, take his papers, check them, and on some occasions would have them get out so they could inspect the vehicle. I nodded to Joe and saw that he was watching as well.

I asked Joe, "Do we get out if they ask?"

Joe just shook his head in the negative. We had already decided what to do in each eventuality. If we took fire at the crossing we would attempt to get back into East Beirut. We knew that the LAF would probably not be friendly if we tried to get back after stirring up a bunch of crap on the Green Line. We'd more than likely receive friendly fire. Best to run down the wall looking for an opening. There were many because the local kids played soccer in no man's land when shooting wasn't going on.

I noticed Edgar was sweating profusely but otherwise he appeared calm. My skin was dry as was my mouth. I looked down at my hands and they were white, as I had a death grip on my weapon. I relaxed. Not good for weapons control if I had to engage.

We pulled in behind the tail vehicle. Edgar had his papers. All we had were diplomatic passports. Our story was that we were headed to the embassy on the west side to check on the facility that was still guarded by Lebanese guards. Muslim guards.

We hired and trained Muslims for the west side and Christians for the east side. No Americans were at the embassy but it still remained and we were still paying the guards. We stopped and went, stopped and went, as the line was slowly checked and permitted to pass.

The vehicle directly in front of us was ordered to empty. A guy was driving with his wife as passenger, and two young men in the rear. All got out and appeared to make small talk. I noticed that they all had that survival smile that Edgar had used several times before. The guards checked the vehicle with attention to detail. There was a shopping bag in the trunk that must have had something that the guards wanted. The driver objected and was shoved back against the car. He was bold because he appeared to be unarmed but he shouted back. His wife was even raising hell and shaking her fist. Eventually an agreement was reached. The carton of Marlboros was taken out and each guard received a pack. They all laughed and shook hands then went on their way. *Baksheesh,* or payoff.

Now it was our turn. We rolled up and I was trying hard to look at ease. I glanced back at Joe and just about shit. We all had collections of t-shirts, berets, and hats. We even had bad guy hats. Joe had put on his maroon PSP beret, had his dark glasses on, and was sittin' in the middle of the seat with the MP5 in one hand and the Shorty 870 in the other. What the hell I thought, too late now.

As we pulled up, Edgar said, "*Yah tic a laffee,*" which loosely means "Take it easy, don't work too hard." Edgar produced his Lebanese papers. Joe and I just sat there looking straight ahead but watching everything in our peripheral. The guard didn't say anything at first but just bent over and looked at Joe and me. He looked at Edgar's papers and back at us.

He asked, "Their papers?" Edgar had a set of balls. But he knew the Arab mentality better than us. Power, Force, Be in charge, and Don't be weak.

He responded, "They are with the American embassy! They don't have to show you papers. They are diplomats."

"How do we know that?" the guard said. He pointed to Joe and said, "He looks Arab." I picked up just enough to know where this was going. So far, Edgar was in charge. That could change at any time. The guard took Edgar's papers back to the shack and showed them to the guy who must have been in charge. The boss got up and walked out to the car.

"*Wayno enta roha?*" ("Where are you going?").

"To the American embassy," Edgar replied in Arabic.

"*Stanana shwya*" (Wait a little); he went back to the shack and made a radio call. He then walked back over and said he needed proof that we were Americans. I knew that Joe's impatience was showing. I waited for the click…click of the safety. These guys didn't know us or we them and we weren't in an armored vehicle. It would be teeth, hair, and eyeballs at this point.

There were six of them, as I recall. A couple were behind us with AKs, a couple on my side with AKs, the guy checking papers, and the guy who was in charge. On the opposite side of the shack was a belt-fed machine gun of some type. Wasn't an M60 but it was menacing enough. I think most of the teeth, hair, and eyeballs would have been ours.

I told Joe to hand me his passport. I could tell he didn't want any part of that, but he complied. I fanned out mine and Joe's so that the guard could see the passports but I made no effort to hand them over. He looked at us again, then at Edgar. He then handed Edgar's papers back and waved us through. My butt was suckin' that seat so hard it would have taken a crowbar to break me loose. Edgar still had his survival smile and Joe was lookin' grouchy as ever. I handed back his passport and he just grunted. I swear, I think that guy was lookin' for a gunfight.

West Beirut was a striking contrast to the east. It was bombed all to hell. There was a new Holiday Inn that had been completed just before the war broke out. I don't recall how many stories, but it was tall. Bomb holes were everywhere. Some floors had gaping holes from artillery impacts and you could see the entire interior. This hotel was the home of several militias. Floors one, two, and three would be the PSP. Four, five, and six would be the Hezbollah, etc. When they were fighting, it was floor-to-floor instead of block-to-block. Crazy place. Reminded me of the movie *Apocalypse Now* but without the music.

Edgar maneuvered through the bombed-out buildings and vehicles like a pro. I'm thinking,' All we need is a flat tire. People lived in blown-out apartments with sheets hanging over the holes created by artillery. The streets were strewn with bombed-out vehicles and debris. At one point, guns at the ready, we made a right turn just in time to interrupt a soccer game that was goin' on. All of the players were young men and really hyped up with the game. We eased through and it seemed to really piss them off.

Edgar, being ever prepared, yelled, "Who's winning?" That broke it. They all started yelling and pointing at each other and laughing. Edgar gave the thumbs up and eased on through, seemingly unnoticed.

We traversed through scenes like this unmolested. We were tense and on our game. Edgar pulled behind a building that had huge metal shudders pulled down over all the doors and windows. It looked abandoned.

I asked Edgar, "Is this it?"

He said, *"Naam"* (yes), before he realized he had spoken in Arabic. He was wired but didn't show it. We got out and covered our weapons as much as possible. We walked to the rear of the building; there was a small door that looked like a basement door. It was half below ground level. We knocked. I told Edgar to knock harder while Joe and I posted security.

I was straining to cover the numerous apartment buildings that surrounded us. Every floor and every window was a threat. In Beirut even a kid with an AK was dangerous, perhaps more dangerous than an adult since he wasn't held to adult standards. Unless he was shooting at me—then the only thing he was to me was a smaller target. I would just have to hold a tight group.

Finally there was a commotion on the other side of the door. Joe spun around and covered the door. It slowly opened a crack and a frail, old lady's voice came through. Once again I heard the *Yah tick a laffee…*Take it easy. I think it really meant "Don't shoot." I was to use it many times during my trips to Beirut.

Edgar addressed the old lady respectfully and asked if our contact lived there. She asked where we were from and I pushed my diplomatic passport in front of her. I wanted out of that alley by then. The door opened and we excused ourselves in. What I saw amazed me.

A very classy, frail, little old lady stood before us. Very humble and hospitable. We took the short flight of steps up to her spacious living area. She wore a Western dress with mid-level high heels and a beautiful shawl, and had on tasteful makeup. She could have been anyone's mom. She was the arms dealer. She led us into the living room and we were seated.

The room was tastefully decorated and extremely clean. The old lady reminded me of my grandma, always sweeping. I felt so out of place. MP5 across my lap, Browning under my travel vest, and a 70S rubbing a hole in my back. She left the room and the three of us just stared at each other. This was the norm for Edgar. Just common, normal people trying to eke out a way of life amidst the hell of war.

After a few minutes a young guy of about twenty-two or twenty-three came into the room. His leg was in a cast and he was on crutches. Very handsome and groomed to the tee. He introduced himself and we did the Arab handshake: hand over heart, etc. We did the cheek-to-cheek kiss. He sat and the old lady came back into the room with a tray of tea and cookies.

My mind was whizzing. Just stepped out of a world where I expected a bullet at anytime or a car bomb or capture. Now I'm in a living room sipping tea and munching on cookies with Grandma and her grandson.

By now it was about 1500 and we had to get back across the Green Line by dark. Well before dark would be best. Especially before afternoon prayer. If we hit the Green Line just before prayer the guards would be cleansing and preparing and we would have a better chance of crossing because they would not want to be hassled.

I got Edgar's attention and told him to politely ask where our guy was—the kid's dad and the old lady's son. I pictured a fat, greasy, cigar smokin' Lebanese who talked faster than he thought. Not so fast. Arabs have a ritual to business. You must talk, drink tea, eat, talk some more, then ease into the deal. We waited for the dealer. Finally the young man, who spoke through Edgar in Arabic, asked, "What is it you need?"

Edgar translated for Joe. Joe said, "We want RPG-7s."

The young man got up from his chair, and just like in the movies, he moved his chair and a table. He pulled a lever under the curtains and opened a false wall. Behind that wall was a sample of everything. The secret room was about twelve feet by twelve feet. On the walls were hung every form of weapon I could imagine. Sub guns, hand guns, rifles, sniper rifles of all types. It was like a professional display. Examples of ammo were mounted on wooden boards. Most amazing thing I've seen. In reality it may not have been much, but to move from this serene living room to a weapons cache with the pull of a lever was mind-boggling.

This young guy was the dealer, and in his absence his mom was the dealer. There was no fat little greasy, cigar smokin' Lebanese guy. This was as good as it got. Every turn, every social experience in Beirut seemed to blow my mind. The way that people adapted was probably the most amazing thing about it all. They seemed to be able to switch it off as though it weren't happening. I guess it's been the same down through the ages, including our own Revolutionary War and Civil War. People just adapted. Brought me back to college when I studied Charles Darwin's theory of evolution—survival of the fittest.

Negotiations went on, more tea, more cookies. Talk and more tea. Junior and mom would leave the room and discuss the latest stages of the negotiations. It occurred to me that many militia men probably sat right here doing the same thing we were doing. They were making purchases to attack Americans and we were trying to purchase to protect Americans.

As things developed, a price was agreed upon and Joe produced the cash that he'd gotten at the embassy. I didn't pay any attention as to how much cash changed hands but it was all that Joe had. I strongly suspect that the amount was agreed upon by the seventh floor and we were just going through the motions. (Joe verified that at a later date.)

By then it was around 1545 and we had to get our God-lovin' asses back across the Green Line with new freight. We went back out in the alley after some warm goodbyes and more hand shakes and kisses…See y'all soon. The rockets were in a shed out in the alley. We paid the exact amount that we'd negotiated for. Imagine that.

We stuffed them suckers anywhere and everywhere they'd fit. Another concern we had was each rocket had about two pounds of high explosives. That times one hundred rockets with rocket motors. If we came under attack it was a whole new world. We departed with the springs sagging and Joe lookin' like Granny in the *Beverly Hillbillies* all cramped in between the rockets. Off we went.

We felt more relaxed than when we came across. I suspect that's because we'd all been exposed to culture shock. Even

Edgar was not familiar with this environment. We backtracked but Edgar was smart enough to follow a different route. He actually took us down to the Corniche Highway and we drove alongside the Med. What a contrast—look to the left and see beautiful, emerald-green sea with ships anchored in the harbor, look to the right and see bombed-out commercial buildings, homes, and schools.

We drove by the old embassy, and although there was no activity there were the guards, ever vigilant and on duty. Why not? They were making big money, about $120 U.S.

It was a pleasant drive. We were headed back to the Montemar and a cold Almaza. Just had to clear the Green Line. I again thought of my old buddy at the mom and pop shop. Would I need him today? It remained to be seen.

We were approaching the militia checkpoint. No cars were lined up to cross. Prayer time was rapidly approaching and we had timed it perfect. We saw a few of the guards emerging from the guard shack wiping their hands from their wash-up before prayer. We pulled up and one guard approached, still wiping his hands.

"*Min fud luck*," Edgar announced (Take pity, or please). "We hurry to get to prayer."

The guard waved us through and said, "*Yah Allah!*" (Hurry!).

Once back in Ashrafiya we breathed a sigh of relief. We had to remember—we were still in Beirut. Bad things happen to good people on the east side as well.

We got back to the embassy compound without incident. Back through the gate with the same celebration as always: Yu-Muh, Yu-Muh, *Kaey fuckin,*' grinnin' and grabbin,' hand over heart.

We drove straight to the storage bunker that was located out in front of the embassy building. It was getting dark by the time we finished unloading.

The RSO came out of the building, obviously on his way to his apartment. Struck me as strange that he wouldn't hang around until he was sure that we were safe. As it turned out this guy was sharp. He had eyes on us most of the trip in one form or another. He received a radio call that we were safely back across the Green Line. He then packed his stuff up and came out to greet us. What a guy. Of course he waited 'til we got the truck unloaded. What the hell, he was a diplomat.

We got back to the Montemar about 1930. As we entered we glanced toward the restaurant area and there sat Mike, Imad, and Ernest. Mike was all smiles and began immediately telling us of his successes in training the ambassador's detail. It was obvious that he had no idea what we'd been up to. He even asked, "So what have you gents been up to all day? Sightseeing?"

Ernest had a grin on his face and Imad had his "I know all" smirk.

Joe just kinda shrugged it off as if to say, "Same ole shit."

I acted tired, which wasn't hard. After a day like that day or after a day of living in combat or high potential combat, you feel drained. When I was eighteen in Vietnam it never bothered me. You just stayed pumped up waiting for the next hell. I laid my bag down and plopped next to Imad. He still stared at me with that look. Reminded me of my wife when I told her, "Honest, I only had two beers."

Imad started toying with my arm as only the Arabs can do without seeming gay. Now he was smiling. He looked me in the eye and said, "Where you go today?" Joe just ignored him but Imad wouldn't let it go.

I said, "Looking for some gold *souks* (shops) so that I can take Mama some earrings and bangles."

Now he jerked his head up animatedly and rolled his eyes towards the ceiling. "No gold in West," he sighed. I looked at Joe with that "help me out here" look. Being Joe, he seized the opportunity.

"*Nunya*," he said. Imad screwed up his face as he searched his limited English vocabulary for *nunya*. By now Joe and I were about to split with laughter. Mike was still confused and didn't catch on to any of it.

Imad said finally, "Noonya…what this?"

Joe said, "Not 'noonya,' you have to say exact or it is a bad word. It is 'nunya'."

Imad repeated "nunya" as he filed it in his vocabulary. Kid was smart as hell and remembered everything. Finally he said, "What 'nunya'?"

Joe said "Nunya fuckin' business."

Now this he understood. Then he slipped into his pout. Joe really loved this guy because he was tough as hell. Joe got up and walked around the table and grabbed Imad around the head with affection then gave him a quick noogie. Now Imad was smiling again. The subject was dropped for now.

We ate and then went to our rooms. One beer did us in. I stripped down and headed for the shower. I let the water run for a long time because I wanted it hot. When I climbed in I let the hot water release all the tension that had built up from the day's activities. I felt drained but in a content way. I stretched out on the bed in my birthday suit. Boy, did it feel good. Then I remembered this was Beirut. Might have to jump and run at a moment's notice.

I slipped my skivvies on and made sure my pants and shirt were handy. More importantly, I did a press check on my Browning and the MP5. I wasn't worried about the 70S because if it got to the point I needed my third weapon I'd be in trouble. This was a nightly ritual and a habit I had trouble getting over when I returned to the States. I never felt comfortable laying down next to Susan, in the safety of home, without doing my press checks. I would never get used to it until many years after Beirut.

Boom!! The whole world was shaking!! I jumped out of bed and grabbed my MP5. What the hell was that? Something tremendous had waked me from a deep sleep. The lights were out and I was gonna leave them out 'til I figured out what the hell had happened. (As it turned out, the electricity was off and it wouldn't have done me any good anyway.) I grabbed my Maglite and headed to the hallway to see if Mike or Joe knew what was goin' on. Then: Whamm!! Tharumph!! Reminded me of Vietnam during a rocket attack. That's what it was. The bad guys were shooting Grad rockets from West Beirut. They weren't targeting anything, just firing indiscriminately. As I went into the hall I noticed Joe standing there in his skivvies, eye-blinders pushed up on his head, with a sleepy, dazed look on his face.

"What the fuck was that?'" he asked.

"Rockets," I responded matter-of-factly.

"No shit, Sherlock," he said.

About that time Mike come charging out of his room, MP5 at the ready and muzzling both of us.

"Easy...easy Mike. It's a rocket attack, not an armed assault."

He lowered his weapon then said, "We should head to the basement."

Joe just shook his head, lowered his weapon, turned around, and retreated to his room, pulling down his blinders. The rocketing stopped as suddenly as it started. I glanced at my watch; it was 0340. Back to the rack for me. I also turned and went into my room, leaving Mike in the hallway at the ready. I seriously doubt that he went back to bed. I did, and crashed big time.

The alarm went off at 0600. I dressed and went through my bag to make sure all was ready to go. I had four spare magazines for my MP5, two spares for the Browning (in addition to the two on my belt), and one for the 70S. Once I strapped on my war gear I looked at myself in the mirror. Looked good, in that no weapons were sticking out and everything seemed to be secured.

I grabbed my bag and exited the room, making sure that it was locked. Of course, I had no delusions. I'm sure that our rooms were thoroughly checked after we departed. It did no good to leave tattlers behind such as hairs on closet doors or tape on drawers—the maids came in and cleaned like crazy. You just had to make sure everything was with you. I walked down the hall toward the elevator. It was always a fifty-fifty chance that they didn't work. This was a morning that they decided not to work. When I walked into the hotel restaurant I noticed that I was the first to arrive. That was normally the case with me because, as I said earlier, I don't like being late. I don't like to wait on people and they won't be waiting on me.

The waiter approached and asked, "Juice?" I nodded in the affirmative and he rushed into the back to comply. I sat and dropped my bag next to my leg. I preferred to feel it touching my leg, a habit I haven't lost to this day. The waiter returned with my juice and a hot pot of coffee in a sterling coffee server. He placed my cup and then poured the coffee. It was funny watching Joe and I trying to stick our gnarled-up fingers into the little hole in the china cups. We felt like faggots. The hot croissants started arriving along with the cheeses and jams. Man, was that stuff good. I can only imagine the calories and fat grams that I consumed each morning.

As I was munching and sipping, Mike came strolling in. He was normally fresh and animated. This morning he seemed to be dragging. I attributed it to the fact that he'd probably remained awake all night. I asked, "Well, did you go back to bed and get some sleep?"

"Oh, yeah," he said, "Went straight to bed."

The waiter took his order and while he waited Joe came in. Joe was in a snarly mood that morning. Didn't smile or say good mornin' or any acknowledgement whatsoever. The waiter was perceptive and didn't say a word. He had already fallen prey to the wrath of Joe on a previous morning. We all ate our way through a quiet breakfast. Joe's moods always set the tempo for the rest of our moods.

Mike said that he had another day left to finish up with the bodyguards. Joe just grunted.

I told Mike, "Me and Joe got some stuff to occupy our time, so have at it."

About that time Ernest and Imad walked in, chipper as usual. They never seemed to care what mood Joe was in. Ernest would just laugh no matter what Joe said to him. It looked as though Ernest and Imad were with us for the duration. After yesterday I suspect they got their asses handed to them for not going with us to the west. We couldn't have taken them anyway. First off, they were the enemy. Second place, they would have been trying to finger our dealer for future operations. The dealer and his mom would have no doubt been whacked at some time in the near future.

We fell in and let them take charge. I threw Imad the keys to the vehicle. We loaded our gear and headed to the embassy. Joe directed Imad to let Mike off at the front embassy entrance. Mike bounced out, all-consumed with the importance of the task at hand. Get those BGs trained, making the world safe for democracy. He didn't even concern himself with what Joe and I were up to.

After Mike was well within the bowels of the embassy, Joe directed Imad to drive to the bunker. The Lebanese security boss was already there. A group of Lebanese guards were there and I recognized them as the guys we'd taken to the mountains on our LAAW expedition. They were smokin' and sipping tea or coffee. The embassy fifteen-passenger van was parked nearby. Imad backed up to the bunker and we dismounted. Joe opened the bunker and all of the students started buzzing about what they saw. RPGs!!

They were all saying, *"Mnea*!! *Mnea*!!" (Good!! Good!!) "RPG very good." Imad just winked at me. We loaded a number of the rockets into our vehicle along with a like number of rocket motors. The rocket motors were packaged in this cool little plastic tube, light green in color. These had to have a future use. They did—they became travel humidors for our Cuban cigars.

Once loaded we headed out of town for the mountains. It was a cool but not uncomfortable morning. The sky was crystal clear, and as we headed up the road we could look behind and see the Med sparkling in the morning sun. It was gorgeous. Made me wonder why these people wanted to destroy this paradise. It was a case of two worlds colliding, one of beauty and serenity and one of war and havoc. They just didn't fit in this environment.

Only a few hours before, one side had been shooting rockets at the other. In the near future there would be retaliation then counter retaliation.

Folks from East and West Beirut were employed at the embassy. You would see guys with guys and girls with girls laughing, talking, holding hands, eating and drinking together.

Then after work the folks from the east would go home, the folks from the west would go back across the Green Line to their homes and after dark they shoot at each other. Amazing.

We arrived at the training site and proceeded to hang another sheet on the cliff face. I had no idea if Joe had ever fired an RPG. I watched as he unpacked and checked everything. I suspected that he, like me, had studied the weapon at EOD school, but had never fired one in anger. He was gonna take the first test shot.

All I could remember was that the round had no positive safety features. You fired it and it detonated. Joe got all set up, stuck the rocket into the launcher, and took a long time checking everything. If he didn't know, he wasn't about to let the students know. He eventually fired and got a direct hit on the sheet. He stood and handed the launcher to me. "Your turn." Never asked if I knew the weapon or had ever fired one. It was another of his little tests.

I was slow and methodical. The RPG was actually Marine-proof. That is, it didn't have too many working parts. I had watched Joe intently, more for entertainment than for learning, but I had learned. I was all loaded and set. Had my Mickey Mouse ears on, but if the thing blew up they wouldn't be of much use. I knelt down and gently placed the launcher on my shoulder. It was a little front-heavy because the warhead sticks out a good bit beyond the launcher tube. The sights were great. Just a poke and hope weapon.

I kept telling myself that we watch these Palestinian kids running around on the news shooting these things. I knew for sure that a big bad captain in the Marines could do it. Well, maybe not so big, but bad in my own mind.

Once on target I engaged the trigger. A lot like firing any cocked striker weapon. The trigger fell and one hell of a roar took place. You could actually see the trail of the rocket. There was a huge puff of smoke and away she went. BOOM! Right on target.

As a matter of fact, I was closer to center than Joe. That got a cheer and an ovation from the students. Joe and I were thinkin' alike. We should shoot one more each to make sure it wasn't a fluke. This time we gave one of the guys our camera for a John

Author kneeling and Joe standing

Wayne photo op. Joe and I fired together just as the camera shutter closed. It was perfect (see photo). Had it blown up, and I display it prominently wherever I hang my hat.

My Day in the Sun

As a result of my passing the test, Joe later wrote a fitness report on me. He specifically addressed the fact that I took a weapon that I had no knowledge of and fired it like a pro.

The remaining RPG training went off without a hitch. All of the rockets fired for the students. Unlike the LAAWs. I can only imagine the ramifications of that entire op. "U.S. Light

Anti Tank Assault Weapon (LAAW) system fails to function so U.S. diplomats purchase Russian weapon systems, train Lebanese embassy guards and protect U.S. embassy facilities and personnel with Russian weapons." Makes a nice headline. It just shocks me that the pencil necks let us do it. I think the embassy bombings were still fresh in their minds.

Having accomplished all of the training and having fired only four guards, we felt that our mission was a success. As we headed to the Landing Zone (LZ) for departure from Beirut, I noticed a lonely-looking guy standing on the small hill overlooking the entrance to the embassy compound. Over his shoulder was his Mini-14 and held at high port was his RPG-7. I knew that behind the sandbag wall which blocked him from view from the knees down were three ready-to-fire rockets. I had no doubt that he would fire if the need arose. We choppered out and had the luxury of spending several more days in Larnaca before our flight home.

I was really anxious to get back to Susan and Stephen. This had been an awakening trip. What amazed me was the immediate transfer back to normalcy. One minute you're facing who knows what at any given time, then in just a matter of a few days you're back in your easy chair sippin' watery U.S. beer.

It was hard attending a neighborhood cookout, and we had a bunch of them in those days whenever I was at home. All of my neighbors at the time were electricians, plumbers, carpenters, and no military. I would attempt to get into conversations and just couldn't go anywhere. First of all, you couldn't talk about it. There was no official classification but it was unspoken word that you didn't talk about what you did or where you went.

I always hated it when you heard a wannabe or a wish-eye saying, "Well, I can't talk about that." Or a better one, "When I was over there with those guys doing those things."

Horseshit!

Another good one I still hear today: When you ask someone, "Oh, I hear you were SAS or Delta or Dev Group." The response is, "No, not actually with them, but attached or assigned." You were or you weren't.

Horse shit again!!

Reminds me of when my folks lived in Sylva, North Carolina, in the Smoky Mountains. Beautiful little mountain town and very scenic. At the time (check it out if you don't believe this one), there was a little town barber shop. It was called Wimpy's Barber Shop. It was called that because Wimpy owned it. On Saturday mornings all the good ole boys would collect for haircuts, or just to shoot the bull, or (normally) both.

When I would go in with my dad, who was very proud of his U.S. Marine son, Wimpy would yell out, "Hey, there's the boy! You a colonel now, ain't you, son?" I later got selected for major but never got higher than captain. In Wimpy's mind I made it to general. Every time I went in he promoted me.

Out of the dozen or so characters who hung out there, they were all retired sergeant majors. Never seen nothing like it. I guess some guys just fell short of their goals and just try to live out the way they wished things would have turned out. I, for one, was proud to be the Cook, Baker, Candlestick Maker.

CHAPTER EIGHT

MTT Training

When I got home at about 1700, Susan had a little surprise party for me. Neighbors and friends were present but I had a surprise for Mama. I excused us and grabbed her and practically drug her upstairs for some carnal activity. It didn't take long. I don't even think our guests missed us. Two rim shots and an airburst and I was done.

We always joked about the float test. When you come home after a long trip, Mama would fill the bathtub. She would sit you in it and watch to see if your testicles sank or floated. If they floated she was waiting with an ice pick to sink them.

Next day I forced myself into the office and trudged to my gray desk. Still where I left it. Off to my left I saw four or five guys in the Abe's MTT office. They were all guys I hadn't seen before but that was nothing new. DS was a big outfit.

Abe looked up and saw me and had that big grin that was so common to him. He said, "Frank, come in here."

I walked in, shook his hand was introduced around. They were all young types with decent builds and Abe said they were the nucleus of his MTT force. Having just returned from Beirut with Joe, they were all asking how I survived—not Beirut, but being with Joe for such a long time. I related some stories but not about the big stuff. I still didn't know what was good to talk about. Most of these guys would be going to Beirut and would find out but it wouldn't be me who told them.

I grabbed a cup of coffee and went back into Abe's office. Guys were going through boxes of gear: Buckmaster knives, gloves, balaclavas, Bolle goggles, rigger belts—all the high-speed stuff.

173

I asked Abe, "Where'd you get all the Cool Guy stuff?"

He said they gave him a million bucks to stand up the MTT and he was determined to spend it before they changed their minds. I was dying to know but wanted to be careful how I played it. Diplomats, even security ones, were no dummies.

I said to Abe, "Guess I made my last trip to Beirut?"

He responded, "Why's that, don't you want to go back?"

"Hell, yes," I said.

He said, "Look, I've talked to the boss and we need a military guy on the MTT for tactics and especially an EOD guy." I couldn't believe my ears. He pointed to a box behind his desk and I saw "Frank" written on top in Magic Marker.

"Grab your box," Abe said.

I did.... I had all my "Cool Guy" stuff. That Buckmaster looked like a sword on my belt. It was huge. Needless to say I never saw a need to carry that thing. It had a hollow handle with fish hooks and survival stuff. I wouldn't be needing that.

Abe said, "Frank, I need to get with you and cover some stuff. When I get done with these guys I'll grab you."

"No sweat," I responded. "I'll be at my desk." Right before lunch Abe walked out and said, "Let's grab a bite." We went to the deli in the next building and got a sandwich.

Abe looked around to make sure no one was in earshot and asked, "Do you have any background in HRT stuff?"

I told him that I'd worked with the LAPD SWAT and Orange County Sheriff's Office and had done some tactical stuff with them. My main focus was explosive entry.

He couldn't believe it. Apparently nobody else had anything close. One guy was a former Ranger but he ended up being the biggest pain in the ass. Never wanted to run or do PT.

Abe went on to tell me that he was working directly for the DASS (Deputy Assistant Secretary of State for Security). He had been tasked with standing the MTTs up in order to get the training out to the embassies world-wide as the embassy personnel were unable to come back to the States for training. I could tell that there was more to the story. Had to be.

Abe took a sip of his Diet Coke and continued, "DASS is also worried about hostage-taking in high threat areas and he's worried about the ambassadors in the scary parts of the world. The DASS wants a unit that can fly in on a minute's notice to bolster the protection of a threatened ambassador and also have in-extremis hostage rescue capabilities. That is, if MTT was there, Delta and Team Six were on the way, and the terrorists started killing Americans, we would have somebody on the ground to save them."

I must have looked a sight. I know my jaw was on the table by now.

I said, "Abe, let me see if I have this right: We are gonna be working in a country under diplomatic immunity, then we shift gears and become an elite hostage rescue force, blowing holes, shootin' people, and grabbing hostages?"

He grinned that captivating grin of his and said, "Yep, that's what we're gonna do."

I said, "Who in the State Department is going to tell MTT to pull the trigger and go get 'em?" State is, for the most part, a den of Liberals who believe they can talk anyone out of anything. Nobody's gonna have the balls to make that decision. Abe looked a little perplexed but stayed the course.

Abe continued, "It's in the hands of the DASS. The DASS has been given direction to respond to the National Command Authority which takes it out from under State."

Dismayed, I thought, That's above my pay grade and I'm sure they've got all the details worked out, including whose balls were gonna be on the chopping block when the hammer falls. Fine, as long as they aren't mine.

Abe looked at me for a moment over the rim of his Coke cup and waited. I looked back with no comment. He then said, "Still want to be on MTT? Want to go back to Beirut?" He had me by the short and curlies. I was in and he knew it. After all, what did I have to lose?

Abe and I walked back to the office and we were both in a light-hearted mood.

He asked, "Did you get your instructor certificate at BSR?"

"Yeah," I responded. "Firearms and tactics, too."

He seemed pleased. "You know, we're going to have to get all the MTT guys certified as well. Frank, I need you to whip some of these guys into shape. You know, start a PT program. You're a Marine; you know how to do that kinda thing."

I know how to do "that kinda thing" with Marines but not a dozen diplomats. As it turned out the majority of the guys fell into it and looked forward to our runs. Normally the one turd always gave me a ration of crap but I finally told him to just drop out. I reported this to Abe and was told, "Well, we can't make them do it."

Once Abe and I got back upstairs he jumped right back into his office. Joe was busy setting things up at BSR. Our first instructor course was to be in one week. It would be a two-week course. I would be one of the instructors. I decided to take off early so I grabbed my "go bag" and headed down to the parking area, threw my stuff in the back of the 'Vette, and headed home.

Traffic was light as it was still early in the day but a drive to Warrenton was still a drive. I never minded the commute. It gave me time to reflect on what had transpired during the day and in the morning it gave me time to prepare myself mentally and to put on my game face. I used to like to analyze all of my important conversations of the day. In the evening I would reflect on that day's meetings and in the morning I would rehearse for what might be ahead. In those days it seemed to make me mentally quick. These days I can't even remember who I talked to much less what we talked about. But I guess the older you get, the less you care.

Susan was waiting for me as usual at the door. She worked in town near my office but for some reason she was home when I got there. We went in and Stephen was with me the whole time. It's like he hadn't seen me in a year. Susan and I began cooking and talking.

I told her about the days events and she wasn't happy. "The only part that I don't like about this is the word 'mobile.' That means travel."

"Yes," I argued, "but this is a tough time and everyone is making sacrifices."

She said, "You've been to Beirut twice; isn't it someone else's turn?"

"There aren't any EOD guys but me," I lamely offered. We dropped it at that point and I honestly don't remember her ever bringing it up again. Of course, she was sad when I departed, as was I, but it was accepted.

I finished out the rest of the week on autopilot. I was excited about the teams but down deep I knew it would be fun and a bunch of good training but that would be it. I doubted that there would be any operational stuff. I was wrong. There was plenty. Maybe not anything as dramatic as a rescue of an ambassador or a good-looking secretary, but worthwhile and necessary stuff anyhow.

We all drove up to Winchester, Virginia, on Sunday afternoon. We checked in separately at the Travel Lodge, which had already become my home away from home. It was a warm day and I'd checked in around 1500. I put on my running gear and went for a long run. I was doing at least five miles in those days. I jogged south, out toward the airport. It was a winding road with no traffic. I looked ahead and saw a couple of guys headed toward me, also jogging. As they got closer I recognized them as two of the MTT guys I'd met in Abe's office.

There were greetings and guffaws exchanged and one of the guys, Doug, peeled off and joined me. As we're running along he asked, "So Frank, you're a Marine and used to this stuff. How do you think this MTT thing is gonna go?"

I jogged on a little farther without answering. I knew that every guy on the team had doubts. They were looking to me to wrap some sense around this effort. Doug was a young, good-lookin' guy and hadn't been with State that long. DS hadn't turned out to be as exciting as he had expected so he was looking for something with more challenge. MTT came along and he jumped at it. He, like so many of the others, had been with DS long enough to know that it would be a tough call to send in a team of diplomats to do a hostage rescue. Especially if they had to whack some bad guys or gals.

Finally I responded. "Doug, at the very least we're going to get some super training that others only dream about. Then to cap that off we're gonna travel to some exotic spots in the world. I'm excited as hell about that." He also fell into deep thought as we jogged. I had my second wind now so I was ready to bullshit.

I asked, "Do you plan on being with DS forever?"

"Hell, no," he said with a loud exhale. "There's got to be more to international stuff than this."

"What are you thinking about?" I asked.

"Agency," he said. "Paramilitary."

I smiled inside. All the young studs wanted Paramilitary Ops with the Agency. Only difference here, about a year later Doug did it.

We got back to the hotel. Abe and Joe had arrived. We were scheduled to be at BSR the next day at 0700. We had a few beers by the pool then went our separate ways. Some of the guys were still grousing but I had most of them convinced that the training was worth the effort.

The one troublemaker was soon to fall by the wayside. On the way out of Beirut he was caught with a weapon in his waistband in Larnaca. A big no-no. That caused mucho problems for the embassy and the MTTs. He went away, never to return. I suspect he was sentenced to UNGAs forever.

We were greeted at BSR by the Director of Training, a smiling, jovial Gary. I could tell right away that he and I would get along. Our first day was to be classroom. We were to cover Accident Avoidance, Vehicle Dynamics, Technical Driving (high speed), Ramming and Attack Recognition. We would then move to the instructor portion of the training. The two weeks went fast. All of the guys got their certificates and were ready to go.

There was another class going on at the time and we saw them occasionally. Young strapping guys with 28-inch waists and 60-inch chests, long hair, and all riding Harleys. There was a huge oak tree in front of the BSR office and on break these guys would hang out under the tree and drink beer. Who the hell is that? I'm thinking. They didn't bother introducing themselves but you could tell they were as curious about us as we were about them.

There was a small general store in the little town of Summit Point. They had the best sub sandwich and super cheap. You could eat a big lunch with soda for about three bucks. Toward the end of training the curiosity got too high and the two groups started eyeing each other. We went to lunch and a few of these long-haired guys were at the store.

There were the casual exchanges of "What's up?" and "How's it goin'?" Just light stuff, but it started breaking the ice.

I had the opportunity to get Gary off to the side, so I asked, "Who are the long-hairs?"

Gary responded, "The more you come here the more you're gonna see strange things and people. Nobody ever asks about the other trainees. The guys you're asking about don't exist."

"Yeah, they do," I said. "I had lunch with them today and said howdy."

These guys would start training at about 0900 and end at around 1500. This all changed when Force Recon started training at BSR for a chunk of the SEAL mission. Recon would show up at 0500, begin shooting or driving by 0600, and wouldn't stop until well after dark. Sometimes, depending on the training evolution, they trained all night. Next thing you know, SEALs are showing up at 0500 and training later and later. It was a fun evolution to watch. Young, hard-charging Marines and SEALs in competition. Only good could come from that.

By the end of the trip we were having open conversations with the long-hairs. It turns out they were a mix of SEAL Team Six and Red Cell. Once they discovered who we were, which was easy because our guys didn't have the OpSec training that the SEALs had, our guys told them everything but got very little in return.

The SEALs were really tongue-in-cheek when one of our guys told them, "Yeah, we're gonna kinda be like a State Department Delta Force." They never really commented but the rolling of the eyes said it all.

Being the good SEALs that they were, they saw opportunity. They started observing our training, making comments and recommendations, laughing and joking with us. Abe and Luke exchanged cards; Frank and Larry were established as the go-betweens. It was really orchestrated nicely. SEALs were thinkin,' Sure would be nice to tag along with these MTT guys when they went to places like Beirut, Cairo, Bogota, El Salvador. What better cover than being a State Department geek?

It was a little comical from time to time. You'd see a group of guys checking in at Dulles, or just hanging around a departure gate. One group would be clean cut, chests and waists about the same size, carrying a leather briefcase. The other group would be in baggy jeans or cargo pants, waists about thirty inches, chests about sixty inches, with arms that looked like small tree stumps. Next would be their long hair and at least a bushy mustache or beard. Let's see now…which group do you suppose were the SEALs? Even with that, the guys did a good job blending in and not drawing attention to themselves. There may have been a young lady or two who let their eyes linger on the muscles but that was expected, at least that's what the SEALs expected.

My relationship with the Navy had started. They were sharp, especially Luke. I always had the feeling that they were smiling, offering their help and assistance with one hand, but their other hand was deep in your pocket. They weren't thieves, only very good at getting whatever they needed to perform their mission.

They also had a unique talent of being secretive without you knowing it because they seemed open and discussed everything. At the end of every day I have a habit of going back over every conversation I had that day and analyzing it. When I analyzed a SEAL conversation I realized that I had been told absolutely nothing of importance, but I noticed that they got something from everyone they talked to. At night over beers they would huddle and compare the conversations that each of them had during the day. Amazing group of guys. Some remain lifelong personal friends that I would trust the safety of my family to...and have.

It was now time for the MTT training to go to the next level. We had a couple of guys drop out. It wasn't because they couldn't handle the training, they just didn't believe in the concept. Can't say that I did either, but I sure was gonna enjoy this training and travel. I knew that eventually I'd go back to the Marine Corps and this kinda stuff would prove invaluable.

After all the guys got certified as driving instructors it was time to shoot. There were extensive ranges at BSR and the 360-degree shooting house that I described earlier. Now, all these MTT guys had gone through the State Department firearms training and they had been through the Federal Law Enforcement Training Center firearms stuff but they were about to get exposed to the high speed shooting. As a Marine even I was about to learn some new techniques that are more applicable to combat shooting.

The first evolution was target shooting. As I later learned, this is a technique that instructors use just to see what level the students were at. Basic marksmanship, sight alignment, trigger pull, breathing, etc. The instructor could observe and see that the students could safely handle the weapons.

Weapons manipulation came next. Most monkeys could stand on a range and point the gun and fire. Now, how fast could you get the weapon from the holster and on target? We drilled and drilled. With the Browning we fired about 2,500 rounds per week, sometimes more. Over and over, do it again, more shooting, re-load, magazine changes. It got to the point that I was shooting in my sleep. We were taught a drill that we could practice at home. Dry fire was an important component of training. I was told that you should have one hundred dry-fire hammer falls for every live round you shoot on the range. We were taught to have our weapon in the carry (holster or concealed). Start watching a movie or TV show. Pick out one character and make him the bad guy. Every time that character appears, draw your weapon and fire at them. I used to hunt for old jane fonda (she doesn't rate capital letters) movies.

181

Susan never got used to that. I think she thought I was being melodramatic. I can tell you this: it worked. My skills improved like you wouldn't believe. Of course, in the back of my mind was Beirut. I knew that I would probably have to use this skill at some point and I knew that some little militia guy was training in Beirut and I wanted to be faster and on target. I was considered a non-shooter at first. Just the Demo Guy...Cook, Baker, Candlestick Maker. I have to admit that by the end of this training I was not only accepted as a shooter, but actively deployed as an integral team member.

While all this training was going on we still had our State Department duties. Now if there were a high threat protectee they'd send the MTT guys to cover it. I felt my first feeling of belonging when we transported the Cuban Foreign Minister to an event and I was handed an Uzi and told "Frank, you're right rear." I was in the follow car and provided firepower to the right flank of the motorcade. May not sound like much but, when you've been on the peripheral (comfortably so) and all of a sudden you're a trigger man, it's exciting.

The training was intense. We fired weapons I'd never even heard of. They called it the Funny Gun class. Autos, machine guns, machine pistols, sniper rifles, assassination one-shot weapons. Good stuff! We attended lock-picking classes, entry classes, a blending course (we were taught to blend in any environment), disguise, you name it. We learned all the "trade craft." During this evolution I was responsible for teaching explosive entry and IED awareness. We were going hot and heavy, twelve hours a day, sometimes seven days a week. In addition, I was studying my Arabic language and culture skills. My plate was full but it was an exciting time and we all knew what we were training for: Beirut. We took it seriously.

CHAPTER NINE

Beirut MTT Number Three

We departed BSR early on Friday afternoon. We felt like kids skipping school because it was the first time in many weeks that we'd taken off early. We headed back to the office to square our equipment away and clean our weapons. That is the first thing you do when you finish training or an operation. It becomes second nature—one of those nagging things that bug you 'til you get it done. Once everything was put away we decided to have a cool one.

Abe's beeper went off and he looked at the number. He said, "Go ahead guys, I have to make a call. I'll meet you there."

We walked across the parking lot toward the watering hole as Abe went back into the range facility to make his call. We walked in and the old gal behind the counter seemed happy to see us after such a long time. We used to go in every night while training at the State Department indoor range. We ordered a round and sat back to relax, as you only can after such an intense past few weeks. That first guzzle seemed to relax me down to my toenails. I realized that I'd have to be careful or I wouldn't be able to drive home.

We were shooting the bull and comparing what we'd learned. We looked like a bunch of pilots sitting around flying their imaginary planes with their hands, except we were pointing our imaginary weapons. The sun was shining in through the plate glass windows with what appeared to be an unusual intensity. The door opened and sunlight filtered through the dust with a silhouette of Abe, the sun at his back. You could tell it was Abe from his outline. He just looked like a big, black outline standing in the door. He didn't even come all the way in.

He just said, "Drink up and pay the bill, we've got to go to the head shed." We didn't say anything but we exchanged curious glances with each other. We knew that Abe had been trying to sell the services of the MTT to anybody who would listen. Thus far we had only been tapped for the high-threat VIP protection details and they were getting old. We suspected that the field agents were naming even the mundane details as high threat so that they wouldn't have to do it. We treated them all as high threat just for the training and experience.

We went out and loaded up. Once underway we almost all said, "What's up?" at the same time. Abe half-turned and smiled, "Looks like some of you guys are going on a little training trip next week. There are people who need training in Beirut and they want it done yesterday." He had that big grin on his face that yelled, "There's more to it than that, boys." We knew better than to ask. He'd given us all the information we needed or were gonna get for now.

We parked the van in the underground parking garage and fairly raced for the elevator. I had not totally realized my transition from Cook, Baker to accepted team member. We went into Abe's office still feeling the last effects of that chug-a-lugged beer. We all gathered in around Abe's desk for whatever tidbits we could get.

Abe dramatically walked over and poured himself a cup of coffee and took his time stirring in his additives. When he turned around he was grinning again. "They want to send four guys. They have fifty new hires to train and some additional duties that will be addressed when you're on the ground. Anybody want to volunteer?" We broke each other's necks getting our hands in the air.

Abe was still grinning. He said, "Unfortunately you can't all go so are there any volunteers not to go?" We all looked at each other. Reminded me of the Miss America pageant when the last few are looking at each other with big smiles but down deep they are saying, "I hope you break a leg or something."

Abe looked at me and said, "Frank you don't have a choice."

I thought, "DAMN, they're only gonna take care of their own and send State Department agents." I understood, I was really an outsider, but that didn't mask my disappointment.

Abe continued, "Frank has to go, he's been there two times in the last four months and knows the players. Besides that," he said, "this mission is probably going to require his skills."

"What skills?" I thought. We'd all just finished the same training. I drove better, my shooting was right up there with the best, but they were all good. What did I have to offer? Explosive entry or IEDs never came to mind, for some reason.

Abe said, "We'll discuss that later but it'll be need-to-know after that. Only the guys who are going will be briefed and that will only be after they arrive at the embassy in Beirut." I'm not complaining. I was happy as hell and it was obvious to everyone. Now came nut-cuttin' time. Who was goin' with me? There appeared to be no bad feelings about me going. It was just accepted, I think because most of the guys realized the importance of having someone on the team who had recently been there.

A couple of guys volunteered to stay behind for personal reasons: sick wife, girlfriend, kids, school, or whatever. Wasn't that they didn't want to go. Just better if they didn't. There was always next time.

For those of you who have trained and trained, you understand the need to go practice versus doing it for real. It's like always being the bridesmaid and never the bride. It was discussed, cussed, and re-discussed. It finally narrowed down to Santiago, Chris, Manny, and me. There was an unspoken transition. The four of us seemed to become one, with something in common that no one else in the room shared. Everyone sensed it. Guys started filtering out, making phone calls. All that was left was the four of us, Abe, and Joe. Santiago was to be the team leader. We had until the following Wednesday to get our logistics set up with a Friday departure.

It was on! Abe told us to stop shaving, and for the team leader and I that didn't matter much. He was a fiery blond-headed guy with peach fuzz and I was a subdued blond with peach fuzz. Santiago and I looked at each other and shrugged. Didn't seem like a show-stopper to us. As I looked around, it dawned on me: we were all blond or light-haired. Never mattered before, so I guessed it would be okay that time.

Abe told us to pack it in and he'd have more information for us Monday. He had a meeting at the Office for Combating Terrorism at main State. Ambassador Oakley ran that show at the time. To my knowledge it was all diplomatic stuff that went on there but in those days who knew? I always thought some of the medical buildings and office buildings in and around Washington were what they advertised on their billboards. Not so in every case.

We walked over toward the gray desk and I plopped down. I entwined my fingers behind my head and leaned back. The other guys grabbed their range bags and headed toward the elevator. The team leader held back.

He looked at me and said, "Frank, you're the military guy on the team. Besides that, you have recent experience in Beirut. I'm gonna really need your help on this one."

I smiled and said, "No problem, Boss—if we had wings we could fly." I used the term "boss" intentionally. I could tell that he was nervous about: 1) Leading a team to a combat zone with no combat experience or training other than our MTT stuff; 2) Being in charge of a Marine captain; and 3) Not knowing exactly what we were to do; or 4) All of the above. My response seemed to relax him, at least on item number two above. I had no ego requirements. They had been satisfied in Vietnam and my first two trips to Beirut.

Santiago and I headed to the elevator, bags slung over our shoulders and heads down, thinking about next week, and more importantly, the weeks after that. One thing I learned at State, people would tell you only generally what they wanted done. If you went out and screwed the pooch, they had plausible deniability. "I didn't tell them to do it like that." "I never said that's our goal." Whatever excuse... "I'm on board, pull the ladder up."

Then came my next hurdle: telling Susan. As I pulled into the driveway I saw her sitting on the front porch, with Stephen playing in the yard. That sure pulled my heart because as soon as Stephen saw my truck he broke into that huge, whole-body smile and ran down the driveway yelling, "Nanny! Nanny!" I stopped and opened my door to allow him to climb in my lap.

As was our custom, he settled in and grabbed the steering wheel. He had to pull himself up to see over the dash. I eased forward and up the long drive. Susan was sternly staring at us in pretended anger.

Stephen turned and smiled a conspiratorial smile as is normally shared between father and son when they're getting over on Mom. We didn't get over often. Maybe we thought we did from time to time but Susan was ever watchful over "her boys." We didn't mind. As a matter of fact, we enjoyed her attention.

I switched off the truck and lowered Stephen to the ground. I grabbed my gun bag then turned and gave her a kiss. We walked toward the house with Stephen skipping along beside us. I guess I was quiet or had a worried look on my face because she stopped and pulled my hand. She read me like a book.

"Are you leaving again?" she asked. This wasn't the normal question, as in "Are you gonna be at BSR all week?" It was a "Are you headed back to Beirut or some other godforsaken place?" type question.

I just looked at her and her eyes turned to damp pools. I just hugged her around the shoulders as we continued toward the house.

I tried to liven it up by asking, "What's for supper? Your Viking is hungry." No jokes were getting through.

The rest of the weekend went fast. Susan turned to preparing my clothing for the trip. She knew I wouldn't be leaving until Friday but it kept her busy, I guess. At the risk of sounding chauvinistic, that little girl takes the natural task of nesting to a new level. She has since the day we married and still does it today.

Monday I threw my gun bag in the seat and headed back on Route 66 toward D.C. Traffic was relatively light that morning. I made it to the office in about forty-five minutes.

Looking back, it amazes me how easy it was to get in to my office, or anyone else's for that matter. You walked in the lobby, got on the elevator, went to the fourth floor, got off, and walked down a long hall and into my office with the gray desk. No security, no checkpoints, and no metal detectors. That sure has changed. Main State was a different story. At least there you had to go through a security checkpoint with walk-through metal detectors.

As was normally the case, I was the first one on deck. I put the coffee on and sat with my feet propped up. I leaned back and stared out over the skyline toward Washington. I wondered what activity was taking place, what decisions were being made, what back room deals were being closed.

I always liked D.C. It was full of intrigue and mystery to me. Later, while working as a body guard, I discovered the reality of the "two worlds of D.C." There is the public world that we all see on TV and when we sightsee. Then there's the back room D.C., where everything actually gets done. The two worlds are totally different and don't even compare. My thoughts were interrupted by the smell of the brewed coffee. I needed a cup in a bad way. I grabbed my mug and strolled back down the hallway toward the coffee pot.

Denise, the secretary, was just arriving. She was a cracker-jack and took all of us MTT guys as her big brother. We joked about her being Miss Moneypenny. I think she worried about us more than some family members when we were on the road.

"Mornin,' Frank," she said in her Southern belle best. "I hear you guys are on the road again this week." It was as much a question as a statement. I could tell she'd overheard bits and pieces and wanted the whole story.

I responded, "Denise, you know that you get the official word before us ole ugly boys." She just shook her head and hustled toward her office with her many bags and purses. I never could figure out what she carried in all those packages.

The MTT boss, Abe, looked like a soup sandwich. He was the kind of guy, like me, who you could dress in Armani, Polo, or Johnson and Murphy's and he would still look like a sea bag with ears. He looked like Denise this morning. He had his gun bag over his shoulder, briefcase in hand, stacks of paper (which were precariously perched looking as if they would go to the winds at any time), and chin holding down a cup of coffee on top of the papers.

I said, "Abe, let me give you a hand."

He said, "If you touch anything, everything else will fall." I backed off. This was apparently a practiced art. Abe said, "Once I dump this crap I'm headed to main State. Make sure the guys are standing by so that I can brief them up."

I asked, "Want to see everybody, or just us?" Both of us knowing that the "just us" meant the Beirut MTT.

"Just you guys," he responded as he rushed toward the elevator. "I'll be back in a couple of hours if all goes well. If not, I won't be back at all, but wait anyway," he laughed.

The coffee was good and I made it extra sweet because I thought I'd probably need the energy that day. The hustle and bustle started gradually as folks filtered into their offices and you started to hear the hum of a bureaucracy at work. Pissing away those tax dollars. The MTT guys started showing up, laughing and joking or making fun of some other agent who wasn't present. My gray desk seemed to be a catch-all as there were four gun bags perched precariously on top.

"Hey assholes, throw this crap on Abe's desk," I blurted.

They all turned as one to fire back but saw my grin and relaxed. "Fuck you, Jar Head," Chris yelled.

"Careful, man—Denise will hear that and we'll all be in the shit."

Chris yelled again, "Sorry, Denise."

A quiet voice responded, "No problem, guys. Didn't hear you anyway." Denise heard everything.

Abe yelled out across the office with scattered desks, "Beirut guys get your asses in my office now. If you need coffee or a piss, do it now!"

We all moved quickly into his office worrying that the first guy might get more information than the others. We were anxious and wanted all available information at once. We were ready to go.

Abe started with, "I'm not gonna be able to give you much more than you already know. You'll be headed out of Dulles Friday afternoon on Pan Am. You'll change planes in Vienna after a seven-hour layover, then a short hop to Cairo. You drunks make sure that you connect. Frank, that's your job…get 'em on the plane."

"What if I'm drunk? Who's gonna get me on the bird?" I joked.

"You guys have been taught all the trade craft tricks. Before you get drunk, win over some cute KLM stewardess and have her babysit you." I think Abe was more serious than not on this comment. We knew that Vienna would probably be our last time to party unless we got hung up in Larnaca again. We doubted that because there was a new RSO in Beirut and he was nervous, and rightfully so. There would be no party delays in our effort to provide support to the RSO. He wanted the team yesterday.

The tempo had picked up in Beirut. Amine Gemayel was the Christian president and his Lebanese Army (LAF) was spinning with corruption and spies from the west. Syria was up to its neck in meddling with Lebanese domestic affairs in an attempt to destabilize Gemayel. Hezbollah and Hamas were working overtime to create havoc in the east with car bombs and kidnappings and outright murder. Beheadings and torture were commonplace on both sides of the Green Line. There were over 300 guards securing the American embassy and we knew that there had to be some tangos who had worked their way into employment.

On the east side there were similar problems. Elie Hobeika ran the Force Lebanon (LF) and he was a Christian warlord. Sometimes on, sometimes off with Gemayel. Then to cap it off there was a nice old guy, Michel Aoun, who had a following that was strictly political. He had no militia but had inspired a following because he was more of a spiritual leader with hopes of prosperity for all of Lebanon.

In my last chapter I will cover some cultural issues that make this work extremely difficult. If you study Arab culture and Islam you will see that there's not much of a chance of reconciliation. They've been fighting and hating for thousands of years. Some Liberal in a three-piece suit ain't gonna go in and change that. Throwing democracy into the Middle East is like throwing ammonia into a beehive. Up until the point you throw the ammonia, the bees are content to fight each other. Once you make the toss, they unite and come after you. Once they accomplish that task they turn right back to each other. Don't want to get too deep into that because I've reserved the last chapter for the study of Arab culture and Islam.

You're saying to yourself, Man, now Frank is a philosopher. Nope, but like Tsun Tsu said, "Know your enemy." We must at least attempt to understand enough to begin to anticipate their reactions and actions. Notice I didn't say "understanding" Arab culture and Islam. That will never happen.

The week's preparation was exciting. We went to the range to get our firepower. Joe was there and he was great. I worried that he'd be jealous that he wasn't going. If he was, he never showed it. He was like a mother hen and a Marine DI rolled into one. We had the thin sheets of lead to cover and mask our weapons from X-ray. The weapons would be sealed in dip pouches but there was always a chance that somebody would get a shot at the bags. My weapon preference was the MP5, which we'd recently been issued when they took the Uzis away. Like any old gun guy, we learned on the Uzi and got proficient. There was some whining until the guys learned to shoot the MP5. Same transition that happened in Vietnam: Halfway through my tour they called us all over to the armory. I had an old M-14 (7.62mm) with a three-round burst selector on top of the receiver. Loved that gun. Shot real bullets, as Joe always said.

We stood in line and as the first guys got their issue they walked back down the line bitching about this little black plastic "Mattie Mattel" that they were carrying.

"What the fuck are we gonna do with this?" was an often-repeated question.

I grudgingly handed over my 14 and they passed me my toy. Seemed to weigh half as much, which wasn't a bad thing. I then started thinkin' about hand to hand combat. This was always my biggest fear in Vietnam. Waking up in the middle of the night with thousands of little screaming rice burners charging through the wire with fixed bayonets, pokin' holes in everybody. Many a night I woke up in a cold sweat with that dream lingering in my brain housing group. That was forty years ago and I still dream about that.

Back to Joe and weapons issue. All the guys were wearing me out. I had learned to shoot as good or better than most but they still remembered how I started out. Never let me live it down. We all had our pouches open in front of us on the student tables. Joe was hovering around like Aunt Bee getting the kids ready for the first day of school. He fingered around in one bag and came out with that Buckmaster knife I mentioned earlier.

"What in God's hell do you plan on using this for?" he yelled.

Chris looked sheepish as he rolled his eyes and shrugged.

Joe threw the knife on the next table and said, "You can pick this up when you get back, asshole." He routed through every bag. Out would come a manicure set, then a porn book, and all sorts and arrays of personal gear. Lucky for me I had traveled with Joe and knew what to have in my bag.

The personal stuff I was to carry was out in my truck. I would simulate sealing my pouch in front of Joe then haul it outside and put my sardines, crackers, and boot knife (which was plastic and couldn't be detected by X-ray). Mama never liked that knife but I wouldn't leave home without it. You just never knew, and the bad guys didn't expect it.

Joe asked, "What are you traveling as?" We all looked at each other in confusion. "Jesus H, you just finished Trade Craft and don't have enough sense to know that you need a travel cover story?" Again, we all looked at each other. The team leader was from the group of agents who didn't really like Joe. *Like* is not the word. *Fear* is the word.

Anyhow, the team leader put on a show of bowing up in order to retain his status and through clinched teeth said, "I think that you're being a little melodramatic now. We have no guidance to establish a cover."

Joe glared at him, "Well, when you're crawling down some alley with one of your guys wounded and about 200 Hamas troops hunting for you, out of ammo, probably dumped your weapons by then anyhow, you've got Frank with a Marine tattoo on his dumbass arm—just tell 'em: It's okay, we work for the American Embassy. You know, those same folks that have been supporting Israel when they authorized the bombing of your homes, schools, and hospitals. They'll love ya. Hell, probably even have you over for some couscous." Joe had a very articulate way of expressing himself.

I watched this exchange with a humor dancing through my mind. I knew Joe and he was serious but he always over-embellished his real feeling. I knew he wasn't pissed, but I also knew he didn't like this team leader. When the team leader was selected I had heard Joe whisper under his breath, "Fuckin' pencil neck diplomat."

As Joe's angry eyes flashed over each of us we just looked down and started kicking horse turds like scolded school boys. As Joe looked at me, I saw that imperceptible wink that only I was to see. I just smiled and looked down to cover my chuckle.

Team leader wasn't done. "I think that determination will be made at main State, not here." Just couldn't leave it alone.

Joe walked over to his phone and picked it up. He dialed and waited.

Finally he said, "Abe, where did you get this data dink team leader? He hasn't even got the balls to make a decision on the ground and you're gonna cut him loose with three other guys and maybe get them killed?"

There was a long period that Abe was talking and Joe was listening. Joe hung up.

He turned to the team leader and said, "Finally, somebody with a brain. We're all gonna meet Wednesday afternoon at 1500. Since I've got more time in Beirut than anybody, I have been made the coordinator for this MTT. Santiago, I guess that means you work for and report directly to me."

You could've heard a pin drop except for the noise created by everyone's ass sucking wind. We all finished packing, with

Joe clucking around without pulling any punches. He didn't let the team leader (TL) off the hook once. If something was screwed up he pulled it out and slammed it on the table. The TL didn't say a word, just looked straight ahead.

We got all packed then stowed our pouches in the gun vault. We headed over to main State to get our courier letters personally signed by Secretary Shultz. That told me something. Normally they are rubber-stamped with some deputy's initials next to his signature. Not this time; this was the real McCoy.

Tuesday was given to us as an administrative day. There was always a pre-deployment day so that you could take care of any last-minute stuff, both personal and professional. I always stayed on top of my professional stuff so all I had to do was my personal checklist. I could take Susan and Stephen with me for what I had to do. Last-minute doctor visit to get my antibiotics, pain pills, and anti-diarrhea meds. That was my "just in case" stuff. You ain't never lived until you get an infection or toothache in a third world country. You're better off to have everything with you.

The next thing was that I had never done a will. We were sent to Vent Hill Farms (won't elaborate on that place) for the will. Supposedly those guys knew what we were doing, when we were doing it, and why we were doing it long before we did. In that environment a thirty-four-year-old Marine walks in healthy and says, "I need a will," they expect it. They also recommended a General Power of Attorney. If you got laid up for a while, Mama would need the authority to take care of you and your stuff. "How long you been married?" the clerk asked. "Fourteen years," I beamed.

The clerk looked up, uncaring, and said, "Guess she's gonna keep you so a General Power of Attorney is what you need."

Having all that done we went back to the car.

As I opened her door to get her settled she looked at me and said, "Be careful. I don't like this."

I just smiled and patted her shoulder in a reassuring manner. No jokes would be welcome now. We finished our day with a trip to the commissary and PX. I wanted to make sure that there was enough stuff at home for the family. Always worried about that. No matter how dumb it seemed or seems today, I have always had a little mental checklist in my mind. The older I get the shorter that list is, but it's still there. At the top of that list is always my wife and boys. I always felt that if they were okay everything else would self-correct. We headed to the house and nothing else was said about my upcoming trip.

Next morning, up early and out for a run. I used to love early morning runs no matter what the weather. It gave me time to think. So that morning I stretched it out and did about four miles at a hard pace. I was breathing hard at first but within a half-mile or so I got my second wind and settled into my practiced rhythm. Breathe in on the left foot out on the left foot. This always kept me oxygenated just below hyperventilation. I had to watch steep hills because they would upset my balance and I would have to adjust.

When I got back it was still dark and I could see that no one was awake in the house. I had my weight bench set up in the garage and decided to punish some iron. This was another stress release for me. I never lifted for bulk because I wanted to maintain speed and agility. I did pyramid weight sets and that kept me toned and strong. I heard movement upstairs as I finished my last set. The aroma of bacon hit me as soon as I opened the door from the garage to the house. Food, shower, shave…I was ready.

I arrived at work a little later than my norm but still early by State Department standards. All the guys were already there. Two of the regular MTT guys were there even though they weren't going to Beirut. Another mission was cooking and they were gonna handle it. Had nothing to do with us, so we didn't have the "need to know." I could tell it had something to do with our mission to Beirut but I never learned what until it was all over. They were tasked with protecting some high-threat folks that might have been targeted as a result of whatever it was that we were supposed to do in Beirut.

The American ambassador to Egypt was always under threat but he was always at the highest alert when negative things happened anywhere in the Middle East. Some negative stuff was about to happen to some bad guys in Beirut.

Abe got the four of us together in the conference room. We went over the threat analysis for the team, not only in Beirut but during our travel as well. We were to stop over in Cairo where the other two guys would peel off and assume the duties of protecting the ambassador. We were covering them and they were providing cover for us. We were going on an announced mission to train the guard force at the American embassy, Cairo. We were then to travel, for all outward appearances, to Alexandria, Egypt. Fact was that we flew straight to Larnaca for another helicopter ride to Beirut. Big difference this trip was that the American ambassador to Lebanon was traveling with us.

We weren't to learn that until just before we departed Cairo. It would be all-too-easy for the terrorists to launch a SAM (Surface to Air Missile) at our chopper. You have to understand, that type of weaponry was easy to get. Those arms dealers were all over Beirut and doing well.

The remaining days seem like a whirlwind to me. As a matter of fact, the entire tour with State seems like a foggy dream. I'm sure that was due to the excitement, but more importantly, to the hours worked. You who have worked protective details know what I mean. Just endless days of go, go, go, with sleep scattered about when possible.

We all took the departure day off with the agreement to meet at Dulles International Airport at 1400; our flight was at 1605. The airports were much easier to navigate in the '80s—arriving two hours earlier allowed us to have an extra beer at the airport lounge. We were on a Pan Am flight to Vienna. It was a 747, and since we were all traveling as couriers we sat in first class. I always felt like a fly in a jug of buttermilk sitting in first class. They hand you champagne followed by caviar and chilled vodka. We had consumed a few beers in the airport lounge and were feeling the effects.

Chris always got comical when he was drinking. He was smart as hell, too, and could come out with one-liners all day and night. He also didn't like the team leader and the more Chris drank, the more he let it be known. We were all slamming drinks that were free at the time. It was as though the stewardesses just wanted to see how much we could drink. Now I'm sure there's a regulation that says you can't drink while in courier status but we had neglected to read that prior to departure. By the time we reached Vienna it was early morning and we were all pretty messed up. Santiago was the only one halfway straight, but that's because he'd passed out and got a couple hours of sleep.

Chris and Manny were hot to find the bar. The bar was in the main terminal and it was a stand-up bar with no seating. We had a beer and decided to head to the gate and get a few hours sleep. Jetlag mixed with a hangover ain't pretty. The two additional MTT guys stayed to themselves. It was a mixture of not being able to tell us their mission, which was nothing more than providing protection, and being jealous that they weren't going with us into Beirut.

We arrived in Cairo sober but feeling rough. Santiago felt fine and he seemed to enjoy the fact that he was the only one. We were picked up at the airport by the embassy expeditor and transported to the embassy. The RSO was an old friend. The two Assistant RSO's were students of mine for their Basic Agent training, so it was a happy reunion. The RSO had us over to his house for drinks and dinner. It was obvious that Daniel, the RSO at the Cairo Embassy, knew we were headed to Beirut but he couldn't understand all of the secrecy. He had hosted several MTTs headed into Beirut that weren't considered hush-hush. He grilled us but all we knew was that we were to train guards and receive further instructions once on the ground.

"Yeah," he said. "That's why you're dropping off those other two gorillas to protect my ambassador. You guys are going to go stir up some shit, then go home and leave us holding the bag." He was laughing as he spoke but you could sense the feeling that he was also serious.

We finally convinced him that the security was for travel precautions. The next morning we all met in Daniel's office. He was all smiles and directed us to the coffee. Once his door was closed he said, "Just found out why the spooky stuff." We all looked at each other. We were told that we'd get our additional information in Beirut.

Daniel stirred his coffee and said, "Bartholomew is flying in with you."

We knew that and had assumed the RSO knew it. It was a surprise to him. We just shrugged and acted as though that was what all the secrecy was about. Hell, we didn't know the full extent of our stay, either.

We were off to the airfield at zero dark thirty. Choppers were standing by with rotors churning and burning. You can rest assured that this timely departure was not in our honor but due to the presence of the American ambassador to Lebanon. He was a small, wiry man and didn't have much to say to the team members. He looked almost comical in his Marine-issued life preserver and Mickey Mouse ear headset. He glanced at each of us in turn, with obvious displeasure at our display of weaponry.

We locked and loaded prior to boarding, making sure that our weapons were pointed in a safe direction. We also tried not to put on a big show with the Egyptian military looking on. They were carrying Beretta submachine guns, 9mm. Typical Arab carry: safety off, magazine in, finger on the trigger. We were hoping nobody sneezed.

We zoomed in over the bay and saw dozens of ships sitting peacefully at anchor. I looked back in the direction of Cyprus and saw only the beautiful emerald green waters of the Mediterranean. It never ceased to amaze me how such beauty and tranquility could exist in such close proximity to hate and destruction. I guess this is the true picture of that which God created laying in stark contrast to the destruction of man. This bird's eye view really made me stop and think. As we approached the city, my thoughts drifted to the old man and his wife in Ashrafiya. Were they still alive? Had the tangos figured out that they were friends of Americans? I hoped to answer these questions within the next few days.

The team leader had prepared a leadership brief for us the night before we departed Cairo. I think he'd read somewhere what he was supposed to say and do. He had this off-the-wall checklist of do's and don'ts.

One thing he said made sense, "You can only go out in two-man teams." Other than that it was a crock of shit. For example, "Don't mix with the locals." "No drinking in town." "No driving if you have been drinking." And the list went on. We listened, guffawed at appropriate times, and stated a couple of "bullshits" muffled under our breath.

After he finished I asked to speak with him alone. He agreed and we went up to his room.

I said, "Look, Santiago, I know that you've got concerns and the rest of the guys have never been here. I can tell you now that I will go to town, mix with the locals, drink with the locals, and then drive that fucking rental car back to our apartment, with one eye closed if necessary." I continued, "That is the only way we're gonna survive here, is with local intel."

He looked at me for a few seconds and it seemed to dawn on him that I wasn't challenging his leadership. During his brief I had not guffawed or made any comment. I just stared at him totally straight-faced. Then afterwards, when I told him, "We've gotta talk," it seemed to unnerve him.

After thinking about what I'd said, he replied, "Frank, I know you've been here before and that you may be doing some things that we won't be made privy to. I just want to take everyone home," he barely whispered.

"Don't worry man, we'll all go home," I solemnly added.

Kevin told us that there was a rental car downstairs and we could follow him to our apartment. No fancy Montemar with fresh breads and cheeses this trip. No Joe to cook for us, either. We were tired, jet-lagged, and hungover. A shower and crisp sheets sounded good to me. We unpacked our dip pouches and stowed our training gear. We locked and loaded our extra weapons and positioned all of our hardware. We inspected each other to make sure that nothing showed or poked out. I laughed to myself.

Here we were, four blond-haired, blue-eyed Americans in Levis, short-sleeved shirts, and travel vests to cover our weapons. We stood out like a hooker in church. I looked over and noticed Chris staring at Santiago. He wore a look of disgust and noticed me watching him. Chris just rolled his eyes and shook his head.

Chris broke out into a huge grin and asked, "Frank, now that this little shit is out of the way, how about something more important. How's the local beer?"

"The best," I laughed.

"Figured you'd have the intel on that," responded Chris.

Santiago said, "Stay focused guys, we have a job to do."

For some reason, that really pissed me off. I pride myself on not having an anger emotion. I learned early in life to control that emotion because I had a terrible temper. I controlled it to the point that I no longer got angry. It flashed in my mind for a second then went away. What the hell, let him be the big shot.

We loaded up our car and headed to the apartment. I fully expected to be in the same apartment that we were in on the first trip. We exited the embassy and turned left, which was my first indicator that we were staying in different quarters. Apparently the seventh floor directed all visiting personnel to rotate living quarters. Made sense until we arrived and I had a look around. No security, no secured parking, nothing.

"What the hell!" Manny said. We were shocked because Manny rarely spoke. "Trying to get us killed, Kevin?"

Kevin was a jovial, good-natured dude and laughed it off. "You guys can thank the seventh floor for these accommodations."

We pulled up behind Kevin's embassy Suburban. We parked right on the street. On the opposite side of the road was a new building under construction. Now, you must understand Arab construction. They bring in dozens of Hindus and Pakistanis and pitch a tent on the vacant land. The construction then begins. When they finish the first floor, they move out of the tents and onto the first floor. As the subsequent floors are completed the labor force moves upward.

I noticed that this building was working toward the completion of the fourth floor. All the Hindus and Pakis were living on the third floor. My experience with these guys was generally good. They seemed to let nothing bother them. The Arabs, whether in Lebanon, Saudi, Kuwait, Egypt, or anywhere in the

Middle East, always treated them like the lowest form of whale shit. These workers would just grin and bow and continue what they were doing. Most of them spoke English so I enjoyed shooting the bull with them from time to time. They always seemed to thoroughly enjoy a conversation where they were treated as equals.

I always looked around when doing any arrival, especially at a place where I was to spend any time, like my temporary residence. Parking on the street didn't thrill me nor did the layout of the buildings around us. It was a sniper's heaven and we could be surveilled from any number of positions. Once we unpacked, Chris and I decided to go find some beer and Cuban cigars.

Santiago nervously looked at his watch but said nothing.

We walked outside. I moved out of the doorway to the left and Chris covered the right. We did a fast glance at the surrounding buildings and were satisfied that the coast was clear. Chris stood watch while I did a quick search of our vehicle that had been parked outside. The thought was that even if we didn't find anything, we were putting on a show for surveillance. Hardening the target, so to speak. Theory being if you look aware, they will probably pick an easier target.

I finished the search and gave the all clear to Chris. I heard a noise and looked up to the source. The Pakis and Hindus were arguing like hell. The normally docile workers apparently had gotten some cheap booze and were all drunked up and fighting. Chris and I thought it comical and watched for a moment.

I yelled up, "Hey, anybody speak English?"

It got very quiet, the fighting stopped, and finally a little brown head peeped over the ledge and said, "Yes, mister."

I said, "What in the hell are you guys doing up there?"

"We do nothing mister. We do nothing."

I said, "Well I'll tell you what, you guys like good whiskey?"

"Yes, mister, we like but we don't drink much."

"Bullshit, you guys are drunk as hell on the cheap stuff!"

"No, mister, we not drunk."

"Okay, okay, I'll make a good deal for you. If you guys watch my car while we are at home I'll give you a new bottle of Scotch every day. Is it a deal?" I asked.

"Yes, mister, we watch for you," he bobbed his head in excitement.

When Chris and I returned with our beer and cigars I walked over and presented a bottle of Johnny Walker Black, cost all of $4 U.S. Man, you'd have thought I gave them the Holy Grail. They grabbed it, passed it around, rubbed it like a newborn baby, and beamed with pleasure. Every day I went through this routine; it was the best investment I ever made.

On one occasion we had to go to the embassy compound in the early hours of the morning. It must have been about 0300. As we exited the apartment and went through our clearing procedures, several flashlights came on at once and blinded us. These guys were on the ball and had posted a duty to watch the car.

I heard the small voice of my new friend, "Good morning, mister."

I never could get them to call me Frank. It was always "mister." I was never concerned about our vehicle from that point on. You can bet that I still did my searches. You never know who's watching. I was a realist also. What if the bad guys came along and offered two bottles of Scotch?

The next day went without incident. We met with Kevin early and he had the Lebanese guard supervisor with him. Maroun was his name and we were told that he was a former Lebanese Army colonel. We were to learn that most of the U.S. embassies had a "former local military colonel" in charge of security. He had about twenty new-hire guards who needed the full training cycle and another twenty to twenty-five who needed refresher training and weapons re-qualification. We hadn't been briefed on what our additional job was to be and we didn't bring it up.

I set up for my IED recognition and search class that we gave all guards. This prepared them to search vehicles, personnel, and buildings in the event of a bomb threat. There weren't many threats in Beirut but there were plenty of actual bombings. These guys knew it and took my training very seriously. The other team members took the other group to the firearms range for re-qualification. We were all moving through this MTT routinely, just getting the guys certified.

On day three we all met up in the RSO's office for a recap of the day's activities. The RSO was very meticulous and concerned about his guard force. He quizzed us daily about the quality of the personnel and wanted to know if there were any glaring problems. During those days everyone was conscious of the fact that we could have hired a bad guy who would set things up for an attack from the inside. Screening was critical.

As we talked, a new face walked into the office.

Kevin said, "Gents, this is Larry." Larry shook hands around and we gave our names. He was a clean cut, younger guy and it was always hard to tell who was who. Of course you never asked. Larry wasted no time.

"I hear one of you is an EOD guy?" More of a question than a statement.

Santiago responded first and said, "Yeah, Frank is our EOD type."

Larry looked me over and I could tell that I was being evaluated instantly.

I must have passed because he said, "When you get done I need to ask you about some stuff." He looked at the RSO and said, "Show him where I'm at when you're done."

I don't know who this guy was or who he worked for but he was used to giving orders and the RSO had no problem following them.

We finished up shortly thereafter and Kevin told Santiago, "I'll bring Frank back to the apartment."

Santiago nodded but I could tell he wasn't happy being left out.

Chris spoke up, "I'll drop Santiago and Manny off and come back to get Frank."

Santiago looked at him immediately and said, "That violates the two man rule."

"Jesus H. Christ, everybody else is running around this country alone and the best-trained of us has to be babysat,"

Chris vented. He jammed his hands in his pocket and his shoulders sagged. We all knew that Chris had given in, but he had to go down fighting.

I followed the RSO to the stairwell and we went up to the next floor. We had to press a buzzer then wait for the electronic release from the interior. There were a couple of overweight guys fooling around with some oversized communications equipment.

Kevin didn't introduce me but both guys seemed pleasant, and nodded as we walked through. We entered a small, cramped office that was littered with paperwork, pamphlets, and assorted other junk. Reminded me of the mad scientists' libraries in the old movies. Larry was behind the desk with his ear glued to the phone. He motioned for me to sit with no regard to the RSO.

Kevin said, "I'll be downstairs when you get done."

I nodded as he left.

Larry shook out a cigarette and offered me one, which I refused. He was speaking to someone on the phone in what sounded like fluent Arabic. I spoke a little Levantine Arabic by that time but not enough to distinguish fluency levels. He seemed to be rattling on and I was pleased to realize that I understood a word every now and then. I heard *goombala* (bomb) more than once. Larry laughed from time to time, so that told me the person on the other end of the phone was probably a friend. Shortly he hung up, took a long draw on his cigarette, and exhaled toward the ceiling, pretending courtesy to me as a non-smoker. It was a waste of time as the room and its contents were permeated with the stink of cigarette smoke.

"Want a beer?" he asked.

I shook my head no. My mind was racing like hell.

He started the conversation with, "Are you up on military ordnance?"

I responded that I had been primarily working with IEDs but I still had some ordnance knowledge.

Taking another draw, he said, "I have some Lebanese army types who need some training. They are the Lebanese version of our EOD but without the formal training. They have learned 'on the job'."

"Sometimes that's the best teacher," I agreed.

He further explained that he had a friend who was a colonel and he wanted to help him by getting his guys some training. They wanted military ordnance identification and recognition and they also wanted safety precautions. I told him that I could do that but that I couldn't teach render safe procedures (RSP) to foreign nationals.

"They don't want that," he said. Then he corrected himself, "They want it but they know they can't get it, not from us anyway." He continued by covering the need and how much it would help his position if I could set aside a little time to hold some classes.

Not a problem, I told him. He stubbed out his cigarette and stood. The meeting was over. He told me to meet him in Kevin's office in the morning and he would introduce me to the colonel and we'd have a look at the training site. Larry told me that I should keep our conversation to myself. What was I to tell the team leader? I knew his panties would be in a huge bunch if he felt left out. I shared my concerns with Larry. This guy was wise beyond his years.

"Just tell him that you're going to do some frag analysis for me. It will be technical intelligence and he's not cleared. Yeah, that'll work."

Now let's pretend that I'm not real stupid. The U.S. military was recently in country and they provided tons of training to the Lebanese military. Given the number of IEDs encountered, I strongly felt that at least some EOD training had been provided.

The Lebanese Army (LAF) was the country's only military formally recognized by the United States. All of the militias, including the LF, were considered rogue forces controlled by warlords.

Even though the LF was not formally recognized, the U.S. was on friendly terms with Hobeika and his thugs. If the truth were known, I'm sure that the Spider folks had also done some useful, if not edgy, missions for the U.S.

I went back down to the RSO's office and Kevin was pounding away on an old typewriter.

He looked up with a scornful smile and said, "So, how did that go?"

"I ain't sure, Kevin," as I plopped in the chair across from his desk. I knew that Kevin liked me. He was one of those Foreign Service guys who saw a need for the military. He also had huge respect for the United States Marine Corps because of what had happened to the MAU headquarters. He was waiting for me to say something as he watched my body language. This is something else that I noticed from day one with State. People watched your reactions and body language as much or more than they listened to what you said. My wife said that I developed the same trait and watched everybody. I still do.

Kevin finally asked, "What was on Larry's mind?"

I didn't want to sound like a spook but didn't know how much I should share. I trusted Kevin so I opened up more for him than I was going to with the team leader.

I responded, "I'm not real sure what just happened."

Kevin laughed and shook his head. "That's Larry for you," Kevin said, more as a statement than as conversation. He continued, "When we have staff meetings, Larry leaves the room and everybody asks, What was all that about?" Larry had an unbelievable mind. He could remember the minutest details and recall the most obscure conversations.

Kevin leaned his elbows on the desk and stared at me for a few seconds, "Be careful Frank—those guys don't give a shit about people like you and me. We are just tools that they use to get whatever they need. They'll then deny the fact that they ever even knew you. They'll throw you under the bus in a heartbeat just to save their own asses."

I nodded in agreement as I tried to reflect on the conversation with Larry. Enough was enough. Time for a beer. I asked

Kevin to join us at the apartment for a cool one, which he refused. Said he had a shitload of paperwork to get out. We all knew that Kevin had a girlfriend on the side but he was keeping it secret. He was going to marry the girl but didn't want State to know because they would bring him home. It was against the rules to fraternize.

The next morning we all collected in the RSO's office. Santiago was busy shuffling paperwork, timecards, notes, and lesson plans he'd prepared for upcoming classes. Manny and Chris lounged with a cup of coffee and spoke in hushed whispers with sideways glances at Santiago. For a moment I felt sorry for him. It was lonely at the top, especially if you were an asshole.

Larry came strolling in and helped himself to a cup of coffee. He had his cigarette dangling from his lips, which brought a dirty look from Santiago. He was a reformed smoker and thought everyone who smoked was lower than dirt. You can imagine how he felt about me and Chris and our Cubanos. Larry made casual conversation with a few one-liners thrown in to lighten things up. He and Kevin got into a discussion about things that were happening around the city and who was in power this day. The warlords literally shifted back and forth from strong guy to weak guy within a twenty-four-hour period.

Finally Larry turned to me and, as if our conversation of the afternoon before never happened, asked, "Frank, can you give me a hand today? Got some military ordnance I'd like you to look at. We can't figure it out."

He then turned to the team leader and asked, "Santiago, can you spare Frank today? We never get an EOD guy and I need to milk his brain."

Not knowing what was going on, Santiago responded, "Sure, we can handle the range today."

I glanced at Kevin and all I got was a rolling of the eyes and a "watch your ass" wink. I grabbed my bag and followed Larry out to his old white Mercedes.

I commented on his vehicle and he said, "Fits in better than those damned Suburbans." Hell, every other car was a white

Mercedes. I threw my gear in the back seat and hopped in the passenger side. Larry slowly pulled out of the embassy compound. All of the guards were watching us intently. Apparently Larry had a mysterious reputation with the locals as well.

The Lebanese underground telegraph was so good, they probably had all the information they needed on him. I knew there was something because all of the guards looked at me with those familiar dancing, laughing eyes; they were genuinely happy to see Yu-Muh. But when their glance moved to Larry, the eyes became those smiling, knowing, defensive stares.

We drove down the winding narrow road toward the Mediterranean. Once we reached the beach Larry turned right and followed the beach highway towards Byblos. Byblos is the resort area right on the Med. Another example of the beauty disturbed by periodic bursts of violence. Larry seemed right at home zigging and zagging through traffic like an old Lebanese taxi driver. He blew the horn at just the right times and held his right hand up with all five fingers together, the Arab sign for patience please… *swaiya…swaiya.* During all of this activity he managed to fish out another cigarette and light it one-handed with his Zippo.

About ten miles outside of town he turned right and headed back up another winding, narrow road, more like a trail than a road. We approached a checkpoint and he rolled down his window. The guard recognized him; they were obviously old friends. We had the handshake, the hand over heart, the cheek kiss, and machine-gun-sounding Arabic back and forth.

Larry asked, "Is Joseph here?" I was impressed with myself. I understood the entire question.

The guard replied, "Yes, straight ahead. Second tent on the right."

"*Hum Du Allah*'s, Go with God, Peace be unto you, etc., etc.," and we headed to the tent. Having seen the guard and the flag I knew that this was no LAF camp. It was an LF militia camp and we were headed to meet with the head of the Spider people, Joseph Sphere. Now some stuff started banging around in my head.

When Larry cut the engine off I asked, "I thought you said LAF?"

"No, no you must have misunderstood. The LAF can get EOD training easy through the ATA program (State Department's Anti-Terrorist Assistance program). I knew that I hadn't misunderstood, but Larry gave me no time to respond. He bounced out of the car and headed toward the tent, motioning me to follow. What the hell, it was all government. We entered the tent under a flap.

In the center was a table with a few chairs. Seated in one chair facing us was a tall, relatively handsome Arab with a huge mustache and balding scalp. I recall how his head shined under the naked light bulb above his head.

He looked up and saw Larry and jumped from his seat with a huge grin and literally bounced over to shake Larry's hand and do the kissing thing again. After exchanging pleasantries, Larry turned to me for the introductions. I hadn't seen Ernest and Imad but didn't want to ask about them either. This was a world of keeping your mouth shut and ears open.

Joseph spoke perfect English with hardly a trace of accent. As it turned out, he was educated in the U.S. and had family in the states. There were two other men in the tent but they came and went as if on errands. Joseph yelled at one to bring coffee. The guy jumped up and ran out of the tent. A few minutes later he came back with a tray of fine china cups and saucers and a silver pot of coffee. That stuff sure seemed out of place.

Joseph and Larry conversed for ten or fifteen minutes, making small talk of family, politics in the U.S., the weather, and women. Finally, with all the preliminaries out of the way, Larry said in English, "Frank is the Marine EOD officer I told you about. He knows a good bit about military ordnance but he specializes in anti-/counter-terror devices."

Joseph was watching me through narrow slits. It was an appraising and approving stare. It was obvious that Joseph had been waiting on me.

He then smiled and said, "Frank! Yu-Muh. Ernest and Imad speak highly of you. I hear that you met some of my men on your last visit."

He and Larry were both smiling broadly now.

I went along, "Yeah, and they scared the shit out of me."

Joseph bellowed a laugh and said, "They scared, too." We all laughed at that.

CHAPTER TEN

The Spider People

J oseph yelled out, *"Rhakeeb Abdu, ardwa, yallah"* (Sergeant Abdu, come here, hurry). A uniformed man entered the tent. He was somewhat disheveled, as if he'd just woke up. His looked like hammered horse shit. He strolled over and shook Joseph's hand, kissed the cheeks, then did the same with Larry. I was then introduced to Sergeant Abdu by Joseph.

Joseph proudly said, "Sergeant Abdu is my EOD man."

I pumped Abdu's hand with enthusiasm which the kind sergeant didn't return. His hand was like shaking a limp noodle. This is a sign of disrespect from an Arab. I countered by grabbing his right shoulder with my left hand as if in affection. I did it intentionally to return the insult. Arabs wipe their ass with their left hands. Now that we had compared dick lengths, we settled on a mutual tolerance.

It is strange; when two warriors meet there is a certain exchange. Maybe not the same mannerisms, but a similar exchange. Once you each establish your territory you can move forward with business. I didn't know what had been said, or what was expected of me, but this guy obviously had information on me he didn't like. Time would tell.

We sat down and exchanged small talk. Sergeant Abdu was also very good with English. He had received some EOD training from the Syrians and had traveled to France for training. Turned out to be a sharp EOD guy within his realm of operations. He wanted to show me his shop so Larry and Joseph gave the thumbs up. I followed him out and down through a small draw. He explained that his demo range was actually up in the mountains but it was an all-day trip to drive there and back. He preferred the small range that he had here. There was a cleared area once we emerged from the draw. It was clear and sandy.

An old Chevy Caprice sat tireless at the back of the range. It had been the host of more than one explosion. There was a shed that appeared to be about ten feet by ten feet. Abdu unlocked and opened his "shop." There was a workbench down the left side and shelving on the right. The bench was littered with wire, tape, mechanical timers, and electrical gadgets of all types.

I fingered through the stuff but there was no order. Abdu had things organized exactly the way he wanted it. He knew where everything was. We actually started to warm toward each other. I think it helped that we each determined that the other had some knowledge. I also learned that his initial disrespect was toward America and not me.

He, like many Lebanese, felt abandoned when the U.S. pulled out. Abdu had Marine friends who he'd met, then one day they were all gone. This was a sentiment that weaved its way through Lebanese Christian society. To make things worse, Abdu was Muslim and working for a Christian militia. Go figure that one.

I was later able to put all the pieces together but it still made no sense. Abdu had been with Hamas in West Beirut but fell in love with a Christian girl in the east. To make it worse she was not a virgin and had a child. Abdu married her, and he and his family were immediately put on the hit list by Hamas. His life was worthless at that point. He was introduced to a member of the LF through his wife's family. He went to work for Joseph as his EOD guy. Abdu had plenty of experience; he had been a bomb-builder for Hamas.

Now I'm lookin' at this guy thinking, Holy shit! Here's one of the people I've been training to kill. I would never grow to totally trust this guy even though he never gave me reason to not trust him. Joseph was a little more subtle. He had told Abdu, "If you cross me I will kill your wife and her family, then your children, then you." Abdu knew he would. Therefore, the safest place for Abdu was working for Joseph.

Abdu told me about some of the tactics and techniques and told me about some of his old co-workers. He was very open and held nothing back. He missed his family in the west. His father had been killed in 1982, but he still had a mom and several sisters there. Any visits to them would put them at risk. He seemed to avoid any conversations about them. This could have been the Arab mentality of not discussing female family members, concern for their welfare, or both. Our conversation shifted to bombs and explosives. I told him about explosive entry and my passion for explosive effects. He, too, had similar thoughts but his focus was IEDs.

We heard someone approaching. Abdu looked out the door and saw Larry and Joseph headed toward the shed. We walked out to greet them.

Larry said, "How you guys getting on?" He watched me closely because he'd seen the manhood test inside the tent. I suspected that not too much escaped Larry.

"We're doin' okay," I responded non-committally.

"Good, good," beamed Joseph.

I got the feeling that they were all waiting on my stamp of approval. I could work with Abdu but, like I said, I wouldn't bring myself to trust him. I had the feeling that he felt the same way about me. After all, the U.S. had pulled out once leaving them holding the bag. A lot of good people were killed after our forces departed because they had supported the Americans.

We headed back to the tent but I noticed Abdu wasn't going with us.

Joseph yelled for more coffee, then hesitated and turned to us and asked, "You want whiskey, beer?"

I shook my head no but Larry indicated that he'd love a cold beer. Little early for me but any time seemed good for Larry. He liked his beer with the same vigor as Joe and Chris. We sat at the small table and made small talk. I knew something was coming because you don't go to all the trouble of getting a Marine captain from the states to meet a former tango then sip coffee.

Finally, Larry opened the conversation, "Do you think Abdu knows his shit with explosives?"

I nodded as I spoke, "He seems to, and with his former experience I'm sure he adds a new dimension."

"That he does, that he does," said Larry.

I glanced at Joseph, who was watching me intently. When he realized I was watching him he broke out into that masking smile. I looked back and forth between the two and they were now both watching me.

I gave in, "So how do I fit into this?"

They seemed relieved to have the ice broken.

Larry started, "Abdu has access to some unique folks, as you can imagine. None of them can be trusted but they're the best we've got."

Joseph interjected, "I have Abdu by the balls so he can be trusted."

Again I responded, "So where do I fit in?"

Larry though a moment then leaned forward, "As long as we can protect Abdu, we can find out where the bombs are headed before they get there. In some cases we can actually get a look at the devices."

I about shit! "You mean to tell me that you look at these devices then send 'em on their way?"

"Depends on where they're headed," Larry nonchalantly responded. I knew that he seemed detached but now I realized he was a downright cold-blooded killer. He must have read my reaction. He held up his right hand, which clinched the ever present cigarette, and made a circular gesture.

"This place is so difficult to judge that you can't understand any of what goes on. The people all know each other and in most cases are related somehow. They hold hands and kiss during the day, then kill each other at night. We won't stop that. Been going on for thousands of years. But if we're careful, we can limit the attacks on good folks."

I must have looked cynical when I retorted, "Does that mean good Lebanese, too?"

"Yeah, we try to take care of them, too," he said. During this exchange Joseph had remained silent.

Now he leaned back in his chair and said, "Frank, you must understand. There are at least twenty-five different factions vying for power just within the city limits of Beirut. Now add to that the Palestinians and the Israeli Moussad and you've got a real mess." He sounded more American than Larry did. He continued, "We Christians don't stand a chance if they decide to join forces. Our only hope is to keep them at war with each other." I understood his reasoning but it was one hell of a way of life.

"Okay, back to me. Where do I plug in?"

Larry was the first to respond. "We'd like for you to teach Abdu a little about booby traps. We, as Americans, can't get directly involved," which got a roll of the eyes from Joseph. "When we get the chance to look at these things we'd like to send a little message back to the bad guys." Now you have to see the big picture. In Beirut at that time (1985) there were two or three bombs going off every day just in the city.

I gave Larry a "we'll talk later look." He expected it. He pulled out another cigarette and ceremonially lit it.

Taking a deep draw then exhaling, he continued speaking, "We don't have much time. The plan is simple. We will take a look at a few devices and establish a trend. Are they electronic, mechanical, or remote controlled? Once we determine that, we want you to teach Abdu two or three ways of booby-trapping the device so that it fails to function."

"Even better, if it's headed back to the bomb factory, we want to arrange a premature detonation at that point."

"Wait a minute," I blurted, "are you telling me that they will bring the bomb out and let you look at it then send it back to the factory?"

"Not often, but it does happen. It normally happens en route to the site. In that case we want it to go off before it gets to the destination."

"That all sounds a little edgy to me," I said. "What if innocents are in the way?"

Larry said, "That's why you're here. To minimize that possibility."

When you're dealing with 10,000 pounds of high explosives you ain't gonna minimize shit!

Larry knew at this point he was gonna have to speak to me alone. We continued the small talk. Joseph also knew that Larry had some convincing to do. We finished our refreshments and made our goodbyes. More kissing and hand shaking, including me this time.

On the way back to the embassy Larry said, "Let's stop by my apartment."

Sounded good to me. I didn't want many people around to hear this conversation. We turned off the beach highway into a small, gated housing area. There was a guard at the gate wearing an embassy guard uniform. He made a big show of searching the vehicle, mainly because I was there and had trained him on search procedures.

Larry's apartment was nice. He obviously was higher up the food chain than us or even Kevin. We went into the kitchen and he pulled a couple of Heinekens from the fridge. There was an ashtray on the counter that was overflowing with butts. I noticed that not all of them were Larry's brand; some even had bright red lipstick. He saw me looking, and effortlessly picked up the ashtray and dumped it in the trash can. He pulled out another smoke and fired it up. I figured it was my turn to start the conversation and he was happy with that.

"Larry, I'm a U.S. Marine and I'm sure there are laws that govern this type of activity, especially for us Marines. Hell, they wouldn't even let us load our weapons before the MAU bombing and it ain't much better now. The politicians are trying to run the war and that's easy to do from a plush office."

Larry took it all in and reserved comment until he was sure I'd finished. One last thing, "What is in place that will cover my ass if this 'program' goes sideways?"

He outwardly relaxed, obviously experienced in these types of conversations.

He started slowly, "I couldn't be doing this alone. I have orders just as you do. We have been tasked with getting a handle on the bomb situation in Beirut. We receive guidance from the Head Shed and your being here is sanctioned at the highest levels. Granted, there are probably people more qualified than you, but you were easy. You had a diplomatic passport, you'd traveled to Beirut on training missions and that was well known here, plus you have a Top Secret clearance. The bad guys are very familiar with the activities of the MTTs. Hell, you've trained a bunch of them already and they work for the embassy both in the east and the west. We knew that was goin' on."

We at the MTT level didn't know who was who, but Larry did.

He continued, "It's good to have these folks employed by the embassy. It's easier to keep track of them and we've created positions for them that seem important but they are harmless. We pump them full of disinformation which they take back to their bosses. We can literally lead them around by the nose."

Now Larry didn't have to tell me that this stuff didn't leave the room. Whole lots of people could get hurt with this knowledge. Apparently over the next few days or weeks I'd be working with Abdu.

The next morning Larry picked me up and we went to the Montemar Hotel for breakfast. We got a table in the back corner, which the waiter was accustomed to when Americans came in. Larry and I did the usual shuffle that guys like us did when choosing our seats. We never put our backs to the door or to other patrons. The table was positioned in the corner so that both of us could put our backs to the wall and see the entrance. The waiter brought coffee and juice.

Joseph and Abdu walked in dressed in civilian clothing. Abdu wasn't happy with having his back to the door but such is life. Joseph said that there was an area we had to go visit.

Larry surprised me when he said, "You guys can go. Frank is all you need and I've got some things to take care of at the embassy."

I didn't care who was sitting at the table when I blurted, "I go, you go. I need your presence on this first trip. After that I'll know what I'm doing."

217

Larry wiggled in his seat and it was the first time I'd ever seen him uncomfortable. He tried again, "I don't know anything about that kinda stuff. I'd just be wasting space."

I was firm, "Like I said, I go, you go."

He caved in because he knew I wasn't bullshitting. Joseph picked up the bill left by the waiter. I noticed that Abdu was watching the waiter throughout the meal. Couldn't tell if he was suspicious or if he knew the guy.

We strolled out into the morning sun. Man, what a beautiful place. There's just something about Beirut that slays me. It was a pleasant mixture of paradise and Dodge City. Things were cheap, girls were beautiful beyond description, and the guys were nice enough. They were all bitter that we'd pulled out but I think they saw a ray of hope with us being there.

We walked out to the parking lot and Joseph pointed to the new, very big, black BMW. I'd never seen a ride like this in Beirut. Hell, you don't see them that much in the States. I'm not sure of the model but it was a movie star.

Abdu and I got in the back and exchanged glances with nods. Still no warm and fuzzies there. We drove along the seashore and enjoyed the view in silence. I expected a brief on where we were headed but none came.

Joseph turned left between the Juicy Burger joint and a large insurance company office building. The street was so narrow that pedestrians had to step back into doorways so that Joseph's big car could pass. We emerged into an open area that had scattered metal buildings arranged with no thought in mind. We pulled up in front of the largest building and Joseph hit his horn twice. We waited and I could tell that Larry wasn't comfortable. He kept looking around, as did I. The big worry here was that Joseph was a high up in the LF. He had plenty of enemies on both sides of the Green Line. We didn't want to be collateral damage in the event somebody wanted to "cap" his ass.

Finally the big rolling door was lifted and Joseph pulled into the dark opening. Now Larry was spooked. The door dropped behind us and the lighting inside, although dim, revealed a large-bodied, dark blue Mercedes.

One guy was standing next to it, smoking a cigarette. He looked at us with hostile eyes but didn't move. An older guy stepped out of a doorway that, I assumed, led from an inner office.

He walked straight toward Joseph, and in a subservient manner shook his hand. No kisses.

"*Shouf! Shouf!*" (Look! Look!), he said, pointing at the Mercedes as he walked toward it. He was expecting us to follow. Nothing doing!

"*Mnea! Mnea!*" (It's okay, it's okay)

Abdu was the most relaxed and I could tell that the guy by the car had no animosity toward any of us but Abdu. He glared at Abdu but he got ignored for his efforts. Abdu didn't even acknowledge his presence.

The old man walked up to the opened rear window and removed a blanket that was covering twenty to thirty propane cylinders, the same type that you use in your back yard grill. Except in this case they were sitting on top of one hundred or so pounds of Semtex-H (Czech plastique explosives). He dropped the blanket and moved to the trunk of the car. My ass drew up like a shower curtain as he inserted the key and the trunk popped open.

The bad guys know how to rig booby traps as well. No bang, so we were okay. The trunk was similarly packed with propane bottles. There were wraps and wraps of what appeared to be (and was) detonating cord. It was yellow with a black spiraling band. It was everywhere. Looked like a drunken spider's web. There was a medium-sized cardboard box toward the rear of the pile. Abdu tapped my arm and nodded toward the box. Holy shit! Was I here to do a render safe procedure (RSP) or what?

Abdu said, "Let's look at detonator."

I'm thinking,' Let's don't and tell everybody we did. The flaps on the box were folded over on each other so as to self-seal. Abdu reached in and grabbed a tab and pulled it open. I peeked over his shoulder and wasn't surprised to see a ton of electrical wire wrapped all around an alarm clock.

Closer inspection revealed some electronic components but I couldn't tell what they were from where I was standing.

Abdu moved aside. I took a closer look and saw that the clock provided safe separation for the driver, maybe. The rest of the stuff was the receiver unit off a radio-controlled model (Futaba). Tangos usually put tons of wire in just to throw EOD off when we X-ray the item.

I couldn't believe it. Here I was looking at an actual bomb that was scheduled to kill people in the near future. It wasn't set up as a suicide bomb, but it probably did have a backup feature that we couldn't see.

I looked at Joseph and asked, "Do we know who it belongs to?"

I got that Arab I-don't-know shrug and pinching of his mouth.

Abdu said, "No problem this one." He pulled out his wire cutters and cut a couple of wires. He then direct-wired the alarm clock to the detonator but camouflaged it with dummy wires running back to the remote receiver.

Now when the safe/arm timer (provides safe separation for the bomber before the device arms) ticked down they would be in for a surprise. Abdu had made sure that the driver hadn't seen what he did. He dropped his wire cutters into his jacket pocket and stood upright, masking his moves. Joseph walked over to the old man and handed him a thick envelope.

The old man smiled and opened it. I could tell that it was U.S. currency but I couldn't tell the denominations. It was a bunch! Nothing was said as Joseph moved toward his car. We followed as if it were rehearsed. The door rolled open as Joseph cranked his car and backed out.

"Wasn't that easy?" asked Larry as he turned in his seat to look at me. I returned his stare.

I finally replied, "Sure will be interesting to see where they decide to arm that thing."

Getting my meaning he said, "Don't worry, it'll be in Indian country."

"They got little Indians there?" I asked.

He got my meaning and just turned around in his seat. The entire trip had taken less than an hour. We were back at the hotel sipping coffee. Over the next few days, when I heard a distant, muffled boom, I wondered if that was our gift. We were to never know or be told the results of our efforts.

Over the next few days I traveled to the LF camp to meet with Abdu. It was more of an information sharing classroom. I didn't do much training for Abdu. If anything he took me to school. He was meticulous with wiring, capacitors, resistors, and electronic 555 and E-cell timers. He handled volt meters and small hand tools like a surgeon. I realized that there was rhyme and rhythm to his messy workshop. He knew where everything was.

The next two trips went without a problem. We were getting the word that our "program" was not unknown to some of the bad guys. Since we were doing damage to their rival militias, they didn't care.

The third trip presented a real problem and we departed Beirut shortly afterward. Abdu and I went up in the mountains towards Bikfaya. We met with the same old guy except he was alone. We were on a deserted, rocky road that meandered up and out of sight. We pulled up behind the old man's car and got out.

The old man seemed rattled and not his usual self.

Abdu questioned him for a minute or two then turned to me and said, "Maybe problem."

My MP5 was in the car, but I had my Browning Hi Power and my Beretta 70S. Only problem with that is that we were in long-gun territory. Even a reasonable shooter could take us out from cover within one hundred yards. We looked around and saw nothing.

Finally the old man said, "Truck late, maybe we go."

Abdu and I both said, "No, we wait."

Finally we hear the groan of a large-sounding truck working its way up the hill. Gears would grind once in a while. Finally the nose of the truck appeared around a turn and slowed, being engulfed in a cloud of dust. The breeze blew it away, revealing a young male driver.

He jumped out and ran over to the old man. The old man was giving him hell for being late but was also asking him what the problem was. We wanted him to make sure that there was no ambush or double cross.

Everything seemed okay. Abdu and I walked over to the truck and peeked in the back. The truck appeared to be Russian or Italian. I hadn't seen one like it before. Bigger than a large pickup but smaller than a dump.

This thing was loaded to the hilt with propane. Only one of the devices that we'd "worked on" had been all high explosives. All the others were propane. I thought it funny to later sit in meetings at CIA Headquarters or the FBI Academy and listen to the hundred-pound heads talk about how impossible it was to use propane as the main charge. I couldn't say a word.

This truck was an ugly one. It was for a suicide driver. There was a safe/arm switch used to manually arm the device on the dash. Just a small toggle switch that has an off and an on position. There was then a handheld button that laid in the seat waiting for the bomber to flip the toggle to arm, then press the button, becoming a warm, red cloud and a memory.

Only nasty thing about this one was that there was a pressure-release switch wired to the seat. If the bomber armed the device then changed his mind about pressing the button, the bomb would detonate when he got out of the truck because the removal of his/her weight would close the circuit. This truck was on a dry run and the driver was taking it back to the factory. This one was easy.

"Is this driver a bad guy?" I asked, being careful not to be overheard.

Abdu said, "He is very bad. He arranges to kill, but takes money for killing his own."

I said, "Let's reward him for his loyalty."

Abdu smiled.

Abdu cut the toggle switch out of the circuit completely. Now it was hot-wired directly from the pressure-release switch in the seat. When the guy got back to the factory and got out of the truck...surprise! We finished our work and cringed when the driver got back in the truck—we sure hoped he didn't forget something and have to get out.

We followed him down the hill at a safe distance just in case. He turned and headed toward the Green Line. That took a lot of balls. We watched as he crossed unhampered. Sometimes the Green Line was wide open. There wouldn't even be guards. Lucky for him, them, and us this was one of those days. Abdu and I shook hands like a couple of football players who just scored a touchdown.

As we pulled in front of Joseph's tent we heard a loud but muffled rumble. We looked across the bay toward West Beirut and saw the large black cloud. Even in the distance we could see the glittery sparklers created by a propane explosion.

I asked Abdu to give me a lift back to my apartment. We drove in silence until we arrived. The Hindu laborers were happy to see me. They grinned and waved and yelled.

"Abdu, come on up and have a beer," I invited.

Abdu hesitated, then smiled and said, "Okay, good, thank you."

Two or three beers later the MTT guys came dragging in after a day at the range. They looked beat. Chris grabbed a beer and I introduced Abdu to everyone. Manny and Santiago were headed to the Gold Souk shop. Chris was gonna hang back with us and drink beer. After the other two departed, Chris glanced from me to Abdu and back.

Then he broke out into a huge grin and asked, "What have you fuckers really been up to?"

We just laughed and I said, "Admin bullshit, man. Somebody thought it would be good for relations to give LF some training, so here we are."

Chris chugged a gulp, "Bullshit!" That's all that was ever said.

The next morning I rode into the embassy with the team guys. I told Santiago that I had to see Larry. He gave me a disgusted look and said, "Okay, go ahead."

I took the steps two at a time then pressed the buzzer and was let in immediately. The fat guys working on the communications gear barely glanced up.

Larry was in his cigarette smoke-filled office and on the phone. He frantically waved me in then motioned for me to take a seat. I could tell that the phone conversation was one-sided, with Larry doing the listening.

At last, "Okay, okay, will do, I'll take care of it." He hung up.

"What happened yesterday?" he immediately asked.

"Nothing unusual that I know of except the driver was about half an hour late," I responded, starting to feel the need for defense and caution.

"Tell me exactly what went down from the time you and Abdu departed, until you returned."

I went through everything as best I could remember. I told him that the old man seemed nervous so we were watching for anything. I also repeated that the driver was at least half an hour late.

Larry listened intently, never interrupting. Then he asked, "How did you re-wire the detonator?" I told him without getting too deep in the weeds. He nodded and appeared thoughtful.

"We may have a problem," he said.

That's the second time in as many days that I'd heard someone say that "we may have a problem."

Larry said, "Nobody can verify it, but the truck may not have made it back to the factory. He might have stopped on the way."

"We saw him cross the Green Line and enter the west before we headed back," I offered.

"No matter, it's okay where it went off, but now some other groups are involved and they're pissed," Larry said. "They are familiar with the MTT guys and now they are aware that you've been working for me. All of West Beirut is blaming the MTT for this explosion."

Larry never said where the bomb went off and I never asked. Didn't want to know. What I did know was that Larry wanted to know where the other guys were. I told him they were in the RSO's office.

"Good, let's go." He headed towards his door with a fast pace. We busted into Kevin's office and found the other guys sitting around drinking coffee.

Kevin looked up and saw the expression on Larry's face. "Do we need to be left alone?" he asked almost nervously.

"No, this is for all hands," he responded.

"Let's have it."

Larry started by explaining that there were certain elements within the guard force that were well-placed agents from the west. He wanted to keep them in place for reasons stated before. They had, however, been reporting to the west that the MTT guys were actually CIA and that the U.S. was getting ready to come back to Beirut. He continued, "To them this detonation was all you guys' fault. We have to get you to Cyprus ASAP. We can wait out there for a week or two then bring you back when it cools off."

I watched the reaction of the guys and it ranged from happy to be going to Cyprus to being disappointed for not heading home. Only Chris looked at me and winked.

Kevin said, "Let me make a call and see if I can get you guys out tomorrow."

"Negative," Larry said. "I have message traffic, assigning this top level priority. Call the Marine Amphibious Unit (MAU) now and tell them you have a National Command Authority (NCA) level request. Have them depart now—they should be here in about an hour." The NCA was the highest level decision makers in the United States.

He turned to us and said, "Take two Marines and go get your gear. I'll grab the gunny and let him know what's up. Let's do it!"

I asked Larry if he was coming out with us. He said that he had some paperwork to do. Just another day at the office for that guy. Within two hours we were over the Med headed for Cyprus. We got to the hotel in Ionapa and spent the next ten days relaxing and doing absolutely nothing.

On the tenth day Santiago came down to breakfast with a big grin on his face. "We're headed out this afternoon." Manny could've cared less either way. Chris and I said, "Yeah, let's go!"

Santiago looked at us and said, "No, no, we're going home."

You could've knocked me down. I had unfinished business in Beirut: Larry, Abdu, and Joseph. What about them? They were in the shit, too. I told Santiago that I really needed to go back in.

He looked at me like I was crazy. "Look, you might have had fun playing with Larry but it's over now and we're going home."

I wanted to punch his puss-gutted face in. All those people taking chances on a daily basis and this turd wanted to go home and indulge in the valium that he'd purchased in Beirut.

Nevertheless, that afternoon we found ourselves on a British Airways flight headed to London. Nobody on the team asked any questions about what I did. There was a lot of speculation about our hurried departure.

Santiago made the comment that the bad guys probably heard that we were "like Delta Force."

Chris laughed like hell and said, "Yeah, I'm sure you scared the shit out of them." What a month.

CHAPTER ELEVEN

Cairo MTT

After a month like that, anything else we did stateside was boring as hell. When we got back, Abe (our MTT chief) called me in.

"What the fuck happened on this trip?" I doubted that he'd been read in so I skirted the issue.

"Apparently there was some internal politics goin' on in the west and they tried to use us as the scapegoat."

"Yeah, that's what I hear." He continued, "Sure is some strange stuff that goes on in that country."

I'd forgotten that Abe had spent several years there until he got his ass blown away. Abe must have been made happy that I confirmed what he'd heard. Either that or he knew and was told to keep his mouth shut. Neither of us would ever know.

When we headed back to BSR the Navy guys were more actively involved in our training. Some of the guys had even been down to Bragg to train with the real Delta guys. I never made one of those trips—never really wanted to. I enjoyed the training I was receiving and the brief spurts of excitement but I had no visions of grandeur. I developed good relationships with a few of the guys that have lasted many years.

Frank and Larry of *Rogue Warrior* fame and Ho-Ho (Timmy, now deceased) were especially good friends. We trained and partied every day together. Many good times were had and they are those kinds of memories that you wonder how you survived. Boys will be boys. We were slated for another MTT but this one was Cairo. I made several trips to Cairo as a member of an MTT but later I spent a great deal of time there as a private contractor. That will come later.

The Cairo MTT was locked. New team leader Josh. Great guy and one hell of a lot more the operator than Santiago. As a matter of fact, the entire team was good. Chris was back on board with a new addition, Keith. We all seemed to mesh and even Chris didn't find anything to bitch about. Only gripe he had was that Keith was a workout nut and Chris was a fat body.

What saved it was the fact that Keith was a really good guy. We went through all the same pre-deployments as before. We didn't care about cover because we were going to a safe area. We partied all the way there and arrived somewhere around 2000. We got through passport control and went to luggage claim. Our bags were lost.

We cleared customs easy enough since we had no luggage. We were staying at the Nile Hilton. We had a standing operating procedure that we learned from our Navy buddies. We checked in and went to our rooms. We waited about an hour, then went downstairs and told them that our rooms stunk, or there was mold, or whatever. We would insist on another room, preferably on a different floor. We never stayed on the first or top floor. Most hotels tried to accommodate the embassy for two reasons. They wanted the business and the local government wanted access to us. When we changed rooms it threw a monkey wrench into their bugs or surveillance equipment. In some countries we changed hotels at the last minute.

Josh was on the phone with Pan Am non-stop trying to locate our luggage. It was all personal stuff because the training gear and weapons were in the pouches. We had those. Josh did one hell of a job. Late the next day, after we'd checked into the embassy, Pan Am sent a representative over with a check for $1,800 for each of us. The next day we went out clothes shopping.

I was told that Egyptian wool and cotton was the best in the world so I went to a tailor to have a couple of suits made. Never, ever, give top-notch Egyptian wool or cotton to an Egyptian tailor. My suits looked like a shoebox with four toilet paper tubes sticking out for legs and arms. We got by with some jeans and sneakers and t-shirts.

Two days later our luggage showed up at the hotel. John called Pan Am and told them we'd spent the money. They said, "No problem, keep the money." Cairo was a fun trip but not without a few events.

We coordinated with the RSO, Daniel "Don't call me Danny" Wishburne. Another super guy that I got close to. There was a cute blond nurse who worked in the embassy dispensary. Daniel was married and was not the type of guy who would fool around, but like most middle-aged guys, he liked the flattery of a young, cute girl paying attention to him. When we rolled in, I was nothing to look at, but Keith and Josh were pretty boys and Keith was a big guy with a good build. This little nurse stopped flirting with Daniel and turned it on them. She even came to the hotel one weekend to hang out at the pool with us. Daniel never said anything but he was pissed.

Keith and I were in the head taking a leak and I told Keith, "Man, Daniel is pissed. He wants that little nurse and she's shit-canned him for you guys. If he wasn't married he'd be trying to get in her pants."

I heard a voice come from one of the crapper stalls, "Frank, it doesn't bother me at all."

Holy hell, Daniel was in the head when I was talking about him. I felt like an asshole.

I'm sure Daniel shared that feeling with me. On the weekend that the nurse came over to the hotel I was lying next to the pool with Chris, drinking beer. Normal for Chris and I. Josh and Keith were shopping and you could tell the nurse was not happy with their absence. She was in street clothes but had a beach bag with her. She sat and ordered a drink.

I asked, "Do you want to change?"

She nodded, so I tossed her my key and told her to use my room. She headed upstairs and Chris and I continued to drink. I told Chris, "If Josh and Keith weren't so straight they could get next to the nurse."

"Yeah, but those pencil necks wouldn't know what to do with it," Chris replied as he took another drink.

The nurse came back down and crossed the pool deck to our chairs like someone was chasing her. She sat down and looked around and handed me my key.

"What's wrong?" I asked.

"There are two guys and a lady in your room. They were working on your telephone."

I glanced at Chris and we communicated without talking. I nodded toward her, and Chris acknowledged with a nod. He was to take care of her and I headed to my room. All that we had were Model 60 Smith & Wesson revolvers. Not much for a firefight but okay in a hotel room.

I keyed my door and burst into the room. One guy was still there and he was in a hotel uniform. He was standing by my phone and looked like he was gonna shit when he saw the Mod 60.

I held it on him and asked, "What are you doing?"

He was scared shit and responded, "We have phone problems so we are checking all phones."

"Bullshit, get out. If you come back without my knowledge we will deal with management through the embassy."

He scurried out with many apologies. After the door clicked shut I went to the phone. I first unscrewed the ear piece and it looked normal. I then unscrewed the cover of the mouth piece. There was a small, clear green electronic chip wired in with the microphone part of the mouth piece. It had circuitry inside that was visible. We had an embassy number that we were to call in the event of an emergency. This was no emergency but I felt compelled to convey this incident. I went to the lobby looking for a house phone.

Finding one, I called Daniel and told him that I needed to speak to him or someone concerning a purchase I'd made at the *souk*. This was a prearranged signal that there was no danger but important information. If I had said, "Join us for dinner," that would have been a distress code for "Send the Calvary."

Daniel replied, "I'll be in first thing tomorrow." His response that he was on it. I went down to the lobby and Daniel was there in about fifteen minutes. He had a guy with him who looked like he'd just got back from a vacation in Key West: shorts, sandals and a ball cap that had a "B" for Boston.

I explained what had happened and the guy with Daniel said, "Leave it in place, just don't use the phone. I'll give you more guidance tomorrow. Make sure you tell the other team guys." Daniel told me that he'd see me in the morning, and they left.

I went back down to the pool and Chris asked what was up, but he did it with his eyes only.

The nurse was nervous as hell and she rattled, "Did you catch them? Were they still there? What were they doing?"

I smiled and said, "It's okay. They're having phone problems in the hotel so they're checking out the system from every room. You know how these big hotels are, try to make everything perfect."

She turned it off as fast as she turned it on. She grabbed her towel and headed toward the pool. When she got out of earshot I told Chris to go up and check his phone. He knew what to do. He was back before the nurse returned from her swim. He shrugged and gave a negative indicator. He had question marks in his eyes but said nothing. The nurse strolled back over, drying her short blond hair. She said that she would have to head back to the embassy. She pulled on her street clothes, obviously not happy with using either of our rooms. You could also tell that the only reason for her visit was Josh or Keith.

After she departed I looked around to make sure no one was listening.

Sitting on the edge of my lounge chair with my elbows on my knees, I whispered, "They bugged my phone. I called Daniel and he brought by a seventh floor guy." I continued, "We'll hook up with him tomorrow."

I told Chris to let Josh and Keith know so that they could check their phones. I didn't want to do it in case I was being watched as well.

I didn't sleep well that night. I guess the thought of the phone right next to my head and someone on the other end put me on edge. As you travel the way we do, you understand that there's Hostile Surveillance, Friendly Surveillance, and Host

Nation Surveillance. I had no idea which this was. That was up to the guys on the seventh floor.

I was up by 0600 and headed to the gym. Keith was already there, as was normal. He had his Walkman ears on and was on the stair climber. He saw me and threw a friendly wave in my direction. I could hear Bruce Springsteen overflowing from his headphones.

I hit the treadmill. He finished up, grabbed a bottle of water, and waited for me to finish. He bounced around on a couple of weight machines. I cooled down and he walked over to where I was recovering and said, "Neither Josh nor I have a problem." I knew what he meant and nodded.

We all met for breakfast, then decided to walk to the embassy. It was only a few blocks and all of our equipment had been staged. Keith bopped along as always with the Walkman firmly in place. He was counting on us to be observant. We got to the embassy and cleared the Post One Marine. He was having the normal early morning problems. It seemed like all the Egyptian workers arrived at the same time and wanted to go in at once.

When the Egyptian guards saw us they intensified their search efforts in order to impress the team. This further disrupted everything, creating havoc for the Marine. We went into Daniel's office and his secretary brought us coffee. Daniel picked up his phone and called the guy who had accompanied him to the hotel yesterday.

"He'll be down in a few," Daniel said as he replaced the phone. Finally the guy walked in and for the first time I was introduced. His name was given as Teddy.

He asked, "How did you know that the phone was bugged?"

I went through the entire incident and could tell that Daniel was uncomfortable with the mention of the nurse looking for Josh or Keith. Of course those two completely denied any involvement.

"How many people did she see in your room?" Teddy continued his questioning.

"She said there were three: two men and a woman."

Teddy, the seventh floor guy, looked at Daniel (I started thinking that your name had to be Abe, Al or Daniel to work at DSS) and said, "We're gonna do a little psy-op with these folks. Frank, don't use your phone anymore. Don't call out unless you're instructed to do so. I want you to answer every call. Each day I'll give you a sheet of paper that will have a script for you to follow when we call you. At the top of that sheet will be a challenge and response code so that you'll know it's us. You just answer, and ask the questions on your script and we'll have some fun. Here's your sheet for tonight."

As it turned out there was nothing exciting and each day it was just a series of questions and answers that made no sense to me and I'm sure it made no sense to whoever was listening. The seventh floor was having great fun, though.

We were to make another trip to Cairo in 1986 but that is another story. We finished our training in Cairo without incident and packed up to head home. This was, by far, the most pleasant trip as far as teammates go. The most interesting thing was to happen when I got home.

We got back to Washington, D.C. Saturday morning just before noon. We went to the range and the ever-present Joe was waiting like a mother hen. He tried to act like he was just there to shoot but we all knew better. We cleaned and sorted our weapons and training equipment. Joe went over it all with a fine-toothed comb. He liked all of us so he really screwed with us. "What did you clean this with, sandpaper?" or "Wife too busy to wash this shit?" He was full of joy.

We got everything secured at last. Susan had just arrived to pick me up. No secret as to where I'd been or what I was doing. We were super happy. Stephen was strapped in his carseat and talking a mile a minute. He wanted all of my conscious time. We stopped and got pizza and a pitcher of beer.

After Almaza in Beirut, Stella in Cairo, dark bitters in England, and warm German beer, this stuff tasted like piss (or what I imagine piss would taste like). Once filled and at home I fell into my cheap recliner. Susan would have none of that. We had a few things to take care of and talk was just a small part of it. I must say I was very happy to be home. She didn't need to do a float test!

I was up early the next morning, as I was still eight hours ahead. Jetlag seemed to be a constant companion. I worked out on the weight bench in the garage. Went inside to get a cup of coffee from the freshly brewed pot. I had to make the coffee—like the beer, Susan's was weak; it tasted like hot water. I made mine with twice the normal scoops of Folgers. I went back out to the garage and saw the newspaper laying in the drive way. I walked out and picked it up, unrolling it as I walked back into the garage. I sat on the weight bench and opened the paper to the front page.

Holy shit!! Right on the front page in bold type: "Two Diplomats Shot in Cairo." I frantically scanned down and read Daniel's name and his assistant RSO, Hawke. I read the details and it said they'd been attacked under the bridge on the way home from work. Three assailants had opened fire on them when they slowed for traffic. They survived. I quickly went inside and was moving so fast that I awoke Susan.

She came downstairs with sleep in her eyes asking, "Where's my damn coffee?" This was a joke between us as she was mimicking her father who always started the morning with "Where's my damn coffee?" She saw how frantic I was and walked over and poured herself a cup.

"This stuff looks like mud," she evaluated as she looked into the cup. "What's wrong, what are you doing?"

"Daniel has been hit!" She didn't know Daniel from Adam but she was, and always has been, smart enough to leave me alone when I'm mission-oriented. I was digging in my gun bag for my phone index. I finally found it and tore it open to Cairo embassy. I had no hope of reaching Daniel or Hawke but I hoped someone could tell me what was going on. There was an answer on the third ring. I had dialed the number that Daniel gave me that went straight into the RSO's office.

I heard the phone click as it was picked up and I heard Daniel's voice say, "RSO." At first I was thinking "recorder" but the voice repeated again, "RSO, can I help you?"

"Daniel," I blurted with excitement! I told him about reading the story in the paper. At first I thought the article was false but Daniel told me it was true. Just after we departed he and Hawke were working late and decided to ride home together. Under the bridge, the same one we identified as a choke point, they struck. They had to have been watching Daniel for a while. It was a bonus for the tangos that Hawke was along. If Daniel had been the target a more professional attack team would have cancelled the attack. History has proven that tangos plan meticulously, down to the most finite detail. If something happens that is a variance from the norm, they will abort. The fact that another person was with Daniel was a change from the norm. Even a change that minute would have disrupted the attack cycle.

Daniel told me that he would like to attribute his survival to my superior driver instruction but it was only luck. He explained that one guy was on the overpass and two were on the sidewalk. When they opened fire Daniel and Hawke had trouble getting to their weapons. Daniel pointed the car at the guys on the side-walk and floor boarded it. He hit one of the tangos and the other two panicked. The wounded one was dragged away, leaving Daniel and Hawke wounded. Daniel just received a flesh wound; Hawke was a little more serious but he would recover.

I told Daniel that he did learn from us. "Never, ever stop fighting." No matter how hopeless it may seem, take the fight to the bad guys. They don't expect it.

We chatted a while. I told him to tell fat-assed Hawke to get well and don't lay up in bed too long. Daniel said he would pass the word and we hung up.

This incident never got much press. I never saw it on TV and I don't recall this incident being used as a training model as we did other attacks and victims. Never understood why, but I'd learned that there were a ton of things that happened at State that I didn't understand.

CHAPTER TWELVE

United Nations
General Assembly

Once I got back to work and assumed the old routine I was bored crazy. I'd go to the range, get bored. Go to BSR, get bored. I knew what was bothering me but I never shared it. The fortieth United Nations General Assembly (UNGA) was approaching and it was supposed to be a huge event with folks coming in from all over the world to celebrate. I decided to check back in with Abe to see what the MTT schedule might be like. Some of the MTT guys were getting disenchanted and now realized that it took a lot of work to be "kinda like Delta Force" and still didn't make a pimple on Delta's ass.

Abe was in his office and looked up as I walked in. It had been almost two weeks since Cairo, and we were standing down the international stuff to prepare for the UNGA. He was up to his ears in that never-ending stream of unorganized paper. I'm not sure if he ever knew for sure what was under that pile. He grinned and told me that there weren't to be any more trips until after the UNGA. That was a month away. There was a great deal of planning that went into an op like the UNGA. Sight advances, setting up the command posts, renting vehicles, staging equipment, etc. Just when you finished it was time to tear it all down and bring it home. Pain in the ass.

Anybody who has worked protection knows that it's not romantic or sexy as portrayed on TV or at the movies. It is hard work and long hours. Doesn't matter if you're working for State, Secret Service, or some chunky little Arab prince. At least you get a laugh or two with the chunky prince.

Chunky prince details are tougher, though, because you don't carry a badge or credentials; you're on your own. When I worked for the Saudis we normally hired off-duty local law enforcement guys and gals. They were great. Didn't have to be trained, and blended well when we had to do surveillance detection ops. Don't want to get too far ahead.

Abe said that I was to be chopped back to Dignitary Protection (DP) with the rest of the guys. If something came up we could be pulled back but for now our focus was in New York. President Reagan was to be there and there were to be a few joint protection details. We never protected the President or any heads of state. We got everybody else.

I went back to my desk and called Tony at Dignitary Protection (DP). He said that he was up to his ass but if I could get my equipment together he'd have it shipped up to the Summit Hotel. I said that I hadn't unpacked since the last detail. All I had to do was throw in some new batteries for the handheld metal detectors, and I'd be set.

The month passed fast as it does when you're dreading an event. I hated protection work with a passion. One thing that I tried to do as much as possible was to go out and relieve the agents on post. These poor guys and gals would stand on their assigned post for an hour, then "rotate." They would "push" each other. That means that post one would move to post three, three would then move to four and so on. This was designed to keep the agents alert and show a change of face from time to time. The main thing that it accomplished was a bunch of pissed-off agents. At least when I came by to relieve them for a few minutes, bring a cup of coffee, or just shoot the bull, they appreciated it. I made some good friends on those days.

I arrived at the Summit Hotel early and unpacked my suits. Another thing I hated about protection was the suit, and especially the tie. This was an every day suit-wearing operation. In those days you had so much crap to wear under the coat: Radio with all the miles of wire for the hand-button, earpiece, and plug-in. Then came the gun and ammo. Then the handcuffs. I couldn't arrest anybody because of Posse Comitatus but I had to carry all the same crap anyhow. It took half an hour to undress and much longer to dress. Everybody had to do it, so I'll quit bitching.

We went through the normal protective song and dance: to the airport, pick up a principal, then back to the U.N. Plaza, drop them off, and do it again.

Through the airport with badges held up saying, "on the job, on the job." It all ran together after a few days.

One morning Dick called me in and asked, "Have you ever done any penetration-type stuff? Abe tells me that you guys are hooked up with Red Cell and I know that they do that kind of thing."

I told him, "No, I never have."

He laughed and said, "Think you can get some guys into the U.N. before the UNGA?" He further explained that the Agent in Charge (AIC) of the New York field office was an old buddy of his by the name of Pat H. He and Pat had been talking about the physical security of the UNGA and Dick had said that "anybody can get in there."

Pat was also referred to jokingly as the "High Sheriff." He was involved in everything that went on. Big, heavy-set guy who seemed like he could sweat in a freezer. Balding, with an ever-present handkerchief in his hand that he used to wipe the sweat off his head. He walked with his feet out turned and his upper thighs continuously rubbing together, much more like a waddle than a walk. His shirttail was always half out and his tie askance. But this guy would walk into a room and take over. He had that type of personality. Didn't care who or what you were; rank meant nothing. He was a likeable guy and when I first met him he and I hit it off.

Anyway, Dick asked if I'd like to take a couple of my Army EOD guys and try to get in. I smiled at the opportunity to not be bored.

I said, "I've got just the crew."

Dick stood up laughing and said, "Just don't cause a commotion might piss somebody off." He told me to just get inside and try to get a photo. "Don't penetrate the inner perimeter.

The Secret Service isn't here yet but they may have an advance team out."

He kept putting qualifiers on so that finally I held up my hand and said, "Don't worry, Dick, I'll keep my mouth shut and you can deny any involvement." He was as happy as a kid. He and Pat were old-time buddies and this was sure to be a bet of some type. Dick asked when I was gonna do it.

I laughed and said, "I ain't gonna tell ya. My luck, you'd tell him we're coming just to make it exciting."

I went back to the Summit and went to the command post. Three or four of the Army EOD guys were lounging around, waiting for the next search assignment. I asked where the Sergeant First Class was. He was the senior man assigned, and a good egg. The young corporal on duty picked up the house phone and pushed a couple of numbers.

Finally he said, "Sergeant Palmer, Mr. Skinner wants to see you." He then replaced the receiver without further comment. Just a few minutes passed before the sergeant came in to the CP.

"What's up, sir?"

I told him to follow me and let's have a beer. He looked confused but had been in the Army long enough to know it wasn't about the beer. He knew I had more on my mind. We went to my room and I opened the mini bar and told Palmer to help himself, which he did. I gave him a rundown on what Dick had requested. Palmer looked at me deadpan as I talked. When I finished he broke into a huge grin.

"We gonna get in trouble, sir?"

I told him that I hoped not, but I'd take all the heat if it went sideways.

Palmer asked me how many folks needed to be involved.

"The girl and two or three others. You pick 'em." I could tell that Palmer liked my style. I delegated and got the hell out of the way.

He went over and picked up the phone. He told the person on the other end to get a girl and two other guys who he trusted.

Apparently Sergeant Palmer delegated, too. I was amazed. In less than ten minutes all three were in my room. I allowed the sergeant to brief them and I answered the questions. Everybody was on board and looked forward to anything that would break the monotony.

First thing in the morning our young lady and Corporal Rivas would head over to the U.N. and see just how far they could get. They would go in as Army EOD in support of the State Department. The only requirement I placed on them was that they were to produce no ID if it was requested. They were to tell the security folks that since they were U.S. Army they weren't allowed to carry badges and Posse Comitatus prevented them form carrying military ID. We'd see how far they got. In my mind this was just a probe that would test security. This would be our dry run. From that we would come up with a plan. Man, was I surprised!

We planned to meet in the lobby the next morning. I was out of the gym and at breakfast forty-five minutes prior to our scheduled departure.

Sergeant Palmer was already at breakfast so I joined him. He told me that Rivas had just left and would be back down shortly. Palmer had eaten already but was enjoying a cup of coffee. We exchanged small talk about EOD and where each of us had been. I paid the check and we headed into the lobby.

Rivas and Cole (the female Army PFC) were waiting. Cole looked very nice and presentable this morning. She had a dark blue pantsuit on with a crisp, white blouse. (I always liked that contrast, male suit or female.)

We went to the car and loaded up. I drove with Palmer right front and Cole and Rivas in the rear. Rivas had brought his camera and asked should he carry it in.

"Absolutely, even have it hanging around your neck. Don't hide it," I told him. "Let's see how they react. Sometimes if you're overt, security will overlook the obvious." We were soon to find out.

I pulled up in front of the U.N. main entrance and Cole and Rivas got out. They were untrained for this type stuff, as were we all, but they looked good together. He was Hispanic, as you probably picked up by his name, and she was a tall blond, also from from Kentucky and as country as a butter bean.

They walked toward the overpowering entrance to the international governing building. I pulled away from the curb and headed toward the parking lot at the rear.

Palmer and I got out and strolled around the park area behind the U.N. building. We both noticed that the building backed up to the water. The pier was empty of boats or people. It was a large dock that could accommodate several large vessels. None was present. Palmer and I were both thinking what a barge loaded with ammonium nitrate and fuel oil (ANFO) could do if tied up behind the U.N. building. There appeared to be no waterside security whatsoever. Of course, we must remember this was pre-9/11.

We strolled around the park for about an hour and finally Rivas came out with a huge grin on his face. He started talking before he got in earshot.

"Sergeant Palmer, you guys follow me. You ain't gonna believe this shit."

Sergeant Palmer asked where Cole was. Rivas said that she was still inside waiting for us. We followed him, looking back and forth, trying to figure what was going on. I finally asked Rivas if we were walking into an ambush.

He laughed and replied, "Just stand by, sir, you ain't gonna believe it." We went around to the front entrance from the rear park area. Rivas led the way at a fast pace, much like a small child does when he wakes mom and dad up on Christmas morning and has them follow him to the goodies under the tree. We approached a series of big glass doors and Rivas held a set open for us. Cole was inside with a small, neatly uniformed, black U.N. guard.

Rivas escorted us up and introduced us. He told the guard that we were his bosses from Diplomatic Security and could we now see those meeting places. "Yes, sir," the guard nodded, and said for us to follow him. Rivas and Cole both had cameras and were taking pictures like crazy. The guard said nothing.

I whispered to Rivas that there were to be no pictures of the guard. I refused to get this guy in trouble. His boss would no doubt catch hell but it would be up to him to figure out who let us in. Nobody had shown any form of ID.

We went into the U.N. General Assembly area and took turns posing for photos on the lectern and in the seat of the U.S. ambassador; and I sat in the Lebanese ambassador's seat. It was crazy. I'm just glad that a few of these photos are contained in this book; otherwise there would be some "You're full of shit's." We then filed behind the guard as he took us into another room: the U.N. Security Council. I couldn't believe our ability to get in so easy. Rivas must have lain on a line of B.S. a mile long. The guard treated Palmer and me like royalty. God only knew who we were supposed to be. The pictures kept clicking in this chamber as well.

Dick was gonna have a ball shoving this one in Pat's ass. I had only hoped to get enough intel to plan a penetration. We got that and more. I'd get these photos developed by Tony at DP because this wasn't something you turned in to the one-hour Photo mat.

Tony could get them turned around within twenty-four hours. (We didn't have digital in those days.) The guard clearly wanted to show us more. He was enthusiastic about his job and about these VIPs that he was showing around. We wanted to get the hell out before somebody got wise to his absence and found us, then took our film. We smiled, shook hands, and headed for the car.

Rivas, to no one specific, said again, "Can you believe that shit!" Cole was excited, too. Her eyes were dancing. She only wanted to know if she could keep a few of the photos. I doubted it but I told her I'd check with Dick.

We got back to the CP and I went by Dick's office. I told him we'd done a dry run and would get back to him. He held a thumbs up gesture as a "Can you do it?"

I smiled and nodded and he got back to what he was doing. I had four rolls of 35mm film in my pocket and I was headed down to the basement to catch up with Tony. I'd be lucky to catch him in, as that guy stayed busy as hell on the protective ops. Luckily I caught him but he was headed out the door.

I asked if he could do me and "Dick" a favor, throwing Dick's name out there to give it credibility. He told me he was headed out the door—What did I need? I held up the film and asked if he could get it developed. He said that he could, and to just throw it on his desk.

"Not these, big guy. We gotta be careful about who sees them." Now this stopped him in his tracks. Tony was an old retired Army SF guy. He missed the action and this presented itself as a little out of the ordinary.

"What is it?" he asked.

"Common stuff, Tony. You know I can't tell and besides that, I know that you're gonna look at them when you get 'em back."

He laughed and nodded. He walked over and grabbed the film and dropped it into his jacket pocket. I'll have it for you by midnight. "Good man," I told him and headed back upstairs.

The next day, after going through all the photos in my room, I walked back down to Dick's office next to the CP. As usual, he was there. Being the Agent in Charge (AIC) of Dignitary Protection (DP) was second only in stress to the job of AIC of the Secretaries of States detail. Both of these guys were working when they were off. I dropped the envelope on his desk and at first he seemed irritated. He glanced at the bulging envelope and then back to my smiling face. His eyes got bigger than two shit can lids as he tore open the envelope.

"Jesus H., how did you get these? Did somebody have these and you bought them? Pat ain't gonna believe these are real."

I held the other envelope in my coat pocket. The ones Dick had contained no people and could have been taken at any time. I produced the second envelope without a word. He tore that open and slumped in his chair.

"How in the hell did you pull that off?" he sighed. I didn't want to give up my secrets. Sometimes a little mystery goes a long way. I told him that the whos, whats, whens, and whys didn't matter. I had gotten what was asked for and more. He just shook his head and looked at me.

"Buy me a beer sometimes," I said over my shoulder as I departed his office. I heard him laughing until I entered the EOD CP. Palmer was there, as were Cole and Rivas. They looked at me expectantly. I told them that Dick was very happy with their efforts. We would probably see a bright flash and a mushroom cloud when Pat opened those envelopes. Great fun, and it beat hell out of sitting around the CP.

The fortieth UNGA went off without further incident. Dick insisted that I join him and Pat for dinner prior to our departure. Dick also said, "Why don't you pick a couple of the EOD folks to join us?"

I told Palmer, Cole, and Rivas to wear their Sunday best because we were going out. We had a fine meal with wine and Dewar's Scotch. Had to cost a fortune. Pat picked up the tab. I had learned what the bet was. Boys will be boys.

We finished up and shipped all of our equipment back to HQ. I'd run into a few of the MTT guys but they were busy providing security to the high threat principals. Cuban, Iranian, Libyan, Syrian, Lebanese. All the fun guys. Aziz the Sleaze was there from Iraq and he looked like he needed a shower twenty-four and seven. Him and his cigar in the back of a sealed limo was a little much for the strongest stomach. Most of us MTT guys enjoyed a cigar from time to time, but in the wide open spaces.

We got back on Thursday and went to the office. Abe was there and saw us headed from the elevator. He stopped us and said, "Unless it directly affects Democracy, I want everybody out of here 'til Monday. Now, get!"

We checked our in boxes and mail boxes. I had nothing except a reminder to renew my diplomatic passport. I'd have to look into that because mine was still good. It was full of visa stamps but good.

I spent a great three day weekend with Susan and Stephen. Both were happy to have me home. Of course, I got the "When you leaving again?" question.

I answered honestly that I didn't know. We departed in a hurry and no word was passed.

Author in Ambassadors follow car

Susan said, "It scares me when they give you a day off."

I hadn't thought about it like that. Well, we'd worry about that Monday.

Stephen was approaching four and he demanded time which I was more than happy to give. When we adopted Stephen we knew that he had inherited a major medical problem. This was to cause us all a great deal of grief and worry over the next years. We were told on three occasions that he had limited time, but he is now almost twenty-six and still talking 100 miles an hour, normally.

Some of the other guys began to trickle in and the bullshit commenced. Good-natured joking and ribbing. Two guys were still up in New York with the Foreign Minister of Kinshasa, Zaire (now called the Congo). What was funny is that one of the guys had been assigned to the embassy in Kinshasa. He said this minister rode around in an old VW with a fender missing and smoking like hell. He comes to New York and gets a limo and a protective detail. I guess we need to spend tax dollars somewhere. Until the day I hang it up, I'll never understand all the things that I witnessed.

Abe was getting ready to give us an update. We apparently had some new trips on the schedule. We were all curious as to where we'd be headed. I knew Susan dreaded me coming home that night with the news. Abe and Joe had been meeting over at Joe's desk and we weren't privy to what was being said. Abe had his calendar and was writing furiously on it as Joe read some official message traffic. We were anxious, to say the least. Chris and I wanted Beirut and all the other guys wanted anything but.

CHAPTER THIRTEEN
Bogotá to Beirut
MTT Number Four

The straws had been drawn and the decisions made. Abe motioned us all over to Joe's desk. It was crowded, to say the least. Ten of us around Joe's desk. Manny, being Manny, hung back and appeared to not be listening. This guy really didn't seem to give a shit. I think that he did; it was just his persona.

Looked like the guys were splitting up. There was a trip on to Bogota, Cairo, Philippines, Beirut, and several to various countries in Central America, including El Salvador. Things were hot there also. We knew that Delta was operating there at the time. Who was to go where? Typical Abe, we'll play it by ear.

The trips were spread out so that we could all go if necessary but it wouldn't be cost-effective. The first on the schedule was Bogota. Abe said that Joe would like to go on this one even though he wasn't officially an MTT guy anymore. Joe had been to Bogota numerous times and it made sense. Abe was told that Mike also wanted to go so it was to be me, Mike, and Joe. I told Abe he should send another team guy so that we would have some depth. He nodded and asked if anyone else wanted Bogota. There was some looking back and forth and under-the-breath comments, but no one stepped forward.

Chris, in his normal diplomatic demeanor, said, "Come on guys, we can't all go to the Philippines." That got a laugh.

Abe said, "Let's get Bogota done, then we'll worry about the remainder."

I left the meeting and headed out to the range to see Joe. Hadn't seen him in a while and thought that would be a good time. He was there with a couple of agents on line re-qualifying. Joe was raising hell as usual. He saw me and came over to the door.

"Did you see Abe this morning?" he smiled behind his ever-present sunglasses.

"Yeah, I guess we're locked and cocked for Bogota next week," I answered.

He shook his head and made a negative comment under his breath about taking Mike, but Joe wasn't the type to badmouth someone unless they were present, in which case he totally enjoyed it. I had brought my gun bag with my Browning so I decided to put a few rounds down range. After about an hour I headed back to the office.

All of the normal fanfare preceded the departure to Bogota. Once we arrived, the embassy vehicle transported us to the RSO's office. I was impressed with my first exposure to South America, particularly Bogota. It wasn't dirty but the air was thin as we were at an extreme altitude. Hard to breathe.

We went to our hotel and checked in. Mike was a character and it would help if you knew him. (Some of you do.) We were carrying our Brownings but no sub guns. Mike's room was directly above mine. I had been briefed that Bogota was extremely dangerous. Not because of terrorism but because of the drug lords. They would kill or kidnap for no reason if they thought their product was being threatened. To the drug lords, everybody who came from the U.S. to visit the embassy in Bogotá was DEA. We were warned to have an active surveillance detection program in place.

As described before, Mike was a very religious man and a deacon in his church. I don't know if this contributed, but he always acted a little unconscious to his surroundings. It was even true in Beirut, if you recall. Still a nice guy and a pleasure to be around. Mike continued up the stairs when I peeled off to go to my room. I unlocked the door and surveyed the room.

Small, but nice and clean with a TV and minibar. All I needed. I opened my suitcase and then decided to take a leak before I unpacked. The toilets were vented through a pipe that ran from the top floor to the ground floor. By placing your ear to the pipe you could hear conversations in the attached rooms.

All of a sudden I heard the unmistakable sound of gunfire! One round, BANG!! It sounded like it came from above and I heard it reverberate through the pipe. Oh, shit!! Mike needs help. I grabbed my Browning and hauled ass up the stairs.

I flattened myself against the wall next to his door on the opening side. (That way, if someone cracked the door they couldn't see me before I saw them.) I could get a "T" shot at their brain stem before they knew I was there.

I tapped lightly on the door then moved back a few inches. Nothing. Now I'm thinking I'd better let Joe know what's going on. If I did that, Mike might be injured or worse. I decided to solo. I tapped again, louder this time.

I heard Mike's nervous baritone voice inside say, "Yes, who's there?"

"Mike, it's me!"

Then he said, "And who is me?"

Jesus, I thought, what's goin' on in that room? "Mike, it's Frank, the same guy that had this voice ten minutes ago."

The door cracked open and I waited. My gun wasn't pointed but it was at the "low ready."

Finally the muzzle of a Browning extended out the door and I yelled, "Mike, it's Frank, put the gun down!"

It lowered and I peeked around to see Mike standing there in his skivvies with a sheepish look on his face.

I asked him what the hell that noise was. He didn't ask, "What noise?" or appear to be surprised by the question.

He said, "Must have been a backfire or something of that nature." He was a very precise speaker and attempted to articulate words beyond his capability. It dawned on me what had happened. Mike had been screwing around with his Browning, which he wasn't that familiar with, and had an accidental discharge, or AD. Some units call them negligent discharges (NG).

I took a quick glance in Mike's room but he was blocking my entrance. It was obvious. I went back to my room shaking my head. We didn't count or inventory our ammo so nobody would know. I never said anything and Mike never brought it up.

We went to the embassy the next day and met with the RSO. He introduced us to the ambassador, who turned out to be a cool guy. While in his residence he would walk around in his bathrobe with a .357 magnum in his robe pocket. He had been trained and wasn't afraid to use it.

The RSO invited us to dinner that evening but Mike begged off. Joe, the RSO, and I walked past the Marine at post one. Marines were not allowed to leave the compound due to the recent murder of several Marines at a restaurant in El Salvador. The RSO walked up to the young, squared-away Marine lance corporal and said, "Hold the fort Marine, we're gonna go drink some beer and get some pussy."

The Marine didn't flinch or acknowledge. All I noticed, and that was because I was a Marine, was a tightening of the Marine's jaw muscles. He could kill but was too professional to comment. My jaw muscles clinched as well. Nobody but Joe knew that I was a Marine captain.

We went to a nice restaurant and had a large dinner laced with copious amounts of beer. We headed back to the embassy and as we approached this same young lance corporal, the RSO entered the door to post one. Post one was normally a glass-enclosed area from which the Marine on duty could observe what was happening.

The RSO ran his index finger under the Marine's nose and said, "That's as close as you'll get to pussy while you're here."

That Marine's jaw muscles were doing double time now. Mine were, too. I had enough. Joe was a retired Marine and I saw his jaws clenching right along with me and the Marine.

Joe nodded to me and I spun on the RSO.

"We need to talk now! Alone!" I was so firm that it shocked the RSO and the Marine's eyes were even wider. "Your office!"

We walked in and I could tell Joe was tickled. He loved confrontations of any kind. He especially didn't like this little pencil neck prick. I reached into my billfold and pulled my Military ID out. It clearly had my picture, my rank, and United States Marine Corps displayed. The RSO had seated himself behind his desk so as to assume the position of power. Little did he know that kinda shit didn't cut it with Marine captains. Especially ones who came up through the ranks and had been a sergeant. Nobody fucks with a sergeant's Marines, much less a captain's Marines. Nobody! I threw my ID card on his desk and stared. By luck it landed right side up; I don't think he would have lowered himself to touch it and turn it over. Curiosity got to him and he leaned over and studied it.

He slumped visibly. He was cool, though. "I guess I'm in deep shit now," he stated.

"If I *hadn't* been a Marine that would have pissed me off," I said through clinched teeth. I continued about levels of professionalism and leadership, with a few choice action verbs thrown in. I have to hand it to the guy. I guess he was just trying to impress me and Joe and it backfired. He got up and we followed him out to post one. The same Marine was still on duty and he visibly positioned himself at attention when we walked in.

The RSO said, "Marine, I owe you an apology. My earlier actions were uncalled for." He continued as he looked back and forth between me and the Marine, "I regret my indiscretions to you, in particular in the witness of a Marine captain."

The Marine glanced at me with my long hair and bushy mustache and man, was he confused. I winked and a slight smile broke out on the Marine's face. He came to very rigid attention and faced me squarely and rendered one of the sharpest salutes I've ever seen.

I must say I was never a salute nut, but that salute lives as one of the proudest moments of my life. One Marine telling another, I recognize you as a brother and warrior. Even though I had no cover (hat), I smartly returned his salute. The RSO really felt like shit, especially after that exchange. Joe was about to piss down one leg with glee.

The remainder of this MTT was uneventful. We completed the training and headed for the barn. That was my first and last trip to South America.

I was glad to be home. I asked Abe for a four-day weekend and he responded with a laugh, "Including Sunday?" We took the four days and visited my folks in the Smoky Mountains.

My Dad was a staunch Democrat and believed everything that was put out on the TV. He loved to debate politics. He asked one day as we sat outside looking down the mountain that he lived on, "This Beirut mess is something. We should get out of there altogether. Them Arabs (the first "A" pronounced long) will always fight. Them Muslims been fightin' for thousands of years."

I tried to explain a little about the real Beirut and the fact that there were a lot of Christians. Nothing I said mattered, even though I'd been there a number of times. The TV knew the truth, period. I gave up.

When I got back to the office I was curious to see what was up next. The Philippine trip was locked on. Four guys were headed out the following day. Fundamentalist activity down in the Batangas Islands was causing concern for embassy personnel. It had already spread to Manila.

I walked into Abe's office; he looked up and a huge grin spread over his face.

He said, "Hate to tell you this." My heart sank. How could they send anyone and not me? I quickly thought that my last adventures there may have kept me from getting back in.

He continued, to interrupt my self-pity, "You're headed back to Beirut. No funny stuff this time, just training."

That suited me. I intended to find out if Larry was still in country but I doubted it. I would imagine he was on the hot seat after I departed. I hadn't heard any more. It was almost like my previous trip had never happened. I was right. When I did some checking with the RSO and the RSO's secretary, Larry had departed about a month after we left. Nobody knew where he went and there was no way to find out.

Typical pre-deployment operation. Guns, dip pouches, lead sheets, letters, tickets, travel advances, and so on. You've been through a couple with me already so I won't bore you with Joe's bitching and clucking. We had no cover story this trip and were going in as an MTT. I was happy that Chris was going back, but unhappy that Santiago and Manny were also going in. At least they never bugged me about what I'd had to do. I was somewhat amazed that it never once came up when we got back.

The only thing Chris said was that I had to take him along if I did any fun stuff. I said that I would.

There was a new RSO assigned to Beirut and he now had an assistant. The RSO was the desk type, which was good for the ARSO, Jim. Jim was a shoot, move, and communicate kind of guy. He loved the people, the language, the food, and the culture. It showed in his every action and the people noticed it and loved him in return. He ended up marrying a beautiful Lebanese girl. I though that finally State had made a right assignment. As it turned out, State didn't think so. Apparently they didn't like for their RSO/ARSOs to get close to the people. Maybe they were right. But, it did seem to work out well. Jim did an outstanding job and lives happily with his wife in the states.

Chris was going to have a good time. The MAU had given the embassy two M60 machine guns with ammo. Six of the experienced guards were to be trained on them and Chris had trigger time on the M60. I had also been on the gun in Vietnam but that was a long time ago. We trained every day and in the evening I watched as the MTT guys gathered around the dining table and went over their time sheets. Being a Marine I worked 24/7. These assholes were getting overtime. I started to think about the training.

We'd shoot until about 1400 and Santiago would say, "Let's secure. We've reached the point of diminishing returns."

This happened every day. We'd head back and drink Almaza. On Saturday and Sunday Santiago would say, "We've got to shoot on the weekend because we lost so much time during the week." They were getting double time for working Saturday and Sunday. Screw that! I was working seven days a week so that they could scam.

The following Monday at 1400 Santiago again said, "Shut it down due to the point of diminishing returns." I didn't say anything but kept my guys shooting.

Santiago yelled, "Hey, Frank, secure your guys."

I turned and glared, "My guys are doing fine so I'm gonna stay out and let them shoot so that they don't have to work this weekend." Chris was grinning like a possum. Santiago glared back but he knew I'd read his book.

He shook his head and said, "We're not going to train this weekend."

Thus ended the overtime.

Chris later asked why it had taken me so long to figure out what was happening. Chris hadn't been comfortable with that situation either.

During the next several days, Chris and I took the machine gun guys to the mountains. We had a ball. Our guards were hard as nails and absorbed everything like a sponge. There wasn't a limp dick amongst them. Training went well.

Jim approached me the evening of our third day on the M60 range. Jim said that there might be an opportunity to go west. I still hadn't heard a word about our last trip and Larry's replacement hadn't even shown his face. My last trip I'd been clean shaven and I was with beard this time. I told Jim to let me know because I'd love to go with him. He wanted the firepower but he'd heard that I'd been over a time or two. He said it would be within the next day or two.

Chris and I went by the old man's store in Ashrafiya. He was tickled to see his old drinkin' buddies Khdees and Fdraunk (his pronunciation). The old lady was even happy to see us. Their daughter was present and she was a dark-eyed beauty. I said that she looked like her mom and this really made Mama happy. We bought some Cuban cigars and the old man broke out the Almaza. We tried to pay but he refused.

We had a side deal with Mama. When he went to piss we gave her the money. She never objected and it was like our little secret. She probably told him about it but it was his way of saving face. Mama fed us with hummus, breads of all types, and tabbouli (which she knew I loved).

The daughter floated around, serving us and smiling. It was uncommon to allow an unwed daughter in the presence of strange men but it was like we were now part of the family. I suspected the old man was working his way up to fixing his daughter up with Chris. He knew that I was married.

The next day Chris and I were preparing for the M60 range when Santiago and Jim walked up. We turned from the storage magazine and watched their approach.

As they came alongside, Santiago opened the conversation, "I'll be going to the 60 range today. Frank, you go give Jim a hand."

Chris bellowed like a wounded bear, "Shit, Frank has all the fun and I get stuck with the pencil neck."

Santiago gave him a stare which had zero affect on Chris. He didn't like the guy and didn't care who knew it.

Chris was really pissed. He was more pissed that he wasn't going with us. He didn't know what it was but he figured it was something interesting. It was.

Jim had rented or borrowed—I never really knew—an old four-door sedan. It was silver and looked like a pile of junk. It seemed to run good and as long as it got us home I was happy. What seemed unusual about this job was that the RSO hadn't requested it and Santiago was in the know. He didn't object but I think he was happy that he didn't have to go.

The embassy area was getting hammered by Grad rockets every night. We were told that there might even be an incident where the bad guys would try to take over the embassy compound. If they did it would be a different story than Tehran.

We had orders not to give up the embassy at any cost. The Marines had the same orders. Even the ambassador couldn't supersede our orders. They came straight from Secretary Shultz. Jim tossed me a little brown thing that looked like a big pinto bean or a kidney bean. It had a small wire coming out of it about an inch long. I looked at it, then at Jim. He was laughing his ass off.

"Goes up your ass."

"Stick it up your own ass," and I tossed it back.

He tossed it right back and said that he had already installed his. He further explained that it was a transmitter. Once we departed the seventh floor, they would be monitoring our progress. If we were kidnapped they could find us.

Bullshit! If we hauled ass with their money and passports they could find us. They didn't give one shit about us. Before we departed I went to the potty and did my thing. I won't go into that anymore. Use your imagination as to how I got it out upon return.

Jim and I loaded up and headed west. I had my MP5 between my legs; an 870 shotgun leaned against the console by my left leg; my Browning was under my right ass cheek. Before we departed the embassy compound Jim and I both took the time to lock and load. We did press checks on all our weapons. The 870 and MP5 were off safe but I left the Browning safety on. It was too close to my family jewels and an AD would have definitely been an ND.

We rolled out. I still didn't know why we were going over. Jim began to explain. When American diplomats pulled out of the west they had left a Mosler four-drawer safe because it was too heavy to move on such short notice. The safe contained passports, visa stamps, and cash. We weren't told how much but we later learned that nobody knew the exact amounts. There was Lebanese and U.S. currency in the safe. We approached the Green Line checkpoints without hesitation. Because of the current tensions and the nightly rocket attacks, the Green Line checkpoints were manned.

Jim spoke fluent Arabic and I was much improved. The Lebanese loved to listen to me because they said I sounded like a child. We pulled up to the LAF checkpoint and Jim shot the bull with the guard. Like I said before, Jim was a good guy and the locals recognized the fact that he respected and liked them.

They have a saying in Lebanon, *Eel Mach tube, El JaBean, Ashuff u Al Ein (eye een)*. This means: It is written on the forehead for the world to see. In other words, you express your true feelings. We crossed and headed to the next checkpoint that would get us into the west. It was impossible to know who was manning that checkpoint. Could be Hezbollah, Hamas, PSP, or whoever else had the most thugs that day.

Jim was a big, young, good lookin' kid with curly blond hair and blazing blue eyes. In his youth and excitement his eyes seemed to dance. They were never still. He wasn't afraid, just spun up tight. I felt that familiar rush of adrenaline that I'd become addicted to. It is worse than heroin.

Believe me, as I bang away on this etch-a-sketch, the déjà vu is killing me. I'd go back in a heartbeat.

The militia guard motioned us to stop, which Jim did.

Jim said *"Safara Merikee"* (American embassy). Why not? We were obviously not Arab. The guy was all smiles but he motioned us to get out of the vehicle. Jim talked a little more and explained we were diplomats and it was unsafe for us to get out. The guard said that we weren't in an armored car so if he wanted to shoot he could do so through the car.

I bent over and looked up at him with an intentional crazed smile.

I said, in Arabic, as I motioned to my MP5 and 870, "We can shoot out, too. Big problem is that I see your weapon is on safe. Probably doesn't have a round in the chamber. Mine are loaded and off safe." I could tell that I called his bluff. His look of confidence waned and he motioned us through. Thank yous and Go with Gods were exchanged and away we went.

Jim looked over and said, "How did you know his weapon was on safe? That side of his AK was against his body."

"I didn't. I took a chance. Three things could happen. His weapon was on safe and he knew I had him; he had been playing with it and couldn't remember what position he had left it; or he was squared away and knew the condition of his weapon and we had a gunfight on our hands. I bet on the fact that he'd been playing with it."

Jim just shook his head and drove toward the American embassy in West Beirut.

I had finally learned my lesson about the Arab mentality. He who is in the position of power…wins!

We arrived at the main gate without incident. There was a crowd of young men watching from the Corniche (the boardwalk on the Med). The stares were nonchalant until they saw us turn into the gate. The stares then became hostile. They'd put two and two together. Two blond guys headed into the American Embassy compound. If you see duck shit, there may be a duck in the area.

The guards were very happy to see Americans. A couple of the guys recognized me from previous training trips and yelled out, "Yu-Muh." They then turned to their co-workers and rapidly explained the Yu-Muh greeting. I know they didn't know the real meaning that Red Fox had in mind but it was still great to them. The rest of the guards started to chant, "Yu-Muh…Yu-Muh!!" The gates were opened and our vehicle was checked for IEDs. It was a check more to prove to us that they did their job than to look for bombs.

The guard supervisor had been notified and he walked out of the building to greet us. The entire compound—bigger than a football field, including the buildings—was surrounded top to bottom with a cover over the top of chain link fence. It was supposed to stop any RPG. That would work if the nose of the rocket precisely hit a wire. Otherwise the RPG would squirt through and maybe make it or the back up fuze would detonate it. Better than nothing, I guess.

We shook hands, hand to heart, kissed the cheeks. Mohammed was the on-duty supervisor. He escorted us into the office areas. I was impressed. I expected to see the place a shambles. It was neat and clean and even had a receptionist at the counter. Post one was abandoned, as were the offices. There was a secretary here and there but overall the place looked to be what it was, an abandoned old embassy. We told Mohammed we would come to his office when we finished.

We had to go to the "seventh floor." Locals were not normally allowed on the seventh floor and they knew it. We had no visions of innocence here. Without a doubt, these folks, out of curiosity if nothing else, had been through everything on the seventh floor. We didn't know if the safe was there, empty or what. We headed up the steps. Elevators hadn't worked since the bombing. There was a keypad lock at the main entrance. Jim pulled out his wallet and produced a small piece of paper. He grinned at me and said that he'd violated OpSec (Operational Security) by not memorizing the combinations. Said his memory wasn't that good. I agreed. I would have never memorized one, much less two or three.

The door opened and we entered. The condition of this office space was not as presentable as downstairs. Of course, if the locals had cleaned up they would have given themselves away. We did a cursory look around and saw no safe. Nobody had been able to tell Jim its exact location, plus it could have been moved. Not an easy task, but not impossible either.

We entered a small room off to the right and I could see at first glance it had been the communications room. All non-essential electrical stuff was still there. Workbenches with half-full ashtrays, rolls of black electrical tape, and rolls of wire and solder. No safe.

We noticed the second office had another keypad lock. Jim looked at me and rolled his eyes. He said he only had two combos. One for the door and one for the safe. I shrugged and told him to try the door combo. After all, it was the CIA. He did and it worked. We were rewarded with an immediate sight of a big four-drawer safe with papers stacked almost to the ceiling. Nothing was stamped with a classification so we tossed it on the floor. Jim looked at me and then looked at the safe. He rubbed his right hand on his jeans. Looked like a true safe-cracker.

He tried the combo once and nothing happened. All he had was the combo and not the directions of spin or the number of rotations. He tried again—nothing.

Finally I said, "Let me try." Jim handed me the note. I spun left about a dozen times just to clear its throat. I stopped on the first number. Spun right three times and stopped. Back left two times, then right to zero. The handle pushed down easy and a gentle pull opened the drawer to expose stacks of cardboard boxes. Jim grabbed one and opened it. Passports. We didn't count them, just pulled them all out and laid them on the floor.

That was the second drawer down because that was where the lock was located. We then opened the top drawer and there were a few documents and a number of rubber stamps and ink pads. Visa stamps. A U.S. passport with no stamp was bringing $5,000 on the black market. There was a small fortune just in these two drawers.

We then opened the third drawer and it was packed with cash, Lebanese currency in the rear of the drawer and U.S. currency toward the front. I didn't recognize the denominations of Lebanese pound notes but I assumed they were big. The U.S. currency was bundled and banded. There were $20 and $100 bill bundles. The fourth drawer was all U.S. currency.

Jim and I looked at each other in dismay. What the hell were we gonna do now? This would require no little amount of effort and we had to accomplish it without the Lebanese knowing what we had. If they knew, there would be a call made to the local militia and poor Jimmy and Frankie would be stopped before getting to the Green Line, never to be seen or heard from again.

We needed a plan. We replaced everything in the safe. Jim asked if we should relock it and I said Yeah, we can open it again. The alternative really sucked. It was still early, maybe around noon. I told Jim that we would need some boxes and a good cover story that Mohammed would believe. We knew that he had probably seen the safe and was curious as to its contents. If we came down with large boxes from the seventh floor it would be obvious.

First we had to get the boxes. We told Mohammed that we needed about six decent-sized boxes. We figured five would carry the stuff but I had started to concoct a plan. Mohammed returned and a few minutes later a guard appeared at his doorway with the requested boxes. Where in the hell they got them so fast amazed me. Jim and I grabbed the boxes and went back to our task.

When we were behind closed doors I hatched my plan. We would empty the safe, then refill the drawers with the useless documents we'd found on top of the safe. We would leave enough out to fill one of the boxes. We took all the visa stamps, passports, and currency and put it in four of the boxes. We then sealed the boxes up with the many rolls of electrical tape that we'd found.

We went back down and asked Mohammed if he could grab a senior secretary and come give us a hand. You could tell he was excited about an official visit to the seventh floor. He yelled a female's name down the stairwell and a very pretty middle-aged professional lady came to the foot of the stairs.

Mohammed motioned her up. She looked at Jim and me for approval because she knew that she wasn't allowed on the seventh floor. Jim and I nodded and motioned her up. We went into the offices where we'd been packing up.

It looked exactly as I'd hoped. Most of the paperwork was gone. Five boxes were packed and sealed. The safe was locked and appeared undisturbed. There was a stack of loose documents on the floor waiting to go into the empty box. Jim explained in Arabic that we had packed all the documents in the five boxes. We weren't Administrative so we don't know if this stack is important or not. We wanted a senior secretary to have a look and tell us what we should pack.

It worked. She efficiently sat in a chair next to the stack and started going through the papers. She had a question from time to time but two equal stacks began to grow as a result of her efforts. When finished, she pointed to the first stack and said, "This maybe important." Pointing to the second stack, she said, "This only papers for building and supplies?"

"Good," we said together. We took the first stack and placed it in the empty box. We took care to tape it exactly as we had the others.

I looked at Mohammed and told him that the boxes of papers were very heavy. Could some of his guards help us? He was all too happy to assist. But he looked at the safe and asked, "What about this. It is important?"

We told him that it was but that we weren't cleared to open it. It would be up to him to protect it. Now this really pumped him up. We, as Americans, couldn't open it but he had been charged with keeping it safe.

Four guards came up and we began to shuttle the boxes down to the car. Three in the back seat and three in the trunk. We prayed for luck crossing the Green Line. We didn't want to seem too anxious so we just lounged around and paid no attention to the car. This drove Jim and I nuts because we knew what was in the car. It was all we could do to go into Mohammed's office for tea. It was then about 1500 and we should have been headed back to coordinate with afternoon prayer.

We were sipping our tea and a guard came rushing in and spoke in such rapid Arabic I couldn't understand anything. Jim understood though, and motioned me outside. Mohammed had jumped up and exited in front of us. He rushed to the gate. There were a bunch of folks outside the gate and they weren't happy.

There was yelling and screaming going back and forth through the iron gate. Hands and arms poked through with clenched fists. The guards were harmlessly slapping their hands away. They weren't about to piss these people off because they were their neighbors. Jim and I both had our Brownings but the MP5s and my 870 was in the car.

We walked over and Jim unlocked my door. I retrieved our weapons and we walked toward the gate. Mohammed seemed to have changed. He looked back and saw us approaching. He yelled at us and pointed back at the compound.

Jim responded with, "What?"

Mohammed yelled again for us to get our asses to his office now. I looked up and one of the guards was pointing a Mini-14 straight at me. Now this sucks. We're in an American Embassy, with guards that we pay, and they're pointing guns at us. I indicated the Mini-14 to Jim.

He said for us to follow Mohammed's instructions.

We headed back inside but stayed glued to the bullet-resistant glass that gave a view of the gate area. The gate was now shaking violently as the crowd outside had grown in size and anger. What the hell was going on? It was getting late and if we were going to get across the Green Line we had to do it soon.

It was clear that we weren't going out that gate anytime soon. I told the secretary to see if she could get a line to the RSO in the east.

In about five minutes, which was good time, she called out that the RSO was on hold. Jim went in and filled the RSO in on what was going down. The RSO asked if we wanted a helo lift and Jim told him no—it was just a protest now but choppers might really churn things up. We would just hunker down and spend the night and leave in the morning. I was anxious to get back to the glass to see what was happening.

I was rewarded with a view that made my ass draw up and shoot out that pinto bean (slight exaggeration). Bottles, cans, trash, yelling, screaming, and all other hell was breaking loose. Four guards were gathered around Mohammed and he yelled at them above the noise. We couldn't hear but the four men ran toward us with their weapons at high port. Jim and I made ready. I turned Mohammed's desk over and we crouched behind it, Jim with his MP5 and me with the 870 pointing at the entrance. My MP5 lay at my knee. When I fired the 870 at the guards I would transition to the MP5 while Jim covered me. I suspected that the 870 and Jim's support would deal with these four.

I had the smell in my nostrils. It's with me today and will be with me 'til I die. It was the smell of fear, anxiety, apprehension, adrenaline, and the outright thrill of entering combat. I know to you non-combatants out there that sounds crazy, but those who have been there know what I mean. There's no other feeling like it. You are faced with unreal odds, you know that you're gonna ultimately lose but you have nowhere to run and wouldn't, even if you could. When you're alone it's easy to run, but when you're with someone it is impossible—for me, anyhow. Too hardheaded. Now if he runs first, he'd better not stumble or he'll have my footprints up his back.

We were ready. I knew that Jim was okay and could be counted on. He was like me; he took a sick, perverted pleasure in this shit. I noticed that he'd laid out his magazines next to his left knee. Good, he was also here for the long haul.

The four guards ran toward the door and we braced ourselves. It reminded me of when I was a kid in Florida and the folks would take me to the beach. I'd see this huge wave coming toward my little body. I wouldn't run even though I was scared shit. I leaned into and braced. I had that feeling now. It looked like we had a fight on our hands.

The first two guards peeled off, one going right and one going left. The other two headed straight for the door. I started to think about another way in and the first two were trying to get at our rear. If that happened we could be screwed.

I yelled for Jim to cover the rear and I'd handle the immediate threat. He picked up on it and spun around to cover our six. He knew that the 870 would be more than enough for the second two. They rushed headlong toward the door and we still hadn't heard from the first two who were behind us. We were as nervous as a couple of whores in church.

All of a sudden the second two stopped and faced toward the gate with weapons in their shoulders. One, then the other, dropped to one knee to stabilize their platform.

Jesus, these guys weren't attacking. Mohammed sent them to guard us. I felt like an idiot as did Jim. I looked over and he had the same shit-eatin,' sheepish grin that I had.

We were getting ready to light up the guys who were risking it all to save us. Weird shit happens in combat. That would have been a friendly fire incident. Now we felt like a couple of whistle dicks cowering in here while these little guys were willing to risk it all to protect our sorry asses. I grabbed my MP5 and the 870 and headed to the door. Jim was right behind me.

I opened the door and was faced with two very hostile Lebanese guards with weapons pointed straight at our heads. For a second I thought I had been wrong and these guys were gonna take us out anyhow. They gestured for us to go back inside and they did so in a manner that left nothing to interpretation. I looked out toward Mohammed and he violently motioned us back inside. Jim and I gave in and slowly moved back inside.

We watched through the glass. Our appearance had made the crowd react with more violent action. That was it—Mohammed wanted us out of sight so that he could get us out of their minds. Now we had to lay low and feel like a couple of wimps because just the sight of Jim and I tended to incite the crowd.

It was getting close to prayer time and the crowd started to disappear. Several *Mutawa* (religious police) were present, trying to herd the remnants of the crowds to the mosque for prayer. Only about one hundred or so remained and they were mostly the young hotheads. That's the ones you had to be careful of. They hated us more than the old-timers. They had the religious fervor plus and, more importantly, they watch TV and see how our young people live. They are crazy with jealousy and that is understandable. Try to imagine worrying about feeding your family or getting drinking water, and then you see shows like Jerry *Springer* or *Special Edition* that flaunts our privileged celebrities. It would piss you off, too.

As it got darker the crowd completely dissipated. It had dropped to the few teens who were on the Corniche when we arrived. They probably spread the word about our arrival. Mohammed came back into the office and sent the four guards back to the gate. The two who we thought were circling around behind us were actually guarding the rear entrance.

Mohammed was sweating profusely and extremely shaken. It was post-combat come-downs. We got him a cup of tea and he sat at his desk. He was smiling and trying to put on a show of calm. I patted him on the shoulder with my right hand, and he appreciated the human contact. He reached up and patted my hand in thanks. To outsiders that may have appeared gay, but to warriors it has a different meaning and we don't give a shit what it looks like.

Jim asked Mohammed if he thought we could leave tomorrow. Mohammed shook his head "Yes" for a long time. I'm sure he'd have loved to have our asses out of there more than we wanted to leave, pinto bean and all.

Mohammed had guards bring up some bottled water and mattresses from the old Marine house. He wanted us to sleep securely in his office. We did not object. It was obvious that Mohammed had his shit together and that we would be protected to the best of his ability.

Given that, Jim and I decided to sleep in shifts. We turned in around 2200 with Jim taking the first watch, waking me at midnight. I didn't sleep well at all and was up on my own at 2330. He crashed right away and snored like an old man. Ah...to be young again. He was sleeping so well that I let him go until 0400. I shot the bull with the duty guard and practiced my Arabic.

The guard's name was Ali and he was a veteran of the embassy bombing. He knew Abe very well and almost cried when I told him I worked for Mr. Abe. Ali asked hundreds of questions about Mr. Abe and we chatted like that for four hours. Abe was well thought of here. I was now tired and when Jim had washed his face I cuddled up and went immediately to sleep.

Jim shook me in what seemed like two minutes and said that it was time.

I unscrewed my eyes and tried to rub out the sleep. Man, I went down hard. I stumbled into the head and washed my face and brushed my teeth with the hand soap and my forefinger.

I went back out to the office and Jim was on the phone with the RSO. Mohammed was in, but momentarily out on the perimeter checking the situation. It was still too early for the secretary.

Jim hung up and turned to me, "Seventh floor says the earlier we leave, the better off we are. These folks sleep in, and we may have a shot at getting out without being noticed. He told me to see if any of the vehicles they left behind run, but there are no vehicles. Probably the first things to be pilfered after the evacuation. What do you think?" It would have been better to use a different vehicle but now we had to go with what we had.

I told him that we should get the fuck out and don't look back, and do it soon. It was about 0630 and too early for the young bucks to be hanging out. We grabbed our weapons and went in search of Mohammed. He was walking across the courtyard in our direction. He waved a greeting to me.

Jim told him that we were headed back and would appreciate it if the guards could open the gate.

As if nothing had happened he said, "*Moffy mooshkilla,*" or "No Problem."

We shook hands, hand over hearts, and kisses. We made sure that our weapons were ready and we turned the car toward the gate. The gate swung open and we rolled through, greeted by a few weak, "Yu-Muh's." We turned right and headed east, home.

There wasn't a soul on the street. Not anyone on the Corniche. I'd never been here at 0645 in the morning so I had nothing to compare it to. At any rate I was happy. Jim drove fast but not crazy. We passed in front of the old/new Holiday Inn and there was no activity there either. A breakfast shop was buzzing but nobody even looked up when we passed. Arabs aren't big morning people. Jim slowed as we approached the checkpoint. It seemed abandoned as well.

We slowly rolled to a stop and a sleepy little guy came out, obviously pissed because we woke him up. His AK was slung over his shoulder and he made no attempt to bring it to bear. Good for us, bad on him. If it hit the fan here we would be at the embassy before anyone could respond. The guard approached my window and looked at the boxes in the back.

Jim told him they were paperwork from the embassy. Office people love paperwork. The guard glanced down at my hand on the 870 and figured it was too early and he was too sleepy to screw with a twelve gauge. Don't blame him—I was sleepy also and didn't want the noise the 870 created.

"*Yah-Allah*," he said. "*Allah Mach*" or "Go with God."

"*Massa lama*," we returned. *Departure* "Go with God." Now we approached the LAF checkpoint and this guy just stuck his head out. Nasty-looking scowl on his face but hurriedly waved us through the gate. He then turned back into the guard house to resume his sleep. If either guard had only known what was in that little car.

We pulled into the embassy and the RSO met us at the main entrance. "You guys okay? No problems crossing?"

"We're here and in one piece. Mohammed did one hell of a job."

The RSO indicated that he needed to get over there and meet the guys. Jim and I looked at each other. "No shit!" We grabbed some guards and moved the boxes upstairs to the RSO's office. I cut the tape with my pocket knife and revealed the contents. The RSO whistled loud and long.

"How much is there?" he asked.

We didn't count it, we were too busy getting' our asses outta there. We were later told that there was well over two million dollars in unaccounted-for funds. We could have filled our pockets and no one would have known. Oh well, maybe next time.

We had a meeting in the RSO's office and there was an even greater concern about the mounting tensions. Hard to believe after we just crossed the Green Line unmolested. On a political level it was heating up and the religious Imams were preaching hate and discontent. There was a call for all nonessentials to depart Beirut. The RSO was staying and asked if there were any volunteers from the team.

Santiago spoke up and immediately said, "This is outside our mission scope so we need to pull back to Cyprus."

I told the RSO that I'd be willing to stay. I was a Marine and an EOD officer. After all, there were a few bombs about. I could be of use.

He agreed.

Chris said, "Count me in, I'm former Army Ranger."

RSO noted that and said, "Thanks, Chris."

Santiago was pissed. Now his tit was in a wringer. Manny hadn't said a word. He just shrugged. Didn't care one way or the other.

Santiago spoke up and said, "We'll have to clear that with main State."

Chris rolled his eyes and said, "Here the RSO is main State if we're needed. Remember what Joe said—we're here at the bequest and support of the RSO."

Now Santiago was really was pissed. Chris hadn't backed him up. We ended up staying until the entire embassy was totally evacuated two weeks later.

In the meantime we continued to train the guards and embassy personnel. It felt more like we were killing time. After work, Chris and I showered and got ready to head out.

Santiago was at the dining table and said, "Where do you think you are going?"

Chris had had enough. He fired back, "Any fuckin' place I want!" Santiago jumped up as if he'd had enough, too. I looked on, waiting for the entertainment.

Santiago looked dejected all of a sudden and said, "Maybe me and Manny wanted to go out for a decent meal, too."

Chris told him in not-so-friendly terms that we weren't going to a restaurant. Chris and I headed out the door without further comment. We were off to see the old man in Ashrafiya. We parked right in front; the old man was outside negotiating the sale of some fruit. He saw us and broke off the sale. Mama took over as the old man wiped his hands on his apron then shook our hands, hand over heart, and kisses.

He invited us in and said that his daughter Samya would be home soon. I think he hoped that Chris would react. She was a student at AUB (American University of Beirut) and walked the three kilometers from school.

We couldn't tell him that Samya had a boyfriend at the Marine house.

We went in and the old man passed around the Almaza, getting one for himself. I walked over and grabbed an Upman from a cigar humidor. I grabbed another and tossed it to Chris.

The old man was very excited today. He told us that a heavy with one of the militias in the west had been blown up. Apparently a slew of his thugs got whacked also.

Mama finally gave up on us after bringing down the hummus and tabbouli and fresh bread. Samya made a token appearance but had to study. Mama wasn't there, so she couldn't stay anyway. As she left she gave me a sultry stare, then up the steps she went.

It was late, about midnight. I told Chris we had to get back but he was having a ball. We were all loaded to the gills. The old man was in deep shit with Mama and Chris and I had to try and drive back to the apartment. We helped clean up our mess and again the old man refused payment. I left the equivalent of about twenty bucks on the register. This was a great deal of money to these people.

We drove out of Ashrafiya. To do this we turned left out of town, down a steep hill, then a winding road up to the main highway. It screws you up even when you're sober. Somehow I got all screwed up and turned right instead of left. Chris was singing and puffing away on his Wilde cigar. I noticed that something seemed strange. Now remember that Ashrafiya is located right on the Green Line. All of the buildings looked bombed-out and the place was a mess.

I said to Chris, "We made a wrong turn somewhere."

He laughed and said, "What chu mean we, white man?" I started to sober up and made sure that my MP5 was ready. I told Chris to do the same.

He responded by coming out of the festive mood to the serious mood. His MP5 was across his lap to the right and mine was to the left.

I decided to do a u-turn at a huge pile of rubble and head back the way we'd come. As I pulled hard right and then backed hard left to do a three-point turn, a group of about fifteen guys emerged from the rubble wearing olive drab and Arab head dress. They surrounded the car. We really had the weenie this time. Indian country, bad guys surrounding us, we were all beered up. Doom!

One of the guys walked up to the car and I passed him my diplomatic passport without a word. I figured we were done anyhow so what was the loss of a passport? The young guy looked at me, looked at my photo, then looked at Chris. He motioned toward Chris.

I looked at Chris and said, "Well ole buddy, is it fight or flight?" He produced his passport and handed it to the militiaman. He studied it for a few seconds then looked at Chris.

I said as soberly as I could muster, *"Safara Merickee."*

So help me, the guy looked at me and in perfect English asked, "What in the fuck are you doing here at night? Don't you know where you're at? You work at the embassy?"

I told him the story about the old man who was our friend and that we'd had a few beers.

"Well, haul your stupid ass back to the embassy," he said tossing our passports through the window.

I had to ask, stupid or not, "Man, where did you learned to speak English so good?"

He looked at me and with a straight, matter-of-fact face he responded, "I live in Jersey. We come over and do our reserve time with Hamas then we go home again. Next guy from Hamas won't be so nice to you. Now get the fuck out of here now!"

I needed no more prompting. I hauled ass without looking back. Through the grace of God we made it to the apartment without further ado.

A couple of days prior to departure I decided to make a run to see Joseph Sphere. I explained to Chris he couldn't go. He understood even though he was pissed off. I drove east along the Med coastline. What beauty. I made the right up the winding road to Joseph's camp. Nothing had changed.

A guard stepped out and I showed my passport and he let me through. I pulled up to Joseph's tent as he emerged to greet me. Handshake, hand over heart, kisses. We exchanged small talk then went inside where he asked if I wanted beer, whiskey, or coffee. I told him coffee.

I asked about Abdu. Joseph said he'd been transferred. I could tell that he didn't want to talk about Abdu. Joseph got a little reflective and said, "Big problem after you leave."

I waited as I sipped my coffee.

He continued, "Not for sure, no hard evidence, but you know device you wired seat to get bomb factory when driver get out?"

I nodded, not wanting my voice to be on a recorder.

He then said that the driver had stopped at the Milky grocery store to get cigarettes. Thirteen women and kids killed.

Now he held up his hands and said, "Now this is not for sure and they may be saying this to start trouble only." No matter what was said after that, I would have to sleep every night with that being my last thought before I dozed off. Sleep is evasive. No confirmation was ever provided.

When the CH-53 lifted off I had a crushing, nagging feeling that this was to be my last view of Beirut. What was the old man doing? Haggling over the prices of the fruit out front? Was Mama on his ass? Was Samya yearning for a life outside this hell that had become my heaven? Where had Abdu disappeared? Ernest and Imad, who we called Hiccup and Fuckup (which was interchangeable) —where had they disappeared? What lives had I hurt or helped? Was Joseph wheeling and dealing for more power for the Spider guys? Would I ever be able to sit at a five star restaurant and order fine wine with my 870 on the table next to me? What impression, if any, would be my legacy to my friends in Beirut? I'll never know.

I did later hear that Ernest and Imad were caught in a .50 cal machine gun ambush and cut to pieces. When I received this news I was shocked, as you can well imagine. I'd lived, worked, and survived with these guys. We'd drunk beer together. They weren't American, but we'd shared some tough times together. Those are the bonds forged from the stress of combat. Not your conventional combat, but physical and mental combat. Having to think together, to out-think the bad guys. Not trusting anyone, even each other at times.

Difficult to explain but for those of you who work the streets, patrol the villages, and interact with the people know what I mean. I'm not sure that I've ever seen it effectively put into words.

Let it suffice to say that it is an emotion experienced by very few. It will be an experience felt by many more warriors as the SO/LIC war and the War on Terror intensifies. Intensify it will.

CHAPTER FOURTEEN

First Ladies Conference

We returned from Beirut and stood down after securing our weapons and equipment. We all had to go through being assholes in the eyes of Joe.

We all just nodded and turned our stuff in. Another team was on the road but we were down for a day or so. I was tied to the gray beast. I had trip reports and travel claims. God, I hated paperwork.

At least it was nice to be home with Susan and Stephen. Having that to return to seemed to make it all worthwhile...plus it was fun.

When I went back to work, Abe told me that he had a three-day assignment for me. Susan was gonna have a kitten. Abe shook his head and said, "No, no. Doesn't Susie (everybody called her Susie but me unless I was pissed off) work across the street?"

I told him Yeah, but what did that have to do with anything?

He said the detail was in D.C. It was at a five star and I should have Susie up for a night. It was for the First Ladies Conference on Drug Abuse.

No kiddin'! I reported for the detail with all my gear. I told Susan the first day I'd be too busy but I wanted her up on the second day after work. My room was next door to the first lady of Mexico. I bounced around as we didn't have Army EOD support for this detail and it was a joint Secret Service detail.

The second day Susan found an all-night sitter for Stephen. At about 1400, the first lady of Mexico was called home. Her husband had cancer and had taken a turn for the worse and was dying. Nancy Reagan sent tons of flowers to her room along with all the other first ladies. Walking into her room reminded me of the jungles of Vietnam.

I called the AIC of her detail, Ronny, and asked what was to be done with all the flowers. He was busy and told me to shit can them or have the hotel do away with them. Light bulb clicked on...flowers...Susan coming to my room after work...a plan was developing.

I called the concierge. Told him I needed some cards. He brought up a couple dozen small thank-you cards. They were fancy and would do the trick. I started transferring the booty. After I had everything moved I started composing love notes on the cards. When I had everything perfect I looked at my handi-work. Man, was I gonna be a hero.

She would be there around 1800. Time dragged by. At 1700 the radio went off, announcing my call sign. I answered. The voice on the other end told me to call the CP on land line ASAP. I did.

My old buddy Dick was on the other end in no time. He told me that a hotel security guard had found a suspicious item on a limo. He didn't elaborate as to whom the limo was assigned to. He wanted to know how long it would take me to get there. The limo was located on Embassy Row. I could be there in about fifteen minutes if traffic allowed.

Dick said he wanted to hold off calling in the locals until I verified the item. Good idea. No sense in calling in the cavalry until we knew. I told Dick to pass the word for everybody to back off and cordon the area.

I scribbled a quick note for Susan and away I went. The item turned out to be nothing but it took me two hours to break away and get back to the room. It was almost 1900 by the time I busted into the room. Susan was sitting on my bed looking extremely cute. From the day I met her she was never a glamour girl or beauty, for she wasn't into that. She was, and always will be, beautiful to me. She was and is also the cutest little girl I've ever seen. It is hard to be beautiful and cute in my opinion. I'm into cute, not fake beauty. She looked especially cute that night. I looked over and saw a chiller of champagne.

"Where did that come from?" I asked as I walked over for a hug. She gives the best hugs.

She had called and ordered it from room service prior to her departure from work.

I had already checked the champagne prices. Eighty-five bucks for the cheapest bottle!!

I asked her which she had ordered and she told me she had them deliver a mid-price bottle—218 bucks!! Captains didn't make that much. Do you know how many six-packs of Old Mil I could get with 218 bucks?

I couldn't be pissed. She worked, too.

Now at this point it is important to remind you that we adopted Stephen. We couldn't have kids and had been to every doctor and Navy hospital in the free world. Susan had an unusual disorder that killed all my little fish.

I sat next to her and she said, "I've got something to tell you." I looked at her and she told me that she'd killed a rabbit. Now, I'm not dumb and I know what that means, but it was so far from my mind that it didn't register. I looked at her stupidly, which is what I did most of the time.

She hit the homer, "I'm pregnant."

My first response, without thought, was, "How did that happen?"

She laughed through tears and said, "The way it normally happens, asshole." That was her favorite nickname for me and it was appropriate. I don't need to tell you what that meant to us.

We were to be four. I remember when we told Stephen. He was so happy that he told everybody he saw, whether he knew them or not, "I'm gonna have a brover."

After the First Ladies Conference it was back to routine. I knew that there were a couple of MTTs hanging out there. The number of MTT guys had grown to about sixteen and people were everywhere. Training at BSR, Fort Bragg, John Shaw's, Gun Sight, and anywhere else we could get training. It was a grab-and-go world that I loved. I missed Susan and Stephen but I felt like I was making a difference.

I was sitting at the gray beast reading an area security survey when Abe walked in. He asked me to step in to his office. Sounded serious, so I followed without my normal banter. Abe dropped his armload of habitual paperwork on his desk. He looked at me and surprised me with his question, "How was John D.?"

Without hesitation I told him John was one of the best. The guy was a pro.

Abe wanted to know if I'd like to go back to Cairo.

I told him I preferred Beirut but he said nobody is going to Beirut for a while. A temporary embassy is set up in Nicosia, Cyprus. Abe said, "Only the spooks are operating in Beirut now." I had a fleeting thought of Abdu working with a Delta guy or a SEAL and a wave of jealousy passed through me. I knew I had to leave it behind. But for me it has been the hardest thing in my life.

I still taste the Almaza beer and sense the aroma of a good cigar. I can still see Mama flitting around the store in Ashrafiya, bitching at the old man. I can still see her appreciative glance when I slipped her money. I can also see the eyes of their daughter Samya as they stared at Chris longingly. Not longing for Chris as a man but longing for the promise of a life in America. Longing for what he represented. It was tough to leave them all behind. Beirut was in the history books for me and that was where it must stay.

The team for Cairo was settled. It was to be the old Cairo team. Josh, Keith, George, and me. The fearsome foursome. It was now early 1986 and the Middle East was a time bomb. When would those people ever wake up and quit being lead around by fanatics? With their oil and natural resources they could be living a far better life than our middle class.

In 632 Muhammad was poisoned by a Jewish lady. Hard to recover from all those years of being pissed off.

Abe said he had a pre-departure brief for us. We had to meet in the SCIF (Secure Classified Information Facility). This was a room that was safeguarded against eavesdropping of any type. The meeting was set for 1500 that afternoon. I had a few hours so I headed to the range at Lorton.

Joe, ever present, was in the vault cleaning a new gun that he'd just bought and fired. I walked in and he glanced up and then returned to his work. "Headed back to North Africa, I hear," he stated without enthusiasm.

I entered a long rendition of emotion. My mind was cluttered. I'd seen a lot. Desired to see more but couldn't get my mind wrapped around what was happening to me. Was I nuts? I trusted Joe and he'd seen more than me.

I asked him how he moved from the MTT scene into sitting at the range teaching boneheads how to shoot. How in the hell could you make that transition?

He dropped his oil rag and wiped his hands on the machinist's apron that he had been sporting lately. He reflected for only a moment before he answered.

"Frank, you're exactly where I was six years ago. It's more intense now because of the terror situation but the drive was there just the same. We bounced in and out of Africa, Central America, South America, and it was different guys but the same crap. I made friends in places that I'd never see again and I'd lay awake at night worrying."

He shifted gears after a few moments of internal reflection. "When you do what we do, people tend to rely on you and your word. When you leave knowing that you'll never be back, it takes a chunk out of you. I suspect that you have more than one chunk missing from your ass as I speak. I got tired of losing pieces and decided that I was done. I volunteered for Bogota because that was my last shot. I left a very good friend there who I'll never see again. It's our life. It's what we do. They say in the mafia, 'We make no apologies, 'tis the life we choose'."

That's more than I've heard Joe say at one time in his life. That came from the heart. He wasn't the kind of guy who wanted to dwell on things said, then lean on your shoulder to recover with a bunch of tears. Neither was I.

I nodded and walked out the door. I was never to see Joe again. But that comes later. My departure and return coincided with a trip that he had to make. He wasn't there to bitch about our packing or complain about our return. I transferred out after my return from Cairo. Many times I thought about pissing him off, the Delta guy in Larnaca, his antics with new agents, and the list goes on. Another friend I left behind.

Fortunately for me, I was at home when Susan gave birth to our second boy. Miracle child. After thirteen years of not being able to have kids, we'd adopted Stephen. Four years later out pops Mikey, and a *Mikey* he has been since day one. From the time he was two years old he would play games with the airport security when welcoming me home. The security guys got to know his little blond head. He would scoot between their legs, go around, over, under, or whatever it took to get to me. I'd throw Stephen on my shoulders and carry Mikey, along with my luggage. Once in the car the two of them would tear apart my bags lookin' for their presents.

Susan was like a kid, too. She'd roll her eyes to the back seat and watch the boys, more to see what was in the bags for her. Homecomings were very joyous but the departures were getting tougher and tougher. Stephen was more of the careful type because he has Neurofibromatosis (a genetic disorder that produces tumors on the nerve endings). We were told on three occasions that he had limited time. At one point there seemed to be no hope and he was granted a "Make-a-Wish." He wanted to go to Disney. That trip and the greatness of many people is a story in itself. He is now twenty-six years old and doing well. Toughest kid I've ever known.

Mikey, on the other hand, was and is a roughneck. He had his first motorcycle (a Honda Mini Trail) at the age of three. I had to put it in first gear and remove the shifter just to keep him from killing himself. We had no landscaping in our yard because Mikey kept uprooting all of Mom's flowers. We didn't care. We were all happy and enjoying our limited time together. I don't think that there is a body part on Mikey that doesn't have a scar or break. He is now twenty-two and still going full steam ahead. He kinda reminds me of someone else I know.

CHAPTER FIFTEEN

Cairo and Libya

I got back to the office at 1430. Went to the gray beast and settled in with the new *State Magazine* I found on my desk.

I didn't notice Keith walk in but he got my attention when he commented on the magazine.

"Company man now, huh? Trying to impress the boss so he'll send you back to Beirut?"

"Naw, I think we're restricted to North Africa now 'cause all the chicks are missing you in South America."

He threw a paper wad at me then we both headed for the SCIF. We went in to find everyone present but George. There was an intel weenie over from main State which alerted us to the fact that this might have been above the Abe level. What now?

Ken, the director of training, walked in with a cup of coffee. He naturally sat at the head of the table. The little guy from main State looked at him and said, "Ken, I'm making a short presentation and will need your seat."

Ken looked at him, shook his head, and slid his coffee and coaster over one seat. He then shifted his body and reseated himself.

Robert was the name of the guy from Intel. Robert sorted through some papers he'd taken from his briefcase and looked at us all in turn, indicating that he was ready. He proceeded with the statement that the Middle East was really in a state of flux. There were about sixty groups that wanted to be in charge, and of those sixty maybe eight were viable organizations that had a significant following. Two of those eight were operating from Libya. Kaddafi was sponsoring their activities throughout North Africa, Lebanon, and other Middle Eastern countries.

He continued that plans were underway to disrupt Kaddafi's activities. At this point Robert interjected that he would not brief us on those plans. For our purpose, all we needed to know was that something would probably go down in the next two or three weeks.

"Now," he said, "where do you guys fit in?" He rambled on, mentioning several other countries in the region such as Morocco, Algeria, Tunisia, and Egypt. He was focusing on North Africa.

Lebanon was skirted. That was because all U.S. personnel were then out of Lebanon, again. Algeria was a hotbed with its own civil war going on. They seemed to be fighting amongst themselves, the Algerian government versus the GIA, a terrorist group that had formed from veterans of the Afghan war against the Russians. They were seasoned fighters and had declared war on the Algerian government. Bombs and armed attacks were a daily occurrence in and around Algiers. For that reason Robert said that Algeria and its neighbor Morocco were not of any great concern to us. Tunisia and Egypt were of great concern.

There had been an increasing number of attacks in Egypt, especially at the tourist sights. A busload of Brits had recently been attacked and killed at the pyramids. Robert said that there was concern for the diplomatic missions in Egypt and Tunisia when the U.S.—then he corrected himself—the United Nations plan was put into effect.

We all looked at each other and rolled our eyes. It was common knowledge in every American household that at some point in the near future Kaddafi was gonna get his pee-pee smacked. Robert said that the "plan" called for beefing up the security at the embassies in Tunis and Cairo. We would also beef up security at the U.S. Consulate in Alexandria.

The MTT was expected to go in and take over the Ambassador's protective detail. Now I started to understand. Chris beamed and looked at me and winked.

He then said to everyone in general, "Frank wants to go protect the U.S. interests in Beirut."

Robert didn't understand the inside joke and said, "I'll say it again, we have no U.S. interests in Beirut at this time." No shit; MTT had evacuated everybody. If anyone knew, it was us.

Robert said that the operational deployment and control would be all up to Abe and the MTT guys on the ground. He wanted two teams deployed within the next seventy-two hours. We had three days. The brief ended and Robert was surprised and disappointed to see that there were no questions. There would be many, but only after this guy left. We would do the job our way, and without interference from main State. We didn't have much time.

Robert gathered his documents and looked around hoping for at least one question.

Abe said, "Teams, keep your seats, we'll meet here for about the next hour. Take a leak and get some coffee and asses in seats in five minutes. I don't have to remind you not to discuss any of this in the hallway."

After reconvening, Abe looked us over and said, "This is no democracy. I have made the team assignments. I based it on past performance and feedback. Priority number one is the Ambassador in Cairo. Josh, Frank, Keith, and George."

He made assignments to a "home team" that would be held in reserve. This home team would be on standby in the event the deployed teams needed reinforcement, and they would serve as the support element logistically. They would be on twenty-four-hour standby. Santiago was the team leader for the home team. He beamed at that. Chris didn't. When Abe assigned Chris to the home team, he bellowed like a wounded cow.

"I ain't no supply pogue. You've got enough pencil necks here to cover the home team. Let me go with John!"

Abe glared at him and reiterated that this was no democracy.

Chris later told me that he almost got up and turned in his resignation. He was hot. I also later discovered that a couple of the pencil necks had expressed concern over Chris' drinking habits. I drank too, but I was EOD.

I was happy to be on Josh's team with Keith and George. We worked well together and Josh stayed the hell out of our way. For a young, non-military guy he had the leadership thing down pat.

Abe adjourned the meeting and Josh gave his team the heads-up to remain behind. The Tunis team was doing likewise down the hall. Josh handed out our pre-deployment assignments and asked if there were any questions. There were none.

I had been assigned to the range to work with Joe getting our weapons ready and packed. I would be able to get that done before the day was out, then I could help George with the admin weenie stuff. I was out the door in a flash. I looked forward to going over the trip with Joe. I couldn't tell him anything about it but he was no dummy.

When I walked into the range facility Joe was, as usual, in the vault cleaning a new addition to his collection. He looked up and seemingly ignored my entrance. He continued to clean as he started to talk. "Which team did you draw?" Apparently he knew more than I thought. It was stupid of me to think otherwise.

"Cairo," I said.

He continued to talk slowly, "Good, nothing is going to happen in Tunis. That will just be a vacation. Kaddafi hates Mubarak so if anything goes down, it will be Cairo. Of course the rest of the Middle East is going to piss down one leg but we've got nobody there. Syria, Iraq, and Iran have their own problems, so it'll be Cairo." He looked up with a smile.

I looked over on the ready table and he'd already laid out the weapons. MP5s, Brownings, and the ever-present Remington 870, twelve-gauge shotguns. I pulled out the Beretta 70S from the small of my back and broke it down. I grabbed some cleaning gear and started the process of making the little gun ready for a long trip. Cleaned it until it was perfect, then a light coat of oil to keep the rust off. I was going to feel naked until we left.

Joe asked if I wanted an issue Model 19 Smith but I declined. He just shrugged and continued cleaning. I checked out the weapons and realized that Joe had already cleaned and oiled them all. How long had he known about this trip?

With Joe you never knew. The "hard cases" were in the storage room. I dragged them out and positioned them next to the table. Joe stopped cleaning and came over to give me a hand. Not a word was said. The shelf under the table contained the thin sheets of lead.

We started breaking each weapon down and wrapping the parts in the lead. Each team guy had his own case. When all the weapons were packed we labeled them with the team member's names. By 1500 I was done.

I said farewell to Joe and noticed he had returned to meticulously cleaning his weapon. He just nodded when I left without looking up.

I truly wondered what was in his mind. I knew that he loved action and the hairier the better. This had to be killing him. He was a disciplined guy with a ton of common sense. I guess that when he decided to hang it up, he was done. Nothing else to be said. The next few days went fast. We were told to tell our families that we were headed to Cairo for an MTT. Nothing out of the normal for us.

We made the trip without incident and checked into the Nile Hilton. We had made friends with some of the desk guys and waiters. They recognized us when we checked in. It was like old home week. Even with that warm welcome we went to our rooms and waited until our individual prescribed time and went back down to the desk. I complained about the musky odor in my room. I sniffled and coughed to emphasize my displeasure.

George had already moved so I was the second guy on the team. The clerk made apologies and promised to have housekeeping in to de-musk it. After a little song and dance he finally agreed to move me. I'm sure he was pissed by the time the fourth guy wanted to move. Then again, he probably knew what we were up to.

This was no training mission. Two other guys had traveled with us and needed to get up to Alexandria. The RSO had locked on ground transportation so they were to depart early the next morning. We had nothing to do. We finished out the day unpacking, getting a little workout, laying by the pool, then having a nice dinner in the outdoor café area behind the hotel. We were like tourists.

Josh said we would meet with the RSO in the morning after the Alexandria team got on the road. That meant we didn't have to be at the embassy until 1000. We had to find something to do or we were gonna be in trouble. Too much down time for guys like us presented too many opportunities to screw up.

We met in the lobby and walked the short distance to the embassy. We had turned in our weapons cases the night before and now only had our Brownings. We checked through security and made our way to the RSO's office. His secretary was happy to see us. Daniel was gone but the new guy seemed pleasant enough. Boggs was his name. I'm sure it was his last name but everybody just called him Boggs. He was a veteran DSS guy having been around for twenty-plus years. His plan was simple, sit and wait.

In the meantime he was talking about all the trouble he was having with the director of AID (Agency for International Development). The AID guy didn't believe in security, thought it "foolish and Rambo-like" to prepare. Boggs said he couldn't get any cooperation. We banged it back and forth and Josh finally mentioned that they needed a Red Cell-type operation to wake them up. It hit me—we had nothing to do and our foray into the UNGA was legendary. We started to plan.

The AID office was a tall building within the embassy compound. I don't recall exactly but it was seven or eight stories, maybe taller. One floor in the middle was some Egyptian company that was doing contract work for the U.S. government. I never figured that one out. Why didn't they have a separate building, or put them on the top floor? U.S. government on the bottom and top floors with these guys right in the middle. That required a complete separate security system to get into the top floors.

The Director's office was on the top floor. Getting through the first floor would be easy. We could just tell them that we were going to the contractor's offices. That would get us halfway up. Then we'd have to get by the Marine to access the top floors. We wanted to have a look.

I asked the RSO if he had any large-scale building diagrams or blueprints.

He asked what area I wanted and I said I don't care—I just want to carry a half-dozen or so under my arm as a cover. He made a call to the GSO and a box full of tubed blueprints was delivered within five minutes. Now we settled down to plan.

I had the secretary provide me with a large envelope. I stuffed it with some wires, paper clips, and my wrist watch. I sealed it, then wrote on the outside in pen:

To: Director of AID

U.S. Embassy, Cairo

As a return address I wrote:

From: Muammar Kaddafi

Tripoli, Libya

Keith and I were set to go have a look. We would use the afternoon to poke and hope then do our thing the following morning. There were no weapons at security for the top floors. We didn't have to worry about being shot, just about having some young Marine beat the shit out of us with his night stick.

We didn't carry any weapons or cover materials such as the blueprints. We just wanted to have a look. We went through security on the first floor with no restrictions as we weren't going to the top floors. The security guards did a cursory check of our tourist passports. (We carried both diplomatic and tourist passports. We also had a separate set in the event we had to travel to Israel. The Israelis wouldn't let you in if you had an Arab visa stamp.)

We got to the middle floor with no problem. There was a large reception area with people moving everywhere. We were happy to see that there were Americans moving about as well. We fit right in. We moved around a good bit and were never challenged. I looked up and saw a fire escape sign with a lighted

"Exit" above the door. I pointed it out to Keith. We walked over and opened the door.

An Egyptian guard was seated on a folding metal chair in the middle of the landing. He had a small stove that housed his tea cup. He stood immediately when he saw us and blocked our way. He spoke little English and I didn't want him to know I spoke Arabic. He pointed back inside then yelled at another guard who was working the security checkpoint alongside the Marine. Once you went through that checkpoint you could board the elevators to the top floors. We saw that would be very difficult.

When we rode the elevators to the first security level we noticed that the lifts were very crowded. Probably would be more so in the morning when folks reported for work.

The yelling got the Egyptian guard's attention and the Marine as well. When the Marine saw that we were not Egyptians he motioned us over. We smiled and walked over. He asked where we were headed. I told him that we didn't want to be on the crowded elevator and were going to take the stairs down.

He shook his head in the negative. "Sorry, sirs, only way up or down is in the elevator except in case of emergency."

We apologized and moved to take the elevators down. The Marine watched us closely as we boarded the down elevator. Wouldn't be easy and we needed some luck. We hadn't caused a commotion so I doubted that the Marine would make a log entry. He didn't.

We exited the AID building and made our way across the courtyard to the main embassy. We walked into the RSO's office to find Boggs, Josh, and George shooting the bull and drinking Cokes.

"Want a Coke, guys?" We declined.

We started our brief hoping that Boggs could fill in the holes. The guards assigned to AID had not been required to take the training provided by previous MTTs. They were "separate hires." Boggs said that they were very loose and undisciplined. They felt themselves above the embassy guards. The guard that intercepted Keith and I seemed to be partially wired.

We would be going back in the morning and a different Egyptian and Marine guard would be on duty. We gathered some additional equipment to make us look real.

Boggs had obtained some hard hats, like those worn by construction guys, and a couple of clipboards. He also had the secretary make up some bogus, clip-on name tags.

We were set. Workers would start showing up around 0800. We were going to go in at 0755. We needed some luck because we were just going to try and pull this one out of our butts. Boggs gave Keith an unloaded Model 60 Smith & Wesson revolver.

We were at the embassy at 0700. We were cranked and excited just to be doing something, anything. Like grown men playing Cowboys and Native Americans. Keith and I prepared ourselves, then looked at one another. We looked the part. I had my make-believe bomb inside my shirt, half a dozen rolled up blueprints under my arm, and my clipboard. We had attached our name tags to our collars.

Keith was all set with his clipboard and hard hat. He was to appear in charge. He was a huge guy and tended to intimidate. He had the Model 60 tucked into his belt. We had our real IDs within easy reach in case something went to shit. We headed to the AID building. The guard on the first floor could have cared less. Once he realized we weren't going to the top floors he gave us a cursory glance and motioned us toward the elevators that stopped at the contractor's floor.

There was a courier headed toward the top floor elevators so I slipped in behind him. He had a manila folder under his arm that was cluttered with what appeared to be inner embassy correspondence and mail. I eased my "IED" from my shirt and slipped it into his folder. It was so crowded that there was pushing and nudging. The courier didn't notice.

Keith had been watching and when I glanced up at him we made eye contact. He had a smirk and just looked up at the ceiling in disgust.

Phase one done. Now let's see if it made it to the target. In all fairness, it was pre 9-11 and I'm sure this wouldn't be possible today. However, something else might be possible, which is why awareness and training are a must. The bad guys are watching at all times.

We traveled up to the contractor floor and exited to find the reception area more crowded than the lobby downstairs. There was talking and chatter and laughter. You couldn't hear yourself think. We again went unchallenged.

From now on we relied on luck. We had no plan and were just looking for a target of opportunity.

There were two hallways, one to the right and the other to the left of the elevators. We wandered a short way down each and saw nothing that would benefit us—a window, a door, anything that we could use to move upward.

Finally I looked up and saw the familiar "Exit" sign. I looked at Keith and he shrugged a "Why not?" We eased toward the exit door with Keith in the lead. We didn't want to attract any attention. Thus far we were not even noticed. Keith cracked the door and peeked through. I couldn't see but when he looked back at me he had a huge grin. I knew we were in luck.

We eased out onto the landing and found the folding metal chair and the stove with teapot, but no guard. The Marine was so busy managing the crowd and his area of responsibility that he hadn't even seen us.

Keith and I did a hasty high-five on the landing and headed up the flight of stairs. At the first landing we tried the door—locked!

I looked at the system and there was no picking this lock. We had our pick sets with us but there was a tamper plate and a swing hood over the keyhole. No way. I pointed up toward the other set of steps. Keith turned without comment and headed up, two steps at a time.

We arrived on the second landing and the door swung open easily. Not even a lock throw for the doorknob. I guess they figured bad guys couldn't climb this high. There weren't any people immediately visible. We removed our hard hats and stowed them with the plans behind a chair in the reception area. We removed the home-made name tags. The layout on each floor was the same. The top floor was directly above us so we elected to take the elevator.

We pushed the "up" button and waited for alarms, but nothing happened. The doors opened and we stepped in. The doors closed and the upward movement began immediately. We couldn't believe our luck. I do believe that if that little guard had been on the job we would have not been able to go up. We would never have gotten by the Marine.

We stepped off to another empty reception area. The hallway to the left seemed to have more folks walking around so we headed in that direction. There was a small desk located in an alcove about halfway down the hall. No security or guards were present. There was a pretty young Egyptian girl sitting at the desk and she gave us a heartfelt smile as she greeted us.

Keith, being ever in charge, smiled back when she said, "May I help you?"

Keith asked, "Is the Director in?"

"Yes. Do you have an appointment?"

Keith moved past her with me in tow saying, "He's expecting us."

"Sir, sir," she said, trying to stop us with her voice only.

We had seen the office marked "Director." Keith walked into the Director's office; he went left and me right. We faced the Director's desk as he looked up, snatching off his glasses.

"Who the hell are..." but he stopped in panic when he saw Keith's Model 60. There was a pending basket on the filing cabinet that held a stack of mail. I walked over and leafed through and, sure enough, there was my IED. I didn't say anything.

Keith said, "Mr. Director, you are the victim of a mock security terror attack. You can be considered dead at this point."

The Director was shaken. The little girl had hauled ass.

He started to fluster, "You wouldn't have gotten in here with a gun if you weren't Americans."

I pointed to the pending basket and said, "Check your mail, sir."

He walked over and retrieved my "IED." He was shaken by then.

We had a debrief that afternoon in the RSO's office. The NCOIC of the Marines was there, the Egyptian guard supervisor, and the Director. No excuses were made except for the Egyptian who had abandoned his metal chair on the landing. He went downstairs to get food from a friend on the first floor.

So help me, he said, "*Enshallah*, it was in the hands of God." He was fired. That was *Enshallah* also.

Boggs later told us we had created a monster. The director of AID became the most active security individual within the embassy compound. He was so security conscious that he drove the RSO nuts.

I would be willing to bet that a similar penetration would not recur on this Director's watch. It was great fun. From that point on we just hung out and went back and forth from the hotel to the embassy.

We went shopping at the *souk* and bought only those things that a bored person would buy. The hammered brass tables, fake inlaid jewelry boxes, and the other normal crap that gets sold at a yard sale two weeks after you give them as gifts.

We decided to take a trip to the pyramids. We spent the entire morning walking in and around all the tourist areas. We, the security professionals, became unconscious. We were having a blast. We hadn't even mentioned to each other the purpose of our trip. We departed the pyramids for our hotel.

There was an open air restaurant that the Egyptian driver recommended as having the best Egyptian roasted chicken in the world. We were hungry so we agreed to stop. The restaurant was surrounded by a rock wall that was about four feet high. Poles from the wall upwards supported a tin roof. The tables were your standard backyard picnic tables. They were covered with a red and white checkered oil cloth. The place had the air of Key West. The aromas were enough to drive you crazy. Everything smelled good. I had to remember that everything in Egypt gave me diarrhea.

We ordered and were enjoying a Stella (Egyptian) beer. The place was large. There were about forty tables under the tin roof within the wall. Six British tourists came in and sat across the area from us. There were about twelve tables between us. They were obviously tourists and not paying attention to anything.

A well-dressed Arab walked in. He was wearing an expensive European suit and what really struck me was the spit shine on his shoes. He was bald on top but the fringe hair was dark and well kept. He had class. He sat at the next table with his back to us. The waiter walked over and the guy ordered water.

Something about the guy sent my red flags up. Just out of place.

After a few minutes a dark-haired Arab lady walked in with two plastic shopping bags. She sat next to the well-dressed guy and placed one of the bags in front of him. I relaxed as it appeared to be husband and wife. They spoke in whispers with their heads close together.

About five minutes later an Arab in full Arab dress entered the restaurant and seated himself next to the lady. Now all three had their backs to us with shopping bags on the table in front of them.

I watched our Egyptian driver and his nervous eyes were dancing. Either he had recognized these people or he recognized the situation. He later told us that he had recognized the well-dressed Arab. He was a terrorist. (This was later verified by the Israelis.)

George was at the end of the table talking his ass off. I had alerted everyone and was trying to get George's attention. We were all hyped now because something was definitely up. There was something familiar about the woman and the well-dressed man.

The two men had placed their hands in the large shopping bags. They all ignored us to the point it was obvious they didn't want to attract attention.

Josh finally kicked George under the table and got his attention. We stood up and moved to the exit. We paid our tab in full to the objection of the waiter who complained that we hadn't been served yet. The two males and the woman had not been served and they had refused an offer to order. We moved quickly to the van and did a quick search in the event something had been placed.

Josh, wisely, wanted a photo of these folks for the seventh floor. We drove two blocks, then turned right and circled up behind the restaurant, stopping before we were within sight. We got out and John set up his camera. We had retrieved our MP5s and ensured that they were locked and loaded. We moved, with me covering Josh, and Keith providing rear security.

George stayed with the driver to secure the vehicle. We were conscious that if this was an attack team they would have surveillance watching the operation. We crawled up to the wall. Josh, from behind the cover of a palm, took several pictures. This was fun so we decided to push it a little. We moved around the corner to get a different angle. Josh, using his zoom, got some unreal photos. We maneuvered back to our vehicle and headed back to the embassy.

We turned the film over to the RSO and he went through the seventh floor folks. They sent copies to the Israelis and they verified that the well-dressed Arab was wanted by the Mossad and that the female was possibly Ms. Mansur, famous for the Pan Am bombing that killed the young Japanese student en route to Hawaii.

When we went through a recreation of the incident it was determined that they were probably after the British tourists. They didn't even know we were around. The fact that we were there threw a monkey wrench into their plan. When we abruptly departed they probably figured that they had been spotted and aborted the attack. We will never know for sure. Was it really terrorists or was it just a coincidence? I don't regret our actions because the alternative really wasn't a good idea.

We spent an uneventful few days around the pool, at the embassy, and shopping. We were more alert now.

The RSO called and asked us to join him at his office. We went over immediately as we were anxious for work. We filed into his office and took seats.

He said, "Well guys, it's over. The Ambassador departed for the states last evening so the threat is off."

Pyramids

We looked at each other in dismay. What the hell had we been doing for the past few weeks? Now nothing to do?

At around 1800 Cairo time the U.S. bombed the piss out of Libya. At around 2000 the team went down to the disco to celebrate. The place was packed. There was a young blond-headed Australian guy who was the DJ. He was funny as hell. We all danced all over the place by ourselves and drank our asses off.

We finally went over to the DJ and told him to play "Born in the USA" by Springsteen. He about had a kitten. "No way. No way mates, they'll kill me." We told him we would if he didn't. Finally he played it and the team guys were the only ones on the floor. We were getting hatred stares from the rest of the crowd. I finally asked a guy at the bar why everyone acted like they hated us. It wasn't because we'd bombed Libya; it was because we hadn't killed Kaddafi.

That was to be my last MTT trip. It was exciting and adventurous, but all good things must end. We returned and went back through the ritual of weapons and equipment turn-in. I had a deep sense of gloom. I think I suspected that my State Department days were coming to a close.

The normal tour was three years and I was approaching that mark. The head of the training division wanted to contact headquarters Marine Corps and extend my assignment. He was going to send the request through the Secretary of State. I was uneasy about that but as luck had it, the request never got that far.

My tour with the State Department was one that I'll never forget. It was an opportunity to see the internal bowels of the government at work, or sleep, or both at the same time. I met some of the most professional people of my career and some of the biggest goofs. But ain't that life?

I'd been through training that other Marines only dreamed about. I had made friends within organizations that didn't exist. I had traveled to war zones when the U.S. was at peace. I had worked protective details and carried machine guns and hand grenades through the streets of the nation's biggest cities. I had met celebrities and high government officials. I had been present at historic moments for our nation. More importantly, I had been present as security when we transferred custody of "Carlos the Terrorist," and not one bomb has gone off against Americans in Beirut since my last mission. I wouldn't trade one second of it, but I would not do it again…Yes, I would! In a heartbeat!!

I was sitting at the gray beast in the middle of the afternoon. I had just finished a conversation with a fellow speaker at the Monday afternoon Awareness Seminar for soon-to-be travelers.

Her name was Mary Pat and she represented the Agency. She was very interested in the places that I'd traveled. Had she bothered to be present for one of my presentations a year or so earlier I might have been able to help her. She wanted photos of everything I could get. I didn't tell her that my traveling days were done. She departed all excited about the prospect of me getting Intel some information for her presentations. After reading some popular fiction novels I realized that she was a real person or close coincidence. Mary Pat is not a common name but one that appears in more than one current fiction series.

Return to the Corps

After Mary Pat left, I leaned back and put my feet up on the gray beast. Once again, as so long ago, I entwined my fingers behind my head and relaxed. I wondered what tomorrow held in store?

I had received a call from a Major Tenus from Headquarters Marine Corps. He wanted to talk to me. He was a nervous-sounding guy and spoke in a gravelly whisper. I later learned that he sounded nervous because he was a hyper workaholic. He wasn't afraid of anything, least of all senior officers. When he called, he kept referring to me as Mr. Skinner. I was soon to find out why.

295

CHAPTER SIXTEEN

Back to the Corps—MAU(SOC)

I had no idea how long I'd been leaning back with my feet propped on the gray beast. I must have dozed because when I opened my eyes, Denise was standing in front of my desk with her hands on her hips glaring at me.

She said, "Too much travel these days?"

I gave her an embarrassed laugh. "Just checking my eyelids for light leaks," I sheepishly smiled.

She'd tell everybody that the Marine was sleeping on duty then I'd hear about it for days. She told me that I had a call holding.

I asked who it was and she shrugged as she turned to walk away. Over her shoulder she said, "I think he said 'Major somebody'."

I thought, Oh hell, that bonehead from Quantico has a wild hair up his ass again. I vowed that as soon as I pinned on Major I was gonna call this turd and tell him what a prick he was. I never really understood why this guy took such a special interest in me. I think that it was a combination of jealousy from my MTT assignment and his inability to control me. Guess I'll never know and I can assure you, I'll never lose sleep over it. I didn't know it then, but I was to never pin on Major even though I was selected. I did get the chance to tell the good major what an asshole he was. I took full advantage of that opportunity.

I started this book with the concept of revealing the birth of Explosive Entry and the evolution of the U.S. Marine Corps into the special operations arena, or the birth of MAU(SOC). It has taken me a long time to get here but the background and foundation was necessary.

I picked up the phone and answered in my best Marine Corps voice, "Captain Skinner, sir." What greeted me was a fast-talking northern accent that kept me about two words behind him throughout the conversation.

"Mr. Skinner, this is John Tenus at HQMC (Headquarters Marine Corps)," he rapid-fired. Before I could respond, he continued, "I was talking to a guy the other day and your name came up."

I nodded and listened because I knew it wouldn't do any good to try and interrupt this guy. I knew he was a major because Denise said so. I was still contemplating the "*Mr.* Skinner."

He said that he'd like to meet with me if it was convenient. I'm thinking that it is always convenient for a captain to meet with a major. May not be liked but it was convenient at all times. Besides, now I was curious. He was very cryptic in his conversation. He further said that he couldn't discuss it over the phone.

I was starting to sweat bullets now. I started thinking about Beirut, Cairo, Bogota, and God only knew what else.

He asked if I knew where HQMC was located.

I replied in the affirmative.

He said that there was a cafeteria in the basement of the main building. Could I meet him there at 1030 tomorrow morning?

"Yes, sir," I told him.

"Thank you, Mr. Skinner. We'll see you in the morning." And he hung up.

I sat there for a second or two, maybe more. My mind was going a million miles an hour. Well, I thought as I replaced the receiver, it will have to wait until 1030 tomorrow.

When I arrived at the gray beast the next morning Abe was already there. He grabbed a cup of coffee and sat in the chair in front of my desk. He sipped his coffee, eyeing me over the mug. He also had that intense way of looking over the top of his glasses at the same time. Searching, questioning without opening his mouth.

I shrugged and asked, "What's on your mind, Abe?"

He just kept looking at me. It became unnerving.

He slowly sat his mug down on the beast and responded, "What's up with you? You were not yourself last night when you left work and you're even more out there this morning."

I knew that it would not be wise to bullshit at this point. I had no idea what to expect in my meeting with Major Tenus.

I gave Abe a *Reader's Digest* version of the previous day's conversation. He again picked up his mug and contemplated what I'd told him.

After a moment or two he looked at me very seriously and said, "Be careful. I know that you've been around and you have been my go-to guy for a couple of years. I want to keep you here but that is not healthy for your career." Everyone knew that Officer's had to get their ticket punched in various billets for career progression. He ended the conversation with, "Just be careful."

Abe had been around also and had been an Army officer in the intelligence field. I was gonna take that advice. My antennae would be on "receive" during the meeting with Tenus. We finished our coffee and I turned to my last trip report. Every time I had to do a report I reflected back on Top Fox's hatred of paperwork.

I entered the cafeteria at Headquarters Marine Corps at 0930. I was gonna be overly careful. I had no idea what to expect. I was wearing khaki pants, a blue pin-striped Oxford shirt, and a blue blazer.

The only thing that hinted of Marine officer was the highly spit-shined Bass Weejuns. Shiny shoes were a legacy of my father, not the Corps.

I poured myself a cup of coffee in a Styrofoam cup, mixed in one packet of sugar, then seated myself away from the crowd, near the windows. I watched as people came and went. Young officers, anxious to please. Old, crusty senior SNCOs who could give a shit who they pleased. It was good to be back.

I had a feeling it was him as soon as he walked into the cafeteria. Short and wiry with longer hair than was expected on a Marine major. He was very jerky and moved his eyes over the crowd with lightening speed. But I could tell that this was a practiced art, as nothing seemed to escape his glance. I'd seen guys like this before. Photographic in every sense. His eyes passed over me not seeming to notice. He scanned behind, around, and in front of me, then his eyes resettled on me.

A huge grin broke out over his normally serious face. He moved toward me in that same fast, jerky motion that he had projected upon arrival. He was ten meters away and had already extended his right hand for what was to be one of the firmest handshakes I'd had in a while. Ours has been a good and adventurous friendship for many years. Both of us are gray but he still is fast, jerky, and all-seeing.

We sat side by side as John didn't want to be heard. John is the type of person who enjoys the spooky side of our mission. To him it was all a conspiracy.

He whispered out of the side of his mouth as he spoke, "I can't believe that there is a real Frank Skinner. In my effort to get this thing going for the commandant, all I hear is the name Frank Skinner. We have a mutual friend at SEAL Team Six. He told me that the person I needed to help and give credibility was Frank Skinner. So I ask, 'Where can I find this Mr. Skinner? Is he a contractor, Army, Navy…what?' The guy from Six said that Skinner is a Marine officer!"

At this point I had no idea of what, when, where, or who he was talking about. I continued to listen. Apparently this mutual friend had sold me up good. John decided to shift gears and give me a little background.

He started explaining, "General Gray, the current commandant, has directed that HQMC stand up a strike university to train deploying Force Recon units in hostage rescue and other special operations missions. Direct action teams."

He continued, "General Gray has given the task to Code T (Training) and Code PP&O (Plans, Policy and Operations) HQMC. The exact location of this university or training site is still being discussed. There are several options on the table. One option is Weapons Training Battalion at Quantico. We're also looking at Fort A.P. Hill."

I was all ears at this point. Somebody had finally agreed that the Marine Corps was a logical choice for the Direct Action

Missions. We had Marines on float in the form of Marine Amphibious Units (MAU) fully equipped and capable of being on target within six hours.

John continued, "We are putting together a training cadre and would like for you to head it up."

I was shocked! What the hell did I know about the operational requirements of a MAU? What could I possibly teach Force Recon Marines about direct action? I expressed this to John.

He was undaunted in his effort to convince me. He said, "It's not going to be Big Picture stuff. The main focus will be on shooting, tactics, driving, surveillance, and surveillance detection. We also want you to develop an explosive entry program within the Force Recon companies. We're talking entry level training initially, with a big push to train the trainer."

John was so excited that it was hard to not get caught up in his enthusiasm. John is another of those unsung heroes. Today the Corps has finally moved into the special operations force (SOF) community right alongside DevGroup (new name for ST-6) and Delta. I understand from some of the Senior NCOs who I remain in contact with that MarSoc and Spec Ops Battalions (MSOB) within the Marine Corps are going through some growing pains.

True or not, I've been told that the Corps is trying to handle SOF funding as if it were normal Marine Corps money. It is not being freely released to the using units. Big mistake if the Corps wants to keep pace.

I learned early on that "black money" (funds allocated to Special Operation Forces that are outside the normal funding sources) is dangerous and requires strict control but it must be available to stay on the cutting edge of the SOF mission. While the Director of Operations at a Virginia training facility, I witnessed SEALs, Delta and other federal agencies training with top-notch equipment. When the Marine Special Operations Battalions (MSOB or MarSoc) came to train they still had the old, dated gear that I had used in 1990. It was state of the art in 1990 but 2007 is a different story.

At this point I want to qualify the previous statements. I have no connections with any of the Marine units other than what I've heard from several sources. I only hope that it's not true. If true, it takes time to grow into a functional, cohesive unit. How long has it taken Delta and Team Six to get to the level that they enjoy today?

When John finished his explanation I felt excited to be considered but lacking in the skills that the Corps required. He again assured me that I was exactly what the Corps needed. I was coming in from an outside agency with more than a little mystique. No axes to grind and nobody after my ass…yet!

Nobody really knew what I'd been doing. I had the strangest feeling that John knew everything that I'd done.

I was nervous as hell. I wanted the job but had no visions of grandeur. If I had a crystal ball I would never have taken the job. Abe had already told me that I would stay with the MTTs until I retired if I wanted it. With no crystal ball and John's sales pitch I asked, "When would I report?"

He broke out into a huge smile and asked, "You'll take the job?" Without taking a breath he continued, "I can have you transferred this afternoon."

My eyes must've gotten huge because he held up both hands and said, "We can do it tomorrow. That'll give you time to move your gear over to my office."

At this point you have to understand, the Marine Corps doesn't move that fast. I had the EOD Program Monitor who was anti SpecOps, anti State Department and anti anything that wasn't EOD-related. I don't mean that in a negative way because his job was to look out for the EOD program. We were limited in numbers and he had to allocate limited assets as it was. He couldn't afford to have his senior folks running around being Ninja warriors (our sarcastic nickname in those days).

I told John that if he could get me transferred tomorrow I'd do it. I personally thought he was a little full of shit at that point.

He jumped up like a jack-in-the-box and grabbed my hand, saying, "Welcome aboard!"

I just smiled because I knew this was a) too good to be true, and b) too short-fused. I figured it would happen and I thought it was one hell of an opportunity, but realistically I had another one to three months at State before John could pull it off.

I underestimated the power of General Gray. I briefed the big boss when I returned. He didn't really seem to care one way or the other. Abe was disappointed to see me leave but excited about the opportunity for me. He was the Reserve Army Officer and, like me, knew that it would take a month or two. I had a long talk with the MTT chief and he took it a little tougher.

He was disappointed because it was going to create a huge hole in his teams. Not that I was great. He just relied on me heavily because Marines tend to get things done without a great deal of bitching. In the end he was happy to see me going into full time Spec Ops training.

An hour after I got back to the office all hell broke loose. The phone was ringing off the hook. Denise was going nuts. She heard I was leaving and was monitoring all incoming calls. She was in tears several times because we were all "her guys." The first call was from the EOD boss at HQMC.

"What the fuck are you up to now, Frank?" he literally screamed into the phone.

I waited until there was a long pause and told him that I had been requested to assist with the MAU(SOC) initiative. That sent him spinning big time.

"Since when does HQMC go directly to my EOD officers and have them transferred without going through me?" He was yelling again. "What behind the scenes shit have you been up to?"

I didn't know how much I could talk about because John had insisted that everything about MAU(SOC) was classified. Obviously the EOD boss wasn't aware of anything. I decided to play dumb.

"Sir, when I got the call from HQMC, I assumed that it had been cleared through you. This is new to me—I initiated nothing!"

Now I was getting hot because that was the truth. I believed in the Marine creed, "We're all Marines first." I recommended that he give Major Tenus a call. They were both majors and could yell at each other.

The next call I got was from a clerk at HQMC personnel. "Sir, I have a set of orders for you. Can I have a courier bring them over so that you can sign for them?"

I still had a slight smirk when I asked, "Can you tell me the report date?"

The young clerk sounded dumbfounded on the other end of the line when he said, "0800 tomorrow, sir."

Those Marines out there, especially from my era, can understand my shock. Man, what was I getting into? The very next thought was of Susan. That should be an easy sell because I'd be leaving the MTTs. Going to a training cadre with no more trips to Beirut. I put that problem on the back burner as a non-issue.

I told my bosses and they were shocked as well. I leaned back in my chair and gave this situation some serious thought.

Denise walked in with hands on hips and said, "You're quitting on us!"

I gave her a brotherly smile and that pissed her off more. I said, "Denise, I'm a Marine officer. I just do what I'm told and I expect those Marines that work with me to do what I tell them. That's just how the system works."

"Damn you and your Marines," she huffed, spinning on her heals leaving me with my thoughts. A few minutes later the phone rang.

After a few seconds Denise yelled, "It's your Major buddy on line two." I picked up the phone, "Captain Skinner, sir."

"Frank! Got your orders yet? Courier took them over a while ago."

I told him that I'd received a call but hadn't seen the orders yet. It was 1630.

John started fidgeting on the phone and told me to hang on. I heard him yelling at some unknown person, obviously of lesser rank. "Where the hell are Skinner's orders? I've got him on the phone and he hasn't seen them."

At the same time Denise walked in with a large manila envelope. She threw it on my desk. As she turned she said that a courier had just delivered this and she had signed for it.

I ripped open the envelope and there, bigger than shit, were my orders to report to Code T, HQMC by 0800 tomorrow. I calmed John down and told him I had my orders. He was all happy again. He said, "See you in the morning," and hung up.

Damn. I wanted to ask for a day or two to pack my trash. Guess not. I had an hour or so instead.

I got home late and Susan and the boys were waiting. Mikey was still a baby and Stephen was the ever-present big brother. Stephen dragged Mike around the house like a rag doll and Mike loved it. When I walked in Stephen ran up and gave me a hug, and I saw Mike with his huge smile when he saw me come in. Got my welcome from Mama.

I told Susan about the day's developments and she was extremely happy. She didn't even comment about the fact that I'd taken the job without discussing it with her. She was a little concerned when I told her that it hadn't been finalized as to where the school was to be located. To her, as long as it wasn't Beirut she was happy. I think she wanted to see me in uniform again.

Uniforms!! Hadn't worn one in over two years. Didn't even know if they fit. I had to check in wearing class-A greens. Luckily all my uniforms were organized in the spare bedroom closet. They had been cleaned a few months back and were still in plastic. Now for the fit. That was a close one. I'd been working out and needed some tailoring. That would have to wait.

Just finding John's office the next morning was a real treat. I walked in and now *Major Tenus* was his usual helter-skelter self. He took me on a whirlwind introduction tour. I was introduced to colonels, majors, and generals. It was as though I was the major's trophy. As it turned out, I was the test case to see if they could actually make things happen that fast. I saw many a head shake, as they couldn't believe it either.

I was introduced to Lieutenant Colonel Trout, the boss at Code T. At 1300 they took me in to meet the general.

He had the appearance of being half asleep and bored with what was going on and being discussed. I was wrong. He would raise his head and open his eyes and ask specific questions that proved he was not only listening but digesting every word. This was just his way of disarming the speaker. I filed this knowledge away. Apparently Colonel Trout and Major Tenus already had done, too, because they delivered their well-rehearsed brief like the professionals they were.

That entire period of time is a blur to me. John was trying to put the MAU(SOC) training package together for the East (Second Marine Division) and West (First Marine Division) Coast Marines. I realized that there was extreme resistance to this training from HQMC. The Second's Special Operations Training Group (SOTG) was being trained by the FBI's Hostage Rescue Team (HRT) and the First's SOTG was being trained by the LAPD SWAT. There was no love lost between the FBI and the LAPD.

I was cast into the equation as the guy who would make it work or be the fall guy. John figured that nobody could argue the fact that I was the Subject Matter Expert (SME) for Explosive Entry. LAPD, FBI, First SOTG and Second SOTG all agreed that I was the right guy to train the Force Recon Marines, and later the FAST companies from FMFLant and FMFPac.

My first training trip was to Camp Lejeune. I had worked a deal with HRT on the East Coast and Charlie at Orange County Sheriff's Office in California. I had my explosives sources.

We went to the range on Monday morning and started with basic demolitions. This went fast as all Force Recon Marines are exposed to the basics. We then discussed theory, $P = E$, and the three effects of a detonation (thermal, frag, and overpressure). Things were clicking along fine.

On the second day, one of the Marines got injured. He'd live but it required a trip to the hospital. I called the commanding officer of Second Force and reported the accident. I asked, "Do you want me to shut it down?"

"Hell, no! Continue to train!"

I was happy. I was finally back among Marines. The training went well except for the Avon mishap that I discussed earlier. Two accidents and I was still in business. I met with the C.O. of Second SOTG and he was adamant about having me train his instructors. He was serious about the Train the Trainer concept.

I began to understand John's motives. If he could get all the players to request my training from Code T, it would be logical to administer all of the training from Code T. Not that easy. It amazed me as to the small differences between the LAPD and HRT training. For example, LAPD taught Instinctive Shooting. This was also a favorite taught by John Shaw at the Mid South Institute of Self-Defense Shooting. HRT taught Front Sight Press. Both techniques were effective. Instinctive shooting was faster and front sight press was more accurate but slower.

Another difference was that LAPD taught that the breacher laid out the Nonel between the stack and the wall. HRT taught that the Nonel was laid outside the team. I preferred this because it allowed the Nonel to blow out and away from the team. If laid between the wall and the team it could blow out and tangle the feet of the assaulters.

There were other differences—minor, but during this time frame they were monumental to the players on each coast. Now I was to really stir it up.

My Delta buddy was the Director of Training at BSR. John wanted to know if he was available to train the MAU(SOC) Marines. I set it up and we were to travel together to Camp Pendleton. Now there was a third school of thought: Delta. My buddy and I tied our training together so as to ease the tension. LAPD was still anti anything not LAPD.

Unfortunately, one of the Marines was transitioning from his MP5 to his 45 while on the move and got tangled in all that Velcro and straps on the SAS-style drop holster. My buddy and I had complained about all the fancy, sexy stuff that the students were wearing. Result was that the Marine shot himself in the ass. One of the LAPD guys wrote a letter and back-dated it complaining that our training was unsafe. Fortunately the investigation uncovered this and blame was laid on the equipment.

Lieutenant Colonel Stedman was the C.O. of the First SOTG. He was one of the finest officers I've ever had the privilege to work for. He had a deep Southern twang that entertained you while conveying his message loud and clear. He was completely aware of all the issues that faced his command. One of those was the need for commercial explosives. He always referred to my explosives as "dee-mo-litions."

He asked me to construct a couple of charges. First, he wanted an oval made from triple-strand detonating cord. Refresher: Military detonating cord is 50-grain per foot. Three strands equal 150 grains per foot. He then asked what size flex I needed to get through a solid core door. I told him that 40 would do it. He asked that I make an oval out of 40-grain flex. I had no idea what he was up to. Didn't have to know because an officer like Colonel Stedman knew what he was doing.

A staff car pulled up on the range with red flags flying. Each flag had the two stars of a major general. Colonel Stedman met the car and opened the door for the general. They were obviously familiar with each other and the general addressed Colonel Stedman as an equal.

"Billy, what the hell is going on here that is so important?"

"General, I want you to meet Frank Skinner." Colonel Stedman was like that. I never recall hearing him refer to me as Captain Skinner. I shook the general's hand after a proper salute. Wasn't sure which to do first, so I whipped out a smart one.

Colonel Stedman said, "Frank, set up that detonating cord shot on the door." His Marines had hung a solid door from the steel door frame at the shooting house. I grabbed the charge and placed it on the door. I walked backwards, feeding out the Nonel. I was about twenty-five feet farther away from the charge than was Colonel Stedman or the general.

I said, "Colonel Stedman, you gents might want to move back here with me."

"Naw, we're okay here," he drawled. The general wasn't paying much attention and didn't hear our conversation.

I yelled "Fire in the hole" three times, as required by demo range regulations. "I have control."

Five, four, three, two, one...BBBAAANNNGGG!! The blast rocked me and I saw the general bend over in an attempt to mitigate the overpressure.

"Holy shit, Billy—you trying to kill me?"

The colonel was talking away about blast, frag, and overpressure associated with military explosives. In the time it took for him to explain, his Marines had cleared the shattered door and re-hung another in its place.

As if on cue, Col Stedman motioned for me to hang the 40-grain charge on the door, which I did. I knew where he was headed with this. I stepped about two feet back from the charge, shielding myself from the frag with the steel doorjamb. The general was paying close attention by then.

"Is that safe, Captain Skinner?"

I heard Colonel Stedman tell him, "Frank's been doin' dee-mo-litions his whole life."

Once again I yelled, "Fire in the hole," and went through the countdown. I always insisted that every shot be conducted in that manner. Therefore the countdown becomes second nature. Probably drove some engineers nuts after I retired. The shot went off and I saw that the general wasn't even touched by the overpressure. He tensed for it but it never reached him. When the smoke cleared there was a perfect oval that looked like it had been cut with a saw.

Colonel Stedman was closing the deal now. "Suh, that's why we need a commercial explosives allocation."

The general was amazed. He just kept running his fingers around the edge of the cut. He looked inside and saw the intact plug lying just inside the door. He looked at me, then at Stedman, and said, "Get your requirements in for training and sustainment while Captain Skinner is here to help out."

We continued training the First Force guys for the next two weeks. It was twenty-hour days of high intensity training. The instructors were fired up and the students were hungry for knowledge. They kept referring to "another tool in the tool box."

The last night of training we were to conduct a full mission profile with a hostage rescue and snatch at the shooting house.

At noon we turned the Marines over to their command structure and called a meeting. We laid out the scenario.

The ambassador and two of his colleagues had been kidnapped in Beirut. We know the group was the PSP (Peoples Socialist Party) but we had no knowledge as to the location. Camp Pendleton was to now be considered Lebanon and the range complex was West Beirut. Eye-witnesses say that the ambassador was wounded but moving under his own power as he was taken from the Silky Restaurant. The other two hostages appeared unharmed.

There was a great deal more, but I just want to give you the basic outline. The Marines were to come in by rubber boat, infiltrate to the range area, and locate the ambassador. Of course they needed his location and we would feed that to them as time progressed.

When we finished the brief we monitored their questions. The questions would tell the instructors whether the students had grasped the concept of operations. So far, so good. Questions came in like wildfire. We never heard one goofy or irrelevant question.

We had to give them intel quickly so that they could plan. They were told the location of the building but not which room or floor of the building. They would have to clear it all until they found the ambassador. Priority was the ambassador. Once located, they were to "grab and go." Don't wait to retrieve the two friends. If they located the two friends first and they were mobile, they could also be rescued.

Colonel Stedman had invited the same general to witness the exercise. The general readily accepted the invite.

Colonel Stedman took it to the next level, "Suh, would you pose as the ambassador?"

Again the general accepted. Colonel Stedman was slick as a minnow's dick. "Win the hearts and minds."

We fed them intel all afternoon. We had given them general construction of the building. The exterior doors were solid wood or metal, interior doors were hollow core, ladders were required to reach windows. We threw in some other problems such as there was an orphanage housed in the same building. Twenty or thirty kids lived in the building and might be used as human shields.

It was a hoot watching these guys plan, finalize, contradict, revise, and plan again. Just like real life. We would change intel just to watch how they responded. We were very careful not to make the problem impossible or hokey. It was real life.

Their plan was final and the assault was planned for 2400. They had considered everything, including Murphy. They had backups for backups.

Really a nice job. We had finally given them some floor plans. They did a chalk talk then laid out engineer tape on the ground to do a walk through.

We heard comments like "smooth is fast," "careful hurry," and especially, "Not that way, you dumb ass!" A good time was being had by all.

My Delta buddy remained with the shooters and I watched over the breachers. They were constructing two folding ovals with 60-grain flex and two with 40-grain flex.

They made twelve one-liter water bottles so that each team member could carry one in their cargo pocket. They also made twelve C-charges to also be carried by each member. They even made up extra firing systems that they would carry in the event they had a misfire. The Marines were good, and they knew it.

We all lashed up at around 2000. They final plan was taking form. They had developed a stealthy approach to be followed by a breach-initiated assault (dynamic entry). They had included the color-coding system of the building so that if "Red (a) (3)" was broadcast over the radio, the Red would stand for the side of the building, the (a) would be the floor and the (3) would be which window.

Sniper/observer teams were to cover two opposing corners that would give 360-degree eyes-on.

Their backup plan, in the event they were compromised or the tangos started killing hostages, was an emergency assault. High diddle, diddle, right up the gut. All sound and light discipline would go away and hell would break loose.

The exercise would conclude once the ambassador was turned over to medical, which was represented by the general's driver at the staff car located 200 meters from the house. We had set up the house with targets and doors. They had decided to attack multiple entry points. This was tricky because you didn't want the assaulters shooting each other. The team leaders had planned well.

There was more fun to come. The Marines were going to simulate coming from rubber boats. We all knew that Recon Marines didn't need to practice that. We let them form at the hard road about three-quarters of a mile from the house. They had to stealth in, set the charges, then assault. Snipers were in place by 2130 and reporting. At 2300 the general showed up.

We walked around explaining everything and I could tell that Colonel Stedman was very excited. He and I were going to sit in the house as the other two hostages and the general would be there also. He didn't know it yet. He had no idea that he would be inside the room when the explosive breach was initiated. The Marine Corps was still settling in to the "live fire" scenario's. He was the ambassador. We had a radio so we could monitor the traffic. I also had communications with my Delta buddy.

2330. Showtime. Colonel Stedman went first, followed by the general, with me bringing up the rear. We strolled into the shooting house with flashlights and could hear the snipers reporting our activity. Colonel Stedman was talking and explaining as we eased into the target room. The general was enthralled and didn't seem to notice that he was in the "kill zone". Colonel Stedman was explaining the Good Guy/Bad Guy targets that we had set up. He further explained about safety and the importance of target placement. He was on a sales pitch that we weren't just a bunch of cowboys.

At 2350 I walked over and sat in a stuffed chair. Colonel Stedman and the general sat on the sofa. I had noticed that the radio traffic from the assault unit had ceased. Snipers were still pumping them info. That meant they were close, perhaps even outside placing their charges. I listened intently as the snipers quietly kept the assault team informed of our activity. I checked my watch. 2400!

All of a sudden...BOOM!! Then yelling, "GET DOWN... GET DOWN...U.S. MARINES...U.S. MARINES...STAY DOWN!!"

Several more booms occurred as "flash bangs" were tossed into adjacent rooms as the assault progressed. I watched the general and he was frozen, hands on knees and watching the door.

The door swung open as the C-charge functioned and a flash bang was tossed in. Now here is where it gets funny.

We hadn't told the Marines that there would be live hostages, much less their commanding general. You could see the shock in their eyes as they dynamically entered the room using the Long wall/Short wall assault tactic.

Here's what made us proud to be Marines that night. As fast as their eyes registered shock they changed to "get down to business." They focused on the targets that were right next to us and finished the job.

Covering us they yelled at us to "get on the ground!"

They were on the job, general or no general.

We had taught hostage-handling techniques. These included the Stockholm Syndrome, when the hostage identifies with the tango and the fact that the tangos like to pose as hostages when they get their asses kicked.

We were flex-cuffed, asked if we were hurt, then pulled to our feet and escorted out. The general was shaking his head with a huge grin on his face. It wasn't just me—the general was proud of his Marines, too.

They collapsed out of the target area and covered our movement to the "Medical Unit." The general's driver was having kittens. He had no idea about what just went down and was very concerned for his general. Of course, the general was playing a good part as the "wounded ambassador."

It was time to end the exercise. I motioned to Colonel Stedman by drawing my thumb across my throat. He yelled out,

"Exercise terminated. Cease fire. Cease fire. Unload, clear, and lock all weapons."

The general started shaking hands and patting backs. The men were still pumped—this was a dangerous time: adrenaline at the max, loaded weapons, and super-hyped Marines. I had them all face in a safe direction and show me their open bolts with clear chambers. All weapons were safe. Then I let them celebrate.

This little exercise served as a coup for Colonel Stedman and his SOTG. It also helped HQMC in its effort to standardize all training. This general was now a solid advocate of MAU(SOC). He was to show up many times during future training and was more than welcome. Good man.

The next day my Delta buddy and I took the day off. We went to the laundromat to clean our gear. We bought a six-pack of Corona and a couple of limes. As we sat waiting for the washers to finish he looked at me and said, "I don't think we'll live to our fiftieth birthdays, not with this lifestyle."

Now he is sixty and I am fifty-eight. We laugh about that comment and say, "What are we supposed to do now?"

He was normally a quiet guy and never did you see him expose his personal thoughts. I knew that he'd been thinking about that comment before he said it.

Later that day we went for a jog on the beach. He had legs that went to his chin. I'm built for agility (short little turd). When we got back we were stretching and cooling down. I looked back down the beach in the direction from which we'd returned and saw that he had one foot print for every two of mine. I said, "Hey, you gotta go do it again!" He looked at me with that dark, blank stare. He then looked back down the beach and just shook his head.

When I got back to HQMC there was a move afoot to put Strike University at Mot Lake on the Fort Bragg complex. The rangers and Tier Two guys were already training there.

Lieutenant Colonel Densing worked directly for the commandant. Colonel Densing was driving the train for Mot Lake.

A team was formed to go down and evaluate the area and the program.

I was put on the team that was headed up by Lieutenant Colonel Bell. There were two other captains, both with Force Recon. One was from the East Coast and one from the West. We were briefed that our guidance was to make Mot Lake work because it was what the commandant wanted.

As you know by now, I wasn't a Force Recon guy. My interest was explosive entry. My thoughts were that if they had a demo range we could make it work. We all looked around and didn't see anything spectacular. We all had the feeling that we could do it better on our own. But our orders were to make it work.

We returned and worked a couple of days putting together a brief for the commandant and assistant commandant. We were ready. Colonel Bell handled it like the pro that he was and is. As he briefed, Colonel Densing was in the front row. All of us riff raff were in the back. Colonel Bell went through his presentation trying to put a positive slant on Mot Lake. It was obvious that he wasn't in favor of it.

The commandant spoke up to that effect. "Colonel, it sounds to me like you think we can do this better in the Marine Corps."

"Yes, sir, I do."

"Then why don't you brief it with this slant?"

"Sir, we got the guidance from a member of your staff that we had to make this work."

The commandant jumped up and said, "I don't know who on my staff would say such a thing," looking directly at Colonel Densing. He then bellowed, "IT IS MY OPINION, THERE-FORE YOUR OPINION, THAT WE HAVE TO PREPARE FOR SO/LIC. IF WE CAN DO IT BETTER, THEN WE WILL."

"Yes sir, no sir, three bags full!" Off we went with a full thirty-inch step.

The problem remained—where do we put Strike University? Weapons Training Battalion (WTBN) was looming closer and closer. In my opinion, the biggest mistake of the MAU(SOC) introduction was placing it at WTBN. WTBN is the home of the shooting teams and that is the primary focus of that unit.

When I got back to Code T, I had to brief everybody as to what went down. There was speculation as to which personalities were at play and whose egos were getting bruised. I experienced none of that on the trip to Bragg.

East, west, north, and south all worked well together to find a common solution.

Except when Colonel Bell told me to "Shut the fuck up." He was frustrated while trying to comply with the guidance he'd been given. I must have spoken out of turn or he had bigger fish to fry than breaching. Anyhow, I followed my last order and I "shut the fuck up."

On one such meeting Colonel Trout asked me, "Frank, if you had your choice of Marines from the Force units, who would you pick?" I started to answer and the Colonel said, "Write them down for me."

I had identified some sharp guys at First and Second Force. I came up with eight or ten names and gave them to the Colonel without thinking too much about it.

Holy crap!! Based on my list, orders were issued for every Marine who I had listed. Of course they were the cream of the crop and First and Second Force Companies were pissed off at Captain Frank Skinner. All of the guys wanted to come back but were afraid of repercussions. We had to go back to the drawing board on that one. I would also have to be careful in the future about what I said. Maybe Colonel Bell was right—"Frank, shut the fuck up!"

The decision finally came down. WTBN at Quantico was to be the new home of Strike University. Word was out. My orders were being cut.

John came to me and said, "WTBN is going to hold your guys' record books. You will be Administratively connected (AdCon) (administratively connected) only. You will remain Operationally connected (OpCon) to Code T." How bad could that be?

I hadn't met the colonel yet. Commanding officer, WTBN. John had my orders issued and told me to carry my record book and health record down to WTBN so that we could start getting people in to fill the instructor billets.

I had all my gear and was getting ready to head south. Colonel Trout and John wanted to have a word with me first. I went into the colonel's office. We all sat down. Colonel Trout looked stern as did John, which was highly unusual.

Colonel Trout opened the lecture, "Frank, when you report in, just turn your records in and leave. The colonel at WTBN has been briefed not to ask any questions as he will not have the need to know. You handle yourself well, and can deal with him." Here we go again. Frank, the sacrificial lamb on the march again.

I made sure that I looked squared away in my Charlie uniform, then took off. I pulled into the parking lot and headed toward a door with "Admin" painted on a neat red board above the door. One thing that struck me was the cleanliness of the battalion area and the ranges. It looked like a postcard. I knew from experience that places don't look like this without some serious effort. I was thankful that I wasn't a lance corporal again. I was later to learn that rank had no privileges when you worked for the colonel. Lieutenant colonels also cut grass. That tells you where a captain plugs in.

I introduced myself to the admin officer and everyone in the office turned to look at me. Looks like my reputation preceded me. The admin officer was a young warrant officer. I also later learned that everybody here was a shooter first. Oh, by the way, you can cook or you can do admin or you can drive a truck.

The WO said, "I think the colonel would like to see you, Captain." He had a smile on his face that unnerved me. Spider to the fly. He picked up the phone and punched a couple of numbers.

"Sir, Captain Skinner is here. Yes, sir…yes, sir." He looked up at me and at my ribbons then again said into the phone, "Yes, sir."

He replaced the receiver, picked up my records and said, "Follow me, sir." We exited into a long hallway and hung a left. The door at the end of the hall had a large glass window. Above the door on the same type red board were the words "Commanding Officer." I followed the WO and stood back while he knocked. Man, this is gonna be another tight-assed meeting with me bobbing my head and shuckin' and jivin.'

"Come on in, come on in!!" came a voice from inside the office. The WO opened the door and stood aside for me. Wham—was I shocked. There was more memorabilia in this huge office than there was in a museum. There were busts and prints of John Wayne everywhere. A long, highly polished conference table shared dominance of the room with the colonel's desk. Spaced down the conference table were huge bowls of peanuts and candy.

I looked up and had my first glimpse of the colonel. A legend in the shooting community. A legend in the Corps as well. The colonel had developed the sniper program to its present status; it was envied and attended by all.

My first thought when I saw the colonel was, "Hell, this is Popeye the Sailor!!" He was shaved bald but had a tuft of chest hair spilling from over his t-shirt. He had removed his utility jacket and only had on trousers and the t-shirt. He looked to be about fifty, but with guys like this it was hard to tell. He was small but very wiry and obviously in good shape. What impressed me were his huge forearms, just like Popeye.

I locked myself at the position of attention preparing to give the "Sir, Captain Skinner reporting as ordered."

He cut me short. "Frank? That's right, ain't it?" He was holding out his right hand for the shake. I was a little dumbfounded but what the hell, it was his battalion. I took his hand and experienced a firm but not overpowering handshake. Certainly one of confidence.

I answered, "Yes, sir, Captain Frank Skinner reporting as ordered."

"Yeah, yeah…have a seat. Want some peanuts…how about some candy?"

I looked up and saw the WO with an open smile at this point.

The colonel indicated to the WO that he was no longer needed. "Me and Frank gonna get to know one another."

He started his spiel. "Ya know, Frank, takes a lot to piss me off. I can't remember the last time I got really pissed except for my wife. The only thing that really pisses me off is when I'm told I can't ask one of my captains any questions."

With that he stopped talking and stared me in the eye. I knew this wasn't the kind of man that you wanted to avoid eye contact so I locked with him.

I started slowly and with confidence, "Sir, I been around a day or two and I've definitely learned one thing." I could tell from a slight twinkle in his eye that I had his interest. I paused, with eyes still locked on his. "I have learned that when my commanding officer asks me a question, I give him a straight, honest answer to the best of my ability."

He leaned over and slapped me on the back and said, "We're gonna get along fine. I don't have many rules. Main thing is I hate trash. It drives me crazy but I don't make people pick it up. I just don't let anyone go home until it gets picked up. If a screen is tore up in the barracks I don't make 'em replace it…Nobody goes home until it's replaced." I was to discover that the colonel was quite the eccentric.

I found myself liking this guy. Not only as a Marine, but as a man. He had all those attributes that men strive for. He was well educated with Master's Degrees but sounded like a Kentucky farmer. Actually disarmed everyone he talked to. He asked dozens of questions but all of a personal nature. "Wife?"

"Yes, sir."

"Kids?"

"Yes, sir, two boys."

"Education?"

"Yes, sir, UCF."

Not once did he ask about mission, MAU(SOC), my background…nothing. He seemed to genuinely just want to get to know me. As the conversation progressed we were laughing, shooting the shit, and eatin' peanuts.

He had a huge plug of tobacco in his cheek. I later learned it was always there. I think he even slept with it. I was a chewer also so when he offered his Red Man I took a wad.

He said, "If you ever run out it's in my lower left desk drawer."

I later made a habit of going into the colonel's office and grabbing a bag of chew. I'd later replace it. We got a new XO who wasn't familiar with the colonel's and my little arrangement. He caught me in the colonel's desk and landed on me with both feet.

"Who the fuck do you think you are! You Ninja guys think you can go anywhere and do as you please. Your ass is mine now!"

Thank God the colonel walked in. He calmed the XO down but the XO never developed a love for us Trailer Trolls (our facility was three double-wide trailers located on Range One). I later told John that this bonehead was gonna cause MAU(SOC) trouble. I guess that they already knew that because the guy ended up at the Historical Branch of the Marine Corps.

I departed his office after about an hour knowing that he got more out of me than I got out of him. This was one of the good guys. Everybody thought he was eccentric. That was just a tool he used to disarm you. He was on his game 24 and 7.

I went back to Code T the next morning and John called me off to the side. "Got some bad news. The powers that be are gonna put a major in charge of Strike University."

That wasn't bad news. I didn't know anything about sniper school, infantry tactics. All I wanted to do was refine the breaching program.

John seemed relieved. He took me over and introduced me to Major Paul.

The guy had piercing blue eyes that bored a hole through to your soul. He always looked confused and that was always the way he started the conversation if something wasn't clear. At a brief by the assistant commandant a certain point wasn't clear to Paul. He raised his hand and was recognized. He stood, made a show of removing his Copenhagen, then very clearly said, "Sir, I'm fuckin' confused." He was one of the smartest guys I knew. He also used it well.

Paul and I headed to Quantico. We became instant "us against the world" guys. We got along well. He knew that my background was what the Corps needed but he didn't ask many questions. He was true Infantry right down the line. We had many heated discussions about SpecOps not being standard Infantry tactics.

Now it was time to get our instructors. We guessed that we wouldn't get the best that the fleet had to offer. We were wrong. Our guys started coming in and we were well pleased. We had good ole country boys from North Carolina, Louisiana, Mississippi, and we had our pretty boy from New York. We had guys from everywhere in between. They all shared the same interest: Get all the training you can then get it out to the Force Recon and FAST companies. Oh yeah, nothing wrong with havin' some fun while you do it. We had to get spun up fast.

We were no longer Strike University. We were Schools Section Weapons Training Battalion. I could see it falling apart already. More courses were added. Now we had the following formal schools:

- Sniper School
- Small Arms Weapons Instructor Course (SAWIC)
- High Risk Personnel (HRP)
- CT/AT Driving
- Explosive/Dynamic Entry
- Surveillance Detection

It was going beyond the scope. Paul was a career Regular Officer and this would be good for his career. Not so good for MAU(SOC). At any rate, he contributed a great deal to the Marine Corps with his development of the SAWIC course.

Now we were a school house. Meetings were still being conducted at every level concerning the future of Marine Special Operations. There were more senior officers against the concept than were in favor. The prevailing mentality was that "there are no special Marines, all Marines are special."

What they were missing was the fact that the word "Special" referred to the mission, not the individual. There were many good supply people and cooks in the Corps and, God bless them, they were what kept us going. But they could not perform counter-terror operations.

We were in a conflict and it was called SO/LIC. It wasn't in full swing yet but it was looming on the horizon. Beirut, Israel, Palestine, Libya, Syria, Algeria, Iran, and Iraq. We were like the proverbial ostrich with his head in the sand. It was coming.

General Gray read it, John read it, and a handful of others read it. We had lost almost 250 Marines in Beirut as a result of it. I was in shock when I attended meetings and someone would stand up and say "Special Operations is not a Marine Corps mission." We had suffered more casualties than all the other services combined.

Another famous Marine saying: "First to fight." What happened to that mentality? There was "black money" available for the SOF units but the Marine Corps took pride in the fact that they could turn back money each year. It was all mind-boggling to me. Not one anti SOF individual ever convinced me otherwise, nor will they—I can see what's happening on the news every day.

John called me one morning and told me that there was to be a meeting in the colonel's office at 1300. Code T, PP&O, FMFLant & Pac, the colonel, and I were to be the attendees. The local Education Command at Quantico (MCCDEC) was twisted because they felt that MAU(SOC) training should fall under them. Code T and MCCDEC were in a huge pissing contest.

I had been told in the past to not allow any MCCDEC people to observe any training. WTBN fell under MCCDEC. What a mess. The colonel had to walk a tightrope, as did I. Code T had tasked the colonel with writing my fitness report. That meant I also worked for MCCDEC. This was to bite me in the ass later.

We all showed up at 1300. The colonel offered up the ever present peanuts, candy, and Diet Cokes. We all settled around the conference table. There was a colonel that I didn't recognize. John did.

John asked the colonel, "Sir, where are you from?"

He responded, "MCCDEC." He had a look on his face that he knew what was coming.

John continued, "Sir, this is a classified meeting and I'm sure that you have a clearance. Need-to-know is required here."

The colonel said, "My boss heard about this meeting and advised me to attend." He made no effort to get up.

John stood from his chair and excused himself and left the office. We were all uncomfortable as hell with the exchange that had just taken place. After a couple of minutes, John walked back into the colonel's office and told the colonel from MCCDEC, "Sir, there's someone on the phone who would like to speak with you."

The colonel, with a smile on his face, excused himself and left the office. He returned in a few minutes and began collecting his gear. He said, "I guess my presence here is not required after all." He departed without further comment from anyone.

John sure had a set of balls for a young major. I couldn't help but think, how much more could things be screwed up? After all, we were all Marines and saluted the same flag. I was to later understand that there was a huge effort to do away with MAU(SOC) and it wasn't gonna happen on John's watch.

We had a full complement of instructors by now. Force Recon guys, rifle and pistol shooters, tactical guys, and one counter intelligence officer. Our guys were training everywhere then bringing the training back to Schools. They went every-where—Shaw's, Delta, ST 6, HRT. You name it we went. We would look at the material and have the instructors teach us what they'd learned. We adopted the good and flushed the bad.

Our High Risk Personnel course was extremely popular with everyone: CIA, DIA, State Department, DEA, and anyone else headed to a high threat environment. All of the courses were really taking off. The SAWIC course was a required for-mal school for FMFLant and FMFPac. Sniper School had been around for a while and was very well received.

The explosive entry courses were being attended by the SEALs, Rangers, FAST Companies, DOE, DEA, and Force Recon Marines. I was traveling with Jaime at HRT and SEAL Team Six. I also traveled to California every time Charlie found new targets. I had befriended a sales representative for the explosives company GOEX. When they produced a batch of flex or Nonel, the product had to meet some stringent requirements. Not all material passed. The explosives were still good but some minor flaw would fail it. They couldn't sell it and disposal was expensive.

John A. was my contact at GOEX and he told me about this stuff. I asked the good Marine question, "Can I have it?"

John A. was tickled. He said, "Hell, yes. All you want. I'll even pay for the shipping." It was cheaper than disposal. I had enough powder to train the world.

The days of storing explosives in my garage were over. I was to become legit.

An important thing that will come up later is that during this time frame I received a call from Frank at ST-6. He said, "I've got a little over 900,000 rounds of silver tip 9mm that has been put in grade III." This is when, for whatever reason, it is determined that the ammo is unserviceable. They may find a few bad rounds so they s-can the whole lot. Frank asked if I wanted it.

"Hell, yes to that also." The ammo and explosives were perfect for training. If you had a bad round you could practice transition to your 45. Frank also paid for the shipping. Our bunkers runneth over.

I alluded earlier to training the first MAU(SOC), the Twenty-second MAU commanded by Colonel Myer (later to become a general). This guy epitomized everything that I imagined a Marine officer should be. He wasn't a big guy but he cut a big path. MAU(SOC) survived only because of men like him. He wasn't afraid to say what was on his mind and was so squared away that senior officers didn't take offense. He didn't care if they did. They should write books about guys like this for the lieutenants to study at Quantico.

The Twenty-second MAU, Force Platoon First, met up with us at BSR. The first evolution of their SOC certification was driver training. They attended a condensed two-day course. Red Cell knew that we were there training so all the boys showed up. Frank, Larry, and Luke. Red Cell had just moved from Dulles Airport to Eli's hardware store at Indian Head, Maryland. These guys were a huge asset helping us conduct the training. They had been there, done that, and had made all the mistakes. We benefited from their experience.

The young Marines ate it up. After driving they moved to an intense firearms and tactics course administered by my Delta buddy with the aid of the Red Cell guys. At this point I separated out the breachers and the snipers went with Craig. This was a week long then we tied it all together with exercises. We trained from 0500 until whenever we were done.

Just being associated with these guys was a privilege to me. I brought explosives knowledge to the table but guys like Larry, Frank, Luke, and Lee were the true heroes. They'll probably want to kick my ass for saying that but it's true. What these men did during their tours completely restores your faith in our fighting forces and the American spirit. But they are the kind of guys who would never mention it and would deny any involvement. That's what makes them what they are.

An example of the intensity of the exercise phase of training: We had rented some minivans from a local rental car company. We removed the back seats and the marines would roll up to the shooting house and conduct an emergency assault at full speed. We instructors were standing outside the house waiting for the first assault.

Here they came, hauling ass in from two fast laps on the 2.01 mile formula racetrack. They were all zapped up with adrenaline. The van came to a sliding halt and the Marines started piling out. The next to the last guy had his weapon on automatic instead of safe. He had his finger on the trigger. As he jumped out his weapon fired four or five rounds before he got it under control. Yep, all the rounds went through the side of said minivan. Shit, there were several gaping holes and the metal had flowered outward from the hole.

No sweat. Went to the local auto parts store and bought some of that match-a-color paint. We took a mallet and banged the rough edges back into the holes. Chewed some bubble gum and filled the holes once we got all the sugar out. We smoothed it out as best we could then applied the paint. Looked pretty good. At least good enough to get turned back in without being charged for the damage.

In those days we kept nothing from the boss. All it got was a "boys will be boys" comment. No reprimand, no office hours, no punishment. Of course, the team leader had some extra duty for the knucklehead that had the AD. Those kids were so good and professional that we didn't have to punish them for a mistake. They punished themselves much more harshly than we could have.

The biggest hurdle to overcome was having the Marines refer to each other by first names. Rank and protocol in the Marine Corps makes this an ultra taboo. We were at the hotel loading up to head to BSR. The lieutenant was on the second floor balcony and a young sergeant was down in the parking lot. They were Marines and it showed. It was a slow evolution for the Marine Corps to transition to the SO/LIC type warfare.

The young sergeant yelled up, "Sir, did you load your bag up?"

The lieutenant was on his game. He said, "David, please come up so that we a have a talk."

It dawned on the sergeant and he responded, "Be right there, Jules."

I don't know what the lieutenant said to "Dave" but I never heard "sir" or "lieutenant" again. It was especially hard on the senior NCOs. Their world had been a "Yes, sir…One, two… Aye-aye, sir" world for years. I'm sure it grated their ass to have some young corporal or sergeant say, "Hey, Bob, can you come here for a minute?"

The reason was simple. If they were operating in a hostile environment posing as reporters or missionaries the easiest way to blow your cover is throw out a "Yes, sir" or "Captain" or "Sergeant Major." Doom on them. It was a different world and a different war. SO/LIC demanded a new mentality. It was a world of shadows and conspiracy. You trusted no one and no one could trust you except your teammates.

After BSR we would take the class back to Quantico. Tons of physical training and stress courses. One phase of the training required a five-mile run followed by gathering at the FBI (HRT) tire house. Inside we had stations set up in every room. At each station would be a weapon in varying stages of disrepair—all in pieces, a jam, no ammo, with ammo—on the deck. Whatever we could realistically think of. These weren't M16s, MP5s or 45s. There might be an AK-47 at station one. Station two could be a Scorpion 32 cal machine pistol, or an Uzi. We had dozens of foreign weapons that we trained the students with. We called it our "Funny Gun" class. Your never knew when you might be in a theatre and for whatever reason you may only have access to a weapon that is popular in that geographical area.

Later, when we got heavily involved training the FAST companies we introduced them to the "Funny Guns." I told their lieutenant to have the company formed for a run at 0600.

Jim, my Non-Commissioned Officer in Charge (NCOIC) and I went out at 0545 to stretch. We saw that the lieutenant had formed his Marines and was exercising the hell out of them. I looked at Jim and we exchanged the "rolled eye" look.

The lieutenant was trying to make a good show for us instructors. He was really putting them through the paces. Finally at 0600 he put the company in formation. One of his staff sergeants was an old Force Recon guy that I'd trained a year or so earlier. He'd been on runs with me before. The staff sergeant told me at their graduation that he'd tried to warn the lieutenant.

He told the lieutenant, "Sir, I know he looks like an old fucker but he can run your ass into the dirt." Apparently the lieutenant ignored him. Too bad.

Jim took up the rear of the formation, with the ambulance to pick up casualties and dropouts. The lieutenant assured me that there would be no dropouts in his company. I just looked at him.

Off we went. Those Marines out there who are familiar with the Yellow Brick Road and the Washboard at Quantico know where I'm headed. I'm out front with the lieutenant beside me. My pace was not particularly fast but it stayed the same, uphill or down. We got to the Washboard. That is a series of about a million, or so it seems, very steep hills about 100 meters high.

As we topped a hill I looked back and saw the company was starting to lag and Jim had his hands full at the rear. The company guide was behind me and I turned to him, running backwards, and said, "Gunny, keep this pace. Me and the lieutenant are gonna go back and see what the holdup is."

"Aye-aye, sir," he panted.

I told the lieutenant that we were going back to the rear of the company. He just nodded. He was winded as well. I took off, with him on my heels.

We got to the rear and Jim tells me that there were two Marines in the ambulance. Six or seven more were doing the fall-out routine. I ran back to the ambulance and got the thumbs up from the corpsman.

Now I really piss off the lieutenant. "Let's go get the guide and have him come back to give Jim a hand." Without waiting for his response I take off to the head of the formation. Now the young lieutenant is huffing and puffing but he won't quit. When we got to the front I told the gunny to go give Jim a hand at the rear.

Again, "Aye-aye, sir."

We covered about five miles and the company was like an accordion. The lieutenant and I made several trips to the rear of the formation to check on the status of the dropouts. We completed the run at the tire house without allowing a breather. Now we turned up the stress factor. We were yelling and screaming, "Hurry it up...Engage...Engage!!"

When it was all finished I got the lieutenant off to the side and told him that he'd made a serious mistake.

He gave me a confused look and I said, "You have to plan for the unexpected. Conserve the strength of your command. Never, ever, underestimate your enemy." He had underestimated my ability to run.

When the First MAU(SOC) completed their training they headed back to Lejeune. FMFLant was the first sanctioned MAU(SOC) for the Marine Corps. Both FMFLant (Lejeune) and FMFPac (Pendleton) were to stand up future MAU(SOC) capabilities. We continued with our in-house training and instructor development. I was proud of all my guys.

We had one old gunny who had been on the pistol team for many years. So many years that he'd forgotten how to be a Marine. He was a good shot but that was about it. He had been forced on me by the Colonel Dave because he was a fair-haired boy due to his shooting ability. I shoved him off on SAWIC and that was the end of him.

I had no "yes men." I would have fired any of them who were and they knew it.

I still believe in General Patton's comment, "If we're all thinking the same, then somebody is not thinking." If all leaders would practice this adage the world would be a better place.

I can't tell you how many times I've had a young Marine say, "What if we try it this way?" It would work...and better!

Let me take a second to introduce you to the boys.

"TRAILER TROLLS" Schools Section, WTBN. The pioneers of MAU(SOC) Training. *(A few of the guys weren't present at the time of this photo)*

The political battles were raging. All of the stumbling blocks realized that General Gray would only be the commandant for four years. They were all hoping to end this SOC nonsense once and for all. Within the Marine EOD community I was under constant fire from the old guard. My response was always immediate: "The only reason you don't want EOD involved in SOC is that you're a bunch of old fat asses that can't even pass a physical fitness test (PFT)." I made many friends during this tour.

Twenty-second MAU had received their SOC certification. There was a huge exercise that was conducted and the commandant required that they passed all phases before he would let them attach the (SOC) after the MAU. As I expected, the Twenty-second performed exemplary. Colonel Mike was very happy and extremely appreciative to old Frank.

Steve and his wife came over one Saturday night to play cards. Steve and I turned early on to the cold beer and by 2200 had risen to the level of solving world problems.

The phone rang and Susan answered. It was Colonel Mike. I took the phone.

The colonel proceeded to tell me that Granada had just gone down and his MAU deployment had been moved up. They were heading to Morehead City, N.C. as he spoke. Damn, that was fast. His logistics folks were going over requirements and the deploying Force Recon platoon had no explosives for breaching. I had planned on augmenting their training allowance just before deployment. He asked if I had any suggestions.

I asked, "Sir, when do you need it?"

"Frank, to be honest, if I had it tonight it may be too late."

My Old Milwaukee-fuzzed brain started working overtime. I said, "Colonel, let me call Joe, C.O. of Second Force, and see what we can do tonight."

The colonel said, "Frank, I realize you can't do anything tonight. I was being facetious."

"Sir, I can and will do it tonight. I'll call you back with the plan."

I hung up and called Joe. He was at his office, half in the bag, but in his office.

Joe said, "Man, am I glad to hear from you. My tit is in a wringer."

"Do you have access to any military vehicles tonight, Joe?" I asked.

"Yeah, but what good will that do?"

I responded, "Can you have a couple of guys meet me at the 301 exit off the 95 in about three hours?"

He told me that his breachers were there and he'd put them on the line. In less than a minute I was talking to one of the hard-charging sergeants who I'd recently trained. Another "get it done" kid. We worked out the details. He'd meet me at 0200 behind the gas station at the 301 exit. He said his guys had been so busy getting ready that they hadn't eaten. He was well aware of Susan's ability to satisfy the heartiest Marine or SEAL appetite. I told him I'd bring food, just to get his ass in gear. I hung up.

Everyone at the table was looking at me when I turned around. Steve was the first to speak. Susan was used to these weird calls.

"What the hell was all that about?" he asked.

I told him what was going on and he wanted to know how I planned on getting explosives out of the ammo dump at 2300 on a Saturday night. Susan knew the answer but said nothing. I didn't tell anyone that I had a bunker in my garage.

The Marine Corps wouldn't allow commercial explosives in the ammo dump but I was expected to train and supply MAUs for deployment. The GOEX explosives hadn't arrived yet and I had no idea what I was gonna do with it when it did. Cross that bridge later.

I told Steve to follow me. I headed out to the garage. "Holy Bat...Fuck, man!" he said. Under my workbench I had all sizes of Flex Linear and cases of Nonel. I knew that the Force guys could get the deta sheet and other military explosives from their attached EOD unit.

I backed my CJ-7 into the garage and we started loading it up. Susan had received her cue and was inside making sandwiches. When it came to taking care of the Marines, just making sandwiches wasn't enough. Those pricks got all my Fritos, Twinkies, and dill pickles. She had filled a grocery bag with food.

After a big hug and a couple of "Be carefuls," Steve and I were on the road. He laughed the whole way.

"Only Frank Skinner...only Frank," he said, shaking his head. "A full colonel calls Frank at home and says, 'Hey Frank, can you bring me a couple hundred pounds of high explosives tonight?' Jesus Christ, what's next with you?" And so the conversation went.

We arrived first and had been drinking coffee like crazy, trying to abate the effects of the Old Mil. I think if the cops stopping us DUI was the least of our worries.

Adrenaline again—that shit is worse than I imagine crack is. The green truck pulled in about fifteen minutes after we arrived. Three guys were in the cab, not two. Word must have gotten out that Susan was providing food...at Captain Skinner's expense. We made the transfer in the shadows and headed our separate ways, them to Lejeune and Steve and I back to Accokeek, Maryland.

CHAPTER SEVENTEEN
Gas/Oil Platforms (GO/PLAT)

In the late '80s the U.S. and Iran were having a tiff. The MAU was faced with having to assault an oil platform in the Persian Gulf. I was told that the Force commander went to the SEAL detachment and asked the officer in charge for his "playbook" for taking an oil platform. The commander was told by the SEAL that he didn't have or need one. His SEALs were well trained on oil rigs and needed no playbook. That wasn't the answer the boss was looking for.

He then turned to the MAU commander who, in turn, called up his Force Recon platoon commander. He was told to bring up his playbook for a GO/PLAT. God help that young lieutenant if he said he didn't have one. The commander reviewed the plan and gave the mission to the direct action platoon of Force Recon. The EOD detachment was included in the event they encountered booby traps. The platform was successfully taken and blown up by the EOD team. Staff Sergeant Goley was the NCOIC of the EOD team. Goley and I had been stationed together before. I couldn't wait until he got back.

When the MAU returned, the EOD platoon at Lejeune had a welcome-home party at Goley's house. That was one party I wouldn't miss. Besides, I always liked Staff Sergeant Goley and was glad that he was home in one piece.

I asked what he used to blow the rig. He said, "Whatever I could get my hands on. I had some 155mm artillery shells, some C-4 and other assorted junk."

Man, that sounded like disaster waiting to happen. Had to do something about that. Monday I called John and told him that I needed to talk to him. He was always worried that I'd get fed up with the politics and request out. He was a good Marine officer and liked to take care of his people. My request to meet with him made him anxious until I explained.

I related what I'd learned from Goley. I emphasized my concerns about an oil rig fire, or worse, a major oil spill. We were just lucky this time that the platform was not a producing well. The Liberal news media would love to get hold of that one.

General Gray had done another wise thing. He had enlisted the assistance of the FBI in developing the MAU(SOC) program. It was so well-received that the FBI assigned two agents full time to the commandant's office. Bob on the East Coast and Ben on the West. These guys were our facilitators during training in the civilian community. They were our "Get out of Jail card." They also put together a "Blending Course" for us that was second to none. I'll cover that later.

John contacted Bob and almost overnight we were invited to use the Exxon facility in Grand Isle, Louisiana, along with several platforms in the Gulf of Mexico.

For the first training evolution we all flew in to New Orleans. Of course we had to overnight in the Orleans House on Bourbon Street. Won't go into that night, not that it was hush-hush—just don't remember that much about it.

We all met at a local airport the next morning and were loaded on Marine UH-1 choppers. We flew to Grand Isle in style. We were all wearing our nomex flight suits and black web gear. The balaclavas felt good because it was a little nippy. We landed at the Exxon compound and stowed our gear. Once we had that done we were free to have a look at the small fishing village. It was off season and all who were in town were the locals. We had caused quite the stir. Black helicopters loaded with guys wearing black had descended on their little island.

Master Sergeant DC was from the Second EOD platoon. I had set it up that an EOD guy came along. In those days it was difficult to get EOD support to the MAU(SOC). All of the senior EOD people were against the program and anti Frank. Staff Sergeant Goley's experience had opened some eyes but not all. DC and I sat in a local pub having a few beers. The barmaid was a local Cajun girl and was totally awed by how we had rumbled into town.

"Did you fellers fly in on them black helicopters?" she shyly asked.

"Yes, Ma'am," we told her.

She went on and on about how she'd never even been in an airplane and how she'd "shore like a ride in one of them there black helicopters." I turned to DC and said, "Sergeant Major, do you still have the keys to my helicopter?" He picked up instantly, "Yes, sir." Then he held up some of his personal keys.

This girl's eyes were bigger than shit-can lids. I continued to jest back and forth, with DC keeping up with me like a champ. I asked her what time she got off; she closed at 0200. I consulted with DC and asked him if he'd noticed any place for us to land nearby. He said that the beach out back would do.

I turned to the barmaid and asked if she'd like a ride. She was clapping her hands like a kid. She was so excited that I couldn't go through with the joke. Finally I told her that I'd better not because of government regulations prohibiting civilians. She was disappointed, but took it in stride.

The next morning we flew out to the platforms. This was just a look/see trip. There was a worker on the platform who was a huge help. He opened our eyes to other hazards besides fire and spill. As part of the production process certain toxic byproducts were created and stored in large tanks for later disposal. We learned that the downwind lethality was amazing. Had Goley penetrated one of these tanks the entire assault force would have become casualties.

Now I was hungry. I wanted to learn all that I could about the GO/PLATs. The first level on the platform was referred to as the twelve-foot platform. It was nothing more than a floor that facilitated loading and unloading equipment and supplies. I'm sure that it was structurally important, as well. In heavy seas it was awash. The size of the platform determined how many levels there were.

The well itself is topped off by an assembly referred to as the "Christmas tree." The Christmas tree, beginning at the bottom, is a series of "casing spools." The number of casing spools is dependent upon the depth of the well. These items are called spools because they resemble large thread spools. When they go to a certain depth they add a casing spool. They then continue to that max depth and add another casing spool and so on. Once they are at the desired depth, the tree is capped off by a "tubing spool." This houses the business end of a well. The tubing runs from the bottom of the well to the top. It is through this tubing that the product is pumped up and diverted to a processing platform.

All Western wells are required to have certain safety features. One of these is the down well shutoff valve. This valve serves to stop the flow of product if the tubing is severed or punctured, preventing a spill or fuel for a fire. As we saw in Kuwait, not all wells have this feature.

Also, if the tubing is completely severed it will drop down into the bottom of the well. Experts told me this would cause the biggest problem to the owner if the well. They would have to bring in another rig and go down inside the casings to retrieve the tubing. A real nightmare, they say. It would, however, prevent a fire or spill.

My brain housing group is clicking. P=E. Exxon gave me a couple of old casing and tubing spools. We had them shipped to Quantico for experimentation. I found that a standard fifteen-pound military shaped charge would cleanly penetrate and severe the tubing. It would do this without exiting the other side of the tubing spool. Perfect solution.

Goley had used a large amount of explosives. (I'm not being critical—he worked with what he had available. If it was anyone's fault, it was mine for not seeing the need for this research.) We had developed a fragmentation-free manner in which to safely accomplish the task.

I was to learn a great deal about GO/PLATs. McDermott is a manufacturer of oil platforms just outside of New Orleans, on the way to Grand Isle. Over a six-month period I was to travel to McDermott to study the bowels of the platforms. I took this information back to the direct action platoons as a course within the breaching course.

After retirement I was to use this information while bidding on the oil fire contracts in Kuwait. It also helped me while working for Kellogg/Brown and Root as the security manager for two liquified natural gas plants in Algeria. After retirement is another story and another book.

The Blending course that the FBI set up for us was phenomenal. They came to Quantico and presented all of the classroom stuff. Later they were to take the training directly to the Special Operations Training Groups (SOTGs). They then took us to New York City and we had to actually conduct blending operations on the street. These operations could be several hours to several days. The NYPD was involved in that they were hired as off-duty officers to try to locate or identify us.

It was amazing to me as to how much you could change your appearance with just minor effort. Thinning your eyebrows or darkening them. Makeup to shadow facial lines. Wearing clothing that is indigenous to specific areas. It was excellent training for the MAU(SOC) mission.

CHAPTER EIGHTEEN
Court Martial (Article 32)

Marine Corps MAU(SOC) training was working overtime. As it grew into what John had envisioned, it took on a life of its own. Paul transferred out as did John. Paul headed out to take over a Marine security detachment and John took a tour with Defense Intelligence and was posted in the Philippines (PI). All of my sugar daddies were gone. I should have seen the freight train coming but I was so engrossed in getting the Marines trained that I didn't even sense it.

We had trained four MAU(SOC)s and had developed volumes of information across the full spectrum of Special Ops. We had the respect of our brothers in the Army, Navy, and other mentioned and unmentioned special units. We Marines respected the classification of "Secret."

John and his wife had gone through our HRP training prior to posting to the PI. He asked what type of weapon his wife should train with. I told him to bring her down and we'd let her choose. Whatever she felt comfortable with should be her weapon of choice.

John and Sue came down and I had the guys spread out everything. A wheel gun is always the best for anyone not firearms literate. A revolver. She looked them all over and I told her to grab the Smith & Wesson Model 19. It was a .357 Magnum that shot real bullets. Loaded with Hydra-Shok, it would stop an elephant. She liked it. John selected a M1911 45-caliber pistol, of course. They went through the training. They both departed.

I was right in the middle of the oil platform training and very preoccupied. When I got back, my number two told me that John had called. John told him that DIA had screwed up and failed to ship his weapons to the PI, could we arrange it? I told the number two to check with the supply folks (TMO shippers) to see how we'd go about it. The captain at TMO said that as long as we shipped the weapons to a Naval installation it was legal. I called John and he set it up for them to be shipped to the Marine barracks at Subic Bay.

I departed again for McDermot. I was gone for about two weeks. When I returned all hell had broken loose. My number two came into my office and closed the door.

He said, "Sir, we have a problem. We shipped the guns to Tenus and apparently there is some obscure Navy regulation that says you can't ship personal weapons through the system."

My reaction was immediate, "What the fuck are you talking about? You went to TMO, correct?" He nodded that he had.

"TMO said it was okay, correct?" Again he nodded.

"Well it ain't our problem, then."

One of our sergeants had been given the task of making it happen. The sergeant knew John and where he was at. Being a good sergeant he decided that the guns weren't gonna do the colonel any good without ammo. He stopped by the ammo dump and got 3,500 rounds to ship with the guns. I still didn't see a problem.

He went on to say that he'd been contacted by my old buddy, the boneheaded major from the Marine security battalion when I was in Beirut. This major buddy of mine had been appointed as the Article 32 investigating officer. The major wanted to see me ASAP.

I asked my number two if he'd made a statement. He had. It was unethical for me to ask what he said and he didn't volunteer. This guy was a shooter and not an operator. He was a Regular Officer and was brought up using survival skills.

I called the major and he was all laughs and jokes. "Yeah, Frank, not a big deal. Just been assigned to clear up this little gun deal with Tenus. Can you come by this afternoon?" I told him I would.

I went to his office at around 1400. We sat down and he offered coffee, which I declined. He then pulled out a tape recorder and turned it on. He asked, "Do you object to being recorded?"

I shook my head. "Is that a 'no'?" he asked.

I nodded. I wasn't gonna make it easy.

"Please just answer, Captain," he said.

So now it was "Captain," not "Frank."

I said that I didn't mind being recorded. He then advised me of my rights under Article 32 of the Uniform Code of Military Justice. One of those rights is to have an attorney.

I stopped him and said, "I'm aware of my rights and now wish to not answer any questions without an attorney."

He reached over and turned off the recorder.

"Frank, this is really gonna piss the general off. He just wants to clear a few things up and it will all be over," he almost pleaded.

"Major, you and I have a history together. It ain't been the best from my standpoint. I respectfully submit that if you told me the sun was shining outside I would grab an umbrella." Man was he pissed. He pushed his chair back and glared. I glared back.

He said, "Once you get a lawyer, have him call me. I've got to go brief the general now and he's already pissed off."

I went straight to the Judge Advocate General's office and made an appointment to see an attorney. I couldn't afford a civilian lawyer so I had to chance it with a Marine. Looking it all over, the lawyer told me that based on the pending charges I could be facing up to eighteen years in Leavenworth. I was charged with illegally shipping personal weapons through the Marine Corps supply system, misallocation of funds and the illegal shipment of ammunition through the Marine Corps supply system.

I couldn't believe what was happening to me. Decorated Vietnam and Beirut veteran. All the things I'd been through to help out with MAU(SOC), all the chances I'd taken, the family separation. I just couldn't believe my Corps was gonna do this to me. To say that I was in shock is an understatement. After I calmed down I realized that it wasn't the Corps. It was the obstructionists who were finally getting their shot at Captain

Skinner. All of my protection was gone. I had nobody running interference for me.

To top it off, I was notified that I'd been selected for Major. That was bittersweet. Might be in prison as a Private. To compound all of our problems, we'd recently been told that Stephen had a terminal illness. We knew that it could come to that when we adopted him but we never thought it could happen. My life was spinning out of control.

My neighbor was an attorney at JAG. I asked him to take my case. He was young and inexperienced but I thought he might fight harder if he knew me. Nothing doing. Don't know what he'd heard at the office but he didn't want my case.

I had to tell Susan something, but I wasn't about to give her the whole story. She was almost insane with Stephen's illness, and this would probably have pushed her over the edge.

I made up my mind to fight. I would continue to train Marines and not let it get me down. Easier said than done. Every time I met with my attorney I was less convinced that I would win. Everyone was telling me to accept a letter of reprimand and I could retire with honor. I was gonna retire with honor anyhow, fuck them! I'd done nothing wrong.

I went in to see my C.O., the colonel. I could tell he was under a lot of pressure from the general. The colonel had been the C.O. of WTBN for an unprecedented fourteen years. WTBN was his life. It would make his life so much easier if I were to take the reprimand. He told me so. I told him that there was no way I was gonna admit guilt. No way!

The colonel almost pleaded with me. I had been put in for a Meritorious Service Medal and it had been approved. I was also to be frock promoted to Major as I was filling a major's billet. Neither happened. My medal fell through the cracks and the promotion never happened. My mind was set—they could stick all that up their asses!

I really feared that my attorney was incompetent. I was wrong about that. This was another guy who disarmed you with feigned lack of concern, then swept in for the kill when you least expected it. He had contacted Tenus and had an official letter saying that John was authorized to have personal weapons for the performance of his duties. I knew nothing of it.

Finally, the day before my Article 32 (like a grand jury) was convened my attorney wanted to meet with me. I sat in front of his desk and he began his brief.

He read the charges against me and explained what would happen if I were found guilty at General Court Martial. Sounded bleak but I listened. When he concluded, he said that the general had offered to drop it all if I would accept a letter of reprimand and retire. There ya have it! They were trying to get rid of the last of the SOC boys.

That just pissed me off more. I told the attorney, "Hell, no!" So help me, the attorney stood up and offered his hand and said, "I didn't think so. I'm happy."

He told me that I had to wear my "Class A" green dress uniform. I asked, "What does everyone else have to wear?"

He said, "Short-sleeved Charlies." I nodded. I also wore short-sleeved Charlies the next morning. Fuck 'em!

The proceedings started with all the pomp and ceremony. The little girl was banging away on her little steno machine. Never could figure out how that worked.

Various witnesses were called up, laying the background. The gallery for observers was empty. Legal procedure was bounced back and forth. I'm thinking that I'm glad I didn't finish law school. What a pain in the ass.

A steady stream of character witnesses and rules and regulations experts. The prosecutor was laying the groundwork. Looked as though they were going after me for the ammo that was shipped also. The Marine Corps ammo was given to a Naval attaché. Marines can't give sailors bullets even if that sailor is wearing a Marine colonel's uniform. What the hell, bring it all out.

I was watching my attorney and the little prick seemed to be asleep half the time. I started to feel like the movie *My Cousin Vinny*. He wasn't sleeping, just lying in the weeds.

The prosecutor slipped and my attorney pounced. The prosecutor said, "Colonel Tenus was shipped unauthorized personal weapons through the Marine Corps supply system."

My attorney asked for a delay until the afternoon, which was granted. We came back at 1300 and took our places. My attorney called his witness. A warrant officer walked in with a briefcase handcuffed to his wrist.

My attorney said, "We have proof that the weapons were not only authorized but required."

They couldn't open the briefcase in open court. It required a SCIF (Secure Classified Information Facility). They had one.

The judge, prosecutor, and my attorney adjourned to the SCIF. About a half-hour later they all returned and the prosecutor was pissed.

The prosecutor opened, "Your Honor, the government concedes that the weapons were authorized."

"...and required," piped in my attorney.

Damn, I had to look at this guy again. He was smiling at me.

Next came the TMO officer that my number two had worked through. He made a fool of himself because he wasn't allowed to hear the other testimony. He didn't lie outright but he sure embellished everything in a negative way. I hope he's reading this now. He told of how he had received a call from my number two and how he had explained that personal weapons couldn't be shipped. He said that my guys had camouflaged the fact that they were private weapons.

That was a lie. The guns were delivered to TMO in a soft, civilian carrying case. He told of how he'd met the sergeant and how sneaky he was. Then he said, "All of those guys in that area are up to sneaky things, so I suspected something was up."

Folks, I didn't flower any of that up. This was a fellow Marine officer who was trying his best to crucify me for no reason.

Next, my colonel was called up. He tried to be funny but he jammed me as well. He was asked about my character. He hadn't heard the TMO's testimony.

As a joke he said, "Frank is a good guy but he's sneaky." He went on to say what a good officer I was and the sacrifices I'd made for the SOC program, etc.

My attorney asked, "Captain Skinner has one charge that relates to 3,500 rounds of ammo being shipped from Marine Corps inventory to a Navy billet. Are you familiar with that?"

The colonel was uneasy, as he didn't want to see me nailed. "Yes, I am."

My attorney nodded and walked back over in front of me. I had no idea how he knew about the 900,000 rounds of silver tip. If you recall, my buddy Frank, with SEAL Team 6, had given us 900,000 rounds of 9mm silver tip ammunition free of charge.

He turned abruptly for effect, "Are you also familiar with the 900,000 rounds of silver tip 9mm that Captain Skinner obtained from the Department of the Navy?"

Now the colonel was tracking, "Yes, sir, I am."

"Colonel, did the Marine Corps pay anything for that ammo—shipping, storage, or anything?"

Again the colonel said, "No, sir, didn't cost the Corps a dime."

Now the prosecutor was rubbing his temples. I think he expected an open and shut case.

Now my hero was having fun, "Colonel, I'm an attorney, not an accountant, but wouldn't you agree that a trade of 3,500 rounds for 900,000 is a huge win for the Marine Corps, saving hundreds of thousands of dollars? Isn't it also true that Captain Skinner is the type of officer that would never look for pats on the back or accolades, unlike some of the previous testimony?" (directly referring to the TMO prick).

"Yes, sir, that is also true," the colonel responded, obviously enjoying this line of questioning, but my defender was done.

"No questions," stated the prosecutor.

All through the proceedings the gallery was empty. It was announced that Captain Skinner was gonna take the stand the next morning. That rumor hauled ass all over HQMC. When I got to court the next morning the hallways were packed with majors, lieutenant colonels, colonels, and a few generals. I recognized most. Only one or two greeted me and the others either ignored me or just nodded. Nice to be loved.

I was in full battle mode now. I had a taste of victory the day before and I was ready. I enjoyed the fact that most of these people knew what I'd done to make MAU(SOC) work. They were either directly "in the know" or were aware of the shortcuts I'd taken. They were here to see what I had to say about them. Good. Let them sweat a while.

I knew it would accomplish nothing but damage to the Corps if I threw a bunch of folks under the bus. I wouldn't do that anyhow. Just gave me the opportunity to know who were the real men and Marines. Tenus had agreed to appear at his own expense, if necessary.

I took the stand and was sworn in. All eyes were locked on me. I realized that there wasn't one founding father of SOC in the crowd.

I had a prepared statement that I hadn't even shown my attorney. I will paraphrase:

"I realize that my attorney will be upset with me, but the following should be part of the record:

I want to make it clear. My number two and the young sergeant were working under my *Implied or Direct Orders*. [This meant that all charges against them were dropped at that point. I looked at my attorney and I don't think he was surprised.]

In the accomplishment of my tasking from HQMC, I developed the program and trained numerous MAU(SOC) and Fast Company Marines. We also trained various federal agencies that now look to the Marine Corps for this specialized training.

With the knowledge of senior Marine officers we bypassed the system in order to avoid another MAU headquarters bombing like the one that killed almost 250 Marines and a sailor.

Every mission that I performed and every task that I accomplished was done under the knowledge and guidance of those appointed over me.

I broke no laws and followed Marine Corps procedure by tasking the SME at TMO to assist in the shipment of the weapons to Colonel Tenus.

I have no regrets, and given similar circumstances, I would do the same thing again. I violated no article of the UCMJ.

That is my statement."

The prosecutor didn't know what to say. I think I'd answered every question he had planned on asking. He stood and looked at the Judge (Convening Authority) and said, "Your honor, the government rests."

My attorney stood, "Defense has nothing more, your Honor."

That was it. We just had to wait. It was lunch time and my attorney asked me to join him. I declined, saying that I just wanted to be alone and think. He nodded.

I desperately wanted to be with my family. I couldn't, because I didn't want them to worry. To Susan we were just waiting to retire...no problems.

I was back in my seat at 1245 awaiting the 1300 start. The gallery folks were still there. They were friendlier now that Frank hadn't harpooned anybody. There were even a couple of pats on the back.

The judge came in and called everything to order. He began to read.

I was listening, but my mind was racing like the flipping of a photo album: Vietnam...Beirut...PI...Bogotá...long training days...adrenaline.

Then I heard the words that still make me proud.

"This inquiry finds no grounds for the pursuit of a General Court Martial against Captain Frank P. Skinner. Captain Skinner reacted as he was trained. He heard a cry from the trenches for guns and ammunition. He responded to the cry...paperwork to follow!" I still have those words framed and hanging in a prominent location in my study.

I would have to live with my punishment:

1. No promotion
2. No Meritorious Service medal
3. No retirement ceremony (my boys would have enjoyed that)

I want to make it very clear. My Article 32 was a necessary thing. It was part of the system that keeps everything in check. Without that system people can run amuck; serious injuries can occur when things get out of control. I am proud of that system. It worked.

I sincerely loved and still love the United States Marine Corps. Like everywhere, there are self-servers, but I ran into very few. I can think of no other career that could put you in such close contact with such exemplary people. I thank God each day for the people I served with, the people who supported me, and the support of my family.

I especially thank God for this generation of kids. Makes me wonder where they come from. Who are these young men and women who take back-to-back tours in a godforsaken place full of such hatred and animosity? Again, it restores my faith in humanity and the American way.

As I was writing the last chapter, all of the memories flooded back. Susan has been doing the proofreading for me and when she got to this part, she exclaimed, "Eighteen years in Leavenworth!! You never told me that!!"

Ooops!

Islamic fundamentalism

When you hear a talking head on the television explaining the Islamic mentality and espousing their point of view, that is the first person you should turn off. We will never understand the thought process that assigns more importance to their death than to their survival.

I have studied fundamental Islam culture and the Arab language for about twenty-five years. The more I learn, the more I am mystified. There are nagging questions that we will never answer or understand.

What possesses an eighteen-year-old from a middle class family to strap on a bomb and blow himself to pieces just to kill innocent people?

We have to look at their social environment. You can look at life as a series of "wants and needs." To most people in that part of the world there is no "want" list. It is too far out of reach. The "needs" list can't even be satisfied. Something as simple as having a relationship, not necessarily sexual, with a member of the opposite sex. Something as small as not having bottled water for your family but seeing Americans discarding half-full bottles, because if they want more they'll just get another bottle.

Men and women were created—depending upon your beliefs—with certain biological and physiological needs that cannot be dictated by man or written material from centuries ago. The biological clock ticks. Human nature will always be human nature. People flirt, people make contact. In some countries you can be lashed or imprisoned for either. Depending upon who your family is, you could even be executed.

When I worked in Algeria as the security manager for Kellogg I noted some interesting social issues at play. I would take the expat workers to the LNG plant and return to the camp in a small village called Bethioua. People were simple, didn't have a lot, civil war going on. Bottled water was a commodity and showers were permitted once a week for a fee.

The maids and maintenance folks were permitted on our camp after the expats departed. There were fifty-two double-wide trailers that were our quarters. A maid normally cleaned three or four homes each day. Our TV was satellite and came in through the chow hall. Only problem is that every house had to watch the same channel. Most of us had VCRs to avoid the arguments. At around 1145 each morning the bravest maid would approach me.

"Mr. Frank, we watch TV at 1200?"

I'd go to the chow hall and turn on the system so that they could gather in one house and watch TV during their lunch hour. After a week or so I got curious because they wanted the same channel each day. What could they be watching? Any guesses before you read on?

Jerry Springer! Yep, and they all thought that was exactly how we lived in America. They just couldn't understand how we, as a people, could have so much and have so many problems.

We were paid by Kellogg but our payroll had to be approved by the Algerian plant manager. This guy was a big shot and was rolling in money. He made about $600 usd per month. I made a little over $10,000.

These are only a few examples. They see us as a spoiled and wasteful people. While they fight for the small things we take for granted, they see us complaining like children.

They have hopes and dreams just like any human being. Fathers want the most for their kids but those same kids are asking why. When they see television, if available, and they are subjected to rhetoric from religious leaders that call us "the Great Satan" a state of confusion and jealousy is planted in their thoughts. Mothers want for their children but can only provide the basics, if that. When they witness the western cultures, via what ever media, it is hard for them to comprehend. It creates a backdrop that is ripe for the recruitment of terror trainees and ultimately suicide bombers.

In Islam, Muhammad was considered to be the Holy Prophet. If you read the Koran, you'll see that there were some violent years during his time. People were murdered and Muhammad's response was "It is like two goats butting heads" or "Nobody will care."

What is the basic difference between Sunni, Shiite, and Kurd? We should all at least know the basic differences. It ain't much, in our minds. It is huge to them.

Muhammad was poisoned in 632 by a Jewish lady. There was nobody designated to replace Muhammad.

When he died he was replaced by Abu Bakr. Outlying tribes refused to pay tribute and taxes because Muhammad had died. This was known as the era of the "Wars of Apostasy." Abu Bakr was the first caliph.

On his deathbed Abu Bakr appointed Umar b. al-Khattab as his successor (634-644 CE).

Umar was assassinated in 644. Before his death he appointed a six-member committee which was to choose his successor from amongst themselves.

Uthman b. Affan was selected as the third caliph. I'll define *caliph* later.

Uthman was murdered by unhappy Egyptians in 656 and the notables of Medina selected Ali b. Abi Talib as the fourth caliph. Ali was murdered in 661.

The death of Muhammad brought about the caliphate. The caliphate was, only as a loose comparison, similar to the papal system. Again, don't be confused. They were not even slightly similar in belief. A caliph is the central religious leader of his caliphate.

The Sunni believe in the legitimacy of the first four caliphs. They likewise accept anyone descendent from Muhammad's tribe.

Shiite only believe that Ali, the fourth caliph, was the legitimate ascendant. They believe that they must live under a descended leader. Ali was Muhammad's son-in-law.

The Sunni believe that the Shiite are apostates and don't follow the *sharia* law. Saudi Arabia is predominantly Sunni and practice Wahhabism, the conservative form of Sunni teaching that everyone must live by the strict interpretation of the Koran. Apostates are backsliders or non-believers who have lost their way.

Iran is predominantly Shiite and they believe that the Ayatollah Khomeini was the next legitimate heir to Muhammad.

Kurds are predominantly Sunni but with a new twist. They have their own language and culture that varies greatly from the Sunni of Iraq. They seek their own national identity, much as do the Palestinians.

I don't know about you, but to me those don't seem like reasons to be a suicide bomber.

Explosive Entry has taken on a life of its own with SWAT, Special Operations, and other Special Groups. One thing remains the same: Plenty Equals Enough. The same scientific theory that can be applied to a two-liter Coke bottle can be applied to an expensive commercial item that resembles a Coke bottle. Two liters is two liters no matter how you add it up! Some water bottles even look like milk jugs. Same thing, folks. Just apply the "use of force continuum" and you'll be fine.

"Better to be tried by 12 than carried by 6"—*Arleigh McCree*

I retired from the Corps in 1990 without pinning on Major. As a young sergeant I had dreams of being an officer, but as I reflect back it was a dream. I am proud of the fact that I was a captain. I took care of my Marines…and they took care of me.

Semper Fi!

Since retirement I have worked extensively in the private security industry. I have served as a bodyguard to the Saudi royal family and to the Disney on Ice show (Cairo, Belfast, Europe, Central and South America). I have trained the Saudi Royal Guard Brigade, Saudi air police, U.S. sky marshals, various SWAT units, SEALs, and Marines. I worked as a security manager for Kellogg/Brown and Root in war-torn Algeria. Unlike the stories you hear, Prince Khalid and his family were very gracious and courteous to all that they encountered. They were especially kind to the security detail. The princess even paid to have our spouses visit us in Paris for a week as we had been on the road for several months during Desert Storm/Shield. I can honestly say that had Prince Khalid known about Stephen's illness he would have provided for my family. I was too proud and vane to let my problems be known. It was the entourage that caused us the major problems.

As pictured below, we were called upon to train SOF in personal security details (PSD).

Arab philosophy: If you're the anvil, be patient. If you're the hammer—STRIKE!!

I hope to continue my journey with you in my next book. This will be an interesting tour through the world of private security, bodyguard details, training, and intense adventure.

I retired in 1990 and immediately entered the private security world by co-founding Training Resources International. Our first contract was to train the Boston Metro Police Department SWAT.

It went uphill and downhill from there. For those of you interested in leaving the military or law enforcement to join the private sector, this will be a must-read.

Author acting as protectee for SEALs on protective operation training exercise. (Note the curious reporter, far left.) Author, center, with khaki trousers. Girl walking away broke the security perimeter.

CPSIA information can be obtained at www.ICGtesting.com
Printed in the USA
LVOW051749131212

311547LV00009B/1231/P